I HAVE ASKED TO BE WHERE NO STORMS COME

GWENDOLYN N. NIX

Let the world know:
#IGotMyCLPBook!

Crystal Lake Publishing
www.CrystalLakePub.com

WELCOME
TO ANOTHER

CRYSTAL LAKE PUBLISHING
CREATION

Join today at www.crystallakepub.com & www.patreon.com/CLP

PART I:

HELL

CHAPTER 1

I have desired to go
Where springs not fail,
To fields where flies no sharp and sided hail,
And a few lilies blow.

And I have asked to be
Where no storms come,
Where the green swell is in the havens dumb,
And out of the swing of the sea.

"Heaven-Haven" by Gerard Manley Hopkins

DOMINO LEARNED HE had to be adaptable.

He may have died sometime in the twentieth century, but the world still spun on above. New-fangled ideas, technology, and culture leaked into Hell's subterranean world. He'd noticed it before: the women sporting blue jeans, the short leather jackets, the abandoned picket signs with painted mantras calling to *burn the bra* alongside *frack the Bloody,* but it didn't truly hit him until he found a contained black box of glass. Something from the Brightside—the East-side. Nothing so fancy would be found in the West, on his side of the Dark and Bloody, no matter how much time passed.

That was the problem with adaptability. If you didn't do it, *refused to,* you ended up stranded in your own time. Locked in a whirlwind of denial, because life had moved on without you and you weren't ready to be forgotten.

It fractured his heart when he found people like that, like the young thing before him, sitting crossed-legged in the desert with her fleshless fingers curled in boned zen. His throat cracked as he called out to her, too long silent on this never-ending peregrination. Her long bleached hair swept across a face blistered and peeling from the sun. He snapped his fingers inches from her nose, but she didn't blink. Didn't move. Returned to dust.

He eyed her ripped jeans, her canvas tennis shoes worn through the soles, and the square black metal brick balanced on her bent knee. He took it, steadily working through the mechanics of a touch screen. Hellish burble cooed through the earpiece, but he ignored it. This was damnation, after all. What did you expect? This was how you survived. Stealing, hijacking, and fast-talking just to get what you needed.

His face remained passive as applications opened brightly colored hieroglyphic bubbles. He sat, hoping this wasn't a laid trap and mimicked her crossed legs. Their kneecaps brushed.

It might've been minutes or a whole year that he sat next to her, figuring out the black box. Time had conditioned him to approach things with childish glee, instead of like a frustrated fogey. Puzzles kept him sane, taught him to accept new appliances that were only science fiction pulp in his time.

He tapped the glass with his fingernail and scrolled through her pictures: three smiling friends, a chocolate-colored puppy, and a rainbow cutting through the gray from far away. He stared at the picture until the screen blacked out. He thought about centuries of black skies full of peace like the good book said. He thought about a horizon that wasn't red-lit with hellfire. He looked up. No rainbows here.

Pocketing the device, he patted the girl gently on her shoulder and wished her well on her journey.

———•———

Domino found his mother in a bar.

It was one of those self-proclaimed humanity plots where some tired group had clasped hands, made a vow, and built a one-story hovel complete with a tumbleweed thatched roof and a proclamation hammered on the door.

This is like Earth, it said. *Blessed the peacemakers: for they shall be called the children of God.*

Beneath it, scratched into the wood: *Now God be praised, that to believing souls gives light in darkness, comfort in despair.*

God doesn't exist was written underneath it.

I HAVE ASKED TO BE WHERE NO STORMS COME

And underneath that: *Of course, He exists, you cocksucker. You're in Hell, for god's sake. How much proof do you need?*

Dust covered Domino's body as he stumbled inside. He slid on a barstool made of driftwood and femur bones. A bartender—hot young thing—dried a chipped whisky snifter and raised an eyebrow at him.

"I ain't got nothing," he breathed out, rusted. He licked his chapped lips, his tongue scooping up the tender ooze of blood from a particularly deep crack. Everything was dry here.

"Not like the economy's crashing," she answered, and put the glass on the scored table. She brought out a big bottle of Glenlivet and poured the amber liquid. He wanted to smile, but even his mouth felt exhausted. He wasn't sure if he should be happy that alcohol was the Devil's drink and therefore found in copious quantities throughout Hell, even the hundred-year-old golden stuff. He rinsed his mouth, wishing water was just as abundant and watched a group of men play some version of pool with the balls smoothed white. He coughed and tipped his head down low, hunching his shoulders. He didn't want to talk to anyone, wasn't sure if he remembered how to anymore, but he entertained the idea of hustling the other sharks for a hardball win.

The square glass brick sat heavy in his pocket. He pulled it out and set it face up on the bar.

"You know what this is?" he asked the bartender.

She peered at it for a moment and then nodded once. "Looks like a fancy new cellphone."

"A cellphone?"

"Yeah, like a telephone? You know what that is?"

He nodded slowly. Rotary dials. Curlicued wires.

"It's a newer version. Compacted and mobile so you can take it on the go."

"Do you know how to use it?" he asked, even though he had a pretty good idea at this point. Never one to assume, though, better to ask questions now than pay for them later.

"Before my time, sweetheart," she said.

He mulled the word, *cellphone*, over in his head, always shocked at what came down the pipeline. He stretched his legs out, muscles taut from walking miles without rest, and his knees popped. His body ached in a multitude of ways.

"Looking a little worse for wear," he heard at his elbow.

His gaze slid over to see the dark-haired woman with a cocky smile and glossy eyes. In her early thirties when she died.

"Don't think I signed up for any beauty pageant," he chuckled, both on guard and delighted with the company. He'd sworn off people ever since a band of no-good friends tried to sell him to the highest demon bidder, but too much solitary was lonely, on the verge of being dangerous. Sanity had to be cradled as carefully as a newborn.

"It would be nice to know you're taking care of yourself, but that doesn't appear to be the case." The bartender set a drink in front of the woman and she added softly, "Hoped you wouldn't end up down here."

He looked at her full on and wondered how he hadn't recognized her immediately. After all, it was one of the things his father hated and loved about him so much, the way he looked so much like her. "Mama?" he asked, nearly breathless.

"Hey, baby," she said, putting the glass to her lips.

He felt like he might cry, but Hell was a dry place that sucked out any kind of moisture that wasn't blood. A rough rasp ripped from his chest. "What are you doing here?"

"Should ask you the same." She crooked a smile. "Thought I raised you right."

He laughed then, a rusted choke, and greedily watched her prop her elbow on the bar and lean back on her stool. "Nobody told me life gets harder when you grow up," he said.

She grinned then, and she looked like she did the day before the fire when she'd baked a cake just because it was Sunday and smeared frosting on his nose before chasing him through their house with a spatula. Wicasah, so small he couldn't keep up, floundered behind them. His giggles became wails when they got too far away. He remembered her scooping Wicasah up, planting kisses up and down his neck while his little brother squealed from the attention. The grass had been high; it was a good but dry summer and he had watched the cottonwoods shed their pods. They'd floated in the air like clouds.

"You die at that age, or you just making yourself look like that?" she asked.

He swallowed hard. "Died," he admitted. Some arrived in Hell with eighty-year-old bodies and had to buy and peddle spells to make them fit for a rough afterlife.

"Too young," his mother noted.

"Older than you," he said, downing the rest of his drink in one smooth gulp. The bartender, bless her heart, was good at her job and filled it back up neat.

"And Wicasah?"

"Still up top from what I know," he said. The look of relief crossing her face echoed his own. "Now *that* would have been too young," he added.

"How have you been riding?" she asked after a pause.

"Alone, mostly."

"Think you might want someone to ride shotgun?"

His heart climbed in his throat and he realized he didn't want anything more. "As long as it's just you."

"Always has been, baby."

They stole a car a few days after. A beautiful vintage Shelby Cobra straight from the Brightside, paint still shiny and red as the sun, parked in a concrete lot in the middle of nowhere. Domino didn't think twice and shoved his bag in while Thessaly swung her legs over the open top and slid in the leather passenger seat. In the driver's seat, Domino rested his twitching thighs for a moment before yanking the panels down to get at the wiring. Sparks shot out with the scent of electrical discharge. The metal-girl revved with a full tank. His mother laughed like she was sixteen and this was her first joyride.

They pulled out of the parking lot and rolled on broken sand, idling for a moment as Hell rearranged its punishment into a long stretch of blacktop extending into the horizon.

Maybe dreams do exist in damnation, Domino thought as he shifted into third gear.

"Thank god ostentatiousness is a sin," his mother said, lifting her hair and letting the wind take it up and ripple behind her like a dark wave.

"Thank god so is gluttony," he said, breaking a smile. He didn't think the car would ever run out of gas or that her tires would ever turn ragged. She was down here for another purpose entirely, but luckily, her punishment wasn't for him.

It wasn't no rainbow, but as Domino shifted into fifth, he felt like things might end up okay.

———•———

Domino huddled deeper into his jacket, his hands shoved so deep into his pockets he could rub his knuckles together through the fabric underneath the zipper.

"You know the first time your daddy asked me out proper," Thessaly began, pulling her dark hair over her ears for warmth, "it was to the country fair. Biggest night of my life. I wore my prettiest blue dress, stiff and starched, and my mama said it brought out what color existed in my eyes. Said I looked like a proper Brightsider, that I should be on the other side of the Bloody looking so posh."

Her hazel eyes traced the ember sparks floating across the hellfire sky like stars. In the distance, a howl and immediate choked whimper made Domino cringe. He wondered what would bring him closer to a semblance of safety: relinquishing his pride to cower in his mother's arms or preserve it to maintain the man he was.

"He walked me there with a flower in his buttonhole. I couldn't stop shaking, being eighteen and desirable to a boy. He bought me cotton candy. That spun sugar tasted like strawberries."

The cold night left frostbite in his marrow, especially with the Cobra's blasted top down. He couldn't feel his fingers. His legs trembled violently for hours until he ached, desperate for morning, only to have the daytime fire making him yearn for dusk.

Land of extremes, this Lady Hell. Bone-dry heat sucked him into a desiccated husk by noon and made him liable to shatter in the freezing dark by midnight.

"So naïve," Thessaly barked. "So simple. To think those were the greatest moments of my life. The chaste kiss at the end and the promise to be called on the next afternoon. So fucking simple. But I wanted that. I wanted out."

Thessaly wanted to talk about Daniel. She wanted to know, but she wouldn't ask, too afraid Domino's answers would confirm suspicions. Domino wouldn't say anything unless she goddamn asked outright.

Because he couldn't explain it right, either. Daniel was a beloved son of a bitch who hurt Domino in a hundred ways, who shaped Domino as a man, who put Hell's document in front of Domino and told him to sign on the dotted line. Domino had a fucking list of vendettas against his sire. So, where was his father? If Daniel was that much of a bastard on earth, and Domino knew for a fact he was—full of suicidal tendencies and bloodied with witch-hunts—then where was he in this forsaken land? What grace did Daniel possess that made him Heaven-worthy?

Questions like these, Domino was sure they were there to torment him. He didn't like to think about Daniel, let alone talk about him because it brought about feeling cheated, feeling lost, knowing that something fundamental he saw as evil in his father God saw as pure.

He touched his breast pocket, half-expecting to feel the letters there.

CHAPTER 2

IF THERE WAS one thing you didn't want to be in Hell, it was a witch.

Domino had learned that lesson early on, even before he'd bit the dust, and it served just as well here where Hell was as flat as a Dakota Territory prairie.

Other lessons, like trust, were things he had to break himself of, especially when he associated them with time. He'd almost ended up as trussed meat served on a silver platter for demon slavers after *that* accident. Getting drunk with the crew he'd traveled with for years —friends whose stories he knew forwards and backward—and letting his guard down, had been a deadly mistake. He'd gotten out of that fix with stained fingerbeds and the wobbly shake of a looming nightmare-migraine that always followed on the heels of heavy magic. All the while wondering if it had been like that for *him* if *he'd* been betrayed just as quick—but no. Now was not the place.

Thessaly had a habit of breaking Domino's careful rules about *liars* and *secrets* and *isolation*. Snapped them like twigs.

She fiddled in the car seat. Had been fiddling for days. Her fingers scampered over the Cobra's leather, picking and smoothing in an endless procession from soft to violent that irritated Domino to no end. Driving his customary ninety-five miles an hour blew a maelstrom of sand grit around them.

"Need something?" he half-shouted. He knew she'd shake her head or shrug, sometimes look out the open passenger window as if she hadn't heard him.

"I think we should stop," she said. Unexpected.

"Where?" Domino asked. He didn't like stopping. Would keep driving for hours if he could. He felt exposed more often than not, but that was Hell for you. A landscape that changed depending on whose hell you stumbled into.

I HAVE ASKED TO BE WHERE NO STORMS COME

She squinted into the boiling sun. Domino waited, his tongue probing the parched desert of his cheeks. "I'll tell you when," she murmured.

An hour passed. Domino frowned at the horizon. The blacktop wound needlessly up to a set of wooden stakes crossed to make two X's sticking high into the sky. Stark, like black assigned gender letters from a biology textbook.

"Head over there," Thessaly said, jutting her chin in that direction.

"Don't have much of a choice," Domino growled, but the wind stole his voice. The road took him there whether he liked it or not and he certainly wasn't going to abandon the car.

He downshifted and slowed to a rumbling crawl. Domino squinted, a chill winding up his spine when he saw the dark figure stretched high up between one of the two crisscrossing poles. The other one waited, empty. The asphalt took them right past the corpse, like a roadside attraction where you could take a whole five minutes out of your day, enjoy the local cuisine and culture before heading on your merry way.

"This yours?" Thessaly asked with a crooked eyebrow.

Domino's mouth crimped. The body had been beaten black and blue. Road rash had rubbed half of the face raw. A kneecap stuck out at a strange angle. The pale white gleam of a tibia peeped through the torn pants. Yeah, it was his.

When he woke up for the first time in this punishment land and crawled to the nearest band of travelers—who patted his cheek, told him where he was, and called him baby face—he figured Hell would be brutal when it came to his actual sins. He never figured small insignificant moments would be exploited, or that imagined worst scenario like this would pop up. It gutted him every time. He didn't want to think of Match strung up like that . . .

"Pull over," Thessaly said.

That was the last thing Domino wanted to do, park the Cobra from someone else's past next to a piece of his, but he complied. At least it was something to take his mind off what might've happened to a good, if hunted, man some dark night.

He felt sunburnt and winded. Inside, a mocking voice told him he hadn't seen the real sun in decades.

Cutting the engine with the hidden key he'd found duct-taped under the carriage, Domino slipped it into his pocket and hoisted his rucksack over his shoulder. Another rule. Never leave behind what you don't want to lose.

Thessaly sidled up beside him, her arm a warm line against his.

It made him shiver, having a partner to lean on, especially when he hadn't had one in so long. This time, they were more than chosen companions from across the wasteland. They were family, and Domino knew the thrum of that in his blood went deeper than anything else.

Across from the X's, a makeshift canopy stuck out of the rolling dust. Cracked earth cupped up like malformed sailboat hulls.

"Trading post," Thessaly whispered, edgy as if she could taste something exquisite.

"Nuh-uh." Domino reared back until he touched the car's blistering red paint. "I'm not going into one of those fucking places again."

Places that smelled like smoke and sulfur, where ropes cut into his wrists and tightened when he struggled, and a shaman dealt out bone prophecies for thimblefuls of water. Where demons haggled over his trussed-up body and cut his arms to taste the grade of his blood.

Thessaly's mouth screwed up in a slanted annoyed line. Her leg edged out toward the desert like she was on third base and getting ready to light out for home. "Bad experience?" she asked.

"We're witches," Domino hissed, anger sudden and hot in his chest. "I don't know about you, but I'm not about to be bled dry to satisfy a couple of yuppies who need to look eighteen again."

She let out a startled laugh. "Baby, that's the whole point."

"Run that by me again?"

Thessaly motioned him around the Cobra until they faced the crucified man and settled in the patch of shade the car cast. Domino rubbed the back of his neck, grateful for the absence of the beating heat. Thessaly pulled her satchel onto her lap, sorting through a thread bobbin, feathers gathered and tied with a piece of deerskin, a Ziploc bag full of cotton balls, three empty glass vials, and four full of dark hemoglobin. She took one between thumb and forefinger and sloshed the liquid inside.

"I trade my blood," she said. "Most buyers don't think twice about the source. Demons don't take the time to smell it. They just want to get their hands on some grade-A witch. Others care even less 'cause witch blood doesn't have to be pure for rituals or even youth spells. I can water it down with vodka and it's still good enough for them. Do you see that, baby?"

Domino pursed his lips, unhappy.

"We've got gold in our veins. Let Mama show you." Thessaly dug through her bag again and found a small leather pouch secured closed with an elk tooth and a strip of rawhide. Unwinding it reverently, she pulled out a syringe and hypodermic needle. She fit the tool together gently and motioned for Domino to hold out his arm.

Domino had a blind spot when it came to people he thought he could trust.

He winced when she stuck the needle into the big pulsing vein in the crook of his elbow. Blood, too black and thick, shot into the syringe, filling it up quickly with every thud of his heart.

"Don't get worked up," Thessaly warned him.

"We shouldn't be doing this," Domino whispered. "Fuckin' mistake. Someone will smell us. We'll be hunted."

"You haven't been living right. Why do you make Hell harder than it needs to be? You have any idea what one vial can get you?"

She slipped the needle out and pressed a cotton ball onto the small wound. He took over and watched her hold his blood up to the light for inspection with a furrowed brow, like reading tea leaves. She added a clear droplet from another miniature bottle and shook his blood around. "Won't let it clot," she explained.

"This isn't a good idea." It made him nervous, having his blood and scent outside of his body.

"Don't worry, sweetie." She reassured him with a hand on his arm. "I've done this a hundred times. It'll go off without a hitch. Just follow my lead, okay?"

"Okay," Domino said, but reluctance vibrated in his marrow. Witch blood was a coveted luxury and announcing they were full to the brim of it near a trade post full of degenerate no-goods did not sound like a wise survival tactic. Standing up, they broke away from the asphalt. Thessaly stayed half a step ahead. Domino threw the cotton ball, watched it drift across the cracked dirt like a tumbleweed, his blood a pinprick staining the soft fluff.

The trade post's canopy overhang balanced on two vertical logs. Barely concealed beneath its shade lay a pit with a ladder leaning against the side. Thessaly hooked her leg around the pole and settled her foot on the first rung, shooting Domino a devil-may-care grin before descending.

He still had a hard time consolidating this woman with the woman he remembered. His mother *then* was soft and enigmatic, while this one was wild and uncontrollable. To preserve her in his memory, he thought of them as two separate people. It wasn't an easy distinction to keep up.

Quelling a tremble and reminding himself that he was older than she, he tested his weight along the ladder's first rung. It bowed under his boots. He wondered if he'd ever find another time when he wasn't uncomfortable, terrified, or so nervous it could almost be considered a mental breakdown. Inside, a chuckling voice reminded him: *Hell, Domino. Did you expect rainbows and puppies?*

At the bottom, his boots crunched thick mud balls to dust, like cowpies that had dried too long in the sun. Thessaly swaggered into the small hollowed-out cave while Domino blinked in the low light to get his bearings. White graffiti from demon warding to rough stick figures painted the walls and ceiling. An unusual fellowship lined up behind a white line to throw a set of green plastic winged arrows at a corkboard. A hooded creature nursed a drink in the corner and the bartender cleaned a fresh glass with a dirty rag.

This wasn't at all what he'd expected. No demon or monster could force its way in here, not with all the pulsing magic from the blessed symbols of mass collaborated power.

Thessaly smiled at the bartender. "Have any water?"

The bartender looked her up and down and gave her a sad smile: *poor girl doesn't know what she's gotten herself into.* She sat a vial down on the tabletop, leaning far enough over to push her breasts together. The bartender changed his tune. Domino loomed behind Thessaly. He had to work at it, especially since starvation brought his usually broad shoulders down to an old man hunch. "I want a glass of water," Thessaly reiterated, "and a little something to perk up my mood if you know what I'm saying?"

The bartender motioned with his hands to something behind the bar. An androgynous child, eyes hollowed out with black paint, scrambled up on a stool. The rest of his—her?—body was covered in white chalk and she—he?—smelled like bloody dysentery. He. She. They. Domino blinked hard to clear his head.

The muscles around his scapula tightened to the point of aching numbness. Thessaly's stance kept a half-cocked swagger, but Domino felt it in the air around her as the child—not just any child, a psychopomp of ancient divine madness from the deserts butting against the plains of his homeland, a kind of trapped *koshare*—put their tiny hands on their legs.

Fear. A thrill went down Domino's spine. The trade post wasn't simply a reincarnation of every dive bar from the boundary of the Dark and Bloody to the West Coast, it was an actual place to trade: information, souls, you name it, the heyoka did it. Psychopomps stole from any world, be it your colonized Heaven, Hell, or Earth, and let the koshare do the dirty work of making both the damned and the saved all fight over the gathered scraps.

His eyes slid off the koshare like oil from water. He remembered stories told to him when he'd been young and alive about them and heyokas, the last vestiges of a culture burned out of his family because of the power corrupting his blood.

The bartender slid a milky-white hollowed-out horn to the child. Their deep brown irises slid from Thessaly's face to the cup. A wide smile curved their lips in excessive glee. Domino tongued the worn ridges of his front teeth behind closed lips, biting down on a grimace as the koshare took a sip of the foul yellow liquid and smacked his lips.

The koshare clumsily slammed the cup back down on the bar as if drunk. The stink of urine wafted through the air. With a flat hand, the koshare rose their hand up like a spider and scuttled their fingers over to the vial of Domino's blood, alarmingly close to Thessaly's bunched cleavage. The spider-hand wrapped around the glass and unscrewed the black top with two fingers then slid the vial across the bar back to them. Sniffing the edge, their eyes nearly crossed from being so close. They dipped a fingertip inside and deposited the droplet on their flickering pink tongue.

Domino shuddered. He'd heard of other koshares like this, who'd donned a spirit in their first life and had been eaten by that magic. A soul split, erased, and rewritten, both fighting for dominance, but a tabula rasa was never completely a clean slate. Twisted stories of Hell. Who knew what was true. Who knew if the tales he'd been told as a child where close to right. Maybe he had Hopi and Sioux blood in his veins from Thessaly, but it was also mutt-mixed with German and Irish from Daniel. A million percentages from a million countries. He didn't belong anywhere.

The koshare tapped the open vial's rim. The bartender relaxed minutely, enough to erase the tension strung between them, and pocketed the vial. He laid a plastic pouch, dyed yellow from reuse, within Thessaly's reach. Transaction complete.

Domino knew demon-dust when he saw it. White like cocaine, only this shit had a slight red-rust tinge to it. Thessaly snatched it like a favorite toy.

Heat built up on the back of his neck, making the hairs there rise to attention. Looking up, he caught eyes with the koshare. Solemn, the child's black lipstick-smeared mouth downturned in a decisive frown and Domino felt the prophecy building in the koshare's body, bigger than their soul and ready to spill out whether Domino wanted to hear it or not.

"There's been talk about you. About how he's coming for you," the child whispered and Domino blinked first in their stare-down. "More importantly, you'll be offered everything, but you won't take it. You love Hell too much to take it. Take it." The child's face split in a lewd grin. *"Take it."*

"What does that mean," Domino demanded. Each word ricocheted in the space between his ears. The world shifted alarmingly to the left as if a hand had cracked his skull open and given a noogie to his brain. Somehow, on some magical level, he was being inspected like a horse at auction.

Sharp pain brought him back and he glanced down to see Thessaly's nails clawing his arm through his jacket.

"Let's get outta here," she said. "Domino, let's go."

His impression, by the hoarse edge of her voice, said she had been pleading with him for a while.

"I have your scent now," the koshare mocked as Thessaly shoved Domino's shoulder hard, pushing at his back to *get a move on, boy.* "Gonna fetch a high price, oh yes, you're an expensive brand in demand, Domino Bluepoint. The heyoka will be pleased. Helia's been wanting her warlord for so long, now."

"How fast can you climb a ladder?" Thessaly taunted over her shoulder to the whole trade post.

"Pretty fast," Domino answered dumbly, double-checking he had both feet on each rung before stepping up to the next one. Thessaly cupped his butt like he was a four-year-old again and needed a gentle shove to make it up.

"I'm trying, Mama," Domino told her as the koshare's soothsaying words accidentally chipped pieces off his insides like cracking a molar on a cherry pit.

I HAVE ASKED TO BE WHERE NO STORMS COME

"You're doing great, baby," Thessaly said, and Domino had to agree. Half-damned, sure, but his glass of water wasn't half-empty, it was goddamned full. Brimming over, hot to the touch, and turning to steam.

———•———

"We are never doing that again," Domino shouted. His hands shook on the wheel. Hell could barely keep up with how fast he drove, blacktop rising from the sand and fitting together like perfect-laid brick just before he sped over it. What would it be like, for Hell to give up on building a road to nowhere and simply let them spin out in the scorching sand, let the engine overheat, and cause a big ruckus that would stop every demon, human, and monster in his tracks for miles around?

"They were trying to scare us." Thessaly bent over to protect her lap. She fumbled with the yellowed bag with trembling fingers. The quiet crinkle of it opening cut through the dust devils kicked up by the car's spinning wheels. Domino had half a mind to take the bag and throw it out the window, let the white powder dust the sand, and see what she thought about that.

"They certainly succeeded," Domino growled. Out of the corner of his eye, Thessaly dabbed her finger in the dust, covering her pad with a cover of white crystal. The digit went promptly into her mouth and rubbed hard against her gums.

"What the fuck do you think you're doing, anyway?" Domino demanded, panic coloring his words with a harsh undercurrent of violence. "Sucking on that shit like you fucking want it, like any other red-light girl."

Thessaly wasn't listening. Her face slackened until all the cunning lines, grit, and suffering faded to reveal the woman he'd known until he was ten. The woman who'd died in a fire. His father thought it was an oven fire, others thought she'd done what would be considered decades later as suicide Sylvia Plath style, but Domino knew better. It was a witch-burning, pure and simple.

Her transformation entranced him: the way she dipped her head to the side like she enjoyed the wind, like she'd found some sort of Madonna quality of inner-peace. Envy, shocked and sudden, churned his stomach. He looked away, unable to bear how much he wanted that simple internal acceptance.

Hell caught up with them and once more, the asphalt extended into the painted hellfire horizon like a winding serpent. His foot backed off the gas. He failed to find a beauty that wasn't overwhelming and terrifying in its intensity. The red shade gave him a headache, brought on by memories of lye and bleach trying to scrub the red away.

Domino glanced over to his mother again. Her chest rose with gentle breath. In the blink of an eye, she was replaced with a boy on the edge of pubescence that Domino had run into once, a boy who'd shown him the end result of what the dust could do. White sores around his mouth and a gaunt hungry edge to him that made Domino uneasy, the boy got into Domino's face and hissed about how he'd taken a gun to his school and shot five children and then himself, that he was a terrible person who'd destroyed what little he thought life had for him, and could Domino please trade anything for a pound of flesh?

Domino couldn't stand the stink of the teenager's breath. He'd shoved him into the ground, dug his boot into the boy's chest, and watched the kid gasp out pleas for mercy.

Domino couldn't judge. He was no better. Still stuck down here with all the other murderers, be they thirteen or eighty-four, he'd been declared unworthy by a soul jury. The tattooed lines on his skin told him so. He had no right to judge.

Thessaly's hand cradled the sealed plastic bag. Domino stared at it, wondering in a mindless circle about forgiveness and confession. He thought about that teenage shooter. The demon's family had most likely hunted the kid down because snorting dust was another kind of murder. Only it was the monsters who were killed, their bones ground for bread.

Maybe the kid understood he was on a downslide into a deeper level of Hell and he'd wanted to tell someone something about his identity, the dirtiest part about him, just so someone in eternal space would remember him. What a relief it must be, to hand off your sins to another and know they still existed, but they weren't your responsibility any longer. What peace.

CHAPTER 3

DOMINO NEVER EXPECTED a funeral to slow him down.

The procession of ragtag men and women had camped in the middle of the road and Hell refused to reroute him. The Cobra's tires crunched over the sand drifting across the asphalt like wind-blown snow. He motioned for Thessaly to stay in the car. Trust felt like an artificial concept he kept falling for time and again. Time to wise up and take no chances.

He hefted his rucksack over his shoulder and approached the group with his hands held out for peace. The group surrounded an older gentleman who paced in tight yet chaotic lines, drawing troughs in the sand with his shuffling heels. The gentleman's hands trembled uncontrollably.

"*Hail ave*, how does the sun treat you?"

Domino shielded his eyes from the sun and blinked at the woman greeting him. "*Ave*, stranger," he responded. "Well enough, I suppose. What mischief goes on here?"

The woman broke out in a relieved smile and relaxed her shoulders. Black spots splotched her tongue as she licked her lips and she put her hands into her pockets. "No mischief here, traveler. Simply sending our next of kin on her way to her next journey."

Domino wasn't so foolish. Anything could become a knife with enough time and concentration, and while guns weren't abundant, they weren't scarce either. He wasn't there to fight or steal—not yet, anyway. He eased closer, hands still out in front of him. The gentleman—fuck, shaman? Could Domino call the man that? Did he have the right to? Have mercy, he was no expert—continued drawing crisscrossing lines with his heels. Domino frowned, recognizing the shape in a vague, teasing way that memory does. A piece of power where connecting lines transformed into a net to harness surging forces. Some kind of dreamcatcher.

"Is that *wise*?" he asked, hoping the woman would recognize his implied question: *Is that cunning magic?*

The woman's eyebrows rose in surprise. She crossed her arms, leaned hard on her back leg. "Come again, stranger, what do you see?"

"In my time, power like that was commonplace," Domino badly lied. "You could practice in the open."

The woman's hardened lips softened with a kind of wonder. "Truly?" she asked.

"Course, ma'am. Don't have the inclination myself, but saw many who did."

Her smile outshone the sun. "Can't believe it," she said. "That we got some semblance of identity back. I must be dead for a long time."

Domino prayed she wouldn't ask for a timeline, that she'd swallow the lie like a salmon swimming into the grizzly's mouth because there was no such thing as universally accepted bewitchment. He would bet his good right hand on the subject no matter how many centuries passed. Some things stayed the same. You didn't want to be a witch, in any timeline, in any culture.

"We're sending our good lady Joan to the next world," she said quietly, scooting closer to Domino's tall frame like a dog who wanted a pet. She motioned to a dark spot far in the distance. "Joan said she could feel it in her bones and she's always had terrible arthritis. Said the wasteland called to her and it was time. She wasn't scared."

Domino inclined his head down so he could catch her gaze. "And what's the old . . . shaman got to do with it? Is he your prisoner?"

"We bought him at auction, but I'm one of the old folk. In my day, our shamans were good people and treated well, not used as whores for spells or trade. We keep each other safe. We're a family."

"You're a good person," Domino said, slightly taken aback. Kindness, now that was new.

"It's not right what people will do to anyone who has power. Every time I find myself in one of those underground auctions I get the wiggles, wondering if someone I know is chained up in those cages. Some of 'em treated like royal dogs, but dogs just the same."

"What's he doing for your Joan, then?"

"Reading her future. Sending good spirits to guide her. Mostly, he's making us feel better. Joan was a grandmother in more ways than one." The woman laughed thickly, and Domino noticed she was missing her pinky finger on her left hand.

"Not sure I believe in next worlds," Domino said, hesitant but a curious cat nonetheless.

"You should," the woman said, all sorrow wiped from her face. "In my time, fucking Christianity may have been a forefront religion, but it's nothing but one pie piece of a whole. This," her hand waved out in front of her to take in the reddish sky and shifting sand, "is just one facet to a big old gem. You just gotta know how to see right."

Domino cleared his throat to avoid responding, hated the guttural rumble that came out. He couldn't stand drabble like this. Hell had its own brand of propaganda that Domino blamed on Dante, foretelling that Hell wasn't one plane or planet, it was an interconnected twelve, no twenty-four, no thirty-eight—no one could decide on a number—and if you could survive through all of them without losing yourself, there was redemption to be had at the end. That if you journeyed into a wasteland where no one dared to build a ramshackle bar or a Hooverville, you'd pass into the next phase and climb your way to some kind of Heaven.

A woman had gone in there once, due to the cat-calling of cruel men. Domino had been drunk, taken to the cajoling with the rest of his crew as the woman, could've been forty for all he knew, was pushed and kicked to the edge of the wasteland. Her terror had been palpable; he could hold it in his hands and feel its swallow-hearted pounding. Gunfire aimed in her general direction meant she ran straight into the stretch of Hell that stopped manifesting responses to anxieties, fears, and hatred. Domino had watched until she disappeared like a mirage.

Never forget that Domino Bluepoint was a bad man.

No one came back from the edge of the wasteland. Hell was like a vortex where all the lost souls circled the outer ring until they were sucked from the rim into the unknown. The worst was it wasn't *black*. He would've preferred darkness, but no, it was bright, like the desert had cranked up the sunlight and let it shine without any sky as a protective barrier. Too many people hoped the wasteland had a fairy tale ending. In reality, it was just another precipice you jumped off of.

The shaman's hands trembled. The uncovered skin at his neck and open shirt undulated, as if something rolled just beneath the surface, eager to be birthed. Domino suppressed a shudder. That magic he knew quite well—how the awakened monsters suckled on power, how the shaman had let them climb up his stomach and into his throat, as they cried to be freed through the mouth. Dangerous. The gentleman must've been powerful to contain them so long without being torn apart.

"Joan's moved to a better place," the woman next to him uttered. "She's better than all of us put together. She'll make it out of here just fine."

Domino dug his fingernails into his palms hard enough to draw blood. He hid his wounded hands in his pockets. He hated it, how good people ended up here, having to justify their existence in fucking Hell as a quest for redemption. Domino didn't belong in Hell and he bet solid gold Joan and this woman didn't belong here, either.

They shouldn't be begging for scraps, fighting like dogs in an underworld ring. The only thing Thessaly had done wrong was teaching her children to survive with the craft inherited from her lineage. The only thing this woman probably did wrong was killing her abusive husband. It wasn't right. Goodness wasn't *right.*

Life might not be fair, but death should be as fair as they come. It should mean something.

He cleared his throat again and looked down at the parched yellow and white sand. Human bones. He could feel the millions of souls vibrating as sand, those who had given up. Like the girl with the cellphone. All those people who couldn't stand Hell any longer and sat down, let the wind erode them to dust, and gave Hell control over their bodies and spirits. They *became* Hell. The worst part was that old Joan probably didn't even know it, didn't believe it. Still as ignorant as the day she fell here.

Fury kindled in the pit of his stomach, the kind that set his fingers tingling and a looming black sun splotch emptying his brain. The urge to send lightning racing across the plains was almost too much to bear. Soon enough he'd expose himself, show these nice travelers he was one of the animals that would fetch a high price at auction and who knew what they might do with that information. Claws might come out. Might try to grab him, sell him, use him.

"Good day, ma'am," he said and the woman gave him a startled, kind smile. "*Vale,* traveler," she said.

He got back into the car, feeling like he couldn't stand inhabiting this skin of his, and drove off the road and around them. He drove over a hundred miles with an endless scream in the back of his head before pulling over without a word. Thessaly looked at him with a raised eyebrow.

"I want some," he said, thinking of peace and reprieve.

"You sure?" Thessaly's hand curved protectively around her bag. "Seemed mightily against it earlier."

"Don't ask me no questions," he said.

"I'll tell you no lies. I've heard *that* folk song before," Thessaly grunted, handing him the yellowed plastic. "Certainly, wasn't from my time."

"Mine either," he said, dipping his finger in the white powder and rubbing it against his gums. Like he said. Quick learner. Adaptable.

"That woman say something to you?" Thessaly asked, studying him as if she looked *through* him and didn't like what she saw.

"She's nothing but a waster," he said. "Hate wasters who think there's paradise in the wasteland."

Thessaly hummed in agreement.

Domino blinked. A giddy rush that demanded he move, walk, run, leap into the air filled him. "Tell me where to go," he commanded.

"You'll know soon enough," Thessaly said, watching him closely. Her dark eyes seemed to sing. "Just wait a minute more and you'll know."

———◆———

He felt like an outlaw that should've been wearing a serape, a flat-brimmed cowboy hat, and a paisley bandana covering his mouth based on the way he lay flat-bellied on the cragged overhang scouting the ravine. Sand dug into his palms—more like bone gravel in all honesty, the jagged sediment got into cuts and wouldn't work its way out again—and ripped out the knees of his jeans as he shifted again to see better, but on the inside, where it counted, he felt absolutely at peace.

He may be damned in Hell, but at that exact moment and at that exact time, Domino felt he was where he was supposed to be. All roads led here. Destiny had guided him to the top of the cliff with his mother, spying on the covered wagons resurrected from a pioneering age that staggered through the pass.

The rush of anticipation hailed from a time when he'd been alive, and he had a gun strapped to his waist with his brother at his side. The only difference was that now, death held no fear for him. His fear of pain remained—that was simply part of being in Hell—but the desperate terror that this might be his last minutes on earth had disappeared. He might take a bullet to the chest and writhe on the bone dust in a blackness that *felt* like death, but which in reality—or *hell*-ality—lasted minutes or days. Yet, a certainty remained. Domino had already died. His soul was in eternal damnation. Ergo, he would rise again.

To make things even better, he could trust his partner. Thessaly wouldn't tussle him up and sell him to the next demon bidder searching for a witch-soul to enslave. Somehow, he felt unguarded, free, like an indestructible force of everlasting youth.

Gone were pangs of guilt too, worries that he might accidentally maul a child or shoot an innocent. If they were here, they all deserved what was coming to them. In Hell, no one was innocent.

Thessaly shifted beside him. The breeze caught her hair and drifted the strands across her face. The sun-bleached ends tickled Domino's cheek, but he didn't brush it away.

"Now?" Domino asked, his tongue flicking out to touch his split lower lip. Tasted the rust and salt coating it.

"Patience," Thessaly hissed back, inching close enough that he could feel the tight coil of her muscles. She was just excited as he. A crow skull tied on a thong bumped against her chest. Pretty piece of magic, cost three vials of blood for Thessaly's crow and Domino's owl, and they'd lit out fast as possible before the two scar-faced gentlemen they'd done business with could ask any more questions. Little bit of hair here, more blood splatter there, a strip of rawhide laced through the eyes and tied tight around Domino's neck, and he had the makings of a beautiful illusion. Hopefully, the pilgrims below weren't quick on the draw to notice the oddity: birds of prey watching from up top.

"Where do you think they're keeping it?" Domino had no idea what kind of owl he might look like, could be snowy, could be a barn, but it didn't matter. Owls had hooked claws and could soar silently on uplifting thermals.

I HAVE ASKED TO BE WHERE NO STORMS COME

Thessaly's eyes flickered over him, her pupils blown with matching hunger. "No idea, but we'll tear the whole place apart if we have to."

In another life, Domino wouldn't have trusted the rumors leaching from the black-market trade posts. He wouldn't have been in those dives in the first place. If he did catch a whiff of gossip, he would've taken his whisky shot and ignored the murmurs about the pilgrims who decided they had no business being in the Pit with all the other lunatics and murderers. These pilgrims decided Hell was just another obstacle to achieve God's love, and the first step in redemption was to find the mystical Lake, which held the tears of every soul in this dump. Domino figured if Hell's only saltwater lake was so goddamn big, it would've been discovered by now, and all of Hell's good citizens would've built their cities on its banks, bathed in its cool waves, and drained it dry.

But that was before the dust.

Before the dust, he ignored those types of rumors. Rumors that foretold the pilgrims' mission, sure, but how they were also cunning enough to carry all the good things in life such as water, food, good leather shoes, and dust.

Dust. Snorting demon dust smelled like rust. When he found bone pieces that hadn't been fully crushed, he ground them between his teeth and scraped the grit on his gums. Within fifteen minutes, he'd feel free. Invincible. Right now, he was high on the last crumbs they had of it.

"Now?" He hated the slight whine to his voice.

"Now," Thessaly confirmed.

They split apart and slunk down the cliffside. Domino envisioned them as two birds drifting close to the ground, hiding behind tumbleweeds and the barebones skeletons of desert trees instead of lifting into the red hellfire blazing in the sky.

The pilgrims spotted him as he closed the open distance between the wagons and the rocky cliff. Domino barreled toward them, hearing the *pfft* of bullets from badly calibrated guns. Puffs kicked up around him. He dodged, still a flying owl, when a shot struck true in his shoulder. It didn't bring him down. Didn't break the illusion. Nothing could stop the absolute certainty that if gods had made him this infallible and ruthless, Domino should accept the idea, too.

Two wagons rocked as the inhabitants shifted from one end to the other. No idiots, these missionaries. Despite their hopes for redemption, they had accepted they were surrounded by those with yearnings for violence, thus kept their weapons handy. Another round of bullets sent tufts of sand shooting into the air. Domino tucked wings and crashed into the first wagon, startling a young man and another old as sin. The old man gripped a pike, levered it at Domino, and lunged. Domino broke the old man's nose, then hissed as the boy's small knife dragged across his ribs. The boy's wrist snapped in Domino's grip and he went down screaming. Domino put his foot into the old man's back and stepped hard until he felt a sickening crunch.

The miniature black hole swirling around his brain, activated whenever he used magic, wobbled and condensed until it finally faded away. He looked down, startled, to see the owl skull had been crushed against his chest. Goddamnit.

With a snarl, he slammed the wagon's broken door open. A woman charged him with a sword held high. He narrowly dodged her wild, sweeping arc. "Get away, you hellspawn bastard! We've asked for no trouble, so give us none!"

"You've got dust," Domino said as the sword's tip sliced into his shirt. "Give me the dust and we'll leave you alone. How's that sound, ma'am?"

"Worthless junkie," the woman sneered. She lunged and Domino sidestepped, letting her ram the blade deep into the wagon's wooden side. She pulled at it frantically, but it stuck fast. Domino's elbow collided with her, sending her sprawling. He wrenched the sword out and cut the woman off mid-sentence by taking her head.

Silence descended like a fast-moving storm. Hell drank the spilled blood, turning the glossy liquid into tacky powder. The sun beat down ruthlessly, making heat lift from the motionless corpses in small, contained waves. Domino scrunched his nose. He never did like the scent of death warmed over.

Inside the wagon, he tore the mismatched beds apart and sliced open the cotton mattresses. Rice and dry beans spilled from burlap bags. The candle of disgruntled rage quickly snuffed out the flame of hope, and in Domino's hands, the sword became a weapon of chaos: chopping divots into the wooden sides, shredding pillows, slicing up trinkets of comfort. The wound on his ribs burned, the scent of old blood lingered in the back of his throat, but it was nothing compared to the telltale pounding of a migraine beginning to wrap around his skull like fingers and dig into his fused fontanels.

Blinking hard, he took a deep breath and focused enough to observe his surroundings, like he would've done before the dust. Amid the grayed cotton puffs of a destroyed couch lay a worn leather scabbard with an attached strap. With shaking hands, Domino picked it up and slung it over his shoulder, sheathing the blade against his back like a second, no-nonsense spine. Once, Domino might've joined their party and the tentative security blanket of offered society, but Domino Bluepoint no longer crept through Hell with a survival mindset. Now, he ripped through the desert on lust, bouncing from one trade post to another with his pockets full of powder as pale as the land.

He stepped outside, empty-handed. The pilgrims would be rising from their Hell-induced death soon. As he rounded the corner to the next wagon, a force barreled into him from behind, knocking the wind out of him. He fell, flat-faced, into the sand. A gasp eeked out of him as a whirlwind of color shimmied before his vision and pain spidered up his spine. His attacker kicked him onto his back just before the grounding agony of a fist drove into his stomach. Domino buckled over, hands protectively covering his belly, and felt the blunt crunch as his attacker force-fed him a knuckle sandwich. His nose collapsed. He couldn't breathe. Multiple non-magic-created black holes sparkled around him, threatening to consume his consciousness completely.

With two hands fisted in Domino's shirt, his attacker hauled him up and pressed close enough for Domino to see the fury that rides on the heels of loss transform the man's face. Domino tried to spit the blood pooling in his mouth, but it only dribbled down his chin.

"You motherfucker," the man growled.

The truth of that festered in his gut—he was nothing but a bad dog that could only be put down with a gunshot. He tensed for the next punch.

"It's you," the attacker said instead, slightly awed, "You're that *kid.*"

Domino chanced a peek: a scared-beyond-belief peek, with the ridiculous inclination to proclaim that he was *not* a kid. "'Scuse me?" he grunted, shaking his head in the negative.

A disbelieving grin split the man's lips and he started hitting Domino in familiar, non-lethal ways, punches that would immobilize and make him blackout. His old crew had beat him like this after they'd turned on him, after they'd found out he had witchcraft carved in his bones.

Domino crossed his forearms over his face and bent his knees, aiming for leverage to kick out, but he ended up balled up to survive the raining blows. The muffled cry seeping from his lips didn't sound like him.

"What the fuck do you think you're doing?" Thessaly's voice cut through Domino's thick rasps. The radiating pain subsided, replaced with a roaring throb. The beating stilled. "That's my son, you fucker. That's my goddamn boy."

The sound of a fist cracking against a cheekbone filled the air. Curled on his stomach, Domino inched up like a stretching cat. His tender, bruised cheek rubbed against the sand as he tried to reorient the sloshy world. He forced his swollen eyes open in time to see Thessaly's arm cock up high as she punched his attacker over and over.

"You touch my kid?" she shrieked. "You lay one finger on him?"

The man cried out as his teeth shattered.

"You ever touch my boy again, I'll make sure your body parts are so far away from each other they won't ever be able to mend together again."

"Don't, don't," the man sputtered with a spit-out broken molar stuck to his chin. "He's *wanted*. We can cash in on him, split the reward."

Thessaly's fist stilled mid-air. She brought her cocked elbow down until it was level with her face. Domino's heart dropped. "Come again?" she asked.

The man fumbled for his pocket and pulled out a worn sheet smudged with fingerprints from bad ink. Thessaly ripped it from his hands and sat hard on top of him, digging her knees into his ribs until he yelped. Smoothing out the page on his chest, Domino watched Thessaly's shoulders still in a way that set off mental alarms. Panic forced him to his feet. He stumbled, hunched over and clutching his stomach, to her. Looking over her shoulder, a reprint of his face stared back at him, poorly drawn but good enough, bracketed by a declaration on top and his full name printed below in big black letters. *Wanted.* No reward, but Domino knew curiosity killed many cats. Thessaly flipped the page over and touched the scrawl: *Come to the Midnight Saloon for this witch's scent!*

Cold terror washed over Domino. In all his time in the underworld, he'd never seen something like that—a poster marking him as hunted in a land of hunters. There was nowhere he could hide. The thought of being without dust crawled over him like a thousand bugs. He tried to ignore the need inside him when the dust ran low, and the absolute panic of possibly going without. He'd been going without for so long.

"Who's selling?" Thessaly asked, deadly quiet. The man hesitated until she leaned forward, her shoulders bearing down over him.

"I don't know," he whimpered. "Rumor goes, the big hit out on his soul is managed through a heyoka, but I don't know who ordered the hit, I swear I don't."

"What does it mean?" Domino whispered, more to himself than anyone.

"Means you're doomed, boy," the man said, solemnly like Domino was a child he'd seen grow up and who hadn't turned out the way he was supposed to. "Hounds tracking you now. Maybe even a Nuckelavee. Not sure you can get anymore doomed."

Thessaly's face reddened like a risen sun bloomed in her cheeks. "Won't let *you* say anything, old man," she whispered, one hand capturing his mouth, a knife bright in the other. The man's tongue suddenly twitched on the sand and he gagged on his own blood.

Thessaly stood, looking sick. When Domino pulled her into a crushing hug, he felt her shaking. They stuffed the Cobra's trunk full of leftover water and food, cracked cups and blankets. The sword's scabbard had warmed to his skin.

And the dust. That stayed close. Couldn't forget the dust.

———◆———

"Give me a little bit more," Domino said.

"If I give you any more, there won't be any left." Thessaly crinkled the plastic bag closed.

"Just one more snort," Domino wheedled. The meager fire he'd built on the side of the road bent sideways with a sudden rough wind.

"No," Thessaly said.

"Thessaly."

"Domino."

"Now."

"No." Thessaly clutched the bag to her chest. "You're scared and worried, but you can't have anymore. There's a limit and we've hit it tonight."

"I haven't hit anything," Domino snarled. Three mounds of dust and he couldn't feel a goddamn thing. One more would cinch it, he was certain.

"Ain't that the truth. You've been everyone's punching bag today." Thessaly's mouth thinned into a mulish line. "You're high as a kite, your stupid brain just can't figure it out."

"Fuck off. I don't need this shit from you."

"This isn't like you, Domino. It's fear."

"Just give me the dust and I'll be on my way."

"You're not going anywhere."

"I can go wherever I want!"

"You're acting like you're thirteen!"

"How would you know, you were dead by then!"

Domino might be a little flame, but he was hot with recklessness, itching to swing with fists and words, yet his energy would only last so long. A match, quick to spark, but a short stick to burn to char. "How would you know?" he asked again, suddenly achingly stranded and halfway to being an orphan again.

He wasn't proud of what came next. Of how she coaxed him, skittish with reluctance, to her lap. How he wept over things she didn't know or understand. How he cried over the names of women she did know and men she didn't. About Christobel and Benedicta. Match. Wicasah. About how he'd searched for them all in secret, hoping he would stumble on them in Hell and praying to all that was holy that he wouldn't. He tentatively spoke of Daniel, about old hurts, thick with scars, that still ached. By then, though, Hell had dried him out and he couldn't do much else but press his hand to his chest, feel the thick paper envelope that once resided there, and wished he could burn the memory like he'd lit up the pages, long ago.

She remembered what it was like to be a mother. He wasn't sure it was something that could ever be forgotten, but it felt good to have her take him in her arms and hold him. When she stroked his hair and told him she'd take first watch, he complied without fear because absolute truth existed within a mother's reassurance, the same way blankets pulled tight over the head would most certainly keep the monsters at bay.

CHAPTER 4

DOMINO HAD NEVER taken to church life. Even so, Christianity cultured his world, so he'd faked his way through sermons and mouthed the prayers and looked at anything but the simple crucifix on the prison's gray brick wall. It wasn't like he didn't think about religion or even his relationship with God, but because he'd been too damaged by it. The psychologist who'd proudly thought up that prognosis had gotten a shrug with open hands from Domino. On the subject of religion, Domino didn't have to play games or hide his feelings. He liked religion just fine. He just didn't like what people did with it. Like Daniel, who'd pretended to wear the solemn black of a preacher for so long it finally became truth.

Domino never kept the church out of his speech, though, and right now a whole slew of *Jesus Christ, sweet mother have mercy, oh god*, flew from his mouth as the hellhound caught up to the Cobra and leapt on the back, claws puncturing the metal trunk with a screeching punch.

Thessaly's scream nearly undid him. Domino barely had two thoughts to rub together before his body decided enough was enough. One glance in the rearview mirror had him staring straight at a slobber-rimmed muzzle bared around sharp teeth. The hound's sunken eyes, wispy with red flames and soot-black pupils, gazed at him like a marinated chicken drumstick.

The Cobra revved in fifth, desperate for sixth. Domino pushed the gas pedal to the floor. The car fishtailed off the blacktop, throwing waves of sand into the faces of the other two hounds galloping close behind. Domino gripped the emergency brake and yanked, sending the car into a drift. In the rearview mirror, he glimpsed a glittering trail kick up from beneath the tires—a glass trail from the heated rubber, turning sand into fulgurite. The candy-red car was a demon in her own right—smoke puffing from under the hood like a snorting bull and all the arrows on the dash pointing to overheated red or empty.

The screech of the hellhound's claws slipping off metal echoed as background noise to the roaring engine. Soon, the beast lay in a bundle of gargantuan limbs behind them. Gears ground as Domino slammed into third, aware he might be hyperventilating as he tried to put as much asphalt between him and the hound as possible. The other two sped past their wounded packmate, their baying howl making the heat-mirages shiver.

"They're gaining on us," Thessaly screamed as she turned in her seat to stare behind them. Domino couldn't help but be reminded of that painting, captured forever in an old art book too dusty for modern interest, of a bald man stuck in an orange swirling background, his mouth dropped in an ever-shrieking O. Thessaly was like that, displaying her panic to the world. In the end, it wouldn't matter one lick. Third shifted to fourth. Fourth to fifth.

"I know," Domino rasped. He'd inhaled enough dust to render his lungs desert-dry, but a wild notion formulated in the back of his mind and ran desperate tingles to his fingers. A precursor to something crazy, something dangerous, just because he was cornered.

"We have to jump ship," he decided.

"What?" Thessaly yelled, spinning to look at him. "Are you fucking crazy?"

"Abandon the car," Domino said, reaching back to make sure he had a hard hold on his backpack. He shifted one final time into sixth, and nearly ripped the door handle off opening the door. He threw himself out.

Roadkill. Bones broke as he hit the sand. The ground scraped away half his face and stripped his coat and jeans to ribbons. Teeth askew in his mouth, his neck nearly obliterated, and with one good eye not blinded by the impact, he saw the hellhounds overtake the suddenly slowed car and began ripping it to shreds. The high groan of bent steel vibrated in his broken bones.

Thessaly crawled to him with both legs shattered behind her. "I don't think we're gonna make it," she gasped.

Domino didn't answer. Luckily, his ankle held his weight. He fumbled with the remains of his pack and yanked out his tiger's eye, the raven's feather, swan's foot, and braided horsetail he'd traded for some sicko's night with his mouth pressed against the bleeding wound on Domino's wrist for a witch-high. He didn't care, too much dust between the both of them, and if Domino couldn't remember exactly what happened after, well it wasn't that much of a loss. He did remember Thessaly gathering him up the next morning, pressing a full canteen of water to his lips, and whatever regrets he had went out the window because *a full canteen.*

He bent down, one hand in an arthritic claw around the supplies of the spell, readying the crooked pointer finger of his other hand to draw in the sand when that bitch Hell changed the sand under him into a small asphalt slab.

Domino let out a choked cry and backed up a step, ready to draw in the fresh sand extending every which way around him but in front. The asphalt block shifted and appeared under his finger before he could touch the sand. If he couldn't scribe, he couldn't summon his power. He looked up, frantic now as the hellhounds finished ripping the stuffing out of the seats.

Domino backed up a step to redraw. Again. Again. His finger hit asphalt every time. Cotton clouds and ruin filled the air.

"God fucking damnit, woman, *save me,*" he roared through mountain-jagged teeth at the blacktop. With a coquettish wink, the asphalt disappeared.

The hellhounds lost interest in the car and milled around the hump of metal, catching their scent and jogging towards them.

In the burning sand, Domino drew a circle with a jagged line and triangle through it, tossed the three offerings with a slurred sentence, and watched them turn to char in the air. He kissed the tiger's eye and experienced his soul falling into a fathomless abyss where a blue nebula waited. He grabbed the pulsing tendrils and unraveled them like yarn, letting the strands expand at the speed of light up his synovial fluid and out.

Lightning, blinding white and thick as a synapse, struck from a cloudless sky. The hounds yelped and shied away from the brightness. Domino grinned, experiencing the electricity in his enamel. Another crack struck one of the hounds between the shoulders, lighting up his insides into a golden throbbing shine before the creature collapsed in a smoking pile of roasted meat and singed hair. Domino felt the lightning release the hound's life and he sucked the essence into his gut, experiencing the leftover throbbing in his belly like a second heartbeat.

Electricity, silent without its thunder, bolted into the second hound. Domino's hair stood on end, waving like cilia. A third heartbeat joined his.

"Jesus fucking Christ," Thessaly murmured on the ground next to him, her legs stuck out in front of her and mending back together slowly. "Now that's some power."

Concentration broken—the moment broken—the air settled into a charged mist around them, heavy with petrichor. Domino staggered as the weightless rush faded, leaving cinder blocks in his veins. He swayed, finding Hell's gravitational pull too hard to resist, and collapsed in the sand.

"Whoever wants you dead sure knows what they're doing," Thessaly said. "*I'd* be looking for you if I knew you could do that."

He sensed Thessaly's pride. As much as he wished to bask in it, he could only whimper as Hell's sunlight split his brain like a lobotomy. Migraine.

"We should start selling your magic," Thessaly added, a sly edge to her tone indicating she had her hands cupped near her mouth as if to hold her ideas close. "Be like the bodyguards of the underworld. We could start small, get people from one end of Hell to the other, then scale it up, attempt the wasteland—"

"No," Domino grunted. "Too painful." His hands covered his eyes and he rocked back and forth. Seasick, that's what it was, nausea that rolled in his stomach where he'd absorbed the hounds' lives. Made him want to vomit and curl up and die. Thessaly's voice struck him like an open-handed slap. If she thought he had impressive magic, she should see what her youngest could do.

"Come here, baby," Thessaly said. "Can't go anywhere on these broken pins yet anyway." Her hand gently gripped his shoulder and eased his head down to her lap. Domino buried his face in the darkness of her knees.

"Where'd you learn a thing like that?" Thessaly asked. "I'm good, but I'm not that good."

"Christ, Mama, shut up," Domino pleaded as the pain ricocheted down his neck and through every neural canal he possessed. Red meat now, this laid-low witch. Any devil could come for him and he'd welcome them, if only they would make this woman hush.

A soft touch rubbed his scalp. He groaned.

"Used to do this for the aunts," she whispered above him, "when their headaches got bad. Do you remember them?"

Domino gritted his teeth and squeezed his eyes shut so tightly he could see wobbly purple circles behind his eyelids. Of course, he did and of course, she would, fishing for information he wasn't willing to give because it linked back to Daniel.

"That old house of theirs was falling apart, I swear," Thessaly mused. "Your daddy fixed every drainpipe and shingle. They were my friends when no one else would be."

Oh, he remembered his mother's adopted coven, deep in the dust bowl of Dakota Territory and their big rickety house that looked as if it had been moved off New England property. Such finery had to have been shipped over from the Brightside of the Dark and Bloody—the eastern side full of innovation and revolution, of experimentation and science.

He used to play with two little girls. One was four years older than he and the other only two, but they cared for him studiously, ensuring he didn't wander off when his mother brought him to visit. They lived in the middle of the prairie, outside of town, where the wide stalks of high grass rustled in the wind like waves and swallowed young boys. The sisters would hold his hand while they scampered through the house as his mother set out her big spellbook and arranged ingredients around her. Eastern magic required tactile things and Thessaly combined the coven's spells with the magic flowing through the West. The magic of the witchery.

Look to the horizon, she'd whisper to him, pivoting him in the direction of a setting sun. *That's how far our magic stretches.*

Money was scarce and with Daniel doing who knows what kind of oil work in the fields, Thessaly sold petty spells and enchantments that wouldn't do much damage. Tactile things. *Look, just a bundle of rosemary for pleasant company, just a touch of lavender with corpse rot on it. Good for the skin.* She never sold witchery sorcery, with its pale roots feeding off evil. Stronger and darker than Brightside power, you could take that to the bank.

The oldest girl was named Benedicta. The younger sister was Christobel. Such Brightside finery even in their names—names fit for antiques and statues carved by masters. They had both lost their parents. The four women living in the house were the aunts: the two witches, the crazy third pacing the attic, and the youngest as a grave marker in the backyard. The living three were off, but kind, surviving in a different type of exile that persisted from a golden goose egg of cash to keep them quiet, a home to keep them content, their silence to keep them forgotten.

Domino basked in their over-affectionate hugs, the small caramels popped into his mouth, the way they let him try hot toddies from their cups with cooing encouragement and laughed when he sputtered at the awful taste. *You'll get used to it one day, they said to him. When you lose all your taste buds, just like you lose everything else.*

Jagged streaks of pain cracked through the haze of remembrance. Domino whimpered, engulfed in agony. Above him, Thessaly bombarded him with a slew of questions and memories even as her fingers stroked his road-rash-exposed cheekbone. Smooth. Lulling. A sharp itch raced over his face like a healing scab, but Thessaly's small enchantment soothed it like a menthol balm. Miraculously, he lost consciousness.

CHAPTER 5

THESSALY'S STRIDE TOOK a hit as her newly knitted legs relearned how to walk. Domino supported her with one arm, repeating under his breath all his self-imposed rules he'd broken for dust. His tongue probed the cuts in his charred lips, eliciting a dull sting and sending a metallic taste like destroyed Cobra-steel to the back of his throat. Sand stuck to the raw meat that used to be his neck, and soon the polished oval exposures of his skull eroded as a sandstorm whipped up around them.

"Not often you see power like that," Thessaly managed. She was getting faster—soon, they'd have to run. "But magic must always be bought and paid for. So, which was yours?"

Domino gave her a sideways look. She couldn't leave well enough alone. "How do you mean?"

"I'm asking a very simple question, baby. Was it necrophilia, incest, or murder?"

Domino flinched at the question's dark undercurrent, her unspoken prayer: *don't let it be incest, please God and all that's holy, don't let it be that.*

He swallowed hard against the betrayal—*you think I'd do that?*—but since he'd ended up here, he understood her reasoning. "None of the above, okay?"

She stumbled, incredulity on her face. "Well, I'll be," she whispered as if she'd finally opened a secret door. "My mama didn't lie when she said boys got the most power."

Uncomfortable now, and Domino desperately wanted to fidget, put some space between them. At least he didn't have to look her in the eye as they staggered across the desert. His knowledge of power was rudimentary at best, garnered from half-remembered rituals witnessed on the aunt's East-finery home's widow's walk. Thessaly was supposed to teach him to control the wildness burgeoning inside him when he reached puberty, but she'd been snuffed out too soon. Sure, he had power, but he had no idea where that magic originated, what it meant, why his bloodline was sick with it and others weren't.

"That's what I get," Thessaly gasped, pausing to twist and test her leg. "Girls who follow the witchery of the smoking lands aren't supposed to fall in love, definitely aren't supposed to have two beautiful strapping boys to call their own." She grinned at him. "Can't become a proper twisted practitioner when you've got kids to take care of."

"What was it for you, then?" Domino asked, his eyes latched to the horizon. An ache had taken root in the rich soil of his heart, reminding him of the dead patches of his heritage. "You're a witch, which meant your mama was a witch. This stuff is inherited. So, back at you: necrophilia, incest, or murder?"

Thessaly took in a shaky breath. "Murdered my sister. Wasn't totally my fault. My mother—who I hope is rolling over in her grave, mind you—knew how to egg us both on, get us at each other's throats. The twisted magic whispered at me for days at that point and I was sick of my mother treating my sister like she was the prettiest bitterroot flower." Thessaly let out an unhinged laugh. "The cycle can't ever be broken. My mama killed her sister, too. The witchery doesn't become diluted by fucking fine Brightsiders or white settlers or wise tribesmen. It sleeps in the blood and wakes when the time is right."

Wasn't that the truth—hadn't Domino appeased the developing magic inside of him by starting fistfights and participating in cruelty? Hadn't he been so desperate for answers he'd put temptation right in his brother's line of sight?

Thessaly let out a sharp breath of pain but continued. "You know, the only thing I know about *where we come from* is that the seed of our family was born and bred in the badlands. Whoever she—or he, I suppose—was, they thought evil and practiced evil, twisted evil into being from normal life, thus created evil in themselves. Her family and community banished her and the evil made her forget the stories of her people, the history of her past. Severed her from all she knew until her memory was nothing but a land of smoke. It's part of accepting the magic. But you know that."

"But our family aren't the only witches in the Territories."

"I suppose not. Poor Annalise. Stupid of her to leave her Brightside life for a witch. Oldest story I know. Abandoned all she knew for him, took a blimp across the Dark and Bloody to be with him, got herself pregnant not once but twice, and he left her for dead. The aunts never forgave themselves. Moved that idiotic house just for Annalise, kept the fine Eastern company from gossiping for all the good it did, but I suppose I'm being unfair. The things one does, for memories."

Words clogged Domino's throat. He hoped she'd say more, banked on his silence as permission. The aunts used to whisper that he belonged to the witchery—a word that followed him around as sure as his name. He remembered being huddled beside Christobel when the heat wouldn't kick on in their hotel room and how she taught him tricks her mother—Annalise—had written on how to exert control over the magical chaos running rampant inside them. Christobel explained clearly that, yes, women and magic were rare, but he had West-magic inside of him while both the witchery and Brightside magic cursed her.

He couldn't quite wrap his mind around it. After all, he'd been surrounded by powerful females his whole life, hadn't seen one strong male in all his years that could compare to the sisters, to the aunts, to his mother.

Except for Wicasah.

Wicasah would always be eight years old to him—growing up too fast, but always tugging on his hand to *hurry up, Domino, let's go.*

Good advice. Dust devils nipped at his heels. No landmarks existed to distinguish their location, but they needed shelter soon before the rising storm took them. Wouldn't it be just his luck if they accidentally wandered into the true wasteland of Hell with nothing? No map, compass, food, water. No dust.

Domino's face crinkled like papyrus as he smirked. Wouldn't his old cartographer buddy Evan, the bastard who'd tied the tethers around his wrists when his little witch-secret got out, get a kick out of that. One campfire night, bellies full on a can of beans and too drunk on sugared vodka, Evan shyly showed his sketched base map and explained with lisping syllables how the outer rim was the "livable" Hell. Inside lay the wasteland and beyond must be where the mountains lay.

"I don't see any goddamn mountains," Domino sneered at him, his mouth sticky like his fingers.

"It's the rainshadow effect, my good man," Evan smiled. He never stopped smiling, even when the bottle was empty. "We're simply on the leeward side of Hell."

Domino hoped that traitor walked into the wasteland in search of the windward west and lost his sanity there.

Now, rising gently in the distance through wavering white heat-mirages, emerged an orange mesa topped with a one-level brick building. Salvation in the form of an off-the-highway pay-by-the-hour dump. Domino nearly cried at the sight of it. Thessaly gripped his shirt collar and, if possible, they walked faster.

The dust devils picked up, urging them to hurry. Domino nearly froze when a glance over his shoulder revealed a wall of dirt, rolling like a tidal wave toward them.

The long rectangular motel, so close. Heat radiated off the brick. Sunbursts reflected off the tin roof. Domino urged Thessaly into a hopping run. He'd filled his quota of terror for the day— things had begun to feel numb. He yanked on the closest door twice before realizing it was locked.

"Look, good sir. See here."

A hand tugged on his elbow. Domino glared down at a man lounging against the wall with bloodshot eyes and a bucktoothed grin who held out a ripped linen square stained with rusty blood. He didn't have time for crazed lunatics who hadn't tended to their sanity like a good farmer should.

"Look!" the man urged, rising to his knees, the cloth cupped in his palm like the holy grail. "Abraham Lincoln's bloodied shirt! Such a loss, such a sad affair, and for only five gold you'll have a relic of that saint's passing. Five gold, sir, please. Please. *Please.*"

"Bother someone else, you nasty rat," Domino growled, shrugging the man off, "and get the fuck inside before the storm blows you away."

He tried the next door. Locked. The lunatic studied him, short breaths hissing through his open mouth, twisting the relic in hands turned to claws. The third door clicked open. Domino hustled Thessaly inside, slamming the door hard on the veteran's scowl and the blood-red sky. At least five different bolts, both ancient and modern, had been installed and he shoved every one into place, experiencing a sense of relief at the satisfying slide and click.

Turning away from the door, Domino studied as Thessaly surveyed the motel room by hitching up the duvets on both twin beds before checking the bathroom. Lightbulbs behind square glass mesh cast a flickering industrial yellow on them. Domino flipped the switch off, but it made no difference.

Thessaly eased onto the edge of the bed, testing the mattress with a gentle bounce. "What now?" she asked.

Domino wondered how fast dislocated fingers would heal if he punched his fist through that wall. His bag hung over his shoulder like a tattered balloon. The supplies, herbs, chalk, spell components carefully, yet carelessly, traded for vials of his blood, had been scattered to the wind. He wished to be the strong, optimistic man Thessaly could've raised because no alpha male would ever feel this helpless.

"Use blood as wards?" he suggested.

"Like ringing a dinner bell," she lashed out. "If you wanted to be found that quick you should've given me the car keys and let the hounds take you."

"I'm all ears for your better idea," Domino snapped.

She put her thumb and forefinger against the edges of her eyes. It had been a while since he'd actually stood in her presence and took the time to take her in. The dull sheen coating her dark hair. How she appeared ragged compared to the days before the hunt for Domino had begun.

"We need to do something," she said.

"That crazy man," Domino said, pleased with a sudden solution. "Bleed him dry. No one will sense him. He's not a witch."

Thessaly's eyes brightened. "Smart boy."

"Just a matter of warming up the old noggin'," he said with a grin. "I'd do it, but . . . "

"Yeah, we don't want any more trackers on you than we need. They've got your description, not mine."

"Sorry you got such a criminal for a son."

"Wouldn't have it any other way, baby. Now lay down before you fall over."

Domino shuffled to the bed, thinking he'd sit on it nice and smooth, but his body had other ideas, including collapsing on the duvet. Thessaly stood, testing her healed legs, and slipped out of the room. Face buried in the pillow, Domino smelled cheap detergent and lingering body sweat. The linen was worn and thin but soft from countless others finding solace in the room. He couldn't remember the last time he'd lain in a real bed with real covers and a real mattress and wondered if this was what a last meal might taste like right before an execution.

Old motels like these brought him back to an age when Wicasah held Domino's hand tight as Domino shuffled them from one small-town soda-fountain shop to the next while their father drank himself to death at the saloon or spent hours interred with hole-in-the-wall psychics.

For all of Domino's bluffs, he wasn't street smart. He never figured out how to get out of the running life. Never had the chance to make a house a home because he figured someone always had an angle to leave him. He simply didn't have the heart to figure out how not to be the one that was left all the time.

He must've slept because he woke up with a start. Uneasily, he used the facilities, even if he didn't need to, not really. Nothing but a familiar routine hailing back to his days alive. The room felt too quiet. Thessaly hadn't returned. He scouted, looking for signs of abandonment, but then again there wouldn't be any because that was a rule. Never leave behind what you don't want to lose.

He cringed as a high-pitched whistle seeped from the small space underneath the door. The sound of a baby rabbit death, he thought, the flash of a .22 stocky in his hands, and the way he could pick off the brown pelted prey by shooting their heads off clean. Good eating. Domino edged closer to the door and turned the knob with shaking hands and a curse. The door stuck but yielded open with a good push. The air rippled.

Through the door crack, the veteran gaped up at him with his legs outstretched. Blood drenched the front of his old brass-button coat like a bib. He looked like a hung man cut from the gallows— limp with a rag doll slouch. Wide eyes, bright with the first cracks of realized insanity, stared at Domino, and it wasn't until Domino pulled himself out of his imposed terror that he realized the whine wasn't really a whine; it was more of what remained of a scream once a throat had been torn out.

He gasped—panic was a slippery slope. Thessaly wouldn't have made such a mess, not for spellcraft. Where was she? Thoughts careened through his mind in vague snippets of *where* and *lost*. Like a rabbit caught in the crosshairs, he couldn't move. The lunatic disappeared from view, stunningly replaced by a huge fleshless rider attached to a horse suddenly rearing in front of him.

The rider had no legs, his torso melted into the horse's sloped back to make them one. A second scream choked his throat.

Time slowed in an adrenalized rush. Domino watched the rider's pink muscles tighten, the white ligaments strain, blood vessels pump, and wetted hair strands damply wave. The sour steam from the steed's nose washed over his face. The monster—it was like no demon Domino had ever seen before—screeched, nearly turning Domino's constitution into soup, but he'd never been smart enough to roll over and play dead.

He dodged to the left, clipping his shoulder against the doorframe just as the demon's hooves came down and demolished the door. A familiar wrenching pain shot from his ankle to his knee as he fell to the ground. An old, alive wound acting up. The sun flickered like a guttering wildfire. He staggered to his feet under slippery sand, not caring about anything but putting space between him and that . . . that fucking creature.

A second screech, like nails on a chalkboard, quivered through him. Blank terror rose from the pit of his stomach as he ran past the dying veteran. He'd never felt so powerless before, transformed back to a child haunted by nightmares that now gained on him with the beat and kick of thunderous hoofbeats. He sprinted into the flat lay of desert, soft mewling cries seeping from his dropped mouth.

Thessaly appeared ten feet in front of him, her hand outstretched to grab him. Blood was smeared across her face, but she only had eyes for what galloped behind him.

"Run!" he screamed. It was the only word he knew. "Run!"

She didn't have to be told twice. Her foot pivoted, her sand-coated hair lightened to the color of wheat stalks or Pixi sticks emptied of flavored sugar. Dust kicked up in his face as she sped ahead of him, putting what felt like miles between them.

Don't leave me, Domino thought. *Don't fucking leave me here with that.*

He let out a sob, half-hitched and ugly in his chest because it felt like she was dying all over again, abandoning him to a horrible man to raise and care for him, twist all the good right out of him.

For one beautiful moment, he thought he might catch her, that he might make it, until agony ripped into his thigh. He went down face first and felt a viselike grip on the nape of his neck shake him hard enough to break his spine. He blacked out.

CHAPTER 6

THERE WAS SOMETHING to be said about waking due to pain stretching across his belly like hunger cramps, only to find dark purple bruises from being flung over a centurion back and jostled over a hundred Hellish miles, instead. Something to be said about the hand-shaped ache in the small of his back from being held steady by the humanoid making up the second piece of this odd monster puzzle, about feeling sweaty like after long travel, about whiplash.

Vertigo. Glancing up through white-hot agony from the clean break in his vertebrae to see the desert flowing by at the speed of the Cobra. He pressed his cheek into the fleshless beast, gagging at the scent of raw meat and sharp rock salt. Something to be said, but language would remain mythic until his synovial fluid drained and his spinal cord finished rebuilding. Something to be said about the strange blinking blackness that foretold either death or a coma overcoming him and stealing his time.

He was still limp and marionette-loose when he was lifted off the centaur's back. A black snake of smoke wrapped around Domino, holding him immobile and upright. The smoke-snake then gently probed his mouth with hands, asking through nudges for permission to inspect: pulling his lips back to check the underside of his gums, fascinated with the lines of his teeth.

"Still pretty, surprisingly. He's the right one," the smoke-snake said.

Domino blinked, seeing the smoke originating from a solid creature that slunk out of sight behind him.

"How can you be sure?"

A hand patted his cheek. His head lolled back. The black smoke kept him trussed like Thanksgiving poultry. The centaur breathed hard and offered an outstretched hand as if waiting. A female demon, not the one he could feel behind him nor the third one who had spoken the question, but an actual hellion, rose from her seat and counted out beaded sacks into the creature's hand. A choked noise made its way out of Domino's mouth, something akin to *help me* because the wild centaur was better compared to the civilized demons of torture he now found himself with.

Three of them. The hellion sat beside the second male, her face blank but her skin tight and wrinkled as if she'd been drained of all moisture. The second male glowered at Domino—disliked already, apparently—and rubbed the edge of his horn curling like a mountain ram's. Domino tried to see his surroundings—somewhere underground, like a basement office space stripped to the basics and smelling of sulfur. He tried to fight against the black smoke-snake but instead sagged into the hands of his captor.

The sharp chin of the smoke-snake hooked over his shoulder. "Not a bad specimen," the demon holding him murmured. "What a marvelous skin to wear."

"Still a fucking exotic," the glowering ram-horned male snarled. "Still an invasive species, just like any other human soul. He's not special."

"You're fine like a good suit," the demon holding Domino rumbled, delighted. "I could wear you all day."

"Helia, why would you want to get inside something like that?" the second male asked, exasperated. "It's not like you need to sully yourself by possessing him. There's no one else around but us. No need to pretend."

"It's a fine adaptation, isn't it," the demon behind him drawled, making Domino's skin crawl. "Once you little human souls invaded our beloved Helia like wildfire, we figured out how to make use of you. How to survive among you so we could stand a chance. Slip inside your squishy bodies. Taste your heat."

The hellion sighed impatiently. "He's not a toy. He's a job."

"You'd like him to be just a job," the smoke-snake demon behind Domino muttered, rifling through Domino's pockets. "Makes you sick to be here, doesn't it?"

"I don't like working for human souls," the hellion said, flat like an expired heartbeat.

"You don't like much of anything since your sister died," the snake-smoke demon mocked in a rich voice.

"You're getting enough out of it, Aiyana," the ram-horned male beside her snapped. "Don't be a boil, Ickto."

"Like you aren't?" Aiyana said. "It's a fucking pretty price for one scummy soul, Manit."

"Don't make it out like he twisted your arm," Manit said. "We came to him."

"Just saying I don't like how it feels."

"Aiyana and Manit don't have anything resembling patience," the demon behind Domino—Ickto—muttered. "They forget that you, our little acquisition, are witchery and must be inspected for foul play." He fingered inside Domino's destroyed pocket, pulled out a thimbleful of bunched lint, and carefully sniffed it. "Dust," he said with disgust.

"Corpse dust?" the hellion—Aiyana—asked, suddenly interested.

"Demon dust," Ickto corrected.

A furious blush lit up Manit's hollowed cheeks. "You human souls just take, take, take. You take our rituals, our ceremonies, and you fucking desecrate them looking for a high."

"Now, now," Ickto tsked. "It's not his fault his ancestors crafted a maze to funnel souls into our homeland."

"It is his fault. The human souls are like mice. They'll never get off our land. We've been pushed so far into our own territory the only thing keeping them from taking *that* is the wasteland fear. You saw the nuckelavee. He's barely hanging on."

"Such a progressive, Manit."

"Such a leech, Ickto."

"Get on with it already," Aiyana said, picking at her dagger nails. "It's too dry out here."

"This isn't going to be pleasant," Ickto said, breathing a kiss on Domino's ear. Domino struggled with a desperate whimper. "But it's necessary. Lots of clean Helia land promised exclusively for us demons in exchange for your puny soul."

The black smoke tightened, drawing Domino's arm straight out. Manit stood and angled Domino's elbow, square nails digging into Domino's skin. A familiar pinch and puncture. Out of the corner of his eye, Domino saw the glint of a barbed needle sliding underneath his skin, smooth as butter.

Domino felt the quiet strings of control being snipped one by one until he crumpled like the dead man he might have been on Earth—loose and limp before rigor mortis. He felt the demonic scrutiny, like leaning too close to the taxidermized eyes of an elk crucified on a hunter's wall and seeing his reflection in the dead gaze. Heavy lidded, he thought, *no.*

"Sweet dreams," Manit said, lips parting in a pleased smile.

"Goodnight," Ickto murmured behind him, ever invisible, ever the devil on his shoulder.

————◆————

"Please no, not again."

"Shh, little soul, it will be alright."

"No more, please no more, *please.*"

"I have to. You have to understand that."

"Why, Ickto? Why?"

"How else do you get cast out of Helia? You have to believe you're alive. Only then can you die again to be reborn into the hands of the white-witch. You have to lose the sanity you love to hold onto."

Muffled sob. Soft gentle stroking. "I don't want to, Ickto."

"You have to. We don't like doing this, you must know. We don't like it at all, but we must."

"Domino. Say it."

"No names. Names can haunt."

"Please, say my name. Please say it. Ickto, *say it.* Say it."

"Shhh, Manit has the next dream."

"*Oh no*, no, no, no—"

Quiet sobbing. Straps tightened. Darkness.

Quiet.

————◆————

Something clanked against the metal door near his feet. Scraping keys fumbled into padlocks and bolts slipped free. Domino became alarmed—so used to the dark, he wasn't sure he could handle what lay outside the coffin space. Every time the door opened, things got worse. The dreams got worse. At some point, he accepted the claustrophobic confines of the morgue slab they imprisoned him in, the way the straightjacket was so tight he couldn't feel his arms anymore. He'd finally finished the latest round of screaming himself hoarse. He could taste the way his vocal cords had ripped on his terror. Blood bubbled on his tongue like a palate cleanser with the silver taste of dusty quarters. He wondered how much longer it would be before the real darkness took him.

That was dangerous. He almost forgot he *was* dead, believed this was a world where pain could end and he wasn't rebirthed over and over. Manit's syringe of dreams made his sanity fragile, allowing him to beg for death and entertain notions of a suicide's nothingness. How many times had they opened the door to infect him with more? He offered them everything he had—he was a beautiful witch; they could love his body, possess it even, and he wouldn't say one word, not one, he swore it.

White light illuminated at his feet. His eyeballs strained like a stallion to see the hand fumbling near his bound feet. A jolt. The rack he was laid out on slid harshly forward, jerking him to a violent stop when the trestle leading it ended. He blinked profusely at the trio standing over him—razor-boned wings and tall as damnation. Another spike of horror rushed through him and came out of his gagged mouth in pitiful hoarse sighs.

Two tall metal IV stands, clipped together like tent poles, shook back and forth like puppets in Manit's claws. He smirked down at Domino. The large IV bags—squished, crunched, and empty like a bladder and flimsy as a kite—fluttered against the metal. The inspection then: Ickto shining a light into his eyes, asking him to do impossible things like focus. Dehydration ripped at him. He tried to stop his desperate keens, but he wanted, he needed, and at their mercy, he'd do anything. Anything to make it end.

Hands tugged at the old buckles securing him down, loosening the suffocating sheath until air cooled the tight layer of grime and dried sweat marinating his flesh. Ickto laid a head on his chest. Domino wheezed from the pressure, feeling searing pain rip through his ruined throat. He rocked side to side, crying with the release, lifting his crossed arms until the demon pushed them down, listening to the quiet rhythm of magic fading from his veins.

Ickto lifted his head and nodded to Aiyana. Quick, no-nonsense, she unbuckled Domino's arms and extracted one weak limb. He almost bucked in the rack from the pleasure of the stretch, the ache in his elbow nearly bringing him to his knees. She tapped the dried and scabby crook and inserted a thick needle. This pain felt quiet compared to the rest of his body's devastation, and she began to pull a slow flood of black-red blood from him. Domino laughed behind his gag and slammed his head down on the rack, reminded that because he used to snort demon bone dust and this was more of the same: using each other's bodies to feel good. They pulled his power out of him for their spells and magic to survive one more day in the depths of this punishment called Helia.

He thrashed as they unbuckled him further, freeing him almost completely. Somewhat hysterical, he wondered if this could be the divine moment when they would end his life. Then, he would no longer exist.

Right? That's what happened. He would die and go to either heaven or hell.

Or had that happened already? He couldn't remember. The thought made him woozy.

Another needle struck his vein. Ickto took him by the shoulders and hauled him into a sitting position. All his blood drained from his head in a tingly rush. He blacked out for a moment, eyesight commandeered by bright flashes of green behind a darkness so absolute it felt suffocating.

Domino flopped in Ickto's arms. Around him, his captors talked in a language he had given up understanding. His mind had degraded and atrophied in that coffin they kept him in, locked up in a bread baker's emptied oven, the space so small it could only fit him.

The gag scraped his teeth as Manit removed it, layers of flesh peeling off with the leather. His jaw ached and he wasn't sure he could remember how to properly close his mouth.

Little puppet, he thought as Ickto snapped his fingers for Manit to haul Domino upright. Domino flopped, legs noodle limp. He thought about the long hours confined when he had cried for his mother before the dreams took hold and sent him on a demonic mind trip into the worst moments of his life.

Dragged out of the basement, the world flashed by in blinking lights. His feet thumped on stairs. Maybe this was redemption, maybe this was beauty, living not for love or affection, but pure release from something so terrible. He'd wanted to die for so long.

The demon holding Domino planted him on his knees. He gagged on a sulfuric stench, but at least it was fresh and new compared to the reek of his own body.

He swayed like a metronome keeping time. Ickto raised his pistol and aimed it at Domino's head. Through the slog of relief, Domino discovered terror never got old. Having a gun aimed at him was nothing new, but it did look ridiculous in the hands of a monster. The barrel stared him down and he couldn't stop his heart from stuttering at the realization that this actually could be the end—that for all its dedicated beating and pumping, the effort was moot when faced with the great and powerful gun.

Domino's mouth still hung open like a dead man's. He shook like a leaf, but experience made him cocky. He'd looked down gun barrels before and they never actually fired.

Only this one did.

Fired with a spark like lit flash paper and the rotten egg smell peppering the air.

Domino had a name on his lips just as the bullet smashed his skull, but he couldn't truly feel that, could he? The way his cranium fragmented and sliced his brain into hemorrhaging paper cuts?

He flopped on the desert shrub. Tumbleweeds spiked his cheek like a thorny crown. Twitching, oh death throes. A concrete building behind him like a flattened pyramid. Body shock. The demons left him, pockets full of poesy and witch blood, on a desolate stretch of desert where even the cacti wilted.

PART II:

THE DREAMS OF THE RESURRECTED

CHAPTER 1
THE KIND LADY

THEY LIVED OUT the week in the squalor of a borrowed room, where oblong mice pellets rotted in the corners and dust layered the broken panels of a ceiling fan. Green grasshoppers with hopscotch legs bounced from the table to the floor onto Domino's legs. The single bed's sheets smelled musty and moth-eaten. For once in his life, Domino hoped for spiders to take care of the gnat balls swarming outside.

His father had left in the night to see this town's favorite psychic and commune with the spirit of his dead wife but must've gotten sidetracked by his good friend Johnny Walker along the way. It was morning now, and Wicasah, all of four, fussed with hunger.

Domino washed him in the tub as Wicasah painted bubbles on the tile with childish glee. At some point, soaked from Wicasah's splashes, Domino dumped himself in the lukewarm water with his brother to scrub off the questionable rings of grime and the dusty snot crusted in the corner of Wicasah's nostrils until Wicasah gleamed, newly minted.

He eased towel-dried toddler limbs into pant legs and shirt holes, tucked bendy feet into scrappy boots, and strapped down tattered suspenders. Wicasah clung to him. What a game it was, getting dressed, and Wicasah snorted in laughter when Domino couldn't get his left boot on. Taking Wicasah's hand, Domino took him outside and down the dusty walk into town, kicking pebbles along the way. Precious pennies and nickels clinked in his pocket. Wicasah frog-hopped, his black locks glossy-blue from the sun. Domino smiled, trying to stop his gut from tightening in a knot from fear—both for his father's safety and his terrifying adoration for his sibling.

They ordered eggs and toast at the diner. The waitress, with a soft spot for the abandoned, added bacon to the mess, needling a cup of rough coffee under Domino's nose. He hated the taste, the acidic burn, but he loved the way he felt awake and warm afterward. Wicasah smeared yolk over his face. Domino sopped up the plate's leftovers with crust, wolfing down the remains. The coffee burned his tongue and he blew on it, held the cup up to his nose like a real man would.

"Coffee?" Wicasah asked, leaning forward with an outstretched hand.

"You have coffee." Domino nodded at the white porcelain cup next to his brother's elbow.

Wicasah peered into his cup of hot water, brow furrowed in thought. "Coffee?" he asked and took the cup in his hands, propping his elbows up and holding it like Domino, mouth curving over the cup's lip.

"Wicasah, be careful," Domino warned quickly. "It's hot."

"Hot," Wicasah echoed but grinned wide at his brother. They both took a slurp.

"Mmmm." Wicasah copied Domino's contented swallow.

Counting his pennies, Domino laid the exact amount on the table and dragged Wicasah out before the nice waitress noticed he hadn't left her a tip. On the dusty road, the wind conjured dust devils. Sediment ground between Domino's molars, swirling deep in his lungs with each inhale. Wicasah swayed, his belly pudging out. Domino experienced a sense of contentment at the knowledge that he could keep his brother fed and happy. Taking Wicasah's hand again, Domino pulled Wicasah down the street, determined to search every saloon for the broad shoulders of his father.

But Daniel wouldn't be found that day, and after the third peep through hazy smoke and bourbon scent, facing inquisitive looks Domino didn't quite understand, he was on his last straw, strung out on worry and fear. Wicasah leaned into him, face scrunched up in a way that foretold the arrival of a fit. Domino picked him up—heavy for how small he looked—and propped his brother on his hip. Wicasah laid his head on Domino's shoulder, thumb stuck deep in his mouth, eyelids fluttering with naptime. Domino's arms began to ache as he whispered in Wicasah's ear and the little legs obeyed, wrapping around Domino's waist to help hold him up.

Domino turned in the direction of the rented room, certain it had been lent out already to another, and wondered whether their father had pawned the truck, or how cold it would be sleeping among the tall stalks of a hayfield. Sometimes, when Daniel disappeared, he didn't come back for days.

A beep sounded behind him. He turned with blooming hope. A rusted green flatbed truck nosed behind him. He swallowed the bitter pill. The truck pulled up beside him, window rolled down and a slender elbow hooked on the outside of the driver's side window. The driver peeked her head out of the shadows into the blinding sun and Domino momentarily wanted to weep at the curling honey blonde hair.

"Need a ride there, kid?" the woman asked, her face almost too big for her small features. She offered them a compassionate smile. "Looks like your little one is dead tired and you're about to fall over yourself."

He paused, realized he was too out of breath to speak, and tried to whet his desert-dry mouth. The top layer of his soul felt tossed and blown like a tumbleweed. Domino glanced down to see the side of Wicasah's face flushed pink, on its way to sunburnt. He imagined the pouts he would get trying to rub lotion over that tender skin. "Don't know exactly where we're going," he mumbled. "My daddy's missing."

The woman smiled brighter, lines like commas around her mouth, eyes crinkling into flat teardrops. She was younger than his father, her skin tanned smoothed and brown.

"How about I take you to my place. Got a farm on the outskirts and I'll phone up some friends, put the word out about your daddy. He can't have gotten far in a town like this."

Domino bit his lip. Strangers, after all, had their own set of rules.

"I'm Helen," she added as an afterthought. "I'd love to get some meat on your bones, kid. I've got cookies and milk at home. Sounds refreshing, don't it?"

Domino wanted to get in the car so bad, but he was scared about driving away without any word to his father. Then again, Daniel up and left them anyway, so what did it matter if this lady made kind inquiries? He suddenly wanted someone to take care of him so badly.

"Can get the little one some water. He'll be needing a change, I reckon." Helen's smile sharpened.

"You sure about the phone?" Domino asked.

"Of course," she said. "You can make the queries yourself if you're so inclined."

Domino nodded and walked around the front of the truck. He jiggled Wicasah, who woke with a slow start, mouth opened in a drooling O, rubbing his eyes fitfully. "Gotta climb in the truck, okay?" Domino whispered to him. "Then you can get back to sleep."

The car door, in need of good oil, creaked open. White stuffing peeked out of the seat's ripped seams. Domino pushed Wicasah's bottom to help him climb in, then hauled himself up and slammed the door behind him. Wicasah clambered back into his lap, both of them not quite sure what to make of the lady sitting next to them. Domino rolled down the squeaky window, grateful for the brisk dry air across his face as the truck rumbled to a start. He squinted. Everything was colored a green tinge from being out in the sun too long.

"Hello," Wicasah said conversationally from Domino's lap. "Who are you?"

"I'm Helen," the woman laughed, delighted in Wicasah's sociality.

"I'm Wicasah," his brother said. Domino fought the urge to roll his eyes. Of course, the kid would be friendly as pie all cradled in Domino's lap. Wicasah tended to be shy at the worst of times, hiding his face in Domino's side until he got used to whatever new thing had entered his world, but apparently, Helen had passed some unknown toddler test with flying colors.

"That's an interesting name," Helen said with a sidelong look. The truck jittered up and down as it rumbled over a rough patch. Wicasah's giggle only got louder as his voice jumbled with the vibration.

"Gotta be associated with the land," Wicasah quoted, the word 'associated' lost in the s's. Domino hushed him, too many words, too much information, too many sparking memories.

"Not many folks know that," Helen said, her smile fading.

"I know," Wicasah said, solemn as a funeral, and scooted off his brother's lap. "What's that?" Wicasah pointed at the talisman hanging off the rearview mirror.

"Stop asking so many questions," Domino snarled, ignored.

"Sage," Helen said. "Some cattail and a little bit of Big Bluestem. Dried pussytoes."

I HAVE ASKED TO BE WHERE NO STORMS COME

"Pussytoes?" Wicasah asked, head leaning back as he repeated. "Pussytoes, Domino. Pussytoes."

"Pussytoes," Domino echoed back. It was a game they used to play when Wicasah learned language, a call and echo where Wicasah would say a word as an incredulous question and Domino would repeat it back as a wild exclamation.

Domino studied the talisman, cataloging the way a longer piece of dried grass and twine wrapped it neatly together. It swung back and forth over the windshield. It reminded him of spells in the kitchen, walks in fields where no trails lay, and a butcher's block table with the aunts at one end, bubbling trouble over their crockpot, and the milky scent of his mother when she hugged him.

Domino realized Helen had a keen eye on him, a second too long looking away from the road. Straight as an arrow though, these Midwestern territories, no rolling mountain paths, and you could look away from anything and be reassured that the road stayed steady as breath beneath you.

Wicasah was babbling, talking too fast for his mouth to keep up, a half mixture of proper English language and baby-talk that meant nothing to anyone but him. Sudden anger washed over Domino at this small bundle he had to care for, irritated at the way he jumped to talk to this kind stranger. Domino wanted to cry, but it was a dry day, and his eyes felt gritty. He wondered if those herbs were a protection spell, or a warding spell, swinging to and fro.

"There's my house," Helen pointed a long finger over the steering wheel. Domino strained forward to see a small cabin between mismatched aspen trees, leaves reflecting golden sparks from the sun. She parked at the end of the road. The engine rumbled in idle and then sighed like an old bulldog as she turned it off. She leaned forward, resting her folded arms on the steering wheel, and peered out the windshield up into the blue sky. "Think it's going to rain stars?" she asked.

Domino's breath caught in his chest, taut with tugging memories. He almost choked out the answer, one witch to another. "Stars are nothing but rain."

Helen grinned and poked a finger at him. "Knew it the moment I saw you. Got an aura about you, kid."

Domino thought he might come undone. Wicasah pushed into Domino's face, mouth in a deep frown because he didn't like what he didn't understand. "Aura?"

"Aura," Domino said back. Wicasah's frown deepened and he glanced between Helen and his brother, deeply suspicious of conspiracies.

"Better get inside," Helen said, sidetracking Wicasah moments before he lost his temper. "How do you feel about oatmeal cookies, kiddo?"

All forgiven and forgotten, Wicasah jumped on Domino's thighs, breath coming out in excited huffs. "I think he'd like that," Domino replied, relaxing in a way he hadn't since his mother burned to death and his father lost all sense of self.

They jumped out of the truck and Wicasah stumbled on his little legs, powering himself over the dirt path to the front porch. He yelled something insensible, but Domino couldn't catch up. He'd burned through his caffeine and the only thing left was a bone-deep exhaustion and learned parental awareness.

The air smelled fresh and clean, like crisp laundry dried outside. High grass waved hello in undulations, and he glanced at the golden stalks before following Helen inside the small house.

Within was a room with a bed, a built-in kitchen complete with an icebox, a table against the wall, a repaired record player, open cabinets with cracked porcelain dishes, wooden floors, and square windows. He smelled the contradictory scents of lavender and frankincense, zinging pangs through him for people he loved and moments he'd lost. He barely noticed Wicasah jumping up and down next to Helen as she poured two glasses of milk and set them on the table. She motioned for him to sit in one of the wooden chairs around the rickety table. Wicasah manhandled himself into his chair, making squawks of protestation when Domino tried to help. He swung his torso on the seat and twisted so he could fully sit, grinning at his brother, who had already taken two gulps from each glass with a serves-you-right smile on his face.

Helen set a plate of cookies in front of them and Domino bit into the softness, tasting cinnamon and nutmeg, a hint of sugar, and the wholesome weight of grain.

Wicasah grinned messily at him and tried to speak.

"Don't talk with your mouth full," Domino ordered. Wicasah stuck out his tongue, padded with balls of saliva slick crumbs.

Helen chuckled and pulled out her seat next to Domino and started to munch on a cookie herself. "Mind if I ask?" she said after eating the first half.

Domino wiggled in his seat, suddenly shy, but he nodded.

"Mother or father?" she asked.

"My mama," he whispered. "Thessaly."

"Pretty name," she said.

Domino glanced away, wasn't sure he could impart how beautiful his mother truly was—her name, her voice, her smell.

"She teach you the witchery?" Helen asked.

"Some," Domino choked out. "She died, though. Just us men now."

Helen softened with pity, something Domino despised. Quiet, Wicasah's eyes flickered from Helen's questions to the emotional trauma radiating from his older brother.

"Wicasah never really got to know her." Domino faked a smile at his younger brother, feeling his heart running out his mouth. Wildly, he could see Thessaly's face in Wicasah's—the turn of his nose, his small frown. Wicasah let out a distressed whine and looked at Helen, begged her to stop, stop hurting his Domino.

Helen pulled her lower lip between the slight gap in her upper teeth. "That's too bad. How did she die?"

"Burning," Domino whispered and felt the dam open. The waterfall rushed in, all those held-back words wanting space to be spoken and heard.

Helen stood and patted Domino on the back. "What's your daddy's name? I'll make some inquiries."

"Daniel," Domino choked out, glad she was going to ignore his breakdown. "Daniel Bluepoint."

Wicasah wasn't having it, never knew when to leave well enough alone, and he half fell trying to get out of his chair to scramble into his brother's lap. Domino balanced his brother on his thighs as Wicasah trembled. If Domino was crying, something was definitely wrong, thus sympathetic cries from the youngest were required. Domino pulled Wicasah to his chest and pressed a silent sob into the child's neck. Wicasah let out an uncertain wail. Domino wasn't sure how long he could do this, but he kissed Wicasah on the forehead and cheeks, loving the flush on his brother's face at all the attention.

Time passed. Wicasah fell asleep against him, all baby warmth and cookie crumbs. Domino waited for his mind to start throwing up images to make him remember in numb silence. Luckily, his brain had given up on his body to go its own way. Far away, Helen's voice chattered on the telephone and the breeze rattled through the bad caulking between the window and wood.

Wicasah woke and wriggled out of Domino's grip to the floor to play make-believe in the sunlight beams. Helen entered the room and knelt beside him, blocking out part of Wicasah's light. She held a tome with thick yellow pages bulging out from the spine. Old leather and dust.

Wicasah stared at her, and from behind, Domino imagined his face of irritation. Small eyebrow barely arched up in a young expression Domino would get to know like the back of his hand as Wicasah got older.

Unfazed, Helen stared right back, making this a no-blink game. "Do you remember your mama?" she asked.

Wicasah, never one for conquering questions on his own, scooted back on all fours until he leaned against his brother's chair. His hand fisted in Domino's pant leg. "Not really," Domino answered for him. "He's not old enough to remember her."

"Would you like to see her?" Helen asked in a high-pitched tone reserved for children, still fixed on Wicasah.

Sudden disbelief mingled with hope in Domino's chest. He let out a hiccupping breath and looked down when Wicasah tugged hard on his pant.

"Mama?" Wicasah asked him.

"What do you mean by that?" Domino demanded. "Just what exactly are you talking about?"

He felt familiar fury, the same that flowed through his father. Cheated, tricked, and made the fool all at once.

"I know she's been dead for a long time, cause your brother must be what, five? I can't bring her back permanently, but I can call her spirit so you could see her. Introduce her to her son. What do you think?"

"You can do that?" Domino whispered, so soft he didn't think she heard.

"It's my specialty," she said, sounding pleased. "It's the least I can do while we wait for your papa. I think you might need reassurance that she's at peace."

"Did you find him?"

"I told the biggest town gossips that I had Daniel Bluepoint's two sons safe and sound at my place. He'll know in a few hours where to pick you up. People will keep an eye out. My friend said she'd seen someone fitting his description at a bar about an hour ago."

Domino breathed a sigh of relief. One less cross to bear.

"You've got nothing to worry about," Helen said, comforting enough to feel true. "It's going to be okay."

She bent down to draw white chalk lines on the floor, an unrecognizable interplay of diamonds and trapezoids. She lit herb bundles and placed them in the corners of the house. The smell, musky and slightly sweet, clogged Domino's lungs. Wicasah coughed, eyes watering as he glanced between the ritual and the safety of his brother's legs. Helen removed her shirt, revealing a lace bandeau flattening her. She walked the chalk lines like a tightrope, then knelt in the middle, book spread open in front of her. She kneeled over it, nose almost in the spine, and muttered the book's language.

Domino remembered his mother's thick colossal tome, a compilation of different magicks she'd gathered from her own experiences to that of the Brightside aunts. Treasures like pressed flowers hid between the pages, bracketing sketches of demon faces, angel wings, and prophecies, along with the baser, more comforting drawings of the earth he knew. It had burned before he could inscribe his name underneath his mother's, scorched to a crisp just like her, the flames taking away huge chunks of who he could've been.

Domino slid from the chair to the floor, scooching closer to the nearest chalk line. Helen's craft saturated the room. Similar to the aunts, but a witchery taste infused the air. Wicasah copied his every move, so quiet it almost spooked Domino. Domino zeroed in on Helen's stomach, pale with a drooping belly button, and saw her skin stretch as if she had a baby inside her. He remembered how his mother's stomach would sometimes bulge and ripple when Wicasah was still inside her, how he could press his unborn brother's body through his mother's skin and watch him resist within her womb.

Domino shuddered. The animals rolling inside Helen weren't beloved siblings but conduits. Helen tossed her head back as her stomach protruded farther, heavy like she might pop. Hands stretched her skin, hoping to break free. The inklings of magic in Domino sparked awake, eager to copy. Domino caught his mother's name embedded in Helen's chanting: *Thessaly.*

A bundle of threads spun out of thin air in front of him, bright auric and so soft Domino knew this must be what a soul looked like. His heart thudded and he began to cry uncontrollably as the golden spool undulated like a wave, spilling more of his mother's face into the threads. Her face peered out to him with proud, pure love.

"Mama," Domino sobbed. "Mama, is that you?"

She smiled close-lipped, her eyes shining. Disconnected hands from her flowing body of light reached out to openly embrace him. Domino threw himself into the light, no hesitations, no doubt, and felt everything that made her in the bedrock of his bones. Safety, security, laughter echoing from the kitchen, the ripe scent of pie, the heat of her embrace as she picked up his sleeping body and put him to bed. Being *home.* The light reflected his tears like dewdrops. He pulled away, hastily wiping at them, because he could never forget that he had to prove he was doing his best— raising Wicasah based on memories, tips from strangers, and observations.

Wicasah hid his face as Domino wrapped his arms around him. Wicasah gripped his shirt as if Domino had been on the brink of disappearing altogether. Domino knelt and tried to catch Wicasah's eyes, bring him out of Domino's chest, but Wicasah would not be moved.

"Look." Domino petted him frantically. "It's Mama. She's here."

Wicasah's tearful breath caused Domino to paw at his face, trying to turn his little brother to *look,* but Wicasah was as sharp and stubborn as a barnacle, molded to him so hard it would take metal to get him off.

"He's just shy," Domino explained to the shifting light. "Being fussy. Look, baby. Just look once for me. Please?"

Wicasah stilled. Domino forgot how long it had been since he had called him that, *baby,* but that was what Wicasah was. He could walk alright and had a temper like a speeding train, but he would always be the baby Domino rocked to sleep in the backseat of the car.

Wicasah's red and scrubby face peeked out of Domino's chest like the golden light might eat him. His lower lip trembled.

"He wanted to see you, Mama. He wanted to see you really bad. He just doesn't understand, he doesn't quite know. Why are you being so shy, huh? You don't need to be shy. It's Mama."

Wicasah frowned as he tugged on Domino's shirt collar until

Domino brought his head down. Wicasah whispered in his ear, "What does she want?"

"She's our mother," Domino said, exasperated. "She wants to see us."

Wicasah's face transformed into true distress. His breathing hitched. "You goin' 'way?" he asked. "You gonna be with Mama?"

"No," Domino said. "It's just to say hello because she loves you. He doesn't really know you," Domino told his mother and he swore she was going to cry.

"Don't take Domino," Wicasah told her.

"She won't, I promise. I'm going to stay right here with you. But you need to go hug her. She came all this way to see you."

Wicasah worried his lip and pulled away minimally. Thessaly held out her arms again. Wicasah shied back, thumb sticking in his mouth, a long-forgotten trait rearing its infant head. He gripped Domino's thumb tight. Wicasah inched forward, Domino's arm now spanning between them, and Thessaly bent down to be eye level with her youngest. Wicasah suspiciously looked her up and down, kept his round body between her and his brother, and let her arms engulf him.

Thessaly held Wicasah like he might break away from her at any moment and she had to take it all in right away. Wicasah wouldn't let go of Domino's hand. He drew away from his mother and retreated into Domino's arms, mouth still puckered around his thumb. Domino reached up and gently drew the digit out of Wicasah's mouth. Wicasah glared at him and glared at his mother, unsure of what to do and possessive but he didn't know of what, his brother or his thumb.

"Mama?" he asked, quietly.

"Mama!" Domino responded, his smile so wide that Wicasah smiled back in reflex, putting his two hands out to touch the creases in Domino's cheeks.

"Wicasah wanted to see you," Domino explained. He couldn't keep his eyes off her. "He didn't understand. Thought you were going to take me away from him, but it's okay now, he understands. Do you want to say something to Mama, Wicasah?"

Wicasah's smile faded. Domino caught the tell-tale turn of Wicasah's head to hide and maneuvered Wicasah so he faced the glowing light. Thessaly smiled at him just as Domino remembered, beaming like the sun and radiating everything that was good.

"I know you want to tell Mama something, you're always clamoring with words, so why don't you tell her something."

Wicasah swayed and looked at the floor.

"Want me to help you?"

Wicasah nodded.

"We wanted to tell you that we're okay, Mama," Domino started.

"Okay, Mama," Wicasah echoed.

"That we're doing the best we can."

"The best," Wicasah whispered.

"But it's been hard without you. We miss you so much."

Wicasah mumbled along with sidelong glances of alarm at his brother. Domino focused on Thessaly, couldn't look away because this was a gift, even though he knew his voice strained with a desperate note that scared even him. "I think about you every day. Wicasah knows all the stories about you. We won't ever forget you." His voice cracked.

Wicasah nodded fervently, finally looking up.

"And wherever you are, we want you to know that we love you. If we could be with you we would. I love you, Mama."

"I love you." Wicasah crumbled, long trails of snot clogging his nose. "Miss you, Mama. Love you."

She opened her mouth, but the luminous tendrils unraveled like yarn. Domino waited until she was a mere auroral dust mote that throbbed like a heartbeat before winking out.

Helen's chanting stopped. Her strained breathing filled the air. Only then, with the smoke stuck in his lungs, did Domino let the grief and confusion carve him out. Wicasah clung to him, seeking comfort, but Domino had nothing to give. He held Wicasah bruise-tight because he didn't know where else to put this woe, except to hand it off and wait for relief to come.

But he'd seen the reflections of his mother in Wicasah when she'd held him. The sharp reminders left him aching. It meant she was still here in a way. In Wicasah. In him.

CHAPTER 2
THE RESURRECTION

THREE ROOF-SHAKING KNOCKS rattled the house in the middle of the night. Domino's eyes, dehydrated from too many salty tears, snapped open. Helen jerked awake, her hair wild from sleeping on the floor with a book as her pillow. Domino shook Wicasah gently as Helen stumbled to draw back the door locks with two soft clicks. The fresh cleanse of thunder and fierce rain drifted through the opening, filling Domino's lungs with an east wind.

A familiar dark shape encompassed the doorway, one that filled Domino with equal parts relief and awe. He'd always seen Daniel as an unmovable mountain. Domino gave him a wave, *good to see you old man,* and Daniel pulled his worn cowboy hat off as raindrops dripped from the long wool coat pulled over his wide shoulders.

Hard hazel eyes under graying brows inspected his boys before giving Helen the same suspicious once over. His scuffed black boots clomped over the threshold without an invitation. With a growing sense of horror, Domino watched Daniel's gaze shift beyond his sons to the incantation circle drawn on the floor. Watched him smell the misty scents of magic and glare at the half-naked woman swaying from a mystical hangover in front of him.

"Dad," Domino stammered, desperate to explain, but Daniel's mouth had already tightened to a severe line. Domino had seen that look before, one of outrage and disapproval before the unknown.

"Came upon your boys on the road and thought you might be looking for them," Helen said, sweet as sugar, even as she refused to step back and make room for her new guest. "Didn't want them wandering the streets alone. You never know what kind of folk are traveling these days."

Daniel pushed past her, set on his boys. Wicasah spread a sleepy smile for his father. Daniel bent down and inspected his youngest. Mauve and tan bruises dotted Wicasah's arm in the width of Domino's hand. Brushing a gloved hand gently over Wicasah's soft skin, Daniel's crow's feet deepened.

"Dad," Domino started in a panicked whisper. "It's not what you think. Helen found us looking for you. She helped us. Dad, she's a good person."

"Why did you leave the room?" Daniel asked softly, ushering Wicasah into his arms and lifting him.

"You think they'd let us stay an extra night with no money?" Domino replied. A hot flush climbed his chest and settled in his cheeks. They weren't . . . *strays*.

"You've got a couple of wonderful boys," Helen said, her voice pitched slightly high. She caught eyes with Domino and a pucker formed on her forehead at his uneasy fear. "Didn't give me no trouble at all. They're both going to be good men one day."

"Mmmhmm," Daniel murmured, drawn out long like tuning a bow and finding the note a bit sharp. He turned away from Domino. Wicasah looked over Daniel's shoulder. Domino wondered if he would be left here.

On his feet at the thought of being abandoned, Domino shoved his boots on and hurried after his family. Outside, the rain had transformed into a great torrential gush of a plains storm. The scent of displaced soil ripened in Domino's nostrils. Great layers of uprooted dark earth slipped like a mudslide. Vicious raindrops beat up dust currents. Hair slicked to his scalp, Domino shook from his head down to his tiptoes as Daniel stuffed Wicasah into the truck and slammed the door shut behind him. Helen touched his arm gently. Her frown brought back the commas around her face.

"Go back inside," Domino whispered suddenly, digging his nails into Helen's arm. "Put up protection barriers, whatever you have to, but do it now."

The thunderclap was as harsh as the lines on Daniel's face. He turned to walk back toward them.

"Look, sweetheart. I get that your old man is a son of a bitch, but I can take care of myself." Helen's eyes narrowed at Daniel's disrespect.

Too young to be taken seriously, then. When his father's gloved hand pitched back, elbow cocked like a chicken wing, Domino knew the punch was aimed at him. Daniel veered and crashed his fist into Helen's face as she stepped forward to intervene, a protestation kicked from her throat like her teeth. Caught off guard, she staggered. Domino heard her cheekbone crack like lighting. She bent over low, but Daniel's second blow across her back sprawled her flat in the mud.

Domino screamed, but remained frozen as Daniel, a modern-day reaper, suddenly held a gun in his hands. Domino latched on the battered rough wool of Daniel's coat sleeve. Rain filled his pleading mouth like it wanted to drown him. Daniel tried to shake him off like a ragdoll, but behind Daniel's shoulder, Domino caught a glimpse of Wicasah's rounded face fogging up the truck's glass. At least Wicasah didn't see that Daniel had his witch-hunger face on, that deadness indicating he didn't see anything but his charred wife.

Helen stirred, rising with her hands flattened deep in mud in front of her. Domino released Daniel's sleeve and inserted himself between the two adults. His hands splayed out palms up in repentance as he gasped at the stiff beauty and horror of this violent prairie tempest. Daniel focused the gun, straight and narrow, between Domino's eyes. Terror bolted through him, not for his life, but because Daniel threatened to take his very last link to Thessaly. No psychic words or rituals could compare to a witch's raw power. That was stark fact. Helen had it, she knew resurrection, and Daniel simply couldn't kill her.

"Dad, stop," Domino pleaded. "She can help us. She knows how to bring Mama back. Not fully, but enough. Put down the gun."

"Get out of my way, boy," Daniel snarled, finger curled snug around the trigger, a heartbeat away from shooting.

"Dad, stop. Put down the gun. Please, she didn't do anything wrong. Please leave her alone."

"She's one of them," Daniel shouted. "A witch. A goddamn witch that needs to be put down. She's unnatural, Domino. I thought I raised you better than this."

Helen moaned behind Domino. He remembered Daniel screaming at the aunts as they tried to explain Thessaly's murder, how they fumbled explaining that the witchery passed down through bloodlines, that his sons were already one of the fold whether Daniel liked it or not. Daniel only heard things like *mistakes, unnatural,* and *deadly initiation rites conjured by the devil.* The barrel of the gun honed in on Domino like a cyclops' eye.

"Goddamnit," Helen yelled. Domino heard her spit, sharp swift. "Son of a fucking bitch, you wife-beater, child-hater."

Daniel's eyes flashed.

"Dad, don't," Domino cried. Helen's feet squelched as she got to her feet in the muck. She uttered a soft gasp as the gun shifted to her. Domino imagined her lovely eyes widened in terror, black and blue swelling her cheek. This was all his fault for getting in her truck to begin with. He should've known better. Nowhere was safe.

"Perverted witch," his father growled before the gun fired, Domino's *no* like fireworks for the bullet, a blast so loud Domino heard a moment of pure silence before a slow ringing took up in his eardrums. He spun around to see the perfect hole in Helen's forehead, the way her eyeballs rolled up into the back of her head, the slow trickle of blood seeping from the fingers-width wound, and the spray of visceral material behind her. He replayed Helen creating his mother from golden strands, how she gave Thessaly to Wicasah before adulthood swept away his childhood memories like *tabula rasa.*

Daniel turned, but Domino couldn't bear to see where he went. Too fixated on the smell of gunpowder and the sludge clinging to his ankles like quicksand. His knees hit the ground before Helen's corpse, hysterically wondering why he couldn't smell blood. Wasn't he supposed to taste it in the back of his throat the way Thessaly's scorched flesh had? He ran his hands above her body but couldn't bring himself to touch her. He swayed, overwrought on a mental landside.

His tears and the rain mingled with the splatter of Helen's blood and somehow, gravity drained it back to her body. Small shards of bone and white brain matter sucked toward their owner with fearsome determination. Woozily, Domino barely heard the car door slam, entranced by a certain candlelight replacing the dull flat of Helen's irises. Her mouth twitched and re-shaped into a furious O.

"What in the name of god," Domino heard above him, and with the hot smell of gasoline, Daniel splashed Helen with car gas. "Witch won't die shot clean between the eyes? Devil, what have you done to allow something like this to live?"

Helen was resurrection. She would keep coming back to life

until burned. That was the only way a real resurrection witch could go. Fire killed everything and peppered stories of life and the afterlife with eternal flame. Daniel would put Domino down just as fast if he ever admitted to what Domino could be. What Thessaly was. What Wicasah could be.

Helen twitched like a fish out of water. Gasoline slid into her mouth. Domino lunged at his father, knocking the canister and disrupting the spill until it lay gritty all over him. *He couldn't survive another burning.* Daniel flung him back. Domino landed hard in the mud with a thump and a grunt as Daniel aimed the gun barrel right at him.

"You want to save this filth?" Daniel roared. "I'll let you know what it's like. *I'll let you know.*"

The shot scared Domino so badly he almost pissed himself. Mud splattered up beside his shoulder. His father wouldn't miss again. Daniel pulled a matchstick from his pocket and ripped it against the rough starter of his lips, flinging the lit match on Helen's revived form.

Domino prayed the rain would snuff it out, but her guttural screech seared his brain as her whole body lit up in flames. Her hair burned like string and her skin charred. Then, suddenly, her cries stopped. Daniel looked back at Domino with nothing but determination and hate. The gun twitched, ready and battle-hungry.

"Dad," Domino whimpered. "Wicasah's crying."

Daniel cocked his head to the side to listen. The telltale screams of a toddler cut through the death. "Wicasah," Daniel repeated, as if in a haze and finding a light at the end of the tunnel. He staggered to the car. Domino shook, but couldn't help himself and looked. Helen cackled and snapped nearly upright in the flames. The smell of her body-pyre burning bright with carnage and grease collected along Domino's palate and made him gag. *Familiar.*

On his feet with his gorge on the rise, a howl built in his chest and he ran into the house. The spellbook. Scattered and rare across this vast country, belonging only to witch families, it was the one thing Helen would want saved. The door tilted alarmingly on its hinges as Domino barreled inside and slid like he was going for a home run on the floor. He slammed the half-opened book shut, the soft tanned leather cover soft against his fingertips. Hot snot ran down his nose, salty with ash. Blurry-eyed, he cradled the book to his chest and bolted past the leftover oatmeal cookies and a straw hat draped over a nail near the kitchen sink. A worn leather bookbag hung under the hat and he snagged it, stuffing the spellbook inside. He ran out the back door and leapt off the small porch just as the front door squeaked open.

He bolted around the house to the car and saw Daniel's shadow in the house's window. Wrenching the passenger door open, Wicasah scrambled to get in his arms.

"I don't have fucking time for you," Domino screamed, shoving Wicasah off him. Wicasah's head bounced on the seat, a wail of betrayal rising from his lips. Domino stuffed the book under the driver's seat, but it wouldn't fit, *it wouldn't fit,* until the book bag's front gave and ripped. Domino slammed the door on Wicasah's hysterics and nearly took a nosedive slip in the mud.

"Have to get rid of it all," he heard Daniel mutter as he approached the house, and lo, now Daniel had booze as well as gas in his hands. It spilled over the walls and the table. Domino watched, horrified, as Daniel turned to him. "Get in the car, Domino."

Domino snapped to attention like a soldier. Anything witchlike relating him to the mewling destruction outside that was once a beautiful woman would leave him shot and burned on the side of the road. He ran outside, sick on adrenaline, as the familiar whoosh of flames took hold. The house's windows lit up the sky like a sacrifice. Domino wondered if his life would always be characterized by embers, blazes, and coal flakes.

Daniel emerged like a haunt from the burning building. "Get in the car. Get in the goddamned car."

Domino nearly pulled the door handle off trying to get inside. The truck roared to life beneath them. Daniel spun out in the mud trying to find some semblance of a road. The aspen trees bent over double from the wind. Wicasah huddled in his corner, sobbing his heart out, and refused to look at him. Domino joined in—he couldn't keep it inside anymore.

A hundred miles down an unknown highway on one of the longest nights in Domino's life, Wicasah finally calmed enough to stare, amazed, as Domino nearly sobbed himself sick. The young child sidled next to Domino and eased onto his older brother's lap. Domino couldn't touch or comfort him—he was going into shock. The fire etchings burned into his retinas radiated like the stars.

I HAVE ASKED TO BE WHERE NO STORMS COME

Wicasah leaned into him, a warm weight he had to protect from his father, but they weren't safe, not by a long shot. The rest of Domino's life would be a slew of lies and half-told truths so his father wouldn't hold that gun up to his head and shoot him dead, salt him like jerky gone wrong because hate was stronger than love now. Always had been, and now, always would be.

———◆———

Daniel haphazardly parked the truck and checked them into a bed and breakfast. The flickering glow of a poor electric light illuminated the front stoop. Domino clung to the warm sweaty slip of Wicasah's hand. Daniel haggled with the front desk woman *because charging seven dollars a night was outrageous*. Domino swallowed hard, studying the gun's outline in Daniel's coat pocket. The receptionist smiled at him sideways and said, "Fee's a fee, sir, late-night check-in applies whether you got two kids or not."

"Theft," Daniel growled, pawing at his pockets. "This is larceny."

"No such thing if you're willingly paying." The woman turned to fetch a tarnished silver key from the line-up on the wall. "There's plenty more hotels down the road. May be filled, may not be. It's your call, sir."

Daniel ripped the cash from his wallet and threw it on the desk. The woman smoothed out the crumpled bills and arranged them face up, then slid the key across the desk. She opened a ledger and unscrewed her fountain pen. "Name?"

"John Washington," Daniel said, taking the pen and writing his *nom de plume* in an illegible scrawl.

Wicasah leaned against Domino's legs and shame filled Domino at the way he'd screamed at his brother. He bent down, gathered Wicasah into his arms, and lifted him. Wicasah wrapped his arms tight around Domino's throat. Soft breath wetted Domino's neck. He tightened his hold under Wicasah's bottom, hating that Wicasah still shivered from time to time out of what could only be referred to as childhood trauma. Daniel hoisted his bag over his shoulder and herded his boys up a flight of rose-colored carpeted stairs to their room.

Two beds. Domino waddled over to the one farthest from the door and eased Wicasah on the mattress. Wicasah muttered incoherent moans as Domino unlaced his boots and instructed Wicasah to hold his hands up high so Domino could slip his shirt off. Lost in sleep and safety, Wicasah complied. Daniel handed Domino an oversized button-up pajama shirt. Little arms pulled through, Domino's fingers slipped on the buttons until Daniel quietly took over, finishing the job, and slid Wicasah underneath the covers. Wicasah looked so small in Daniel's hands and Domino wondered if he'd ever be big enough for his little brother.

"Your turn," Daniel whispered, turning to Domino. Domino allowed the kindness with terror clenched in his belly, handing over his safekeeping for Daniel to coax stiffening arms and legs into blue striped pajamas. Ushered into bed, his back stuck to Wicasah's under the covers. Daniel's hand stroked his hair away from his forehead, a soothing pet that made Domino's eyelids drift closed. "I'm sorry," he heard Daniel whisper, fighting the creeping black from sliding him under. "I never wanted to scare you like that. Don't know what came over me. I don't know why I get like that."

Domino didn't know how to answer, his tongue had become too heavy, but he wanted to say: *It's okay, Dad, I understand you were scared, but you have to understand I have witch blood inside me and it's not something you can cure with medicine or a gun.*

He heard his father fumble, then the familiar pop of a whiskey plug being pulled free, the most familiar note in his father's lullabies, and Domino crushed the confession down deep. He recalled the terror and his resolution. Daniel could never know.

———◆———

The prairie storm caught up with the bed and breakfast, waking Domino with a start. Raindrops clawed against the grimy window framed by lace curtains. How easy it would be, Domino thought, to be found in this big world and yet how easier to be lost in the blink of an eye. If he slipped away with Wicasah in tow, how fast could their father find them? A week? A year?

Even at nine, he was a worst-case scenario kind of kid. He imagined starving on the streets or using his body for money, being arrested for thievery and separated from Wicasah. Carted off to different families for wholesome lives.

His mouth tightened like he had to hold back his protestations already. Pretending was easier, he decided, than surviving without food or shelter. Easier to deny his heritage and keep his broken family together for as long as possible than make it on his own. He could do it, but Wicasah had one of those faces that made people coo, and cooing led to questions. He understood that better now.

I HAVE ASKED TO BE WHERE NO STORMS COME

Mind made up, Domino carefully extracted himself from the puddle of warmth that was his little brother and slid barefoot on the carpet. His father sprawled face down on the other bed, coat still on, whiskey bottle within reach. Domino padded silently to his father's bedside table and fingered the worn leather wallet open, pickpocketing a nickel and dime. The silver cooled the hot sweat in his palm and he clenched tight, hearing the skritch of metal scraping metal. He slipped out the door, ensuring it remained unlocked and closed it quietly behind him. The electric lights had been cut and the rain thundered down on the roof like galloping hooves.

Domino picked his way down the stairs and out the front door. The outside air wrapped around him like a sheet and stole his warmth. He half-ran to the telephone booth, the rounded blue and white sign declaring its public use. Domino prayed to an empty deity for a sign and the booth door opened easier than the car door. Inside, the rain sounded tinnier and he crawled up on the scratched wooden chair next to the big black receiver. Standing on tiptoe, he unhooked the black phone from its cradle and held it between his ear and shoulder while forcing a nickel into the slot with a metallic clang.

The dial tone buzzed. His middle finger spun the rotary dial in a memorized pattern for the operator. Once put through, the phone on the other end rang once, twice, until a raspy voice picked up. "Hello?"

Domino cleared his throat. "Fiametta?"

"Domino?" Relief coated his name. "Oh god, Domino, *where are you?*"

"I'm okay," Domino whispered, hating the break in his voice. Fiametta rustled on the other end, improperly covering up the voice box and probably calling for Luna. "Fia?" he asked.

"Domino, baby." Luna's voice filled his ear, and Domino could hear them both fighting over the phone. "Tell me where you are, right now."

Just like Luna, Domino thought and wondered if it was the oldest sibling's universal right to be so aggressive, demanding, yet so motherly.

"I had to call you and tell you that I love you both," Domino said. "Kit too."

"We're coming to get you right now," Luna commanded.

"I wanted to tell you that I'm okay and Wicasah is, too. We're still with Dad."

"It's not right that he took you both away," Luna said, hot like a struck match. "Just disappeared in the middle of the night without a word. You're not *okay* without your coven. Your mother gave us rights, too."

"It's not safe for me to contact you anymore," Domino continued, his lower lip wobbling. "He can't know I'm talking to you."

"Are you hurt?" Fia demanded.

"If he knows, he'll come after you. It's better if you don't know where we are. You should stop looking for us."

"Damnit, Domino," Luna cut in. "You're a child. You barely have any training, don't know anything about . . . the rites to become a witch. Baby, you can't do it on your own."

"But I have your number in case anything really bad happens. I didn't want to disappear on you without a word." Domino would've broken down by now, but smoke roughened his throat, and he knew he wouldn't survive if it were the Brightside aunts lit on pyres of Daniel's making.

"You don't have to stay with him," Fia said. "We will come and get you. We'll get Daniel help, he simply doesn't understand, he didn't stay long enough for us to fully explain."

"If he hurt you, so help me god, I will rip him apart," Luna growled.

"Tell Benedicta I miss her. Tell Christobel I love her. I love you, too." Tears leaked past the dam and squeezed out the corners of Domino's eyes. He swallowed with a hard click, just like his father, and the phone dug into his hand.

The aunts immediately jumped in. "Don't hang up the phone, don't do it, tell us where you are, we love you, please come home, *come home.*"

"Don't look for us, okay?" Domino pleaded. "It will be better this way. No spells."

"No, it's not okay," Luna snapped. "What about Wicasah? What are you going to tell him when he's older and starts shooting lightning out of his hands? You're not old enough to handle this!"

"You belong with your coven," Fia said, voice gravel-rough. Domino imagined her smoking a cigarette, her nails tapping her black cigarette holder.

"I'll take care of them." Domino held the phone away from his ear. "It will be alright. I love you."

Their denial cried through the phone in muted laments. Domino hesitated, the phone balanced against the cradle, hating the finality, but it would be a clean break. He silenced them with a click. His change rattled down the phone box's internal chutes into the change holder. He scooped out his pennies and wiped his cheeks with rough sweeps. He didn't understand the magic he'd inherited or the coven rules, but he knew it would be better this way. Resolute, he climbed down, holding his money tight, and hurried back inside the motel.

Back upstairs then, and through the door, closing and locking it behind him. He turned and almost cried out in alarm at the body sitting cross-legged in front of the entrance. Hand clutching his chest, he hissed at Wicasah, "What are you doing out of bed?"

Wicasah's mouth downturned in a frown beyond his years, dark eyes shiny and solemn in a way that made Domino feel like the younger child. "Where you go?"

"Had to make a call." Domino knelt in front of his brother and flickered a wary look to the mound still snoring on the other bed.

Wicasah gripped the front of Domino's pajama shirt tight in a fist. "Trying to go away?" His eyebrows drew together in deep frustration as if he had more to say but was still too young to know all the words. "Going away?" he emphasized.

"No, never," Domino breathed.

"Leaving with Mama?" Sharp as an interrogator.

"No."

"Promise?" Four-year-old uncertainty leaked through Wicasah's voice.

"Promise," Domino whispered and reached for him.

Wicasah settled into the hug. Domino imagined him waking to an empty bed, gunshots ringing in his ears, and Daniel's whisky breath filling the air. He had to be a better brother. He shuffled them back under the covers, tucked them both in tight, knowing he made the right decision.

CHAPTER 3
THE SUICIDE

DOMINO HAD A bucket full of suds and two sponges. The lye and bleach gave him a headache and cracked his hands. *Haven't gotten old enough to grow old yet,* he thought, dipping the sponge into the scalding water and slapping the mixture on the blood staining the floorboards of the bathroom.

Suicide blood, he thought darkly. *Razor-kissed blood.*

Morbid, he thought a moment after. *Fucking morbid.*

Had he said that out loud? He glanced up, half-convinced their landlord would appear out of thin air with a bar of soap for his mouth. Wicasah peered at him from around the bathroom door, too scared to come closer. Wicasah had found Daniel ten minutes to dying up to his neck in dirty bathwater stained red from the horizontal slits in his wrists. Screamed in a way Domino never wanted to hear again. Domino, headed in from playing a game of catch with the boys on the block—the new boy yet again—had dropped his borrowed mitt and ran full-tilt to make the screams stop.

Daniel was stupid, though, hadn't realized the proper methods of self-mutilation worked in a vertical style, and Domino was smart enough to wrap the wounds, hold Daniel's hands high above his head, and yell into Wicasah's terrified face to run for the neighbor, call the police, get someone for the love of Christ.

Ruined his good shirt. Daniel floated naked under the waves like it would be a good idea to be nude when his sons found him as if being fucking dead would make it any more beautiful. Domino almost let those arms drop when he saw his father's slender hipbones lift above the water before slipping back down.

Love, though, terrified and wary but fucking love all the same, made him avert his eyes and pray for his father's life, the man who had held a gun to his head but who—all the same—kept some semblance of food on the table and drove the car from town to town. The car with Helen's spellbook sewn into the cushions of the backseat.

Doctors, then adults who put Daniel on a stretcher and hauled him to a hospital or institution where Daniel's ravings about demons and witches would be medicated with quieting pills. It would be a week before Daniel could come home and, in that time, the priests had been at him. Holy water had been sprinkled and exorcisms whispered under black cloaks, but never performed for the Vatican deemed that a no-no in the eyes of the Lord.

But that was to come. For now, Domino scrubbed his father's blood from the floorboards. They wouldn't be there long, not with such stigma surrounding them. Personally, Domino thought they made a good trio. The father, the sons, and the holy ghost.

"Is he going to be okay?" Wicasah whispered, on the verge of tears.

"Yeah," Domino sighed. "I suppose he is."

Wicasah worried at his lower lip. "Do you think . . . do you think I shouldn't have found him?"

Domino wanted to say *no, it's better this way, he's our father.* "We aren't old enough to be on our own yet."

"You are," Wicasah protested. "You're almost thirteen. Kids are driving tractors at that age."

"Yeah, and what about you?" Domino asked. "Think they'll let me keep you? Stick us in an orphanage, *don't look at me like that, they would,* and being locked up is worse than being free with a crazy man."

"I don't know why you defend him."

"I'm not defending him."

"He treats you like shit."

Domino threw the sponge into the water. Chemicals splashed and burned the back of his hands.

"He's a piece of shit," Wicasah insisted. "You shouldn't have to do this for him. Make him clean up his own mess."

"I can't just leave it here."

"Why not?"

"Because," Domino said, losing his temper, "this blood's got potential spellwork written all over it, and I don't know about you, but I don't want someone using my bloodline for god knows what."

Wicasah sucked his upper lip in and rocked back and forth on his heels.

Domino didn't want to say it, but it cried out from his heart: *what if a new family wants to live here? I don't want Daniel cursing a perfectly good home because us Bluepoints can't function. What about the next family, huh?*

"He's not worth it," Wicasah finished. "That's all I'm saying."

"Come and help me."

"No." Wicasah disappeared from view.

Tears pressed into Domino's eyes. Grief welled up his throat. He didn't want to be alone in this. Daniel's suicide letter nestled in the breast pocket of Domino's oversized coat, addressed to Wicasah.

Domino had found the letter on the table after the trauma left the house silent. Jealousy overwhelmed him and he'd scrunched the letter in his fists, nearly tore it in half. He read it alone, one sentence at a time because it was too painful to do it all in one go. Too devastating to share.

Domino looks too much like your mother, Daniel had written. *Acts like her, is mysterious like her, has her eyes. I can't stand to look at him without thinking of her. So it's okay if I tell you, Wicasah, and not Domino because telling Domino I want to die would be like telling her, and that's something I cannot do.*

That was as far as Domino got before he put the letter away and pulled out chemicals that would cleanse and water that would purify, submerged his adolescent hands under the deep, and felt the burn as the combined two worked into his cracks and crannies to scar him like a man should be.

CHAPTER 4
THE BARNSTORMER

THE BARNSTORMER CRASHED into the farmer's field in a plume of white smoke and stuttering propeller twirls. Domino wiped away the sweat beaded on his forehead and shaded his eyes with a winged hand to see the smoke disappear up into the blue expanse of sky. He tugged the cinched straps of his stained jean overalls further up over his shoulders. A hard clap on his left hurt more than it should and the second farmhand, only a few years older than him—but for some reason that made him ageless with wisdom—thrust a scythe in his hands.

"Finish up the stragglers," the teenager told him, counting nickels into Domino's open palm. "Then get the hell out of here."

Domino couldn't agree more. Wheat grain stuck to his clothes. Grasshoppers rubbed their legs together in the chopped golden-white field. He could smell himself—beansprouts and dehydration, sour and wet. Summer months meant summer work, and he traded hard callouses, knuckle bruises, and tender split fingernails for gleaming coins. He kept his wages close, either on Wicasah or under the foot bed of his shoe where the silver absorbed the reek of his feet.

The chopped wheat waved in short bursts when a cooling breeze hit, lifting Domino's sweat dampened hair off the back of his neck. He paused, letting the physical toll overwhelm him—the way his legs shook and heels tingled, the throb of his hard steel biceps. He spent too much time roasting in the sun. Most days, he'd come home and have nothing to say but a few grunted words before collapsing on the floor. Lulled by the sun setting fast over the plains in rays of pink and navy, with Wicasah's arched knee providing him shade alongside the furrowed brow as Wicasah deciphered metaphors in Faulkner imagery or some shit like that.

Wicasah, baby-faced and still young, worked in the barn milking cows and slipping deft hands between chicken legs to retrieve blue-tinged eggs. He fed goats and threw breakfast slops to the hogs. Dirt and manure stained his fingernails and he smelled like sun-warmed hay and cream. The scent wrapped around Domino, who nestled under the crook of Wicasah's tanned legs, and lost himself in oblivion.

Not this time, though. Today, a down plane overtook a recently harvested field.

"Goddamn vulture better not have scorched our field," the older boy said with a jutted chin to the red biplane. "Better tell the boss."

"I'll do it," Domino volunteered, sweat slipping the scythe's handle. The farmhand shrugged, tucked tobacco in the corner of his lower lip, and swished saliva to whet it. "Brave soul, you. I hate delivering bad news."

Domino swept the scythe in broad controlled strokes, slicing the grain until his arms shook with the weight and the action. He barely finished on time and slid the scythe in the truck's open back. An older man lounged in the corner, sipping from a flask. Two other boys—probably his sons—crowded the other side, heads drooping with fatigue. A good harvest, but a long one. Domino would have to walk home, but it was worth it to satisfy the dying glory of childhood curiosity.

He found the pilot arguing with the bossman. The farmer, red-nosed with a buff-colored cowboy hat, pointed at the candy-red machine nestled in the pale gold spill of evening sunlight. The pilot hooked his hands in the pockets of his brown jumpsuit, goggles perched on his head, and fought a smile.

"Look, sir, it's a simple matter of supply and demand. I would love to get the hell out of your field, but I can't very well do that running on E."

"Then roll that contraption out," the farmer snapped, spitting tobacco juice on the pilot's boot. "Your kind are dead these days. *Dead.*"

"I'm still kicking," the pilot said, spreading his hands. He leaned against the back end of the plane, unconsciously stroking the paint. Domino sidled up next to the enraged farmer. "Looks like you're already handling the situation," he said. "Beat me to the punch."

"I can't have the whole town stomping around on my land," the farmer raged, ignoring Domino.

"Listen," the pilot said with a cocked hip, rubbing a thumb and forefinger over the ended curve of his lips. "You charge to get into the field, you make a profit. I charge for plane rides, I make a profit. This is a win-win situation, sir. Fate didn't just make me land here, it made damn sure I came to you by the grace of God."

The farmer paused and spit out of one corner of his mouth, sucking in air from the other. He grimaced at the pilot with stained teeth.

"You *sure* you ain't got any fuel?"

"Empty," the pilot said, patting his plane. "Old Jenny don't have one drop left in her."

"One weekend," the farmer snarled, holding a finger up for emphasis.

"Excellent," the pilot grinned, plucking a strand of wheat and sticking it in his mouth. A white and red carton of cigarettes peeked out of his pocket. "I've already got my boys distributing flyers in town."

The farmer scowled and spit, the too-large chunk dribbling down his chin. Wiping it, he stomped off.

The pilot took out his carton and tapped it rhythmically against his palm before sliding out a brown-tipped white stick. It dangled from the side of his mouth. A big silver lighter made the end glow. Domino eyed the plane and snuck closer, thinking if he could put one hand on it, it might transform him.

"What's it like?" he asked. "Flying?"

"It's like being in heaven," the pilot said and then reconsidered. "It is heaven."

"I want to do that."

"You want to go to heaven, kid? Go get your angel wings and you can." He blew a puff of smoke and stars ignited in Domino's eyes as the pilot scrubbed a hard hand over Domino's scalp. "Come back later tonight, kid. I'll give you a ride half-off."

—————◆—————

"Where were you?" Wicasah demanded, hands and legs spread wide enough to touch each corner of the doorframe. Paranoid, his brother.

Domino had nicotine breath from the cigarette he'd shared with the pilot, a smoke-rough scratch in the back of his throat, and a headrush. He grinned and took Wicasah's hand in his. "C'mon," he said. "Have a surprise for you."

They raced down the dirt road, away from the rundown rental. Domino's long legs kept him in first place and his laughter floated behind him like kicked-up dust. Wicasah shouted profanities, complained it wasn't fair. Domino slowed down and the two walked side by side to the field transformed into an event of wonder.

Bright electric lights glowed from suspended paper globes. The smell of kettle corn, vegetable oil, and cotton candy suspended above a milling crowd of faces Domino hadn't time to become familiar with yet. Wicasah tugged on his arm, face split into a grin, and Domino dropped five pennies in his upturned hand.

He couldn't see the plane, but he could hear the roar of an antiqued engine and the rush of wind. He squinted into the starless dark, catching a brief glimpse of the pilot's Jenny zooming low enough to make the crowd gasp. Wicasah returned sticky with sugar and Domino peeled off a long stripe of the spun sugar. It melted on his tongue in both smooth and grainy patches.

"There's games, Domino, can we play a game? Can we? Please?" Wicasah bounced.

Domino nodded, mouth full, and followed Wicasah to the booth where four grinning clowns waited. The carnie handed Wicasah five beanbags in exchange for three pennies. Wicasah hustled the rest of the candy into Domino's arm and Domino watched him swing his arm around, warming up like a pitcher, before launching the orange bean bag straight into the clown's mouth. Knocked the teeth out of the middle one. More cotton candy dissolved and Domino swept hardened sugar crystals against the roof of his mouth.

Wicasah blackened enough molars to earn him a stuffed tiger. He waved it in Domino's face in triumph, stroking the white tufted ears with fingers not smeared pink and blue.

The plane whooshed overhead, accompanied by shrieks of delight. A barely clothed woman in kitten heels displayed her black tattoos twirling down her back. A trio of fools somersaulted over the patted-down hay, stopping at random intervals to poke each other in the eye or make loud farting sounds.

Wicasah giggled. Domino fought a smile, rolling his eyes that such childish antics could still make him guffaw. The line for plane rides stretched around the carnival's perimeter. Cigarette smoke grayed the air, and Domino relived the way the pilot offered his, the way Domino took it with anticipation curling his insides but all bravado on the outside. He had coughed once, but took another drag and held it inside like Fiametta did, tapping ash on the ground. The pilot had smiled, respect a warm gleam in his blue eyes, and Domino folded his arms, feeling invincible.

"Can I play another? Domino, can I?"

Domino nodded, took the tiger under his arm, and counted out precious coins. He didn't need to fly. This was heaven right here. He didn't need wings to get there.

———◆———

"Did you see that wing walker? That mummified mermaid in the tank?" Wicasah asked, his shirt tucked up tight under his armpits exposing his stomach.

"What do you know about mermaids," Domino asked as he concentrated on inking a symbol of protection on Wicasah's skin. "She was a siren if I ever saw one."

"I know plenty," Wicasah sang, his arms hooked over the back of the barebones couch, looking like a fledgling about to take the leap. "I know lots of girls."

"Sure," Domino said, pressing harder until Wicasah yelped. "You only know how good old lady Sherman's cookies are."

"Old lady Sherman's daughter's cookies, you mean," Wicasah winked.

Domino didn't answer, a little out of his league with this conversation. He couldn't imagine Wicasah kissing a girl, much less flirting with one. However the kid figured out how to do it, he didn't learn it from Domino. Domino didn't have time for chicks and even if he did, he didn't possess the gumption to talk to one in the first place. Too much on his mind for new, outside love to fit.

"Is it done?" Wicasah looked down at his pooched belly.

"Almost," Domino said, rounding the symbol's last corner.

"You gotta teach me how to do this," Wicasah said. "It must be hard to do it on yourself."

"Can't do it on myself," Domino said, touching up the final lines and leaning back to admire his work that would fade and need to be redrawn in a week. Symbols he remembered Thessaly drawing on him, interwoven lines crafted along the front door of the aunts' Brightside Victorian.

"How come?"

"It's supposed to protect those who are beloved, not yourself. If it worked the other way, nothing bad could hurt anyone." He popped the cap on the marker.

"So, you've been drawing this shit on me for who knows how long, yet you don't have one for yourself?"

"Sounds about right."

"That's a shitty thing to do, Domino."

Domino shrugged. Once, Daniel found Domino drawing the bird's eye on Wicasah's palm after Helen, and demanded to know where Domino had learned it. Learned it from Mama, he wanted to cry, but he kept his mouth shut. Daniel pursed his lips because *he didn't want to see it, not in this house,* so Domino began drawing the symbols secretly on Wicasah's stomach and the top of his feet. In tandem, he'd incorporated magic from Helen's spellbook, crafting half-breed power, just like them. Daniel never took care of them properly anyway and Domino would be damned if Wicasah went wandering around unsafe.

"Did you hear me?" Wicasah demanded. "Shitty."

Domino sighed. "How is it shitty?" He already knew, though, and kept his head down. He didn't want to see Wicasah's cocked eyebrow of irritation, those narrowed brown eyes, and feel like he was the bad guy for keeping secrets.

Instead of answering, Wicasah carefully pulled his shirt down and sat up on the worn couch cushion. He tugged at Domino's leg. "Give me your foot."

Domino rolled his eyes but obliged.

"Teach me how," Wicasah ordered, taking the marker from Domino's hand.

"It's not about just drawing," Domino said. "You have to put yourself into it. A little bit of . . . of the love you feel for me. Otherwise, it won't work."

Wicasah gnawed his lower lip, studying the bottom of Domino's foot like it was a canvas. "How do I do that?"

"I always think of . . . of, you know, how long I can stand your stupid face and how much patience it takes not to strangle you when you're being dumb."

Wicasah's gnawed lips broke into a grin. "Should be easy then."

The damp touch of the marker made Domino jerk back in reflex. Ticklish and feather-light, like air being blown across the plains of his skin. A concentration line deepened Wicasah's forehead. His mouth parted as if ready to command silence. Domino didn't have to tell him how to craft the symbol—after all, he'd been drawing the damn thing on Wicasah for forever—and when Wicasah finished, the symbol appeared a little wobbly and off-centered, but whole. Domino felt as if he'd been locked safe inside his own skin.

"Did it work?" Wicasah asked, head angled haughtily, but Domino could see the unrestrained hope in his eye.

"Yeah," Domino said, breathless. "It did."

Wicasah scooted closer to Domino until they were chest-to-chest. "Who taught *you* how to draw it?"

Domino's face flushed red.

"It's another one of those things you just know, isn't it?" Wicasah said, a bloodhound who'd caught a scent. "Something you learned a long time ago. It's one of those things Dad gets weird about, isn't it?"

Domino couldn't look him in the eye and mumbled something that resembled *sure, yeah, maybe, yes.*

"You have to teach me," Wicasah said, now nearly in Domino's lap. "You have to."

"Don't have to do anything," Domino managed, trapped.

"It's not fair," Wicasah whined. "You keeping all these secrets from me."

"It's not a secret—"

"It is! You never give me a straight answer. I'm owed one."

"Can't you just leave it alone?"

"No." Wicasah's face reddened in outrage. "You don't know what it feels like, but I remember *some* things. I remember . . . that she would've wanted me to know."

Domino snorted, wondering how an outsider would interpret this conversation between two boys accepting the existence of magic. It felt like the noose around his neck had been loosened. The relief of temptation flooded his veins. He smiled lopsided at his brother. He'd never been one to say no and it made him sick inside, how easy he rolled over. "Already taught you one spell already, Christ, what more do you want?"

A brightness lit Wicasah from the inside and if Domino had been a romantic he might have told him the sun nearly shone from his eyes. "How many spells are there?" he asked.

"Loads," Domino said, "but most of the time I'm spitballing as I go."

"Like do you have to give your blood and use bat guano and chant something to cast it?"

"That's more East-finery magic. There are . . . " Domino paused. "Conduits inside of us."

Wicasah looked like he might come out of his skin. "Conduits?

Domino squinted at him, recalling his childhood in flashes— the stark reality of Helen's distended stomach, his frustrated attempts at reading her spell book while locked in the bathroom in the middle of the night one stolen page at a time, the way Luna smeared a potion on his bottom lip to test the taste. The way Thessaly had stood in the middle of a thunderstorm, the earth's own magic flowing around her. He knew magic ran in their veins, but everything else was piecemeal. "Kind of like vessels. They're like monsters sleeping inside us. All we need to do is wake them up."

Wicasah worried at his lip. "How?"

Domino huffed. He wasn't very good at this. When he'd tried waking the conduits, he'd had only a few tiny pushes against the skin of the stomach, like a child's hand reaching out. "Kind of like with the protection eye. You have to put something of yourself in it. Don't try it without me."

He didn't want to say more. He already regretted giving Wicasah the incentive because sometimes the conduits hurt. They wrapped around the cords of his insides and tugged them like testing a climbing rope.

Wicasah's mouth opened to ask another question when the front door banged open. The two of them scrambled off the couch. Domino slammed a sock over his foot.

Wicasah yanked his shirt down for good measure and spread a smile for his father. "Hey Dad, how are you?"

Daniel half-heartedly returned the greeting. Perspiration and grime coated his forehead in a neat line when he took off his cowboy hat. "Just the same. What's on the burner for dinner?"

"Mrs. Sherman gave us leftover sausages," Wicasah said, adjusting to take position near the door while Daniel walked into the adjoining kitchen.

"Thank her for me, won't you?" Daniel said, a fork poking at the uncovered plate.

"Always do," Wicasah said.

Domino held his tongue, feeling spooked—as if speaking about magic had conjured Daniel. The bottom of his foot burned like it had been numb and only now started to wake up.

"Always do," Wicasah repeated. This time, Domino didn't miss his younger brother staring straight at him, struck with the notion that Wicasah was a hundred years older and wiser than he had been a minute before. He wanted to speak, but Daniel was in the room and in times like these, Domino found it was wiser if he remained silent.

CHAPTER 5
THE CONDUITS

BY THE PINCHED set to Wicasah's cheeks, Domino knew his younger brother was trying to wake the conduits lurking under his skin. He first noticed it while dozing propped up against Wicasah's legs with his head tilted back. Wicasah stared at his textbook wearing a look Domino had never seen before. In the mornings, Domino woke to Wicasah's frustrated dark smudged eyes and wished he could be a better teacher. He handed Wicasah his pocketknife and told him, "Don't hurt yourself, Christ. Spellbook pages are sewn in the car seats, but you have to stitch the leather back up right or Dad will have your head."

The sun hadn't risen yet and hope stained Wicasah's bright eyes. One more step down a slippery slope Domino had promised himself he would never descend. Maybe ignorance would be the best safety net for Wicasah, but now Wicasah was like a cat with the cream.

He should've understood his mistake when Mrs. Sherman pulled him out of the field later that day with fierce disapproval, asking why sweet Wicasah hadn't shown up like he'd promised. "First time he's ever done anything like that, he's always so responsible, has he taken ill with the hay fever?"

Domino, out of breath, shook his head, hating that he stunk of cow manure next to her tight bun and flour splotched apron. Sometimes, he felt like talking to a woman was like speaking with an alien race.

"He hasn't taken up with those other boys, has he? Smoking dirty tobacco behind the barn instead of working like good men should."

Domino smiled best he could, feeling dead on his feet. "Don't worry, ma'am. It's just one of those days. I assure you, he'll be there bright and early tomorrow."

Mrs. Sherman studied him, and while Domino couldn't charm worth a damn, he could stand stoic with unblinking eye contact.

"See that he does," she said, "and make sure you eat two of the biscuits I brought for the farmhands, you hear?"

"Yes, ma'am."

Dusk had the same darkened feeling as the dawn as he trudged home, heading straight for the truck. Looking at the mess through the window, he could've screamed at the carelessness. The stitches holding the back panel of the driver's seat had been haphazardly put back together. He unwound the thick waxed cord and re-threaded it through the leather's pre-punched holes. Picking up the pieces—that was what he was good at. Picking up Wicasah's messes.

Wicasah didn't show his face that evening or the next morning. Smart boy. As Domino waded into the overpowering scents of chopped wheat heralding the ending of the harvest season, he quietly panicked until the mindless roar of physical labor ran his thoughts into the ground. Soon enough, the sun gently set with a flash of green as he came home with yellowed stalks poking through his jeans. His left foot ached, his shoe sole wearing out, and he'd have to pad it with rags until he could fix it. Coins jangled in pocket. At the end of the lane by the rental, Daniel's truck was parked at a stranger angle than usual.

Uneasiness lingered in his belly at the unusual sight. He eased up the steps to the front door. The final step creaked like his weight would snap the wood. He paused, armed with the knowledge that shifting, even a hair, would make another creak. He wasn't sure he was ready to know what lay beyond the sound.

Behind him, the road beckoned him to be swept on a journey far from regret-born fear. Fleeing was not his fate—he was a good trench-soldier for the family. He stepped inside the house as a raised voice floated out from the inside. Never been good at leaving well enough alone. Never been good at not sticking his nose in his own shit.

Wicasah turned to him as soon as Domino entered, tears staining his cheeks. Dark-colored, his brother, inherited all the shades of the land from their mother as he transformed from a chubby toddler to a lanky teenager. He didn't look exactly like

Thessaly or Daniel, but Domino imagined he was the spitting image of someone long dead with all that straight black hair and eyes so dark they could've come directly from the heartwood of the earth. The same color of the soil in which Domino had planted his devotion for Wicasah: rich and good.

Wicasah made a choked sound and lurched in Domino's direction, but Daniel's hand around Wicasah's upper arm tightened and yanked him back. Wicasah's bare stomach undulated, the conduits pushing against his flesh, making his face screw up in agony. Dread dropped from Domino's throat to this heart, something akin to broken hope.

"I lost my job today," Daniel said, "and I come home to this."

After being so cautious, so careful, Wicasah had undone all of Domino's work in a matter of days.

"You know what this is, don't you," Daniel asked. The scars on his wrist shone slick as the golden dusk crept through the open windows.

"It's nothing, Dad," Domino said, easing closer, slow as a hunter. Sharp spilled whisky and cigar smoke filled the air. Unfiltered, raw, and cheap. "I think you're seeing things."

"Don't play stupid with me, boy," Daniel growled. "It finally made its way through my thick skull."

"Always treated you with respect," Domino responded. Wicasah whimpered as the conduits pushed against his skin.

"It stares me right in the face, what the aunts said," Daniel said. "That you weren't really my boys. That your mother gifted you into the care of a coven rather than under my protection. That you would do terrible, awful things to each other in the name of power and I couldn't keep you safe, even from each other."

Domino was less than an arm's length away from Wicasah. He secured his hand on Wicasah's other arm and gently but firmly steered Wicasah away from Daniel even though Daniel still gripped him tight.

"That you'd kill me if you had the chance. You'd bring the worst sins upon each other without their guidance because you were born to breed evil. I told them no, I could stop it, but I can't, can I? I can't because I don't know what you are."

"We're your sons," Domino said.

"Yes," Daniel said, and it sounded like a curse.

Wicasah slid out of Daniel's loosened grip and lunged the rest of the way into Domino's embrace. Domino wrapped his arms tight around Wicasah's shoulders. Wicasah's monsters rolled between them and he realized the tightness radiating within his whole belly—hard as a rock and clenched like a fist—was his magic manifesting under an unconscious command to be ready to attack.

"I found something new for us. We'll move tonight," Daniel forced out.

Domino licked his lips. "I have work in the morning."

"There's a carnival group that just passed through town needing a handyman. Who knows? Maybe we can get together an act about the preacher saving his boys from their demons." Daniel cast him a crooked, wild smile. "What a plan. Your mother would be so proud. Her children. Laughing stocks."

Domino swallowed hard. Wicasah's arms tightened like metal bands around his waist. "We'll be ready in the morning, Dad."

"See that you are," Daniel gave in. "I'll give you tonight. That's it."

Domino wanted to see his father walk into the sunset as heroes do at the end of comics. Instead, his old man slouched out the door and stared at the ground as he disappeared into a blaze of fading sunlight. Wicasah sobbed out apologies and promises Domino couldn't quite hear. Domino waddled his brother into the bathroom and took a questionable washcloth to Wicasah's face, smearing dusty tear tracks back from his sun-darkened skin. Wicasah hiccupped with fresh sorrow. Domino wanted him to suffer for fucking everything up. For exploding Daniel's blind eye into one as keen as a hawk's.

"I'm sorry—" Wicasah wailed.

"Doesn't matter now."

"He surprised me, I never meant to let him see—"

"Stop talking about it."

"Domino—"

"Just stop talking, okay?"

Wicasah's shoulders slumped, defeated.

"C'mon." Domino patted Wicasah's back. "Bed."

"Hurts," Wicasah whispered.

"Yeah, it will. Playing around with supernatural forces isn't exactly free, you know? When will you learn that there's always a price to pay, and I'm the one who's been paying your dues?"

Wicasah didn't respond but tentatively laid his forehead

against Domino's chest. Shame radiated from him. Domino felt his magic pulse, trying to reach out for Wicasah's other. The conduit hands stretched his belly and he watched as Wicasah's responded, touching palm to palm with only the sheath of their skin between them.

CHAPTER 6
THE PERFORMANCE

THE BORROWED CARAVAN stank like a leaking gas line and heated up to a hundred degrees easy, even on a cooler morning, but after three years, Domino had become used to it. In that time, he'd gone from mucking up show animal shit to mending costumes to being the star of the Preacher's Monster Boy act. The barnstormer would fly overhead and claim a farmer's field, they'd get word, and move to set up the carnival.

He hadn't liked it one bit when, six months in, Daniel sternly told him that Wicasah was to become part of their act. Wicasah had begged for it, a point that made Domino shake with fury, but the unspoken truce between father and son was simple: Daniel didn't exploit his youngest. Daniel wasn't allowed to make them hold hands like lost souls and then cure them like the preacher man he pretended to be.

He hated agreeing, but he had new shoes to show for it and enough food for Wicasah to shoot through another growth spurt and time to be homeschooled by the bearded lady with an inclination for mathematics. Beyond traditional schooling, Wicasah had mastered his conduits faster than Domino, and they had both picked their way through the remaining pages of Helen's spellbook enough times to attempt the craft themselves. Domino still insisted on a bird's eye of protection, but now Wicasah took to drawing them on Domino with a determination that bordered on obsessive.

All in all, this venture to include Wicasah was better suited to keeping his family content.

Behind the curtain flanking the ringleader's circle, the costume designers helped him don his best overalls, strategically ripped in all the right places for shock value, and clip them over his shoulders. When the time was right, he'd go into convulsions and summon the monsters inside him, yank down the overalls and expose mass writhing inside his naked torso to a stunned audience of ten to sometimes hundreds of people.

Daniel would emerge from his seat placed strategically in the middle of the crowd to speak against the evil possessing this doomed child. The crowd would turn and gasp at the savior. Daniel would put his hand on Domino's stomach and Domino would sink to his knees, feigning agony and then peace as he soothed the conduits within him. It killed every time. Plus, they got to keep the tips.

He had nothing against religion. Just hated what people did with it.

"Ready, kiddo?" Mindy asked with pins in her mouth as she checked the stitching one last time. "Shouldn't even ask, not like you have stage fright anymore."

Domino gave her a polite smile. He wasn't a talkative sixteen-year-old and he hadn't exactly won favoritism with the carnival's matrons, beyond a reputation that he could be relied on to get a job done. His first time onstage had nearly undone him: the audience's collective gasp followed by an eerie quiet, finished with a whoosh as the crowd broke into applause and a standing ovation. Now, he barely broke a sweat.

From behind the curtain, Domino heard the rustle of skirts against the worn board seats and the crinkle of popcorn bags. The abnormal heat from the electric lights made him perspire. He couldn't see Wicasah, waiting on the other side of the circular stage for his cue. There always seemed to be something menacing within the darkness hiding behind the light. The ringleader's introduction began and Domino sighed at the dramatics, wondering if he might be able to sneak away later to watch the tattooed lady undress in her lamp-lit trailer. His bare feet clenched against the dirt floor.

Perhaps the spotlights only served to blind him from the audience, turning them into bulky shapes. Perhaps the spotlight was only supposed to highlight Wicasah, who now strode toward him with the same purposeful determination Domino always felt but never showed. His brother might outstrip him one day, being so tall, and he had obtained a lithe stillness about him that honored the hunters of the long-empty prairie.

"Brother!" Wicasah called out, too brash with just the right emphasis of an actor. Domino couldn't help his genuine smile. They were good at this. Pretending.

Memorized dialogue. Wicasah kept his hands on his hips like a boy that would never grow up. Domino was the first to go into convulsions, baring his stomach for the audience. Daniel emerged from the crowd to lay Domino's monsters to rest. Domino feigned fainting, quieting the stretching hands inside of him. Through slitted eyes, he watched Daniel place his healing hands upon Wicasah and chant a gobbled patchworked passage from the Bible.

Daniel's hands hovered over Wicasah's skin. Domino tensed. He wasn't a fool. The more shows they booked, the more he noticed Daniel's tenderness, as if Daniel believed he slew the witchery infecting his sons. Wicasah's monsters stilled, but then reached up to clasp Daniel's hand in greeting.

Off-script.

Squinting, Domino made out the outline of the conduit's detailed fingers. Wicasah's head tipped back slowly, his mouth parting in unconcealed ecstasy. The conduit's hands opened and curled like a flower, hiding something precious within the center of their bloom.

Daniel stilled, uncertain, until his face slackened as if coming out of a long nightmare. A golden glow, similar to when Helen had summoned Thessaly's spirit, throbbed between Wicasah's conduit hands. The light, like shining a flashlight through skin, illuminated the red veins spanning Wicasah's stomach. Daniel bent closer, peering into the cupped hands like he stared into a seer's pool. The hands quivered but held the vision open to Daniel before sinking deeper into Wicasah's body as if they never were.

Domino trembled. He'd seen that look on Daniel's face before, the expression stating that Daniel might've never truly believed in Hell all the way, but now that he acted a priest, belief was mandatory. The costume was becoming harder to take off.

Wicasah quivered and rolled to his side, curling his legs up as the glow expanded from within to outline him—transforming the young man he was becoming back to an innocent, and beautiful in a way that hadn't been scarred by adulthood and experience. *Redeemed.*

Daniel knelt beside his youngest. His hands shook as he called Wicasah's name, his voice enriched with awe and disbelief.

Wicasah rolled his head into Daniel's touch and smiled sweetly. "They're quiet now, Father."

The crowd lost their mind.

———◆———

"What was that?" Domino hissed as he yanked Wicasah behind the curtain. The roaring applause transformed into entreaties for an encore. The ringmaster placated with promises of a new show. Wicasah's smile was one of elation, as if his triumph had been carved out of stone.

"Just what the hell was that?" Domino demanded. They were supposed to be hiding, not swept up in improvisation of bullshit devil claws and golden angel grace.

"I figured it out," Wicasah said as Domino gripped his wrist and forced them out into the firefly spotted night. "The conduits don't have to hurt so much afterward if you know how to feed them."

"Feed them what?" Domino asked, the arrow of fear struck true in his heart. They weren't supposed to be enchanted with the conduits—weren't supposed to let on that, for Domino, the magic had become stronger and brighter as he shed his childhood like an unwanted second skin. Still, the magic felt immature, like it fought against a chrysalis that wouldn't open without the right condition. Daniel brought it up enough times—they were damned because this power matured with sin.

"Conduits aren't just vessels," Wicasah said, his temper flaring. He wrenched his arm out of Domino's grip. "They say things. They want things."

"Like Dad's blood?" Domino snarled. Continuously summoning the conduits was like revving an engine to overheat while in park. The car still devoured fuel and burned hot to the touch, but never went anywhere. These shows, while lucrative, only served to let the magic gestate in its pupae, never take flight.

"Would it really be such a tragedy?" Wicasah asked, his mouth a mulish line.

"Why stop there?" Domino said, the knowledge cold around his heart. If that's what Wicasah wanted, Domino would give it. "Why not use my blood if you're so interested?"

Wicasah's face went white. "Never your blood. Never that."

"Then what? You'd murder him?"

"No," Wicasah said, but Domino knew enough to see that a

maybe lurked behind that negative. He felt like he did onstage: blinded.

The crowd dispersed and filtered out of the tent. Mothers shouted to see the blessed boy. Security ran them off. A man on stilts snuffed out the oil lamps illuminating the path one flame at a time. Domino had a sudden urge to spirit them away and give up on the encroaching civilization. He was done with ringmasters who hoarded electricity, with the carnival taking a hefty percentage of each show, of existing with this aching terror that never eased and only seemed to increase as the years flew by.

"You want to do something to someone, you do it to me," he said, instead. "You want matured power, you do it to me."

Wicasah's lip curled. "Enough's been *done* to you. It would be for us. Daniel's violence is only building inside him. He won't hurt me, but I won't allow him to hurt you. Not anymore."

"You're just a kid," Domino mumbled, shamed. Wicasah shouldn't have to choose between father and brother. He turned away, his split devotion clogging his throat, and headed toward their caravan.

"So are you," Wicasah said.

"Don't do anything stupid," Domino ordered, scrambling for control. "Fucking idiot."

"Language," Wicasah mocked gently.

Hands reached up from behind Domino and pulled him into a hard hug. From outside their caravan, the windows lit up with new candlelight and Domino imagined his father sitting on the cot with clasped hands, scarred wrists turned up.

———◆———

Domino had to get away from the caravan's stifling interior for a breath of cool midnight air. An itch had begun since his conversation with Wicasah, one of survival that urged him to take Helen's spellbook and run for the hills. What magic could he do that was completely his? He'd heard adrenaline-soaked stories told to scare of curses that required bones, poisons distilled through stripped thistles, children chucked into wood fires after eating candied homes. But had any of these crossed his mind as something he could control and use?

He detangled himself from their shared bed—Wicasah had developed twice the number of legs as he grew, kicking Domino in his sleep until Domino was twice as sore. Daniel, quiet and uncommonly sober, had rolled to the side of his cot.

Slipping outside, the fresh air cleared his mind, chasing away anxious thoughts. He eased down to sit at the edge of a set of dirt tire tracks. His breathing sounded like the loudest thing for miles. With his chin in his cupped hands, he wondered if Helen had lured them to her home for such nefarious purposes only to discover an unexpected kinship at the last moment. What had Thessaly done, the aunts even, to merit their power? Did Brightside magic work the same way? Was it just as rare as the witchery? One day, under their tutelage, he would've had to make a similar terrible choice and think nothing of it because the decision was in his blood, in the magic.

He'd heard whispers of the *'ánti'įhnii* traveling through these parched American lands staked by a European lineage, a claim which did nothing to erase the tales cultivated there, especially myths about the howling *yee naaldiooshii* mimicking a lost lover outside locked windows. Domino wondered if that might be him one day, calling for what he'd lost. Sometimes, he wondered if such stories might be linked to him, but he would never know. Those tales did not belong to him, the culture closed off to an outsider such as himself. Anything would be better than the well-trod twisted thing Christianity had become. He shivered and wrapped his arms around his chest.

Summer was at its hottest with the biting finality that would end in the wake of a long winter. He tried to look at the sky but the stars remained stubbornly dim. Behind him, the cavern loomed and breathed down his back, a direct contrast urging him to return to what meager safety remained within those walls. No matter how stifling. How hot.

He stood, wiped his dirtied hands on his pants, and slowly walked back to the caravan parked in a field distantly surrounded by the other traveling homes holding the slumbering.

Inside, the glow of a single candle shed a bare glow over the stark walls. Domino had his eyes to the ground and his mind down a rabbit hole when a cut-off muffled cry caused him to look up. Daniel had Wicasah pinned to the bed and a hand tight enough to suffocate over his mouth. Wicasah's eyes flickered to Domino in terror. Domino didn't hear Daniel's muttered Latin or the way the knife against Wicasah's throat reflected the candlelight like a mirror. He barely glimpsed the hope on Daniel's face—like an *exorcism* would save them—before he lunged at Daniel with an inhuman snarl. Daniel reeled, flinging Domino over his shoulder. Domino sprawled to the floorboards. The knife clattered in the half-light.

This was war. Daniel wouldn't take away another beloved, wicked or not. His foot collided with Daniel's kneecap. The satisfying joint pop meant his old man took a knee.

"I can save him," Daniel screeched, turning on Domino. "You saw how God came through me to him. He can be saved. One of you can be saved."

Domino scrambled back, searching for a weapon, before reaching out to Wicasah, begging him not to attack, but Wicasah had never been good at following orders. Wicasah launched on Daniel as a clawing pile of limbs. Daniel gripped a handful of Wicasah's long hair and shoved him off, colliding Wicasah's head against the bedpost.

Howling black rage. Maybe that was what the limelight was distracting Domino from, this beast consuming him like a typhoon. Wicasah wasn't moving, there was blood slipping from his nose, and Domino's fists hit hard flesh with the roaring disorientation of battle. A hard punch to the side of his head made his ears ring. His brain sloshed from one side to the other. A hand wrapped around his throat, choking him. He fought not just his father, but the darkness ready to engulf him.

"He could've been good if you'd let me save him," Daniel whispered through the blinking black. "He wasn't going to be like *you.*"

The gunshot exploded so loud it nearly deafened him. Wet splattered across his face. The shot dropped to a ring and Domino sucked in a horrified breath as Daniel's shattered skull dripped on top of him. Wicasah stood behind Daniel's shoulder, the smoking barrel cocked at a sideways angle. His mouth wavered at what he had done. Wicasah said his name as a pool of warm blood started to come for him. Like the police would, like the civilians would. Domino screamed for rationality.

"Get the keys," he stuttered, breathless. Pushing his father off him.

Wicasah, finally broken down, obeyed. Domino was rewarded with a silver jingle. There wasn't time for anything else. The plush tiger, worn near to bits, stared at them from the bed. The sounds had been too loud and people were too close to take anything with them. Blood stuck to his skin like paint. Alarmed shouts filled the outside air, accompanied by slamming doors.

"Out the back," he commanded and shoved Wicasah hard in front of him.

They burst through the screen door, feet hitting the dust and bolting for the truck. Wicasah outpaced him easily and Domino couldn't understand the reluctance holding him back. Everything he'd ever done in the name of protection lay destroyed at his feet.

Shouts turned to cries of persecution and one shrill scream. Domino saw them both hanged for murder, saw the whole country laid out unsafe without anywhere for them to go, not when there wasn't someone to take the fall or responsibility. Wild gunshots sounded around him, and the bullets from their pursuers kicked up the dirt around his feet. Wicasah had started the car and shouted at him through the half-rolled-down window to get in when the decision was made for him. A stray bullet, shot from close behind him, slammed into his thigh. He pitched against the closed passenger door with his heart pounding. There was no time to get in.

"Go," he screamed. "Go, you son of a bitch, get out of here!"

The tires squealed, dirt and rocks kicked up in his face, accompanied by the smell of burning gas and a cold engine being told to go over a hundred instantly. Hands roughly gripped his shoulder, restraining him. He must have cracked a tooth from gritting his jaw shut so tight. He heard cries, accusations, questions, bullets aimed for rubber gone wild while his greatest fear had been realized—they had been separated— and he couldn't stop looking at the kicked-up dust in the hopes of seeing the red brake lights flash, telling him Wicasah had changed his mind, had stopped, and come back for him.

CHAPTER 7
THE MATCH

THE BENCH UNDERNEATH Domino hurt his back, but it was better than sitting on the ground, where the overturned earth would get him dirtier than he already was. Bending over, he hunched his shoulders and crisscrossed his fingers in feigned interest as the sun set over the flat-top plateaus and bluffs lining whatever territory the prison labor had crossed. He wished there was more in his ration bowl than questionable meaty stew and the heel of day-old bread. His jumpsuit wouldn't be washed for another two days and he could smell his own scent of hard work and imprisonment. He bent his knuckles until they cracked.

He liked to sit outside after the grueling day ended, even though he spent most of his time outside anyway, far away from the clink of wooden bowls and spoons, the cacophony of the hungry combined with the crass contained to males in close quarters for too long. A wolf pack, perhaps, of the mentally disturbed and criminals working hard on the new railroad spanning across the land of the West—bought and paid for by Brightside money and policy to help the other side of the Dark and Bloody see advancement. Domino had no idea who'd even use a railroad. It wasn't like anyone except for oil barons had cash to spare and the tribes made them zigzag the layout between specifically ordained plateaus. Brightsiders didn't care about sacred land, but the West knew better than to desecrate that. After all, why start a war in the name of the East when those bastards only saw the west as an expanse of virgin land, when in reality, that land had been ridden hard and put up wet? The East had money to burn. So, the Brightsiders cut their costs employing prison labor, which was how Domino ended up spending part of his murder sentence—daily splitting and moving land, laying iron, cutting thick fresh wooden boards for rail ties.

Domino remembered when he'd first been brought here, two months after his latest runaway attempt from the rehabilitation of young adults, and was told if this didn't break what kept him wild then it was the true clink for him. Dank prison cells and sparse rooms like a chapel, mess hall, cell, and recreational yard would make up his life.

The thin bangles around his wrists had just enough give to move up and down his arm but were strong enough to enforce that he wasn't exactly here on his own terms.

He forced the rest of his bread slice past his lips and quickly swallowed. Two sets of footsteps crunched behind him and he could sense one of them was in chains.

He hadn't officially been told yet, after all, no one *wants* to be here, but he'd found his latest bunkmate strung up by hastily ripped bed sheets—his bedsheets no less—the previous night when he'd come back from the hole-in-the-ground privy. Their barracks were more like horse stalls with a lock on the door, but the guards were tricky and found a way to chain each man to his bed by one wrist and then hitch two men together with heavy iron links between the other wrist. His bunkmate must have planned it out carefully, pretending to sleep while Domino hailed down a guard to unchain him and let him outside. By the time Domino was brought back, the man had breathed his last breath. Domino gave his old buddy the finger before the guard hitched him to a post and left to find something to clean the piss, or ejaculate, from the floor. Domino figured if he'd been a better man, he wouldn't have scraped it up. It wasn't every day you found a hanged man's juices that could birth or feed a mandrake. Heavy magic in that, right there.

Someone cleared his throat. Domino cocked his head to the side and glanced over. The guard tipped back his wide sombrero shading his face from the hot sun. Next to the guard wavered a slight man, older than Domino by a good ten years if the crow's feet were anything to judge by, with scraped knuckles. Had a thinness about him, some kind of inner flame that had eaten half of his candle and was eagerly chewing on the wick. Domino huffed.

The guard pulled on the newcomer's chain and motioned for Domino to raise his wrist. The lock clicked closed and now Domino had a whole new ball and chain to lug around. He tuned out as the guard recited the rules—no fighting, no engagement of any kind, life out here was lived on the buddy system, so don't fuck around with your partner and he won't give you a black eye.

"I'll come for you in the morning," the guard finished before departing. "For your treatment."

The newcomer sat beside Domino, radiating trembling heat, and swallowed hard. Domino didn't look at him, instead watched the sun slink behind the dust-kicked horizon. This man wasn't like him. No reputation, no strength, no magic, and Domino smelled his fear from here, but he wasn't one to play dominance games. He'd had four years before this at some bullshit orphanage prison dealing with that kind of dog-eat-world mixed with therapy. No one messed with him after he cracked a few skulls. Even now, he still had a reputation of being that sixteen-year-old with patricide on his hands.

"I'm Domino," he said into the air and felt his new buddy tense.

A ringing bell indicated it was time to be herded back to the barracks. The sun disappeared. Domino ached, a sharp pain tugging from his shoulder blade down to his lower back. Sleep sounded like the best and worst thing in the world. He stood, and his silent companion followed.

The guards shut and locked the cell just before running the chains through the hook embedded in the creaking bunk bed. Domino could move around the room, but if he had any ideas of going anywhere beyond the three feet of horse stall, he was sorely mistaken. His new companion watched the guards as if measuring how to take them apart. Domino slid into the lower bed, crossed his arms over his chest, his body concealing things he kept hidden under the mattress, all the things he couldn't let anyone see. It was why he didn't move to the coveted top bunk. Sometimes, you knew your cave so well there was no point moving, even if the grass did look greener on the other side.

The newcomer eyed the top bunk. "Sure I can take that?" he asked, hands limp and loose at his side.

"Sure can," Domino drawled back. "Don't have a use for a suicide's bed."

The man flinched but nodded and inched to the ladder, tugging on it carefully before putting his whole weight on it. Domino had to hand it to him; the man had experience in being bullied. He heard the creak of the old mattress being tested, the weight of a new body shifting above him, and Domino could almost make out the way the man lay, first on his side then on his back.

"I'm not going to give you my name," Domino heard from up above, a voice floating down without a home.

"S'all right," Domino responded. "Thought I'd stick with calling you Match if it's all the same to you."

The man didn't answer. Domino listened, hearing hitched, short breaths. The crying eased Domino into a blank sleep. When the bell woke him up in the morning, he found the top bunk empty and his companion gone.

———◆———

Halfway to late morning, Domino's back protested as he swung a pickaxe, deforesting the terrain to lay fine steel. His thigh hurt, and he swore that gunshot five years ago had chipped bone. He remembered the hate, but nothing compared to the widespread detest the people of that godforsaken town had felt for him. Out of his mind for a week on morphine as the hospital fixed his leg up, and even then, the staff showed such reluctance to care for him. Not only because he was handcuffed to the bed, but also because the carnival had scattered after the incident and left only Daniel's rotting corpse in the caravan behind. Open and shut case. No witnesses. Guilty until proven innocent.

He lied. Said he was eighteen so they wouldn't send him to one of those orphan rags, but they called his bluff. His trial, with his court-appointed lawyer, went fast with a signed confession. It wasn't until he was stripped of everything and riding a railcar to a structured asylum for disturbed youths that it really hit him. He was a bird with clipped wings.

In the next few years, he'd moved from disturbed boy to incarcerated criminal to penitent prisoner serving out his time making his world a better place with the sweat on his back. It was a familiar nightmare that never ceased to amaze him when it wasn't a dream. Domino didn't dream of monsters under the bed anymore. In this life, he was the monster.

His brain had a hard time letting him forget that. He nearly missed two guards hauling Match over to Domino's right side and chaining him up. Connected once more.

Match shook so hard he almost couldn't hold his shovel. Domino nearly yelled because they were supposed to work together on this stupid task that neither of them cared one wit about, but at Match's fish belly face he couldn't bring himself to speak. A hard nudge made him glare at the other man besides him, stupid asshole Jim Barkers.

"What's it like, Domino, shacking up with a strange?" Jim asked with a nasty laugh.

"You sound jealous," Domino hissed as things began to slot into place. "Wish your body warmed his bed?"

Jim's face twisted ugly and he swung his ax harder than intended. "Don't need anyone to tell you how," he sneered. "Your daddy probably fucked you just as good as your new bunkmate."

Domino flushed red, but the croon already seeped out his mouth, "Didn't get far did he? I hope it was worth the bullet to the head."

Jim, a thief who'd never spilled a drop of blood, paled. Domino seethed. He should break Jim's nose. The poor excuses for doctors out here wouldn't put it back together right and hopefully, the shit would breathe with a whistle for the rest of his life.

Match, chained next to him, remained silent. His throat clicked with anxiety. Domino still felt vicious towards *anything*. "What's the matter, Jim?" he taunted. "Is it hard to imagine? Too hard for that puny brain of yours to figure out what's worse: rape or murder?"

Jim glared up at Domino, hatred a starlit gleam in his iris.

"Maybe I'll tell you. Better yet, maybe I'll *show* you."

Jim raised his chained hand, yanking his partner closer and Domino saw the next few seconds in fast-forward. Jim would hit him in the jaw. Domino would slug him in the gut with the wooden butt of his ax. Jim would go down and Domino would let out a roar before squishing his skull with the other, sharper, end of the ax.

He didn't have anything to lose. He didn't realize he was defending Match, but it just happened that way and his fury remained strong. His conduits ran talons down his ribs, playing his spine like a xylophone.

His wrist chained to Match jerked, throwing him off balance. A second yank had him stumbling backward. Jim's fist missed him by a breath. He felt Match hold the pickaxe's rod steady, felt Match like a warm shadow against his back, and Match's hot breath on the notch connecting his neck to his shoulder. Suddenly, it was like he *had* been punched because it could've been Wicasah behind him, wrapping his arms around Domino's middle without a word and simply *being there*. A small part Domino had buried and smoothed over until it was unrecognizable cracked and split, letting loose a resounding heartache that nearly brought him to his knees.

"Let it go," Match told him, loud enough that Jim could hear. "We'll get in trouble."

Domino's eyes flickered beyond Jim where two guards picked their way towards them, eyes intent and waiting for the blow-up, hands hovering above their beat sticks. They had to be careful not to kill, after all. This was penal punishment.

Domino shuddered. Jim must've seen the attention shift because he backed up, his chain going slack between him and his partner.

"Sticks and stones will break my bones," Match whispered bitterly, "but words will never hurt me."

Then that sudden weight was gone, leaving Domino unbalanced.

"Problem here?" the guard asked, his fingers tapping the belt on his hip.

"None that I can see," Domino said.

"Me either," Jim piped up.

"Thought there might be some issues with our new prisoner."

"Nope, just a regular lookin' guy," Jim said with a mean wink. "Doesn't look like a strange to me, sir, if that's what you might be thinking."

The guard eyed Jim up and down and didn't look surprised. "Can't learn to keep your trap shut, huh?"

Jim shook his head and lowered his eyes. "No, sir, never learned, sir."

"And you," the guard swung back to look at Domino, "are you starting something you can't finish?"

"Finish everything I start," Domino said. The guard leaned closer. Domino smelled the harsh scent of badly brewed beer and bread on his breath

"Do you now," the guard whispered.

"Domino was just introducing me to the men," Match piped up.

"Shut the fuck up you strange shit, no one wants to actually meet you." The guard's face twisted into a scowl and he shoulder-checked Domino as he walked away. Domino breathed a sigh of relief before turning around. Match wouldn't quite look at Domino, and his shaking had turned violent like he was waiting for the next punch from the hand that feeds.

Domino stared. Match picked up the shovel. It took Domino a minute, with his pickaxe in mid-swing, to realize Match was waiting for Domino to turn and hurt him, punch him, kick him to the ground. The pickaxe hit and broke dirt. Match flinched.

They continued working in silence. Little by little, the sun crept over and above their heads. Finally, Match relaxed enough to look up. His mouth wavered, eager to speak or maybe offer thanks, but shame still flowed through Domino's system. He remembered his question—rape or murder—and felt a familiar dread gather in his stomach reminding him how the world saw him. When the guard said it was time to end their midday shift, he didn't hesitate to leave Match in the dust.

———◆———

Footsteps shuffled beyond their cage. Domino heard the lock being fiddled with before the door slowly swung inward. He stayed still and cracked an eye open, trying to see through the shadows in the already dark room. Two guards pattered in, quiet as church mice, and tapped knuckles on the top bunk. Match shifted and clambered down the ladder. The chain connecting him to Domino was unlatched and a new set strung between his wrists. Match's shoulders slumped in defeat.

Wicasah blazed through Domino's mind, alone and all too young, lost in this wide world. Domino dreamed of a changed past, one where he told his shot leg to fuck off, and he jumped in the car with his brother, and they ran with all the wolves after them.

The trio exited the cell. The lock rattled again. Domino vaguely wondered where Match had gone as a new thought struck him. What if Wicasah had gotten in trouble and eventually ended in some hole like this?

When his mind sunk deep in depression with what-if thoughts like these, he felt crazy and gut-punched with a need to fight and put all his fury somewhere where he didn't have to look at it. Where he didn't have to be reminded that maybe he'd made the wrong choice. God, he couldn't imagine how this imprisonment could be the *right* choice.

Dark nights like these, amongst the snoring of others in their adjoining cages and surrounded by the ghost-roll of the hundred sinners who'd slept in this bed before him, Domino felt like he'd forgotten what it was like to love.

His exhausted brain dozed, but when they brought Match back as the darkness lightened to dawn, he woke to Match's blanched face and his harsh perfume of sick. It took Match two times to climb the ladder and when he finally settled, Domino heard muffled sobs from above that couldn't be held back.

CHAPTER 8
THE STRANGE

"**MIND IF WE** have a sit?" Domino asked.

Match gave him an exhausted blink. The end of the day had come and while Domino generally liked to zone out, today held a different purpose. Match was flagging. He'd nearly sliced Domino's foot to the bone when he lost a grip on the shovel. He'd tripped over their combined chains more than once, shoving Domino face-down in the dirt. He couldn't defend himself when the other inmates rained verbal blows down on him until Domino stepped forward and make a show to get them to back the fuck off.

Babysitting exhausted *him*. He didn't think he could go another day like today and not lose his temper. He didn't want to become mean street trash that had one more cruel thing to say. So, Domino took the lead and went outside to his favorite bench. Match shuffled behind him like some leashed puppy. Match *had* to be stronger. The others were cannibals that favored a slow feast. Match made the hunt too damn easy.

Domino eased into a lounge. Match exhaled in relief when he settled down, too. He reached up to rub his neck.

"Look," Domino said, clipping his heels together, keeping a weathered eye on the milling guards. "I'm not your mother and it's not like you're innocent being here and all, but Match, man, you gotta be smarter than this."

Match's relaxation disappeared. "I know," he whispered. "I'm just not very . . . "

"Strong?" Domino suggested.

"I'm not the same kind of guy as all of you."

Domino bristled, hating being lumped into that category. Nasty retaliation sat on this tongue, but for the most part, he had a slow-burning fuse. "For one, you've got something in common with us mongrels to be placed in the same boat as us. Problem is, you're looking for an excuse to drown."

Match snorted in disbelief. "You know who Oscar Wilde is?"

Domino tilted his face up so the sun could blind him. No, he didn't have any idea, but he could hear the contempt leaching into Match's voice and that was enough.

Match plowed into the silence. "He was a writer, but more importantly, he was a socialite with a secret that he didn't keep quite so secret." Match waited a beat. "I wanted to be like him. I thought there wasn't any harm in being who you were. In fact, it was much more daring to flaunt it than conform to all the twittering hands of high society. I dressed how I wanted and made love with whomever I wanted and I didn't care that there were people who disagreed or frowned at what I did and who I was. It was simply a game. I couldn't be touched."

"But you could," Domino said softly.

"Don't ever fall in love," Match said. "Someone fell in love with me and I didn't love him back and that meant I was in for some harsh revenge. Slandered my name. Made up some bullshit accusation that actually stuck. Sentenced to hard labor and therapy." His voice quivered over the last word, and if fear was an ink, Match dripped with it.

Domino felt very young suddenly. His world was piniomed to day-by-day jobs. He could harvest wheat, write and read a little bit, knew how to mold the earth and clay with his bare hands into rudimentary tools. He knew little of therapy, barely grasped the word *twittering*, was completely ignorant of status unless it pertained to the fighting pits. He knew how blood looked in the dark and how slippery it could be, how it stained the skin deeper than any acrylic. Silence was always his best defense and he used it here, letting it grow thick between them.

Match didn't take to the quiet. Now that the sieve had been opened, he became angry and accusatory. "You know what the fuck conversion therapy is?" he demanded. "You know that they think they can cure me of this psychological disease by giving me drugs that make me sick and make me watch porn until I vomit?"

Domino swallowed hard. "I don't know anything about what you have."

"What did old Jim call me? Strange? I'm that. I'm sure you can figure out what a faggot is without a dictionary or a demonstration."

"Yes, I know," Domino said, laid low. "It must be hard to change an inclination that's born in your bones."

Match quieted as a tumbleweed somersaulted in front of them. "You're nicer than the rest. Even the people I thought were my friends, old lovers even, didn't want to be seen with me."

"I'm not exactly an angel here myself," Domino said with a half-stifled laugh. Of all the things the witchery commanded, being a homosexual was not one of them. Couldn't be *that* sinful.

"Maybe not, but at least you're decent."

"You have to say that. You're my ball and chain."

Match didn't laugh. Domino shifted, uncomfortable. He wasn't a good man. Match should see that.

"You're decent," Match reiterated, and Domino wondered how it had come to this, that Match had to reassure him.

———◆———

The guards brought Match back long after the lights had been smothered and the inmates had settled. Mattresses had stopped squeaking and quietness that bespoke of rest and peace, at least for a little while, lay over the paddock. Domino had remained wide-awake on the bottom bunk, counting the bars of the mattress frame above. Alone, he felt sick to his stomach. Match should've been back from conversion therapy by now.

An hour passed, maybe two by the way fatigue dragged at his eyelids. When the lock rattled and the door opened, two guards dragged Match across the room. His limp legs trailed between them. They prodded him until he climbed the ladder up to his bed, feet slipping in his worn slippers. The guards didn't speak, almost looked sad with responsibility, but the jingling keys were their only apology as the lock closed. The sound of their shoes whispered across the floor as they disappeared.

Domino waited. Tension ignited the air. Above, Match wasn't moving. Maybe he'd slumped down and passed out. Domino couldn't figure out what counted as his business or not, but when a strangled sob cut through the room, almost as if Match was stuffing the sheet into his mouth, Domino tossed business out the window. He'd stayed up so long already; it seemed pointless to feign sleep now.

Another sob cut through the quiet. Domino bit his lip at the sorrow rippling around the room, perfect to fit a spell, but now it reminded him of Wicasah crying against his shoulder. Wrapping his arms around Domino's neck, face buried in Domino's shirt, trying to find some semblance of safety in Domino's arms. Match may be older than Domino, but Domino boasted the oldest soul and if he wouldn't let Wicasah cry himself to sleep, he certainly couldn't let Match. He slipped out of bed and scaled the rickety ladder. Darkness shaded Match's curled position, his face pressed into the pillow, the muffled cries cutting Domino down to the quick. Unsure, but the darkness helped him hide, and Domino put his hand on Match's shoulder. Match cringed.

"Shh," Domino whispered and laid down, wrapping his arms around Match.

"Don't, don't," Match said. "Don't touch me. Just leave me alone."

Domino considered obeying, but he knew what it was like when you had to stand against a whole slew of shit, and while denial worked, it wasn't always a solution.

"I don't want to touch you." Match's breath hitched. "I don't want this. Please, don't hurt me."

Domino didn't move. He wasn't offering sex, he was giving comfort, and he put on his best eldest tone. "You're gonna wake everyone up if you keep crying like that."

For a split second, Match went absolutely still before he rolled over in outrage. "Get the fuck out of my bed."

Domino had him where he wanted him and pulled him in close, dropping Match's head on his shoulder to take the comfort with arms that said *I'm here, I'm strong, I'm sorry, I'm not gonna leave you, and if I could stop them I would.* Match cried until Domino's shirt was splotched and Domino sat his head on top of Match's, rubbed his back before just holding on. He wondered what they did to him, but he couldn't find the strength to ask. For now, Domino did what he did best—weathered the storm.

———◆———

"So, I've been thinking," Match said for the fifth time that day.

Domino tried to stifle a sigh but didn't quite succeed. He bit down on the question, *been thinking what?* because he'd already said it four times today and Match's answer hadn't been anything worthwhile. Match had been 'thinking' all kinds of screwball things from the frequency at which the supply boxcars choo-choo'd their way to the town's holding station to how many miles did Domino reckon the train traveled in an hour, to did the weather look like rain, or were those clouds just faking it?

The problem was that since Domino fell asleep butted up against Match and woke up just in time to scuttle down the ladder to his hard-as-rock mattress, his brain kept throwing up ugly words like 'strange' and 'conversion' and all the chilly shakes that went along with it as he sweated under the hot summer sun.

Match's mouth shut with a clap and Domino used his peripherals to see concern bunch in his crow's feet. Early this morning, Match had looked death-like with dark circles under his eyes, yellow crust flaking from the corner of his mouth, and a deep-set shake like a persistent hangover. Domino hated that he loomed, daring anyone to say anything, do anything, c'mon just try him.

It seemed like the silence that should've existed since last night, a quiet acceptance of *I understand what you did for me and I'm grateful* didn't seem to fit into Match's vocabulary. He'd gone off like a shot whenever they were alone, setting Domino's ears buzzing with fun facts about the evolution of moth color due to increased pollution in England that Domino could give two shits about before querying him endlessly about the boxcar schedule.

"What's on your mind?" Match asked, so slight next to Domino's tall bulk. "You're so quiet all the time."

Domino sighed. "Thinking about those fucking moths, Match. Run it by me again, why don't you?"

Jesus something was wrong with him. He felt loose and tight at the same time, like a stitch that was desperately trying to keep it together and failing.

Match gnawed his lip and blurted. "I need you to do something for me."

Domino rolled his eyes.

"You know about the," Match paused, "well, the therapy."

"I know *of* it, not exactly what it is."

"Well," Match licked his lips. "You're going to find out. My therapist thinks it might be a good idea to meet the man I'm bunking with."

"We're not bunking," Domino said like a maiden with a wounded reputation.

"Not like that, I didn't mean it like that, like you're my prison mate."

"Not exactly prison either," Domino said.

"Exactly," Match said like he'd hit the jackpot. He jabbed a finger at Domino. "Exactly."

"Why does he want to meet me?"

"*She* thinks," and here Match put his finger to his mouth, bit down, and ripped the white nail off from one side to the other in one neat tear, "that it might be best for you to sit in on it. She thinks I'm scared of you."

Domino paused, his pickaxe deep in the earth. "Are you?"

"No," Match said. Domino heard it, the quiet stillness that came with Match's truths. "Not really. You *are* scary with the way you stare at people like you're thinking about how it might be to put the ax through their ribcage, and you did do that thing to your dad, but no I don't think you're scary."

"Who told you about my dad?"

"People around here cluck like chickens." Match shot him a crooked smile.

Domino grunted, avoided agreeing.

"They're going to make you come with me this evening."

"They can't exactly do that, I'm a prisoner."

"This isn't technically prison, remember. We're rehabilitating," Match said, using his foot to dig his shovel deep in the dirt. Domino laid the next rail tie, replacing the conversation with hard breath that tasted like hot metal in the back of his throat.

"What are they going to do to me?" Domino asked, panting.

"Nothing," Match said, hands on his hips. "It's what they're going to do to *me* that you'll have to sit through."

Domino tried to stomp down on the urge to pace.

"Just don't say anything, okay?" Match said, catching Domino's gaze. "Whatever happens, sit through it and don't make a sound. Don't trust anything they say, okay?"

"Sure," Domino said, lifting the pickaxe high over his head. It splintered the ground and spread cracked fingers like the warnings of an earthquake.

CHAPTER 9
THE THERAPY

DOMINO IMAGINED THEY'D be smuggled out of their cell in the middle of the night. Shamefully, like bad baggage. Instead, he put down his empty bowl with the last taste of brown stew lingering in his mouth, when a guard placed a hand on Match's shoulder. Behind Domino, a similar firm touch urged him to stand. Match's mouth became a pinched frown. The shocked silence of the mess hall lasted only one awful moment.

"Converted, eh, Domino?"

"No hard feelings, Domino. A strange like that would make any weak man turn."

"They'll take good care of you, Domino. Turn you back around the right way."

The clatter of utensils banged a drumline on the table. Domino's face flushed. It took effort not to stare down at his boots, give the hecklers a flirty wink, instead. A soft touch brushed his arm. The prisoners jeered in an uproar. Match stood too close to him, the downward bob of his throat as he swallowed, and his retreating fingers.

Shoved into the back of a Brightside-imported car with windows grated like a police carriage, Domino fingered the seat's worn crushed velvet as the world sped by in a blur. He closed his eyes, thinking against the red curtain of his eyelids that he wished he'd prepared more.

Forty minutes to the closest town. It felt like a lifetime. Fields melted into streets with a wooden boardwalk lining a direct path to the general store, the post office, and the nondescript bar where men smoked cigarettes with broad cowboy hats tipped against the sunlight. Domino pressed his fingers against the warmed windowpane through the bars. He was so far removed from knowing what daily life might be like. Picking up horse feed from the mercantile with the money he'd earned on the farm, meandering to the post office to drop off a letter to the aunts, feeling awed by the sight of an imported car from the East, and last but not least stopping in for his favorite treat: whisky and women. Domino didn't know that man he might've been, but he enjoyed pretending.

Turning a corner, the driver pulled up to an upscale stone building. Two suited men approached and flashed the butt of a gun through the window. Match's breath smelled sour in the enclosed backseat. Stillness settled in Domino's gut, the what-if yearnings at it again. He and Wicasah had both escaped finding rest in the back of the truck, eyes to the sky, breath fogging the window, finding home in what the next day would bring rather than in where they were in the present moment.

The car door creaked open. The chain connecting him to Match rattled as they shuffled out. One suit tried to guide Domino by the elbow, but he shook the man off. The front door, some general slab of polished wood with a simplistic knob, waited and Domino cursed. Doorways were portals. An eerie sensation tingled down his spine as if he'd transitioned from one world to a new one.

Inside, the air smelled the same as the outside, maybe warmer, staler, without the kicked-up dust. The closed-door shut out the wind, the soft bite of dirt against Domino's skin, the careful far-off crunch of wagon wheels, and the lift of indistinguishable voices in conversation. The silence made his ears ring.

"Doctor's upstairs," the suit said, like a badly done tour, and he inclined his head for Domino to take the lead. The solid stairs didn't creak and the loft opened like a luxuriously rustic office. A pencil-skirted lady ushered them in and shooed the suits away, gifting a generous smile on Match.

"Good to see you again, Robert," she said.

Match offered up a sincere smile, making Domino's gut twist with the instinct that Match and the doctor had known each other for much longer, that they were playing with Domino like a cat with a mouse.

"This must be Domino." She extended a hand, cool as if he had stopped by for a regular old chat. Domino stared at the outstretched gesture for a moment before letting her hand slip into his. Words caught in his throat.

"Linda," Match said. Domino tried to see him as a Robert but couldn't match the name to the face. "You're looking well."

"Are you ready to begin?" she asked.

Match held out his hands. "There's not much of a choice."

A breed of dread growled in Domino's stomach, something uncomfortable that had him itching to flee. Linda motioned to a set of chairs sitting in front of one of the plain white walls. Domino sat in one and Match the other, while Linda knelt beside Match, one hand strangely white-knuckled on the chair arm.

"Here," she said, dropping a set of round tablets into Match's open palm. Match immediately tossed the pills into his mouth. He extended his arm and flexed, allowing Linda to place a needle into the bulged vein. Match began to sweat instantly, his face dropping to that fish-belly pale. His mouth opened just enough for his breath to whistle through his teeth.

Domino blinked, looked down to see his own panicked grip on the chair arms. The world tilted like he'd been pulled up too fast. The place had that smeared surreal quality. Was this real?

"Now," Linda addressed Domino. "Robert tells me you're a murderer, Domino. Shot your father when you were sixteen."

A metal weight gathered in the back of Domino's head, and he succumbed to it, letting his head loll on the back of the chair.

"Robert told me you didn't care to learn his name. You called him Match one day because you said he was going to burn you up like the sick sodomite he is."

Domino's tongue lodged against his teeth. He didn't remember saying that. He would never say something like that. That was a lie.

"Robert says you've terrified him in ways I never could. That's why you're here. Conversion therapy works on fear."

Perspiration beaded on Match's forehead, echoing Domino's own. Linda nestled a trash can in Match's arms like handing off a newborn baby, support the head, steady pressure. She bridged a pack of flashcards between her hands, ready to deal poker, but these cards were big and bulky like tarot cards. She shark-circled Match. Domino couldn't see her anymore, couldn't even look behind him because the weight in his head was so heavy. His dread transformed into hopelessness, like he'd been here before one too many times and knew how this show played out.

A projector's whir. A yellow spotlight shot a picture of two men kissing carefully, their chests angled away from each other on the wall.

Match rocked gently from side to side but kept his eyes pinned on the screen, even when the light blinked and a new detailed picture came up, so intimate Domino huffed trying to look at the plaster below the model's clenched fists.

Flip. New picture.

Match choked on a wet gag and tried to cover his mouth, but between the chain and the trashcan, he didn't quite make it before he hurled it into the bin.

Flip. New picture.

A strange helpless fury woke the conduits within Domino, but it was as though they'd been drugged, as if his magic had stagnated within him. A sour, pungent smell drifted into his nose, making his stomach shift in an earthlier way, triggered by the stench, and Linda was talking, always talking . . .

"It's a natural process to cure. If you're violently ill due to say, sour milk or bad meat, you don't want to come in contact with that particular food again. Nature traumatizes and your body develops an aversion to said trauma, keeping you away from things that hurt you. It works the same with terror, too. Why actively seek out something that makes you remember how it felt to be so scared? We're giving Match a double dose of this. Sickness and fear."

But he isn't afraid of me, he told me he wasn't, why would he tell her I scare him? The poison twisted his organs, made his head reel as if he'd spun around one too many times. A sulfur tinge ignited the air. Domino closed his eyes, hoping the darkness would settle him. No such luck.

Match vomited again. Domino had the unsettling sensation that he could taste it, feel the burn of acid eating away at his throat, the sick gut roll, the way he went sweaty and hot all over.

Linda's heels tread with a pointed stomp on the hardwood floor. She stepped in front of Match like Domino didn't exist. The projector flipped three more slides before clicking off. She bent down and slipped another syringe with a needle into Match's arm.

Somehow Domino experienced this: the skin catching, the cold pierce and flush of chemicals invading his system. It spidered from his elbow out to encircle his organs. In response, something flared, awoken from a long sleep. He doubled over in agony. Whatever writhed inside wanted to tear its way out of him. The doctor—her face elongated like a snake—held up one flashcard after the other. Domino caught shocking vivid sights of a woman's thigh, curving breast, and Match fixated on the pictures as if in a trance, hypnotized.

His vision dropped from color to a flat red that erased anything existing before or after. Billowing power dissolved the chemicals burning his system, suspending him in time, just before the room shimmered—it looked as if the room itself was red—and he wasn't angry, he was fucking terrified. He'd never felt like this before. Magic had never thrummed so easily through his bones. He nearly panicked—where had it come from, he hadn't made the witchery offering to earn such power—when it exploded out of him like a cracking lightning bolt, sizzling the very air an electric purple.

Linda—although the fit buxom woman had been replaced with an unhinged open jaw and swaying lanky body—staggered as if hit with a bullet. Her heart ticked like a grenade and shattered her ribcage, a slivered jaw bone penetrating the wood floor like a knife. Tiny creatures, white and rickety with big heads, swarmed out of the cavity and over her bones like ants. The scraping sound of her ribs being smoothed like river rocks by the creatures' hungry mouths didn't make him quiver in horror, but ecstasy. They diminished in number with each blink until the last one pelted for Domino on all fours and climbed his leg to reach his outstretched palm. The chair he'd been chained to shattered.

Domino brought his hand close to his face. The little beast held a chipped tooth in its humanoid paw, fit the molar around its wide black mouth like a baby ready to receive the bottle, and Domino's skin absorbed the magic monster—his familiar—into the fortune lines on his palm.

Impossible. Match studied him with eyes that didn't look quite right, a golden sheen flickering behind the iris like a guttering candle. His mouth pursed in a tight line, brows drawn in disapproval. His pointer finger tapped once, twice, on the wooden chair. A sense of déjà vu struck Domino like a blow and just like that he knew somehow, he had been here before, done this before, only it hadn't gone like this. He wasn't supposed to tear the room apart—he didn't have the power for such things yet—he should've been handcuffed to the chair as Linda purred in Match's ear. Match was supposed to say, "Yes, you've changed me. You're right, I feel it now, the attraction to you." Linda would lean closer with victory in her smile. Match was supposed to throw the vomit in her face, headbutt her, and then pull her to him, punch her temple and then her jaw until she crumpled. Match was supposed to pick the handcuff lock with one of her bobby pins and free Domino and then and then . . . that was how it was supposed to go. Not like this. This wasn't what had happened; this felt like a dream. The memory was what was real.

Match shot up from his chair and stood in front of Domino. He smelled like the desert. Domino yearned for a drink to quench it, but he hadn't had a sip of water in so long.

"We have to go down the drainpipe." Match enunciated every word like Domino's had an addled brain. Domino didn't understand where Match had gone, and who was this mimicking staring *thing?*

"We're escaping. Do you understand? We have to go down the drainpipe. Nod your head yes."

Domino obeyed, he suddenly *had* to, as if this possessed Match controlled his body.

"We have to hurry. They're after us. Remember, Domino? We're escaping down the drainpipe and we're going to get on the boxcar out of town. Follow me."

Domino didn't want to go anywhere with Match, had the urge to run in the opposite direction. Even better, he wanted to huddle in the corner with his hands cupped over his eyes, pinching himself to wake up. *Wake up. Wake up.*

His head throbbed. An empty black hole opened up in one corner of his eyesight. Match yanked him up to his feet and together they scurried down the side of the house. He ran just behind Match across the town streets, through empty fields, to where a boxcar waited. He jumped in the sidecar and by the time he looked back to Match, the man had become his friend again, beaming with joy, high on exhilaration, and free.

———◆———

"Domino?"

"Match?"

"Are you having problems sleeping?"

"No."

"Then why aren't you sleeping?"

"Because you're keeping me awake with all your chatter." Domino laid on his side, facing the sliding door he'd opened for air. That uneasy feeling was back, like being stalked and hunted. Match settled behind him, close enough for warmth, but right now the man gave Domino the chills. Instinct had him on full alarm, screaming at him to get out, wake up, run away, it was *unsafe*.

"Would it help if I sang to you?"

"I'm not a fucking child, thank you."

The blur outside had been black with the ghostly gray outline of trees, but off and on, he caught sight of that red color. Sand. An endless horizon. A morgue slab.

"I like saying your name," Match said and a sharp thrill ran up Domino's spine.

"Names can haunt," Domino said and wondered why, but he knew this wasn't his Match. This was the Match of before, the one with the gleaming eyes, the one that made him obey.

"Yes. Yes, they can." Match sounded so sad. "You should sleep."

Domino cringed as a light touch like spider legs walked over his arms.

"Sleep."

Heavy-lidded. Barely there. Floating.

"Here's the next dream."

———◆———

"Wouldn't have gotten far without you," Match said with a gentle grin. A soft afternoon light illuminated the rattling boxcar and the rushing scenery of blurred green leaves. "I'm grateful."

"You got us out of that mess," Domino said, relishing their success as if he'd swindled a second ride from a barnstormer.

"I'm heading north," Match said.

Hurt wrenched Domino's heart. He was always losing the people he'd come to trust. He understood, though. It was safer to part ways and maybe Match didn't want to be reminded of their time together. Maybe he had a lover somewhere that he wanted to find. Domino desperately wished he had someone waiting for him, wondered for the umpteenth time if he should seek Wicasah out.

Match rose on his knees in front of him. "I'm going to do something you might not like," he said. "Don't get any ideas. I'm not *into* you or anything. I just need to do it because . . . because it means more this way."

He cupped Domino's face, laid a gentle kiss over Domino's lips. It was goodbye and thank you all rolled into one. Quick and fast, but it spread warmth down Domino's limbs like he knew he was thought of well by a man he respected. Match pulled away, flashing successful fang, and Domino shook his head at him.

"Get outta here," he said.

Match slid the door open wider and crouched, the boxcar slowing as the telltale smoke tornados of an industrial town rose in the close distance. Tears strained Domino's eyes so much that he didn't really see Match leave, only the frozen moment of him jumping, the absence of warmth and the empty space Match once filled.

That moment was as real as he remembered it.

CHAPTER 10
THE LOVER

TWO DAYS AGO, Domino had unfurled the hot-off-the-press daily newspaper and gotten the obituary section stuck to his palm. It had been a fluke, picking it up before he walked into his ten-hour shift at the factory. As a result, he'd been late, and then almost severed his hand with the grinding mechanism spitting out machine-made pellets and bolts. All because the obit had left him in a fugue.

Luna Wilcox. Aged 71. Affliction of the lungs. Survived by two sisters and two nieces. In meager paragraphs, the *Prairie* answered the unknowns Domino had consciously decided *not* to piece together since he made that phone call over ten years ago. He remembered it accurately, honestly, he remembered a lot of things too clearly when thunder rumbled and petrichor wafted in his nose. Others might seek the rain, but to him rainfall meant mistakes.

He tried to stay away. What would they think if he showed up at their door with only the clothes on his back, barely two pennies to rub together, and a desperate plea? Once, in the beginning— fucking Genesis, see there was that Christianity again, haunting him everywhere—he cut ties so Daniel wouldn't find them, but now?

Now he was a wanted escaped criminal. He was the dangerous man. He shouldn't dream of returning to them. He shouldn't spend so much time imagining what it would be like to show up at their door.

But his loneliness was a bull-headed ox, convincing him that this was the time to act, that if he didn't show up to the funerary wake, he'd never alleviate the hurt stewing within him, tasting of guilt and closure.

So here he was, two days later, with the black imprint of words just beginning to fade from his fingers.

Standing in front of the old Victorian was like stepping back in time. The big square home with windows that looked like eyes, the way nobody wanted to cut the grass so the prairie weeds grew tall next to the porch. A little more worn, a little more chipped, but he could see a boy—him—sprinting through the fields with Christobel's guiding hand and a horizon that expanded into forever. Three cars were parked neatly together in front of the gravel where the horse stable used to be. Could the surviving aunts be looking out the window, thinking, *my now, who could that tall man be?*

The porch steps creaked underneath him. The wind hushed through his ears. Behind the screen door, the main door was propped wide in an open invitation. He pushed inside, smelling old cigarette smoke and lingering perfume. Above him, old electric lights looked gray from constant use, out-of-fashion Brightside appliances. The sound of clinking china came from the room in front of him and he veered to the left, away from the staircase leading to the attic where Kit paces, nearer to bookshelves stuffed with herb bundles and glass jars, until he slipped into a parlor room. Faded portraits and rare photographs cluttered the wallpaper, sepia fragments of the four smiling sisters back when they were young standing in front of a waving field of wheat, another of Fiametta holding a baby girl, and even a picture of his mother, waving at the camera. Kit stood awkwardly to the side. Luna had her arm around Thessaly, leaning in as if to share good gossip. His heart dropped, another familiar stitch unhitching. His eyes roved over the pixilated face.

Voices drew him back from the picture's spell. The rattle of cups hitting saucers ceased. He slunk to the kitchen, approached the mourners swathed in black, and peeked through the V created by shoulders. Fiametta stood in front of the group, her hands on the wide butcher-block island. On the counter sat a myriad of items: a Raggedy Ann doll, face-down mirrors, stacks of rustled paper, jewelry. Fia assessed the small crowd, alarmingly the same with her white curls pinned haphazardly with clips. She picked up Raggedy Ann, stared into the black button eyes, and a quiet smile crossed her face as she caressed the doll's red hair, fragile, like it might wake her up.

"When I was a little girl, Luna was the strongest woman in my life. When we followed our Annalise—rest her soul—out West,

I HAVE ASKED TO BE WHERE NO STORMS COME

Luna was the one that put together the permits. Luna repaired our home with imported Montana pine after the floorboards of this house were ruined crossing the Dark and Bloody. I hated it here. I missed the ocean, but Luna loved our new home. She used to say the appeal was in the sun and air." Fia picked up a smoking cigarette balanced in the ashtray next to her and took a shaky draw. Her yellowed fingers tapped the edge before she broke the wax seal on a piece of paper.

Domino craned his neck to see further, noticed Kit with her head down up front, full lips halfway parted. She wiped her eyes with a fist.

Fia began to read. "To my eldest niece, Benedicta, I pass on my finest scarves. To my youngest, Christobel, I give my cameo brooch." Fia handed the items to the younger women, who rose from either side of Kit. Benedicta with everything too wide and Christobel a condensed version of her sister: blonde to Benedicta's strawberry-red, but both with russet irises.

Christobel fastened the ceramic white and purple brooch to the lace neckline of her black jacket. Benedicta opened the box and her tears dropped on the silk. Fia handed out three more items to people Domino didn't know, while Raggedy Ann sat close like her own familiar in a slumped well-loved posture.

"For Domino," Fia said and Domino started. "I never thought I'd see the man you'd become. Fia and I talked about it often." She held out a thick white letter with Domino's name scrawled in a slanted neat hand on the front. He awkwardly eased past the guests, saw Christobel's mouth open in awe, and took the letter, the paper fine and well-made. Always letters weren't they, goodbyes the lot of them, he couldn't read anything that wasn't a farewell.

Fia offered up a heartwarming smile, her tears momentarily one of hope instead of grief. Domino blushed. Too much attention. Someone called his name. He bolted, needing open space to bust into the letter with a soul-hunger bordering on terrifying. He wasn't sure he could survive the next few minutes.

Outside, he braced on the porch railing and sucked in deep breaths—what if he could've been stronger, better, could've run to the aunts in his time of need. Wicasah would've been given, who knows, a fucking vase with some quirky story attached, Domino something just as sentimental. Not a letter full of words that couldn't be taken back or clarified. Luna wasn't exactly alive to explain her intentions if he didn't get her meaning.

A hesitant touch brushed his shoulder. Christobel leaned next to him, her suit jacket bunching at the shoulders, blonde hair straight as straw and smelling of dunes and mint. She licked her lips, asking, "Do you remember me?"

Domino had a story of his own, a memory long-lost but which jolted him like an electric shock, brutal in its vivacity. "You were ten and I was seven," he said, looking up into her eyes. "You liked to stay up late and sneak down the steps to watch the aunts boil trouble over the stove until they shooed you upstairs. You said to me one day you wanted to be like my mother. I asked if that meant you were a witch too and you said yes. I remember the old crooked tree we used to play monkey bars on and how red the sun got during fire season. You tricked me into thinking it was your doing."

He had shocked her. It sat in the sudden silence as she tried to recover.

"I always knew this moment might be graceless," she joked. "I thought a lot about how it might go. We'd meet in a bar. At University, maybe, run into you on the block. Once, I imagined it happening on the train. You've been a topic of late-night conversation in this house for a long time. Where have the fabled Bluepoints gone?"

He didn't want her to know, this inquisitive creature who looked better in a suit than he did, wanted her to think he'd spent his days as sexy dangerous instead of imprisoned. She'd put him on the spot. He wasn't good at this. Small talk. "How did . . . " he trailed off, couldn't ask the question, and wagged the unopened letter instead.

"Slow," Christabel said, head tipped into the light. "But not painful. Bad lungs, probably from Fia smoking like a chimney. She got a, a cough, that wouldn't go away, fluid in the lungs." She wiped her eyes. "It turned into pneumonia."

It seemed too strange to him that old age was a way to go, that your body could one day give out instead of being cut down.

"Would you like to see where we put her?" Christobel asked.

"Yes," Domino said. Simple request. Simple answers.

She took him to that crooked tree where a pile of rocks outlined a rectangle big enough for a body, next to Annalise's weather-worn grave. He cried then, wasn't sure why except that his what-if life seemed a whole lot further out of reach. Christobel put her arm through his and leaned her temple on his shoulder. It was like he had never left, that they had been together this whole time. *Relief.*

———•———

"So, you never thought about looking for Wicasah? All this time?" Christobel sounded out his brother's name, looking at Domino for confirmation. Wicasah hadn't been much to her but an infant, something small that screamed and needed.

"No. Too dangerous."

"Even with . . . your father gone?"

"It's not about him anymore. It's me that's the bad one. What if the police somehow screwed the truth, got him accused of Daniel's murder, too? What if both of us got thrown in the clink?"

"I doubt anyone would think that. He was so *young.*"

"Don't trust 'em anyway. Too risky. Never let anything lay down and die."

She didn't lean away from him at his admission, only paused and opened her intertwined hands to make a roof. "Now what are you going to do?" she asked.

"Find work somewhere. My spot at the factory's probably been taken already."

She knew now, everything he had done. He couldn't keep his mouth shut once she needled it out of him. A bare twenty-four hours and he'd come clean like he'd gone to confession.

"You could . . . stay out here a while. I've got cataloging to finish and Benedicta won't split for another month at least. Please stay. We'd love to get to know you again."

Warning bells clanged but the question melted like sugared butter on his tongue. "Sure I won't be any trouble?"

"None. Good god, none at all."

"Sure no one will think different about me, unemployed at your place? I'll make my way, fix things. I'll make sure to earn my keep."

"You wouldn't need to do anything like that. All we want is to see you again. Stay for as long as you can."

"Okay," Domino said. Easy convincing. A starved cat desperate for a pet. "Okay."

CHAPTER 11
THE BONES

HE SAT ON the back porch a week into his stay, wearing his only other white button-up shirt and blue jeans—soft from wear and beginning to hole in the knee, but still strong as cotton intended to be. Skittish he was, but the inclination had dulled with his stomach full on home-cooked meals of fresh bread and fried eggs, bacon, butter, and cheese. The ache between his shoulders had eased. Now, he slouched in the rickety beach chair picked up from some thrift shop and pulled one leg up. He rested Luna's still-sealed letter on his knee and watched the sun's over-brightness wash out the yellowed hues of the flat land.

In the far distance, a dark shape stooped against the ground. Christobel, her hands dusty-dirty, cataloged the small bones and pottery shards from an uncovered midden centuries old. She'd explained that the artifacts, from a presumed migrating culture, were indicative of a more sedentary lifestyle. He'd smiled gently, asked what the appeal was about going through the trash of ancients.

"Trash is everlasting," she'd said, eyes flashing and hands on her hips. "We make so much of it and can't get rid of it. It tells me what they ate, what leftovers they didn't need anymore, even the kind of dyes used for their clothes and jewelry!" Her white shirt was tucked into her high-waist green army pants and she'd pinned Luna's brooch close to her throat. She spun her hair into a loop with an elastic band. Leather gloves made her hands clumsy.

Domino could've told her all those things. If she lived on the land, she'd find out right quick what she could and couldn't use to survive, but her enthusiasm seemed . . . cute. Bursting her bubble wasn't worth it. On his first day, she'd taken him out to her trash hole—excuse him, *midden*—where she used brushes and trowels to extract small brown triangles, scribbled numbers in her notebook with a lead pencil, scrawled out a label and tagged the piece. Domino couldn't quite understand it, but he wasn't a university man, and Christobel assured him it was important, she'd get a paper out of this, first author even, and that, according to her, was a big fucking deal.

He liked her world: one where she mucked around outside at all hours, came back to the house with her nose sunburned and her hands cracked, and one of the biggest smiles on her face because one blue bead indicated trade with the Pacific Coast.

Domino fingered the blunted edge of Luna's letter. He wanted to read it badly, but the thought made him sick. Christobel hadn't pressured him, but Benedicta had demanded he suck it up and do it already. She didn't have time for his insecurities, *just tell her what her fucking aunt said.* He had a feeling Benedicta didn't quite like him. He couldn't figure out why, but the two of them worked better when there was a third, calming influence. Otherwise, they'd probably break into a store, smoke all the cigarettes, and smash glass just to hear the shatter. Benedicta was chaos to Domino, igniting some dangerous forest fire he believed, no doubt, paved the pathway to the witchery.

He worked his pinky under the sticky seal until it flapped open. With a deep breath, he pulled out the fine paper, saw Luna had written in a variety of inks, favoring a dark blue.

Domino,

I first met your mother when Kit, the littlest and last of us, came down with something nasty that escalated into scarlet fever and fried her brain. Like a saint, Thessaly emerged with a poultice in one hand and willow bark in the other. How fresh she was! She tutted death away and while Kit wouldn't be the same, she at least survived. We were grateful and Thessaly was like everything else in the badlands. Wild.

It's the nature of the game that I didn't see her for a long time after. We both lived on separate farms far from each other and the chance that we would see each other in town was slim. I was getting old for suitors and Fia had all the attention. I was jealous, but the sad kind. Annalise had been confined, but together we ventured to a jitterbug social. A man stood in the back in a shirt worn enough for us peering ladies to catch an eyeful of collarbone. Annalise went to him too soon with a dark spot of lust in her eye. When she came back, three days later, she was almost serene.

That man. We'd dealt with his effects in the East, he changed our whole life for their love, and still, Benedicta came six months later.

Three years later, I bounced my niece on my knee at a newly opened teashop next to the cowboy's old saloon and he was there again. Changed shirt, crow's feet a little bit more defined, but Annalise went to him with a smile on her face like she was grateful and had waited so long. He took her in his arms and kissed her passionately right there in the street. We had Christobel not long thereafter. We lost Annalise soon after that.

Thessaly, married and pregnant with you, showed her face at our door sometime around then. Her man gone in the fields and her so lonely, but she took one look at Benedicta and said, "Half-breed, just like me. What kind of man got to you?"

"She's my niece," I explained. It still hurt that Benedicta wasn't mine.

"Gonna give you trouble one day," Thessaly said. "Who's her daddy?" She ate three shortcakes in a row—three!—but then, your mother was never good at being sweet. I told her the father had wandered into our lives one day and left us with two little girls. That their mother had died.

She nodded. "Witch trying to spread the witchery."

And there it was, out in the open—the admission of magic!— and I gripped my brooch like a cross. The three of us had inherited a branch of it, the Massachusetts-kind that got you burned at the stake. But you never spoke of it. You never admitted it out loud.

Thessaly rubbed her belly and explained: a witch-wanderer was trying to keep the badlands magic alive by bringing as many children into this world as possible. They were a dying breed, Christianity had slain them, and it wasn't anything new because even their own people thought they were rotten. These twisted practitioners had been cut off from their past—she barely remembered hers—and this witch-wanderer had approached her, too. Wanted to make a home for witches who'd been born and bred on this side of the Dark and Bloody. Thessaly liked the idea, but she'd been married to her sweetheart and wanted to stay that way. Daniel knew nothing about magic.

I HAVE ASKED TO BE WHERE NO STORMS COME

"Your girls have it," Thessaly said with a shrug. "My children will. You have to do evil to have evil. They won't be able to resist it. I killed my sister for power. If I hadn't, she would've slain me."

"So, it would be right to let the magic die," I said bitterly, watching Benedicta play with her doll at my feet. Thinking of what would be required of her and how I could stop it. "It's the right thing to do. It took my sister. It changed my life. And now, you say the girls might kill each other for power? How is that right?"

"Is it the right thing to kill the wolves teaching their pups how to slaughter the sheep? It's what I am, what they are, and I'll fight for it until I'm bones."

That's what I should've done for you, Domino. Fight for you until I was bones because I knew it in my bones what kind of coven we were supposed to become with Benedicta promised to you and Christobel to Wicasah.

Without our guidance, I don't know what kind of evil you will commit without knowing. I needed Thessaly's guidance to help the girls learn what Annalise could barely teach them, and it still scares me. The difference between us, the Brightside magic and the twisted power of the West. What's required of them and you. If and how you'll all accept it. Our magic doesn't require so much sacrifice. Then and again, our magic is like sparks compared to the wildfire of yours.

Daniel was a good man. I trusted him, but fear does bad things to you. Remember that. Your father was a good man.

Domino folded the letter back up, took a shaky breath, and touched the headache blooming between his brows. He saw Christobel walking slowly back toward the house, her head bowed in thought and her hands cupped like transporting water across the desert. Her hair had loosened from its tail and flopped over one shoulder. When she ascended the porch, Domino's hands still trembled.

"What you got there?" he asked, inclining his head to her hands.

She pondered for a moment and then held it out to him. He expected gems, gold even. Instead, he saw a pockmarked vertebrae disk. He raised an eyebrow at her.

"This is the smallest one," she whispered. "This is the smallest piece of the spine."

——◆——

Luna's letter nestled in his breast pocket next to Daniel's as dusk shot over the sky in a swatch of navy-blue crafted gray. He gazed at the grass as Christobel knelt in front of the hole and methodically brushed away a new layer of settled dust. Her effort wasn't needed. Domino could see enough of the curving spine to determine its breadth and length.

His heart throbbed unnaturally as he felt the witchery wick inside of him, drenched in oil and aching to light, pant for whatever spark this centuries-old monster could provide.

"Maiasaura, perhaps," Christobel said, sitting back on her haunches in the dirt. "I'm no expert, but I know a dinosaur when I see one."

"Unkehi," Domino corrected, the pit in his stomach expanding wider. The conduits woke at the scent of fossilized calcium, scratching at his insides. Half-remembered stories flooded his mind. Of Thessaly trying to tell him a story from her past, a past that had faded with time like smoke because it was her punishment, as a witch, to forget her roots. He had no claim to that word— *Unkehi*—or the gravitas it held. Shame flushed his cheeks at the easy way the word had poured from him because, even though this land was the only land he'd ever known—the plains lay in his bones, the badlands his homeland—the ancient stories of their creation and gods were not his. They never would be. He would always be a foreigner to the ancients here. Always be a misplaced witch.

"What's that?" Christobel asked, watching him in awe again like he was a creature come from an earthen abyss.

"Water serpent," Domino said. "They managed to flood the world, except for the topmost rock towers. The thunderbirds tried to stop them and killed most of the Unkehi, but fried the land in the process." Domino inclined his head in the direction of the badlands. "You've seen it, the big canyons of dried rock where nothing lives. This one must have been a baby."

"Thunder," Christobel repeated slowly, her face lighting up. "This story sounds familiar. I've heard of this. And then what happened?"

"The Unkehi bones turned to stone. They're all over this territory, but some are bad spirits," he hesitated, wanting to explain, "Bad luck. Bad fossils."

"Then why is there a midden out here?"

Domino shrugged. "Could be an offering. Could be someone settled here before they knew and got out quick. You're the anthropologist here."

"You need to tell me all of this again," Christobel said solemnly. "I need to write all this down."

"These stories aren't mine. They probably aren't even accurate. I shouldn't have even brought them up. I don't have . . . the standing to tell them."

"It will give me a place to start." Christobel smiled.

"Sure, then," Domino stumbled, shy but glowing inside because she wanted to hear what he had to say. Even though he knew he shouldn't tell her half-remembered myths, the words he would give her wouldn't be like the ones in his pocket. He'd give her good words, good stories, enough to make her stay up late and lean forward, her eyes shining from the fireplace glow, hanging on his every word.

———◆———

When Domino came back from the kitchen with two hot mugs in his hand, Christobel leaned against the fireplace, the flames licking her face in a glow of yellow and tawny. Benedicta stood behind her, whispering furiously into her ear. Domino cleared his throat, unsure if he should interrupt.

"Would you like a cup?" he asked Benedicta, gracious, gentlemanly.

"No," Benedicta snapped. Her hands planted on her hips, her elbows winged at severe angles. "I can't drink caffeine. I'm fucking pregnant."

Christobel rubbed her forehead and offered Domino a watery smile. He wondered if that was the secret Benedicta had been telling her.

"Jesus Christ, don't look at me like that, Bluepoint. I know who the father is. We're engaged, for fuck's sake," Benedicta said.

"Didn't say a word," Domino said.

"You hear me, Bel?" Benedicta demanded, eyeing Domino up and down. "Engaged."

"I hear you," Christobel said. "Just stay a few more days, okay? Just a few more days."

Benedicta wavered but her pointer finger tapped her hip. "Fine. Few days."

"Okay," Christobel said, her face white like the request had cost her. "Okay, thank you."

"Don't thank me," Benedicta waved her hand. "Fia finds out, she'll murder me."

"She won't. If she does, she'll think it's reincarnation."

Benedicta groaned and clapped her hand on her forehead. "Good god."

Domino handed Christobel the cup. Their fingers brushed. He had such a dumb crush on her, the way she listened to him. He desperately wished he wasn't so odd, it was so obvious he didn't belong. He couldn't think of a thing to say and didn't want to finish his story with Benedicta pacing like she was caged. Christobel watched her in an almost accusatory way. Domino sat down on the couch instead, tucked his feet up, watching the interaction of a relationship he had never been in before.

"How far along?" Christobel asked, breathing the steam away from the cup.

"Few months."

"Months?" Christobel demanded. "Months?"

"I wasn't sure for a while. You have to wait in case . . . you know. *Miscarriage*. It's not like I planned this."

"You never plan much in the first place," Christobel muttered into her coffee.

"You want to say that again? To my face this time?"

"Are you really going to marry him?"

"Why not? He's not rich, but he's not a pauper, and we need this. You get me?" Benedicta glanced at Domino, almost like she was alarmed.

"I know what you mean," Christobel snapped. "Can we sit down? For a little bit? This is all so much. Domino can finish his story."

"Sure," Benedicta said, too fast, like she wanted to please. Then, too light, "What kind of story?"

"A good one," Christobel said and offered Domino a warm smile that sent a thrill down his spine. Benedicta narrowed her eyes.

The women slid onto the other side of the couch and suddenly Domino had little to no space. Benedicta tucked Christobel under her chin, an old gesture, and Christobel put her mug into Benedicta's care. Domino squirmed, uncomfortable with sharing, but they both watched him with the same expectant russet eyes.

"Finish the story, Domino," Christobel said.

"Yeah, Bluepoint. Let's hear your tale." Benedicta mocked. Christobel pinched her sister's arm, but the undercurrent of anger had disappeared, replaced by wistfulness. Benedicta looked almost happy.

Domino opened his mouth and spoke long into the night, about every story he could remember, as the sisters relaxed and grew amazed at his tales and he wondered if the two of them could ever be separated, the way they wound around each other, so similar yet so different.

CHAPTER 12
THE SISTERS

THE CALL OF MAGIC whooshed through him like a gale and set the conduits to chattering and yearning. His bones itched like they were disintegrating, leaving him boneless and limp. The pain wasn't really pain, but it hurt not to obey, like a sliced finger constantly bumped. He flung back the quilt and leapt from the narrow twin bed, descended the stairs in a flash, and didn't slow until his feet followed the faint summoning trail out to the excavation site.

Christobel, her too-long robe trailing behind her, lit candles around the perimeter. A layer of chicken wire carefully covered the midden, but the huge uncovered spine stretched ahead like a cobblestone path. She beckoned to him. Domino ducked under the hole in the chicken wire and stepped over, strung tight like a fishing line.

His body hummed as her hands flew to pat her blonde hair knotted in the back of her head. Against all odds, he realized she reciprocated his crush and had called him here. Silly witch. She didn't need magic. He would've come if she'd asked with only a coy smile.

She swayed shy in front of him, but so bold to have done this *summoning*. He wondered if Annalise felt this under her witch-wanderer's touch—irresistible. For Christobel had Brightside-power wound around her witchery skills and Domino was a slave to it.

"I would've come if you'd asked," he whispered, honored by the invitation.

"I wasn't sure," she admitted. Her lips parted at the end of the sentence. "Because see, it's not just me."

She inclined her head. Benedicta emerged from the darkness

and stood just outside the candlelight. He blinked, night vision ruined by the flames and a half-hearted moon.

"I give Christobel everything she wants," Benedicta said, coming closer. "And she wants you. But we come as a package."

Domino licked his lips as his world rocked, feeling desperate for clarification, uncertain of what she meant. "So, you've . . . sacrificed to the witchery?"

"You never have?" Benedicta asked in astonishment.

"How could I?" he said, the *wanted* feeling evaporating, leaving him frazzled. He came here on invitation, not harassment. "No sibling to fuck, no grave to desecrate, no family left to kill."

Christobel tucked her hair behind her ear, leaving her face plain and open.

"How have you?" Domino demanded.

Benedicta and Christobel looked sidelong at each other. Domino wondered how he could be so dull, wished he could take it back, bowed his head, and let the shame wash over him. *Of course.*

"Christobel invited you," Benedicta clarified, "but you have to take both of us. That's how we came into the witchery—together—and that's how we'll stay."

Domino fidgeted, the warmth of being chosen plummeting. Still, this chance wouldn't come again. He'd never been asked for before, never been wanted, and he tried not to blush like the prison virgin he was. He nodded. He'd learned that to want was to wait and good things might never come.

"What do you think?" Christobel asked, breathless.

Domino traced her neck, brushed the robe's necklines, and reveled in touching her skin. From behind, Benedicta shoved Christobel's robe off her shoulders, almost challenging Domino as she kissed Christobel's shoulder. When their lips slid together with a slippery sound, Domino refused to show how cowed he felt, just like the first time he'd gotten into a fight at the juvenile center and he'd been punched hard in the gut but had to get up quick otherwise it'd be *over.*

"She's beautiful," Benedicta told him. It still remained—her dark slide glance that reminded him Christobel wasn't his, not by a long shot. "Kiss her."

Domino obeyed, grateful someone knew what to do because while he wasn't a blushing bride with this primal heat pulsing inside, he was still fumbling in the dark. The *summoning* rode him hard, pushed him against Christobel's soft mound, and he watched Benedicta's hand rub small circles at Christobel's clit as he kissed her until her lips came away dark and used.

He kissed her again, flicked his tongue against her, making it slow and filthy as his other hand drifted over her breast's caramel-pink peaks, rubbed his thumb back and forth until she moaned. Caught between the two of them, Christobel seemed to melt. Her hands worked at the buttons of his shirt, peeling it back. A layer of sweat coated his back and he shivered under the night air.

He'd never felt inexperienced, sometimes thought he was broken in that way, but now he was convinced he was as the witchery-power rose against the stiff membrane of his immaturity, a hymen that hadn't been broken. Gasping against *too much*, he imagined puncturing that confining womb with a pin to let out the rising pressure. For the first time, he wished for mature power.

His mouth left Christobel's to explore her neck. Benedicta mimicked him on Christobel's opposite side, observing him carefully for any sign of backing out. He traced Christobel's spine, rested one hand on the top of her buttock, and edged his thumb in the dip there. Her knees wobbled. Together, sister and lover eased Christobel down until she straddled him. Domino sheathed himself slowly, savoring every wet inch. Above her head, the moon acted as his focus point, grounding him. His hands spanned around her hips, keeping her still so he could push up as deep as possible, and he wished he could lay her down on the sea monster's spine, put his head between her thighs, and taste the power of them both—the feminine and the ancient.

Her hips undulated and Benedicta removed her palms, crouched in the flickering light naked, waiting to pounce. Domino couldn't think of that strawberry blonde crow because Christobel's summoning raked his insides, rubbed the orb of his dormant witchery, as his mouth sought her breast. A small cry escaped her and suddenly he was held painfully tight by her convulsing muscles, couldn't move an inch, and he lost focus on the moon—it wavered, inconstant.

The second muscle held him tighter, immobile, either her Brightside-magic or witchery, with roots deep in the earth of his soul, and his bottom ground against the vertebrae as the magic rattled his insides, electrifying his bloodstream. He could only imagine what this could be like if he'd given the sacrifice. Yet, behind Christobel loomed a black void as terrifying as it was ecstatic. Even when the summoning ended, the aftershocks tingled. Christobel kissed him, Benedicta mimicked, and Domino found out just how inexperienced he could be.

CHAPTER 13
THE WITCHERY

AFTER THAT, things started to go too fast, like someone held down fast forward. Domino wanted to cry because these were the best years of his life. He watched, in a dream, as he took Christobel under his arm and guided her back inside. She shivered but then tilted her head up and he had obligations now to kiss her. In front of them, Benedicta wrapped the robe around her tighter.

An anticipatory weight gathered in his chest, and he realized this was a mere taste of a life he'd grown to love, but the sages said it best didn't they? Life always went by in a flash.

In a flash, Christobel and Benedicta waited naked in bed for him, hands drawing fast circles on each other, beckoning him with the sight.

In a blink, he smelled the hospital's aseptic tang as he waited with Benedicta's pacing husband, a thin reporter with glasses, as the wailing dark-haired Naomi came into the world. She was so small in Domino's arms, her big eyes staring into another place beyond this one.

In a year, he bought the small diamond ring he'd spent months saving for. When he proposed and saw the light in Christobel's face, he knew he'd made the right decision. When she kissed him, she tasted like the rare blackberry ice cream they'd finished sharing.

Suddenly, he stood on the coastline during their honeymoon, and Christobel was saying it was worth it, the leave of absence from university. He couldn't speak, mesmerized by how much water rolled against the shore, with her hand belonging in his. He kissed her, tasting the sea spray sticking to her pink lipstick. Then, in their small closet of a rented room, both tipsy on cheap liquor, Domino told her stories while she taught him rudimentary spells he couldn't ever use in between unfastening buttons.

"My mother taught me," she whispered to him. "Thessaly taught me. We're fucking half-breeds, a sky god on one side, the god of earth on the other."

"It doesn't matter," he breathed. "As long as I have you, it doesn't matter."

But then, he held her tight as she sobbed against his shoulder, clutching the rejection letter until her fingernails pierced the paper. Her eleventh one. Publish or perish, and his Christobel was dying.

In a flash, he was getting a managerial promotion and bringing home enough that they weren't surviving hand over fist. While Christobel's smile was slightly bitter—it had been months since her resignation—she still held him tight enough to expel the air out of his lungs in a whoosh from being so lucky, so loved.

Yet the bad existed, too. He hated the fights Christobel had with Benedicta, screaming matches that kept him up at night with how violently they traded threats, how deep the jealousy between them ran. When Christobel came back home once with scratches like talon claws down her back and bruise mouth-marks on her neck, Domino wondered who had the more passionate relationship with his wife: the husband or the sister.

"I'm not going to see her anymore," Christobel told him haughtily like it was his fault she was still half in love with Benedicta. "*You* told me the sacrifice only had to be made once and I've made mine over and over again. I'm done."

"The witchery isn't going anywhere," he agreed. "It belongs to you now. You don't have to do anything you don't want to do."

"It's not right," Christobel whispered, slumping against him. "It makes me sick, the things I do with her."

Domino wrapped his arms carefully around her waist, touched his mouth to the spot where her neck met her shoulder. He couldn't tell her that Benedicta blamed him, that she'd come to his office and tore it apart with accusations of filling her sister's head with lies and deceit to keep them apart. He suspected Christobel hated Benedicta's husband and the reverse was true. Naomi had been so small clinging to her mother's hand. Domino bent to hug her, his chest tight with how fragile she felt, the way Wicasah once had. Benedicta had left a rounded hole in his door with her heel and stormed out.

Christobel's depression lingered like dust bunnies. Once cleared out, they immediately gathered again as wispy regret bundles hiding under their bed. She wrote furious letters until she earned a column in the local newspaper, joined an emerging woman's scientist group, but the activity was stagnant, mere filler for a dream that hadn't come true. By the time Domino truly faced the elephant in the room, it was atrocious how big the dust bunnies had gotten.

He wrote to the aunts. He wrote to Benedicta, who never answered his calls anymore, and who finally showed her strawberry head when Christobel told him she was pregnant.

He hadn't seen the two of them holding hands and sitting side by side since the early days. When they both smiled at him—Christobel pleased and Benedicta close-lipped—something foreboding pressed under his ribs, like an instant side-ache. He smiled back nervously. Christobel held out her hand. Domino took it, guided to sit on the other side of her. He didn't miss Benedicta's checkered suitcase leaning against her skirted peacoat or the way she peeked over Christobel's shoulder at him with a look telling him they could be friends now.

"Domino, I'm pregnant," Christobel said.

He'd imagined what it would be like to hear those words and none of it involved shock. In disbelief, he kissed her hand hard enough to bruise. Christobel laughed and Benedicta copied. Domino wanted to ask simple questions like *when did you find out? is that why she's here?* but he didn't question happiness, especially when there was love between them all again, quick transitions to long dirty nights and hustled mornings to work with Christobel growing bigger between both of their hands.

Christobel rarely got sick, but exhaustion set into her and refused to release its hold. During his day off, he kissed her sleeping form and wandered into the kitchen, seduced by the smell of brewing coffee that didn't resemble the awful dregs found at the office. A question nagged at him, and he felt like an accomplice in a tragedy he didn't mean to star in.

Benedicta leaned against the linoleum counter and poured a cup of espresso when she saw him. He hated how she demanded luxury, but he couldn't deny it tasted good. "Who's taking care of Naomi?" he asked, coming right out of the gate, facing her one-on-one.

She shrugged, nearly took back the mug she had offered to him. "With her father. She's fine without me. They understand Christobel needs me more." Her silk robe loosened around her neckline. She stretched her leg out, pointed her toe, but he didn't take the bait and look.

"Christobel has me," Domino said and added hastily, "if you needed to go home and see them, I mean. It must be hard, being away from them."

"Sure, you're here, but you don't know how to guide her like I do. You wouldn't send me home, would you? *Could you?*"

He swallowed hard and felt an unfamiliar fear of her and her power. Of the witch.

She leaned closer as if to sniff his neck and he felt the same heat build in him whenever she was near. An insanity to set the world aflame, just for the fun of it. "Of course I could," he whispered into her ear. "I'm the one she loves more. Just as you chose your husband, she chose me."

Benedicta jerked back as if slapped, but her breath—smelling of morning sour and cream sweetened coffee—beat against his cheek. He wasn't sure if they were going to kiss or fight, but either seemed possible.

Rustling from the bedroom. The squeak of the bed. Christobel saying, "I smell coffee. There better be breakfast to go along with it!"

"Of course there is," Benedicta called back, too loud in Domino's ear. "Wait a moment, though."

The hustled sound of Christobel running very fast followed by empty retching churned Domino's stomach. Benedicta flashed a smile and he wondered how long she could keep it up, pretending to love him for the sake of her sister.

Another flash, months later. He came home to the apartment in shambles. Splintered chairs, broken plates, nail marks puncturing the wallpaper, and Christobel hunkered in a corner with a feral snarl twisting her mouth. The electricity of magic crackled in the air. Domino winced as he reached her side, barely noticed his shirt smoldering to his skin in curling ash and leaving red blisters.

"What happened?" he demanded, seeing thugs, seeing convicts, all kinds of bad people breaking into his home and terrorizing his wife. "What happened? Are you okay? How's the baby? Where's Benedicta?"

At her sister's name, Christobel tensed, ready to attack. Domino took a second look around the room, finally seeing the fight between witches.

"She tried to get me to leave you, but I wouldn't. I wouldn't go with her. And now she left me. She's evil, Domino. She's the worst thing that ever happened to me."

Domino eased Christobel into his arms. She slumped but finally accepted the embrace. Her hair tangled in his black greased fingers. "No one is taking you away from me," he said. "No one can make you do anything you don't want to. I'd always fight for you."

She shook and he tightened his arms around her, suddenly terrified of being alone again.

The baby—his child—rolled and Domino pulled back, unnerved at the foreign feel. A little hand imprint pressed against Christobel's tight skin as if asking if everything was okay, reminding him that death would be preferable to losing them. "She won't come back here again," he vowed.

"She said I need her for the magic. That I'll lose it without her." Her grip on his shirt tightened. "And I need the magic. I need it."

"You don't need her. The magic exists. You don't have to keep making the sacrifice to keep it. I've told you this a hundred times."

"I can't feel like that again, like it's been drained out of me. I need to make the sacrifice and I can't without her. I hate her, I hate her so much."

Domino rocked her as she sobbed and realized that was the crux of her fear—losing and being *without*. Christobel had been *without* her many dreams for so long that no longer having the witchery would be her undoing. He felt sick with wanting to convince her, but for once, his words weren't enough.

Then finally, he catapulted to the last memory, the final time, when he didn't think anything of the quiet behind the door. He saw her as soon as he stepped inside their home. She hadn't the decency to do it in the bathtub or on their bed. No, she'd scarred him forever by seeing *that:* his pregnant wife's suicide.

She'd done it right, better and smarter than Daniel, and she'd made sure the window shades were open so she could watch the sunset.

He stood in front of her, staring until a small shocked voice in the back of his head—one he didn't recognize—told him he had to send her off right. This was the moment when he did it.

So, Domino dragged her dead body to the kitchen table and washed the blood away clinically, made sure to bind her like a mummy—like he was fucking supposed to—and tried not to look at her still stomach. When she was covered, when she was decent, and when the little voice stopped talking, he tore the room apart. A black hole opened up in front of his vision, something that sucked him in and promised nothingness. He couldn't look at the precision of her process, the bowls left to collect her blood. She'd been so goddamn careful. He kicked them over, jammed his pocketknife into the cushions of the chair she sat in, tore all the photographs and pictures in half. Her inherited brooch crumbled in his fists. He threw it down, stomped on it, and then unzipped his pants and pissed on the last spread of her life seeping into the floorboards. *Desecration.*

Fire immediately sprung from his palms, catching hold of the walls and lighting the room in orange flame and black smoke. Magic, brought to life and finally given the outlet to bloom. Small creatures made of bone exploded from his skin and ran over Christobel like an ant swarm. He burned his hand picking up the phone but managed to dial Benedicta's number. The machine picked up.

"Come and get her," he said, not even recognizing his voice.

A letter, a damn letter, was left for him. He tore it open, knowing it would say: *I can't do this anymore. I don't want my children to do the evil the witchery requires. They shouldn't have to fuck their sister to keep the beauty of the world. I won't bring more evil into this household. Don't blame yourself or me. It was never about loving you enough, it was about loving myself.*

He knew every line, memorized it every chance he got after he left their home because this was the wound that kept on giving. When he opened the envelope, he saw instead: *Are you ready for the next dream?*

Reeling. He wished this were a dream, but this was reality. The words blurred and changed in front of him as if being scrubbed out and rewritten over. *You're ready. Do you believe you're alive? That you can die?*

He threw the paper down as if it were poisoned. He felt the offering to the witchery ignite his veins—his desecration of his wife's last resting place. Power flowed, all-consuming and brutal. Out of the corner of his eyes, he thought he saw someone constructed out of the flames, watching him and judging. Placing hands in his pant pockets. Crumbling dust from their fingers.

Christobel's body jerked like she had been cracked with a whip and crumbled before his eyes. More bone-familiars scurried out of him and dug into her scorched body, devouring her in their tiny maws. Flames licked his skin and he walked into that black hole, let it eat him from the inside out, told it he was ready to die. *Let it end.* Let him walk into the sunset and be free. *Let it be over.*

A weight pressed behind him. This wasn't how it was supposed to go. His body felt limp, like a doll with all the strings cut. He was supposed to leave this place, become a nomad where he forgot how to speak, and tried to abandon his name in the cracked badlands.

How strange. The black hole looked like staring down the barrel of a gun.

PART III:

THE HISTORY OF
THE BEAST

CHAPTER 1

WICASAH NEVER TALKED about his past, so it didn't particularly please him that Crazy Mary wanted him to pick at those scabs. Gooseflesh broke over his skin, but it wasn't easy being nearly nude on his back in the middle of the woods at midnight. Crazy Mary knelt beside him, a black shape against the Milky Way backdrop, and laid a wrinkled hand on his chest. "Relax," she said, her voice still strong despite her age. "You want this, don't you? You want to find your path?"

"Of course I do," he said and tried not to squirm. This was his idea, after all, to sink into a vision and attempt to commune with the spirits of his people—and his past.

"Then tell your story. The ancestors and saints are listening." Her graying braided hair looped over her shoulder and she looked exasperated.

"I'm trying," he whined, wishing that simply telling his tale would be easy. After he killed his father, he'd driven out of the flatlands barely able to see over the wheel and press the gas pedal at the same time. Doing a hundred until the car gave up and he no longer saw his brother shot down on the ground. He'd hitchhiked into the rising mountains and begged for food and work from some cherry farmer who let him sleep in the barn.

"Is it working?" he whispered, cracking open one eye.

"Does it feel like it's working?" Irritation lined Crazy Mary's voice.

"No," Wicasah said, opening both eyes, "but I'm cold and uncomfortable."

"You can't retell your story like reciting facts. You have to relive it. Stop being so impatient."

Wicasah sighed and stared hard at the stars, willing the vision to come to him. He could hear the roar of the waterfalls in the distance, could smell the smoked salmon and whitefish that Crazy

Mary had strung up earlier, remembered the folks dressed in green forest ranger uniforms disturbing their meal and telling them they were on newly minted federal land and it wasn't no place for people to actually live.

Oh, how Crazy Mary and he had laughed when they'd departed. She'd said it didn't mean much, only that they'd have to move further into the slowly dwindling wilderness. She wouldn't go back to living in some asbestos-lined house with a strip of store-bought dirt for a garden. She'd paid her dues growing up in missionaries, had witnessed the angel Michael falling in love with the dreamer-spirit of the whispering waves, and fought back when she'd been told *she could only choose one.*

He'd snorted and said, "Hey, you think this earth is bad? You should see what it's like where I come from. It's sand and clay with nothing rich in between."

Suddenly there it was—that thing sitting ignored in the back of his mind. He never wanted to look at it directly and hadn't since he'd become a teenage murderer. It was heavy with regret and guilt. Mainly composed of what he *should've* done.

Every morning since he'd become a witch, his fingers red from cherry juice and the magic raging like puberty inside him, he'd wake and know, like he knew the sky was blue, that he had to find his brother. Every day, he'd push the witchery down, work until he couldn't function from exhaustion, and not act on the knowledge. Instead, he thought about lost time, about Domino stuck in a hellhole system, while Wicasah breathed fresh air and put his feet in the chilling waters of the nearby river.

For a while, he thought Domino would find him because that's what Domino did: he found lost things. How many miles had the two of them walked in cities or rundown dumps, ducking into any and every bar looking for their father? Yet here, the winters were full of snowstorms and the summers high with sunshine and Domino never showed. Wicasah lost any idea of where he should start to look. He tried once, using the small shadows birthed after he made the sacrifice to the witchery, and failed.

The worst thought of all was Domino didn't want to find him. That the mistake known as Wicasah had been regulated to a footnote in his older brother's history.

A familiar bellyache cramped his stomach. His back arched, signaling the shadow-monsters awakening inside him. Crazy Mary moved her hand away from his bulging stomach. She refused to touch him when his magic woke, called his witch-brand bad medicine. The galaxy began to swirl, sickening him. Crazy Mary pulled a blanket closer around her shoulders and Wicasah caught an obsidian glimmer of an arrowhead clenched in her hand. Just in case he didn't come back the same.

She'd been a mother to him all these years, gruffly taking in this wayward teenager who wouldn't leave her alone after hearing stories about her from the other youths back in town—*she was one of those crazy crones, she ate a bird raw once, I swear*—and even then, she still made him outlast the cold autumn nights shivering outside her tent. He'd been thin as a wraith but wanted someone like him—someone who didn't throw him out for being different, someone who had experience in this realm and others. Someone who was an outcast, too.

Crazy Mary had helped him. By the end of three years, Wicasah could walk as silently as a stalking cougar. The magic had been tempered, matured, no longer boiling over. No longer striking humans like a rattlesnake and sucking their shadows to join his others. Wicasah would do anything for her, worried about her back pains and loneliness, laughed at her dry jokes, and enjoyed her silence when she wasn't up to talking.

An itchiness grew in him, though—wanderlust or growing pains—and he'd learned to live with it until Crazy Mary snarled that he'd better reconnect with his past or she'd feed him to the next bear that came by. Which was how he ended up painted and nude in the middle of the night, picking at his scabs to tell his story.

His body rocked with some unknown force, but Wicasah had left his earthly vessel. He ran through the moments making up his past. How the dust of the plains had been scrubbed away by overgrown forests and large crystal lakes. How he'd decided he was saved in this vibrant land until Crazy Mary told him he'd made the woods imprison him to stop finding out who he was.

In his mind's eye, the endless plains opened up before him. Shrubs and grasses waved as a violent wind shook his foundation, making him teeter. He crouched down and bent his head to keep the sand from his eyes. He blinked furiously as a sudden dust storm transformed into a tornado with him at the center, and he nearly fell at the sight of *him* appearing in front of him—a mirror much older and more worn.

His doppelgänger's black braid was wind-whipped and ratty compared to the fine plait Wicasah always maintained. Wrinkles deepened around his mouth and his skin had become leathery over time. Wicasah wanted to touch this version of himself, make sure it was real, when the mirror-Wicasah crouched down next to him and held out cupped hands like offering water. Fossilized bones filled the elder's hands: eggs, trilobites, and juvenile dinosaur skulls. Wicasah stared, confused, but cupped his hands underneath the elder's. The fossils fell.

He heard his name being called from behind him—maybe it was just the wind—but his elder stared beyond Wicasah's shoulder. His face softened in awed devotion. Wicasah whipped his head around but couldn't see anything. He could only feel some strong presence shelter him. Could only see the shifting spin of his dark shadow-hounds.

Wicasah.

The vision disintegrated like erosion from rough wind. He gasped as he opened his eyes. He tried to push himself up, but his joints felt stiff—*old*—and Crazy Mary watched him from a distance, seated next to her fire. Firelight flickered in her dark gaze. "Did you see what you needed?" She wrapped the blanket tighter around her shoulders.

Wicasah hobbled to the light. Warmth caressed his skin. He pulled a shirt on and sat near her feet. "I think so."

"I'll miss you," she said and he knew it was a painful admission for her, this savior of his, to say.

"This land," he said, digging his fingers into the dirt, "knows I'll never completely leave. You taught me that. We're family."

Crazy Mary reached out to cup his cheek. Her fingers traced his cheekbones, and he knew she was memorizing his face to recall on lonely nights.

"Where must you go?" she asked.

"The Badlands."

Crazy Mary tutted. "You always did need to go back home."

"It's not my home." Home was Crazy Mary. Home was Domino.

"It's where you came from. Where you were born."

"From the dust returned," he whispered and laid his head in her lap, overcome with the prospect of the journey to come and what he must do. Time to stop running.

CHAPTER 2

THREE YEARS LATER

"**WE'VE GOT A** new job, but the boss says there's stipulations."

Wicasah grimaced at his partner and took another pull from his water bladder. "Well, shit, like what?"

"Have to work with some outside contractor." Bates snorted and spit chewing tobacco into the low-lying scrub brush. He folded the missive some pony express Ford Mustang had given him just before they'd left the sad messenger fretting over his steaming engine, both of them shaking their heads. Badlands weren't no place for things imported from the other side of the Dark and Bloody.

Wicasah reined his horse in so he could trot closer to Bates. "Think that's a good idea?"

"Beats the hell out of me. You're the fossil hunter here, being one with nature and all."

Wicasah smiled true then, but still sighed internally at Bates' coarseness. He'd been out in the desert for three years hunting bones. Big monster femurs down to delicate raptor claws to ancient leaves imprinted in sandstone had all passed through his hands. While wind-sore and slightly bent, Wicasah had been his own brand of freelancer before Bates recruited him with his handlebar mustache and bowler hat. How Bates had survived the wind storms and twisters was beyond Wicasah, but Wicasah had learned to never judge a book by its cover. While building trust between them had taken, well, *patience* for lack of a better word, they'd been on the same road for so long, there was goodness in the company

Plus, this dinosaur business wasn't something you picked up strangers for. You had to be vetted. Trusted. There had been too many backstabbers in these fossil wars to take anyone for granted.

"Where are we supposed to meet this person?" Wicasah asked.

"The Lookout, dumbass. Where else?"

Wicasah's smile faded and he pulled his wide cowboy hat lower over his eyes. His legs ached at the thought of riding another ten miles, but he wouldn't complain. Him, being one with nature and all that.

The Lookout wasn't anything that the name implied, just some rundown saloon on the outskirts of some one-lane pioneer town on the edge of where the earth became truly inhabitable. But, in this skeleton business, Wicasah was number one and the Lookout was where the bone-hunters made their home.

Imported Brightside cars parked along the street, more for prestige than use, although one had its hood popped. Steam rose from the engine. Wicasah patted his horse's heaving sides and maneuvered to the Lookout's trough in the back. He hitched his trusty mustang to the pole and put the feed bag around his neck. Out here, it made life easier to do things the old way. No way was a car going to survive the rocky backroads leading to the canyons and bluffs where the good bones were buried. No way he'd trust a Chevy to do what a mustang could do with a little love, rubdown, and water. It was all Eastern finery, anyway. Brightsiders had started to realize the value of the West, sending their contraptions and inventions and second-hand cast-offs for testing.

Stale cigarette smoke filled the clapboard walls of the Lookout. A piano player plinked out an out-of-tune heart-and-soul. Bone hunters—Wicasah's competitors—hunched over round tables, deep in conversation. Bates grinned at the gal behind the bar as she rubbed a rag against the lacquered top and inclined her head toward the backroom. Wicasah took another drink of sun-warmed water from his water bladder. He hated the canteens. The taste of metal was like blood in the back of his throat, much better with this sheep gut one.

Together, they meandered to the backroom, bypassing suspicious patrons and pretending-ignorant bartenders. Bates banged his knuckles in mysterious-succession on the door, heard the same pattern repeated from the other side before locks jiggled and the door cracked opened. Wicasah took his hat off and hung it from his pack while double-checking the integrity of the bones wrapped in soft worn leather within. Proof he hadn't been drinking away his employer's advance.

Inside, bright spotlights focused on the focal point of the

otherwise sparse room. A long table surrounded by badly carved chairs where Edwards, Wicasah's investor, sat. Edwards adjusted his fine suit jacket and fingered the watch chain dangling from his vest pocket—all funded by rich science. Wicasah nodded hello and fell back into the routine Bates and him had down pat. Bates placed a fresh tobacco pinch against his lower lip. Wicasah put on his best holier-than-thou look. Edwards liked to hire local collectors with a shady streak for his schemes—to him, the best of the best. Wicasah was expensive, but he'd networked his way to success and knew how to jimmy his way out of a backwater jailhouse. The best of the best.

"Glad you two finally made it," Edwards said, standing up from the table covered in his prized collection and shaking each of their hands. Wicasah resisted the urge to wipe his hand down his pant leg. Edwards just ran moist.

He studied the amateur reconstruction of the skeleton spanning the length of the table and upended his finds over the bones. Edwards' nostrils flared in anger, but he snagged one of Wicasah's trilobites and held it up to the light.

"Beautiful. Well done. Knew you two were assets to the team," he gushed.

Wicasah rolled his eyes at Bates and was glad to see Bates' pinched mouth suppress a grin.

"What's the job now, Edwards," Bates said, getting to the point. "That pony express probably burned his car to smelt getting your missive to us. We've got wind of a good dig near Black Hills. Like to get up there before Copeland's team gets their grubby hands on it."

Edwards put down the trilobite and fingered the other new treasures Wicasah had dumped. "That will have to wait. There's sound information that Copeland has secured the jaw of a baby *Tyrannosaurus rex.* Can you imagine the information we could learn? What the bone structure could reveal about the life cycle of these creatures? Imagine the funders cooing over it at the museum. We need it. I won't let Copeland take this from me like he did the *Eobasileus.* He might use this to back his idea of changing the taxa. The taxa of all things!"

Wicasah bit his tongue. This intellectual war grew more ridiculous by the month. Squabbles about nomenclature for skeleton reconstructions which, to his mind, looked to have been built wrong, made little sense. He doubted Edwards and Copeland had spoken in years, but they continued to harass each other in print—Wicasah had picked up one of those scientific papers and read the long-winded argument about which name should be used to classify some new raptor and put it down in disgust a half-hour later. This *Tyrannosaurus rex* jaw was probably nothing more than a rat's rib bone.

Bates slid his jaw side-to-side. "I think I know what you're getting at, chief. You want us to bring it back here. Give it a new owner."

"Copeland doesn't know we know. He doesn't yet know for certain his team even has it. I, ah, gave his graduate student a sizable payoff to ensure I received any information on big finds first. We have a window of opportunity and I won't be one-upped by him anymore. He thinks he can steal our *Triceratops* replicate? By god, they won't get away with it. We'll burn their big reveal to the ground."

Wicasah raised his eyebrows at Bates. He wasn't against illegal activity, but he wasn't a pro at thieving jewels or coins. He dealt in ancient bones, but he supposed if a mammoth tusk came to him *accidentally* he wasn't against bartering if the profit was high. It was all just another way to pass the time. For years he'd been waiting for a sign, and so far all he'd learned was how to wait out a wind storm and that it tended to snow in July.

"I've hired a man who knows the site and Copeland's team," Edwards continued. "He's a freelancer, but for the right price, he'll pledge his loyalties. He's a real trader, worked with archeologists and anthropologists about the myths behind these things. You know how much the crowd loves such bumpkis, eats up the stories like nobody's business."

Edwards inclined his head. Wicasah nearly jumped when the newcomer stepped from the shadows. Hubris had gotten him again. He should be better than this, use his skills, not assume he was the best at everything.

The man was shorter, and if Wicasah had been learning how to live off the earth, this man had to have been doing it for much longer and in even rougher territory. His tousled brown hair had a wild edge to it like it'd been knotted far too many times to be combed out and he wore buckskins with a pouch around his neck. Wicasah felt some jiggling warning of recognition in the back of his head that he'd seen this man before, but he couldn't put his finger on where.

"These two are my best. I expect everyone to be treated fairly. I hear of any foul play and you'll be the one future archaeologists dig up in a thousand years," Edwards said, pointing a finger at the newcomer.

The fossil wanderer raised his head and it was the look that punched Wicasah straight in the stomach. He knew that look. God, he could count how many times it had been directed at him. Excitement rushed in his veins, a combination of addiction and brutality and wildness because he was here. *He was here.*

"Wouldn't think about it," the fossil wanderer said. "Traded with your folks before, but this is the first time I've had to take a side in the field."

"How come?" Bates asked. "Why you switch sides?"

The wanderer stared Bates down for a minute, and that was Daniel's *you're an idiot* look. Wicasah remembered it well. "Other side ignored treaties and decency. Can't have that," he said.

Bates grunted. "Jesus, another one of those, Edwards?"

Edwards waved a dismissive hand at him. "Give it a rest. I don't care what your reasons are as long as you're solid."

"Where's the dig? Out in a spot where the flowers grow?" Wicasah asked, and he was proud he could keep his voice under control so well. Bates looked at him like he spoke in riddles.

"One's a wetland, but it's drying up. Has some sage, little bit of green grass, lots of pussytoes, I suppose," the fossil wanderer admitted, just as lost by Wicasah's question.

"Pussytoes?" Wicasah echoed, his heart seizing. "Pussytoes?"

Domino looked like he'd been shot. Wicasah noted they didn't quite resemble each other anymore. Domino studied Wicasah long and hard as if seeking the little brother Wicasah had been so long ago. Wicasah wanted to jump, leap, pull Domino into an embrace and pound his back because here he was. *Here he was.*

"What's pussytoes? Sounds like a good smoke." Bates laughed at his own joke.

Wicasah flicked an annoyed look at his partner. He wanted this meeting to end. "Why don't you go find yourself some pussy," he suggested, instead. "I can fill in . . . " he looked at Domino, in search of a name.

"Domino," Domino supplied, slightly breathless.

"I can fill in *Domino* about the particulars."

"Fine by me, kiddo. Don't hurt yourself," Bates said with a wave and exited the room.

Edwards sucked in his lower lip. "Give me a minute, good men, I don't want Bates running up a tab in my name like he did last time."

"Make sure he doesn't run up the insurance, either," Wicasah said. "He tends to fight when he's drunk."

"I'll find him," Edwards said, nearly barreling Wicasah over as he left.

Wicasah stared at his brother in the empty room over a centuries-old monster and began laughing and crying at the same time. "Holy shit. Holy shit, it's you."

"*Get over here*," Domino said, rough like he hadn't used his voice in a while.

And then Wicasah was clinging to his older brother, amazed he was taller, and Domino's broad arms nearly cracked his ribs. Domino remained silent despite Wicasah's curses of disbelief, and Wicasah decided it was definitely worth it, the waiting, the long time out in the sun with his hands in the dirt, to finally have them around his brother after all this time.

<hr>

The night flew by in a blur. They were older now and drunk from being close again. In tandem, they'd drunk too much of whatever foulness the barmaid let them pour down their throats. Wicasah charged it to Edwards under Bates' name and pounded Domino's shoulder raw. Domino didn't say much, as if he wanted Wicasah to bruise him with enthusiasm. Afterward, Wicasah followed Domino back to his rented room, some closet of a space, and while Domino had huffed in annoyance, Wicasah had shivered because it was all familiar and wonderful.

Domino shoulder-checked the doorframe. Wicasah pushed him the rest of the way inside, helped his swaying brother remove his boots, and then shoved his intoxicated sibling onto the bed. He ripped his shirt up to expose Domino's stomach, frowned at the lean belly, and grabbed a marker from his bag. He popped the cap off and held it between his teeth, and laid the felt tip on Domino's skin.

He had to. It had been too long. The tension of *not knowing* relaxed once the perfect circle had been drawn, the eye in place, the love transferred into something tangible, leaving a space inside him finally at peace.

Domino watched through half-lowered lashes. "Fucking obsessive."

Wicasah smiled smugly, capped the marker, and blew on the symbols of protection to make them dry faster. Domino's stomach clenched and Wicasah uttered some kind of insane chuckle he didn't know could come from him. He elbowed Domino to the side until he had space to share, remembered how pushy he could get, and it felt so good to feel entitled because he was the youngest. The youngest and so beloved.

"Pain in the ass," Domino growled. "Taking over the whole bed, you little shit."

Wicasah's grin felt mischievous and far too broad to be normal. "Not my fault you're too drunk to walk. Not my fault you're such a mess."

Domino swallowed hard. Wicasah's joy faltered, knowing he'd ruined something without knowing what. He took a deep breath to explain—apologize, even—and noticed an odd smell. His nostrils flared and he popped up on his elbows, following the off-scent out to the open window leading to a small outside ledge. The flayed bodies of rats and cats decomposed on the sill.

"You've got dead animals in your room," he said.

"Good Lord, you're observant."

"Why?"

Thinking *serial killer* with a shrug, thinking *fucked up in all kinds of ways,* thinking about how to relieve pain, and finally feeling unnerved at the way all those thoughts didn't bother him so much. He'd get used to it. There wasn't any way he would leave now. Domino could be butchering children and Wicasah wouldn't leave.

Domino tossed his head in a way that said he didn't want to answer. Wicasah remembered the tactic from when Domino wouldn't share spells. Wicasah leaned in and punched him hard on the chest. "Tell me."

"I have to feed my familiars," he said without looking at Wicasah.

When had the witchery overtaken his brother? When had Domino made the offering? Wicasah counted the ways it could've been done. Still didn't matter. Same as before. Kind of stuck together. "Hungry creatures, huh? But to keep carcasses around? Domino, that's not very classy."

Wicasah glanced back at the balcony. A white creature no bigger than his hand sniffed the animal corpses. Big bone head, black eyes flat and matte with a wide mouth that encompassed the whole face. Wicasah stilled, taken aback. Familiars weren't rare, but then they weren't common, either. Wicasah never had a familiar appear to do his bidding. He didn't count his shadow-hounds.

The little thing looked disgusted at the carcass and jumped off the sill, scampering back to Domino. Domino reached over to pick up a pair of pants tossed on the floor and patted the pockets, finally pulling out a fossilized pelvis. He gave the bone to the familiar, and with a crunch, the thing devoured it. It slunk up Domino's arm and faded into his skin.

"Like children they are, I swear," Domino said, glancing at Wicasah as if his brother might judge him.

Wicasah licked his lips, swallowed his questions, and decided to derail the conversation. "The heist is gonna be great," he said. The two of them. Fossil criminals extraordinaire. Screw *Nature*, they'd be in the *Times*.

"Have to be careful." Domino yawned. "*Heist*. You're ridiculous."

"Always am," Wicasah said. "Not my fault you're an old maid too scared to step outside."

"Fuck you," Domino said affectionately.

Wicasah felt settled, too wired to sleep, but when Domino's breath eased and he uttered a soft snore Wicasah nearly came out of his skin. He'd waited so long and now here they both were, reunited. He wanted to take Domino into the forest, introduce him to Crazy Mary. He wanted to take Domino's life and meld his past with Wicasah's so he could know everything. Maybe, it would feel like they hadn't been separated at all.

CHAPTER 3

WICASAH WASN'T SURE how he swung it, but three days later—his pack bulging with rations and water, his pockets heavy with money and goods—he'd successfully convinced Bates to take a long-needed hiatus, and Wicasah had Domino next to him, riding silent on his mare.

Wicasah wasn't in any hurry. He'd been in a hurry to get out of the godforsaken Lookout. He'd been in a hurry to leave Edwards, duty, and whatever honor there was in being a man who picks up bones behind. He wanted the harsh wilderness of the world, empty of anything but the two of them so, if the time called for it, they could fight and scream or sit and stare. They could freely talk about what it meant to be in the witchery. They could talk about Daniel.

Wicasah had so many things to say, but he didn't know how to say them.

Domino seemed too calm, nothing like the bossy boy who nagged Wicasah about his cleanliness or gave him second servings from their small dinner while saving none for himself. This stoic Domino allowed Wicasah to skirt down old deer paths through ravines, skirting the edge of the plains, sometimes edging too close to a canyon's edge without so much as a peep. Multiple times, Wicasah opened his mouth to engage in conversation, but when he looked over his shoulder at Domino, Domino had his head down, focused far away. Unreadable face. Chapped lips pursed together.

Wicasah coughed and adjusted his hat. Within an hour, the routine would start again. The wanting squelched by silence. Confidence slain by fear of awkwardness. Wicasah with nothing but the butter churn of his own thoughts.

It felt the same as the first morning he'd woken up in Domino's bed hung-over and alone, petrified that the day before had been a lie. He checked the boneless carcasses warmed on the sill for familiars. He rinsed his mouth with tepid water from a pitcher and flew downstairs only to find Domino trading for a horse. He'd been startled at Wicasah's frantic entrance. Fear did that to him. Made him rage.

Now, old painful doubts seeped into him. He wondered if Domino was rethinking this reunion of theirs, pondering whether it was the best policy to keep Wicasah by his side even though Wicasah had burst out of the inn, livid. Maybe all Domino saw was Daniel holding him down, the gunshot cutting through the night, fear clogging the back of his throat as they barreled for the car, the way the taste of silver from the car keys mingled with the blood. Everywhere metal, from the car to the bullet that shot Domino down.

He didn't want those memories to be their only ones. He knew there were others, like the iron bird soaring above the electric lights. The way Domino held his scythe after returning from the fields. The way dried vomit on the stairs from Daniel's late-night drinking made Wicasah's lip curl in disgust. Blood on the floor that he refused to touch because he wanted it to stain. He wanted to rub Daniel's face in it like a bad dog, and tell him, "Look what you've done."

The late morning sunlight lit the orange and tan bands of the ravine rocks, some appearing smooth and water-worn, others triangular like a castle's turrets. Wicasah swayed on his horse, overcome, and focused on the bumps and divots of the badland ridge. The spine of some sleeping giant, comatose under layers of stone, waiting for the right time to emerge. His stallion's hooves kicked up pebbles from the low grass. He couldn't stand it. He turned to say something to his brother but realized he rode alone.

He tugged on his reins, pivoted his stallion around, and paused. Domino had dismounted and crouched on his haunches, combing through tufts of sparse yellowed grass. Wicasah uttered a sound of disgust—he despised that he'd lost the ability to keep tabs on Domino. The pit of his stomach expanded into an even darker abyss. His squeezed knees urged the mustang forward until their combined centaur-shadow cast over Domino.

Wicasah tipped his hat back, but his mouth remained too dry to speak. Domino dug up a handful of curiosities from the earth— bones if the so-called professional could get his head out of his emotional ass one moment to identify them—and brought one of the eroded half-ovals to his mouth. His tongue flickered out to lick, pausing for a brief moment to taste. The damp spot evaporated. Domino smiled briefly, tucking the items into the pouch around his neck.

"Good find," Wicasah blurted out. "You can buy a decent meal with those."

Domino's smile widened momentarily in answer. Wicasah's stomach dropped as he waited for a response, internally pleading for a sign, and he wished he could find a rock big enough to hide under. The sun ticked down the minutes. Domino mounted and once more Wicasah took the lead, wondering why defeat had to feel this humiliating. Maybe he had sunstroke, maybe he was dehydrated, maybe his ass chafed from riding for so long, but he had to turn his brain off. He'd even be okay with the silence if the silence wasn't so damn terrible. He missed Bates' companionship.

The afternoon rolled around, slipping into evening, and as the sun fell behind the horizon Domino spoke, "Let's camp here for the night."

An hour ago, Wicasah would've rejoiced, but it had been one hour too long. He shrugged, too fatigued to disagree. He dismounted and tied his horse to a lone white-barked tree, coaxed some water into the creature, fixed the feed bag, and rubbed the stallion down. Thorny grass crunched underfoot. Darkness raced across the sky in bands of twinkling starlight. By the time he finished, the heat of Domino's cookfire taunted him.

Always fast, the nighttime, greedy to hunt them once their solar guardian departed. Sweat cooled under his arms and on the nape of his neck. He unrolled a blanket, wrapped it around his shoulders, and felt his amulet thump against his chest. A gift Crazy Mary had given him, something acceptable that came from his side of the Midwest, ended up in the North, and finally straddled the country by going wherever Wicasah went.

Domino had built the fire between two tall rocks and crouched near the flames. Wicasah sat against the other rock with a groan and stretched his legs out. His muscles throbbed and felt like they'd been tied tight. The outline of the plateaus, buttes, and canyons was pitch black. The sparse firelight cast Domino's face in eerie ghost-like illumination. Domino cradled a bowl and dropped his newly acquired fossils inside. Using a pestle from his bag, he ground the bones, making a rasping noise. Wicasah cringed. He wanted to ask *why* but figured he'd be met with fucking silence again. A curl of dust rose from the bowl. The layered star-cake of the Milky Way extended above him like a trail he would never reach the end of.

Wicasah's stomach rumbled. Domino snorted. Wicasah had an urge to tip over the bowl just to get under Domino's skin. Piss him off. Just *because*. He did neither. At some point, this stranger across the fire had been a parent, brother, and best friend. Now, Wicasah feared their connection had been lost.

Domino dribbled water from his canteen into the bowl, sprinkled what looked like rosemary on top, and swirled the mess around. Sniffing it, he tilted it in Wicasah's direction. "Brightsiders think the dinosaur bones are to be reconstructed, but their ghosts linger in the remains. Good for tapping into power."

"Not likely," Wicasah said, sharper than intended, and was met with silence again. He heaved a sigh and covered his eyes. He hated this.

He thought back to Crazy Mary, remembered how the first time he'd begged her to teach him, she refused to talk until he brought her a gift—a loaf of good bread from the bakery in town. His mistake coiled like a snake around his spine and he nearly sobbed at the realization. He'd forgotten how words—*stories*—were possessions that shouldn't be given freely. He'd simply never expected he'd have to buy his brother's past.

"If you're waiting for me to trade you something in exchange for your words, you're out of luck," he said. "I don't own anything you might want."

He heard a shuffle of quickly moved earth and sensed a presence over him. He parted his forefinger and middle finger to view Domino on his knees in front of him with sparking embers shooting up behind his shoulders like an aura. He sipped his bone tea, his lips reddened and glistening. A concentration line appeared between his brows. Wicasah waited, stubborn in a four-year-old way he was certain he would never outgrow.

"Can I share your blanket?" Domino asked.

Wicasah blinked, considered saying no out of childish spite, but unwrapped the blanket from his shoulders. Domino sidled up beside him, stretching his legs out, and Wicasah dropped the blanket over them both. Shared warmth seeped into Wicasah's limbs and a more comfortable quiet rose, the kind he'd pined for—

one where he knew everything Domino was thinking and feeling from one shared look.

"This is all the payment I need," Domino said, quietly.

Wicasah snorted. "Should've bargained for more. New horse, maybe? Upgrade to a car? You settling?"

Another soft smile. "Guess I didn't think too much about it."

"How you've survived this long, I really don't know. This world is on the cusp of a technological revolution. You could've owned a rocket ship."

Wicasah saw a flash of teeth from his peripherals.

"I'm not . . . it's been a long time since I've been around someone. I've traveled alone for a while." Domino bit his lip.

Wicasah nodded, thought it wasn't a very good excuse, but let it pass. Like he'd said before, he wasn't going anywhere. The silence stretched, but Wicasah decided to fill it as he focused on the constellations: the hunter, the coyote, the dipper. The serpent and the scales.

"You know after I murdered Daniel—"

Domino's breath whistled through his teeth. "What a way to start."

"After I murdered our father," Wicasah repeated, "and I ran away, a woman took me in. I had traveled far, worked shit jobs, slept outside, nearly froze to death. Barely ate. Stole. When I came to Crazy Mary, begging her to take me in and teach me, she made me wait even longer. Made me stand outside her tent in the rain, wouldn't share her meal. She judged me, Domino. It was hell. I thought if I couldn't convince her—this madwoman of the mountains—then I wouldn't be worth anyone's time. It didn't make sense, but sitting in the rain, starving, shaking—somehow, I passed whatever test she put before me. Then, later, she and I sat kind of like this, looking up at the Ghost Road."

He pointed his finger into the sky, tracing the Milky Way. "I wasn't in a good place. I was coming out of my skin, felt like the world was closing in on me, and the worst part was I didn't know it. I thought it was just something I had to get through—growing pains, teenage angst, the works—and Crazy Mary told me about the starry path I had strayed from. Each star might be a boiling mass of rock or plasma—*whatever*—but so are our spirits. We're all elemental. The stars are our campfires and at the end of the road waits an old woman who judges us based on the tattoos of our life—

marks on our soul as proof that we had lived. The judge determines the quality of the spirit's life to either send it to the next world or return it to Earth. Crazy Mary told me I had become a shade, that I had lost my connection to the Earth I had come from—even if that Earth was dry as bone. She helped me retrace my steps and I found my way back out here. In the badlands."

"Do you think you found it?" Domino asked, his voice hoarse. "Your path?"

"I know I did. I knew for sure a few days ago when I met up with you." Wicasah remembered the man he had seen in his vision, the elder roughened Wicasah whose face was struck in awe at some sublimity.

"I'm a wanted man," Domino blurted out as if the words boiled and he had to get them out, fast.

"You shouldn't be," Wicasah said fiercely, blinking back sudden tears.

"If I got caught, it can't lead back to you."

"Even though I'm the guilty party."

"Not . . . not just that. How I became part of the witchery."

"You're a real witch, then."

Domino nodded.

"You got more *umph* than just feeding bone fellas." Wicasah nudged Domino with his shoulder.

Domino's lip cured. *Obviously.*

"You don't have to justify what you did," Wicasah said. "Not to me. You don't have to explain unless you want to." Wicasah wanted him to explain more than anything else in the world, but he wanted trust even more than that. He wanted Domino to come to him out of security rather than pressure.

"It's why I'm here," Domino said. "After I became a witch, I crossed this whole side of the Dark and Bloody trying to take it back. I'm wanted for a lot of things I didn't do, but on paper, it's me who signed the dotted line."

"So, we'll be careful. You won't get arrested."

"More than careful."

"You have any idea how much money we'll make from this heist?"

Domino opened his mouth like he couldn't even guess at a number. Wicasah had a feeling Domino struggled to answer not because the dollar amount was huge, but because Domino hadn't thought about it.

"It's enough to go to New York on. Buy a blimp ticket, light out for the Brightside, if we're so inclined."

Domino looked startled as if he'd never considered it before. "New York," he repeated in astonishment as if the city was as foreign as Mars. As if there could be more than wide-open spaces where the wind howled and the grass undulated like waves.

"Not the city," Wicasah clarified. "I hear the city's a shit show, but up north it's nothing but wild times and backroom brawls."

"Tell me more." Domino's voice had an ache to it. "You want to pay me for my words? Tell me yours. Please."

The intensity of Domino's desperation shocked Wicasah.

"I tried for so long not to think about you," Domino continued, his voice hitching. "I tried to keep you out of my mind because I felt like they would find you, that you'd get caught and taken somewhere terrible."

"Who? Who would find me? Daniel's dead."

"I don't know. The law? The police? Executioners? Anyone. It could've been anyone. I didn't want to know. I didn't want to find you because I've got a paper trail and I didn't want you to have to bear that weight too if something happened." Domino covered his face. His breathing, low and ragged, drowned out any other sound.

"You're an idiot," Wicasah said. "All I *wanted* was to be found. Took you long enough. Why'd you have to wait so long, huh? Was this some big brother lesson?"

Domino wiped his face with the back of his hand. Pleasure suffused Wicasah's heart, bold and strong and loved. So beloved.

"That's what you get for shooting a man in the head," Domino croaked. "That's what you get."

"Some lesson," Wicasah snorted. He paused, licked his lips and saw across the fire, poking with an inquisitive turn of the head, an outline of the bone familiar in shadow and flame. "Some lesson."

CHAPTER 4

TIME—**THE RISE** and falling sun, the constant twinkle of the Milky Way, the way the land flattened—made things easier. Wicasah rediscovered how to earn a smile from Domino, how to poke and prod and joke, recalled how good they were at setting traps for lizards, foxes, and long-eared rabbits. Domino kept the bones, fed his magic with them. Common knowledge beyond shared history, things like bones and fossil beds, kept them trading stories of stupid mistakes when youth still felt like immortality. While they were both older now, Wicasah at least had his brother's back.

They detoured to a bustling town chock-full of batwing door saloons and resupply general stores for the hell of it. Wicasah convinced Domino to rent a room after he saw his brother wince and dig thumbs into his back after all the nights they'd slept on the ground. The mercantile down the way had old portraits of past presidents and chiefs and an even bigger map outlining the boundaries between tribal and allowed territories, the Dark and Bloody schism, and the claimed European East with twinkling stars notating cities. Wicasah rolled his eyes when he saw it. Those declarations of land meant nothing to anyone anymore except for the congressional and spirit leaders back East, who squabbled and made laws that never reached the West. The embargo on the Brightside didn't just encompass laws, it also included discoveries and technology. If he hopped on a zeppelin and crossed the Dark and Bloody, he'd see finery he'd never thought possible. Airplanes that weren't just for war, but travel. Cars that could push over a hundred and not burn out. Diesel that didn't clog the air with toxic clouds.

Sauntering down the aisle, Wicasah tallied up dried stock, food, and water rations. He calculated shoe repair and clothes, horse treats and saddle gear, new blankets, and matches. His mind was full of numbers when a crash came from the other side of the store and he saw Domino clench his chest through the shelves.

Wicasah didn't know how he made it to Domino, only the crystal-clear way he could smell Domino's distress. He yanked Domino up, wrapped his arm around his brother while Domino clutched his torso. "It hurts. I think there's something wrong," Domino gasped, leaning hard into Wicasah.

Such a sensation, to hold Domino up. Domino had always been an immovable giant. This was the man who excavated man-sized femurs out of ravine beds, who burned the dinner beans over the fire, who rode without complaint for days. This man who doubled over in agony was not the heroic god of Wicasah's memories.

Alarm? Too mild. Wicasah tried not to slide into a full-blown panic. He hefted Domino's arm over his shoulder and balanced Domino against him as he bore the two of them out into the street, screaming for a physician, a healer, a fucking bone medicine man, whatever would get the job done.

"The hospital. I haven't ever felt like this before," Domino whispered.

The mercantile manager followed them out and flagged down the only taxi in town, pointing the driver in the right direction with a click of the tongue to the horses.

"Breathe," Wicasah coached, gripping Domino's hand so hard he could feel Domino's fingers bend under the weight. While Wicasah had grown stronger and taller than Domino ever could— and for a moment, he saw red, thinking of Daniel feeding them like shit when they were younger—he felt like a child, praying to any kind of kind deity that Domino would be okay. The fear was so real he almost wouldn't be separated when the nurses took Domino into the back-emergency room. What if this was the last time— what if they couldn't find each other a second time?

Hours passed. Wicasah stared at the white-painted wooden walls and listened to the carriage clock tick. Workers and mothers milled in and out with ailments from a cough to severed fingers lost in a farm accident and still, the time counted down. When the doctor finally emerged and put a hand on his shoulder, Wicasah knew it was the end of the world. The doctor gave a half-hearted chuckle at his drawn face. Wicasah couldn't handle it, couldn't handle the fucking joke, wanted to take him out back and beat him viscerally. Strangle him with his stethoscope. Wouldn't even bother with a gun. It wouldn't be intimate enough.

"Your brother is going to be fine, Mr. Washington." The doctor straightened the lapel of his off-white lab coat. "Does your family have a history of degenerative diseases?"

Wicasah stared at him. Silence stretched between them.

"There's something wrong with your brother's bones, John," the doctor reiterated to him. "Do you have a history of bone cancer? Generational diseases? Any of this ringing a bell?"

The words struck like daggers. Wicasah didn't know what they meant, could've been asked if they had any bloodline curses for all he understood. He shook his head. "Not that I know of."

The doctor shook his head as if puzzled. Wicasah decided he wouldn't kill him. It terrified him, the rage he felt, the wrongness sitting deep inside him, slick and growing like a brand-new organ. The good, non-witch thing to do was resist the urge to kill.

"I don't know how to explain it, but you'll need to bring him in again for tests," the doctor said. "We're going to release him, mainly because he's causing too much of a ruckus and I'm short on beds, but essentially, his bones are dissolving. One of his ribs looks like it's about to collapse. We can rebuild it, but it's a risky procedure. Most people can live without a few ribs, it's not a death sentence, but if the progression holds he could collapse his ribcage. Does this make sense, Mr. Washington?"

Cold shakes. Wicasah nodded, pushed his black braid off his shoulder, and nearly twisted his hands off.

"Now for the long term. If this is cancer, it will move quick. It might infect the rest of his skeleton and start the degeneration elsewhere. Schedule an appointment for tomorrow and we'll do some tests, see what this thing really is."

Another nod. The doctor retreated. A nurse helped Wicasah collect his brother, soft from some sweet drug. He tucked Domino into bed in their rented room, hoped their fake names wouldn't be noticed, and pressed his hands against Domino's side, felt the squishy indentation where his ribs were supposed to be.

Then, he finished his purchases at the supply store. At one point, while counting his coins, he fought through the fog to think about how bones created blood. How the skeleton was the mother source of magic. He had to close his eyes least he puke on the spot.

Back at the room, he made a concoction of calcium—milk,

cream, and cheese. He balanced the spread and walked into the bedroom to see Domino feeding a piece of bone from the recently-caught rat carcass. That little white beast. His familiar. The creature sucked the bone like a popsicle before swallowing it whole. Its slit eyes pursed even smaller in joy.

Domino cooed, breaking another rat rib to feed his magic child. Wicasah nearly dropped his tray in sudden fury. If it wasn't his family, it was the magic. He imagined Domino's skeleton, eroded by the hungry machinations of the witchery.

"Domino," Wicasah said, putting every ounce of command into the name. "Can I talk with your familiar for a moment?"

He knew it was an odd request. Confusion crossed Domino's face. The impulse to say no.

Wicasah tried again. "It's about your health. About this pain you're feeling."

"I know they're eating me from the inside," Domino said. So simple. He fed his monster a bit of spine. The creature licked it and then spit it out. Wicasah could see a line of muscle and white sinew still attached. "I didn't want them killing other people when they're hungry. They're always hungry."

"Then we need to feed them more," Wicasah said, like it was the easiest thing in the world. On the inside, he rolled in terror. If Domino knew—*if he knew*—but Domino had always been stupid when it came to Domino.

Domino petted the top of his familiar's curved head and stood up. "Taking a leak," he said, and clapped Wicasah on the back. "Have your talk."

Wicasah let out a deep breath. He'd won a big battle. Wicasah put the tray down and the creature scooted back as if appalled—betrayed—that his master would abandon him this way. Wicasah picked up the rat's skull—it stunk to high heaven—and let it rest in his palm.

"I understand you're hungry and you need to be fed," he said, and it was probably the first time the thing had been talked to on a one-on-one basis with someone who wasn't Domino.

The little thing stilled and focused all its energy on Wicasah.

"He's told you not to kill the living, but if you continue to eat him from the inside, I swear you'll wish you hadn't." Wicasah crushed the skull in his palm, felt something brown and slimy streak across his skin, and a secondary scent rose to hit the back of his throat. "Do you understand me? Do you understand how powerful I am?" Wicasah's shadow-hounds pressed against his voice, eager to immobilize the familiar, devour it.

The familiar rubbed its belly.

"I know it hurts, but I can make you hurt worse. You don't want to be locked in a place of meat, do you? With all that blood, cartilage, and muscle? Do you want me to bury you in a carcass without bones, that won't rot?"

The familiar didn't say anything, but Wicasah knew his point hit home.

"I need you to promise. I need you to show me."

The familiar reached out and swiped at the rot on Wicasah's palm. It scrunched its face in distaste and smeared it over his cheekbones.

"Good," Wicasah said.

He realized then how deep his love went and it wasn't pretty like the songs he heard girls coo on stage. No, real love was visceral, as heavy as those intestines of meanness growing inside him, something ruthless and cruel. He'd do anything for it, he knew. He'd do fucking anything. C'mon. Try him.

———◆———

The town's welcome sign was almost indistinguishable against the falling night, but Wicasah could still make out the wood blackened from the pounding rain. It was just like every other little town among these *mako sica* lands with one exception: this place had water.

Rolling plains pockmarked the fading badlands, marked by lone derricks rocking side to side as they harvested oil underneath the earth. Mining dinosaurs remains, just like him. It was an old way of resource extraction, but the schism splitting the country reminded the world that sometimes, old ways worked best. Wicasah had always lived too far west to see the Dark and Bloody, that ravine descending miles deep into the earth, but he'd heard the stories centered around greed interpreted as need. About the richness hibernating beneath the crust, a vein of natural resources so plentiful that the government and corporations had shaken hands and began harvesting with drills and pulleys, pipelines and pressurized water spouts. Too far they'd gone, too deep, and soon enough the miners came back not right, marked by the dark, nearly deaf from seismic clashes. It wasn't magic or a god woken from the core—but the realistic terror of earthen instability.

I HAVE ASKED TO BE WHERE NO STORMS COME

When the first earthquake hit, almost a million were killed. Cities built on stilts along the ridge toppled into the darkness. The second earthquake, when the tectonic plate threatened to shift and break, ruptured the surrounding area, pockmarking the territory like bubble wrap, causing sinkholes where any new development might occur. The Dark and Bloody split the country unfairly—the developed East and the Wild West—but nothing could be done while the continent barely hung on like Pangea, fragmented and divided, but still one.

It became a pilgrimage for some—to walk into the fractured land and see the split wider than any ocean, deep as a marine trench. Wicasah had heard of suicides diving into that split, and he'd always wondered how far they fell until they lost their voice from screaming. It became a symbol of adventure for Brightsiders who dreamt of the open space and a wish for Westerners wishing for that soft-callused life in the East. Wicasah's world was stuck in a time zone that siphoned off Brightside technology and moved at the speed of molasses, somewhere between the outlaw west and the industrial revolution where everything was new, but somehow still ancient and rusted.

Wicasah had a good notion of where the dino-dig would be, even if he couldn't quite see it in this downpour. A shallow canyon northwest of town beside a bird refuge, a small wetland of reeds and tall grasses where the ponds appeared just as flat and still as the prairie, marked by bobbing waterfowl huddled in groups.

Mud caked his horse's legs. Beating rain soaked him through his duster and dripped from the brim of his hat. "Bet you're glad I got your boots patched up, eh?" he said to his brother.

Domino looked miserable next to him. He had drawn a blanket up in a hood over his head. They rode close together as if it might provide some sort of cover by simple proximity. "Fuck you," he said, muffled.

Wicasah took solace in the response. The horizon lit with heat lighting, the yellow kind that spread brightly across the sky instead of striking through it. He could barely make out the water gushing like a river next to them, washing away the topsoil, and sending it into a slurry down towards the canyon. Lifting his head, the rain pattered over his face, cleansing the half-memory he had of a resurrected woman on fire, the terror generated in the backseat, and the two men who shaped his early life opening a locked car door and cursing, reaching for things that weren't him even though he'd cried for comfort.

He didn't quite know what had happened that night, only that Domino had been on the verge of departure. Wicasah had waited by the door for him to return, enraged at being left behind. He hadn't been, but the feeling was enough. A feeling which never really left him.

The rain tasted refreshing and cold. Petrichor filled his lungs and nostrils. He shook, but he felt so alive. Pausing on the incline leading into the town, Wicasah followed Domino's gaze away from civilization to where a dark shape, hunched over like a crone, waddled through the mud in the close distance. Rags clung to the creature as it bent over, sifting through the mud. Startled, Wicasah figured it was a woman searching for freshwater clams or distracted birds for her breakfast. He nudged his horse into Domino's line of sight and Domino shook his head as if clearing it, gave Wicasah a weary smile. Wicasah wanted to be inside, dried by a fire, and asleep.

They gave fake names at the boarding house and were still forced to take a one-bedroom stable shack outside of town. The innkeeper—Penny—sighed at their sopping coats and Wicasah's broad smile, apologetic for having no more rooms, but slipped them extra firewood. They took a table. Wicasah accepted her offer of whisky, while Domino croaked for coffee. Black.

"Travelling through?" she asked as she sat shepherd's pies in front of each of them.

Wicasah's mouth watered, the delicious scent of beef and crumbled taste of buttered crust. Domino sipped his coffee. Wicasah rolled his eyes as Domino tried to hide his grimace.

"Just for a night or two," Domino responded.

"I figured you'd come to see our monster," Penny replied, sliding Wicasah's whisky in front of him. "We made state news. The Copeland group's here to investigate. It's the reason we're booked up. Made such a splash, papers even said my cooking was the best they'd had yet." She beamed with pride.

"I wouldn't deny it," Domino said.

Penny's smile widened. Her wash-roughened hands played with the necklace around her neck.

Wicasah realized he'd already eaten half of his pie, but he still frowned. "A monster? Big bones?"

Penny nodded.

"I heard it was a novelty," Wicasah said slowly, shooting Domino a concerned look. "Something never seen before." They'd be in trouble if they came here looking to steal a baby dinosaur and find it was a lie.

"Oh goodness yes!" Penny said. "Like a bird, almost. I never knew something so large could fly!"

Wicasah met Domino's eyes and wondered if the frown he saw was the same he wore.

"Have you seen it?" Domino asked.

"Oh, no, they keep it guarded day and night. One of the diggers told me about it, how it's one of the most fragile creatures ever uncovered. Bones so weak that anything could disturb it. They have to be careful excavating it."

"When you've got a moment, could I have some more coffee?" Domino asked, sugar-sweet.

Penny looked almost scandalized that she hadn't noticed and left to fetch the pot.

Wicasah leaned over the table. *"Bird?"*

"Wakinyan," Domino said. "All the lightning storms, of course, it's a thunderbird."

"What the fuck is that?" Wicasah demanded. Hearing the unfamiliar words on Domino's tongue, the way he rolled parts of the word like he sometimes would Wicasah's name, made him know the two words had roots in a related language.

"It's a great bird," Domino said, his voice small. Wicasah sensed he was afraid. "Or so I've heard. I need to see it."

"We need to see if there even is a baby *T. rex* here," Wicasah snarled. "Edwards had better not've sent us on some wild goose chase to fetch a skeleton that doesn't exist."

"We could bring back the thunderbird skull," Domino mused. "Might be comparable, if not worth twice the price of a dino."

Wicasah worried his lip between his teeth and gulped the rest of his whisky. It burned and warmed, but did nothing for the sick twist of uneasiness. Things weren't going according to plan. They should abandon the venture altogether.

"No one has preserved a thunderbird skull," Domino continued. "We probably would've come out here anyway if we knew the right rumor."

"Maybe Edwards' contact wasn't as trustworthy as he thought."

"This business has never been about trust." Domino leaned back sharply as Penny filled his cup.

Wicasah put his elbows on the table and leaned forward, holding the empty shot glass up to cover his mouth. He suddenly felt caged. "I don't like being lied to."

The silence stretched. Wicasah polished off his food, resisted the urge to lick the bowl, and decided he needed to sleep on the whole ordeal. Yes, the fabled flying dinosaur fossils were worth more. The few that had been uncovered had been botched—fossils broken or crumbled and only a mere outline where the remains had lain in stone. Edwards wouldn't have lied—Wicasah knew he'd have sent more resources to haul the thing back home. Maybe he'd gotten the location right, but not the source. Maybe the source had hoped they'd wing it on their own. Information changed, sure, but Domino had already cut to the chase. There was no way they could pack the wings, feet, or ribs, but the skull? That could survive on their horses. The payout would be monumental. Edwards would get his petty revenge, just in a different way.

Domino was on his third cup of coffee and looking better by the moment. Wicasah kicked back and shoved his foot up on Domino's bench. He stared at the soft glow of the electric lights above while his stomach settled. People milled in and out of the inn, apparently a surrogate bar for the locals. Hardworking men sat on the benches sharing drinks. Women swooped between bar and piano, some in dresses, some in breeches looking just as rough as the men. A girl, ten or twelve if he had to guess, rapped her knuckles on the bar and was rewarded with a dark-colored soda. She pushed her short dark hair behind her ear and sipped from a straw. Wicasah rubbed his face, scrubbing away the families that would be caught in this academic war, and figured it would be better to go home with something than nothing at all.

"Okay, we scope out the scene tomorrow. Don't look so smug, Christ."

Penny slid the bill across the table and Domino cleared his throat. "How old is this town anyways?"

Penny scrunched her face up in thought. "Got five generations of kin on my side. Older than you'd think. We were the first to get radio. Excuse me, gentlemen."

"Mean something to you, does it?" Wicasah asked as they started to stand.

I HAVE ASKED TO BE WHERE NO STORMS COME

Domino laid coins on the table. "An old town means an old cemetery. I know you and me do things differently, but I like to be a ghost in situations like these. In and out. Nobody the wiser. I'm not *just* a bone collector, you know."

"There's no way I'm body snatching in this blasted weather," Wicasah snarled. His braid lay across his shoulder, damp at the crosses.

"No way I'm walking around tomorrow in this skin. You have a steel stomach?"

Wicasah raised an eyebrow. "For the most part."

"Might want to take another shot, then." Domino grinned and called Penny back over.

———•———

Standing in front of a barely marked cemetery, Wicasah grimaced. He was wet through and through *again*. "You're really making me do this," he said and even to his own ears, he sounded outraged and prissy. He couldn't feel his toes. Even his palms had pruned.

"Don't be such a baby," Domino said, sauntering past the rickety fence like there wasn't a torrential flood happening.

The cemetery wasn't much of one, at least, not like those Wicasah rode by in other towns where white-picket fences surrounded the plots and simple crosses indicated where the bones lay. This town must have been a boomer once, especially since this graveyard was one of the hundred-year-old ones, situated on space without a view and where the unbaptized and poor were laid to rest. Potter's fields.

Domino prodded the ground with his foot, tracing the outline of rocks overcome with grass and weeds. Even so, someone had taken the time to bury this unknown person.

"Don't even think about it," Wicasah growled. There was no way he was digging through stone to get to some corpse.

Domino whispered something, a kind of hissing sibilance, and one of his familiars wiggled out from the bottom of his pant leg. The stark white creature was almost lost in the sudden monsoon of rushing water. More followed and scurried across the wet ground, away from the rock-surrounded grave. They sniffed a patch of not-so-special earth and dug in with paws before a sluice sent them tumbling down the slope. One rose and gave a silent sneeze.

Domino beamed and plodded to the spot. Pulling out a trowel, he dug into the mud. With a long-suffering sigh, Wicasah leaned down to help, but his efforts were worthless. Rain filled the hole up, mud splashed into it. Soil darkened under his nails. Finally, Domino paused and closed his eyes, concentrating hard. Above them sheet lighting lit up the sky in waves of yellow-white, outlining the clouds in a dark blue. Within that moment of light, more bone-familiars writhed and wriggled beneath Domino's skin, like insects pushing up and out of his flesh. A sudden pulse of power not his own flowed over Wicasah—almost like adrenaline, the rush of seeing someone beloved for the first time in ages. Wicasah's power stirred, responding to this call-and-answer from his performances on stage.

Another flash of lighting, but this one struck in a lone bolt of purple. The familiars birthed from Domino's skin tumbled to the ground in small rolled-up balls. They pawed the earth and, as one, sank into the mud, digging and widening a hole until they had made a pond constructed of teeming bone creatures searching for whatever Domino needed most.

The skull emerged first, slick and goopy with mud. Old hair and roots pocketed the eye sockets. Thick planks of moldy pinewood outlined the skeleton, catching the rain like a bowl and making the body float. Wicasah couldn't smell anything but the green scent of rain and lighting. The familiars gnawed at the dead man. Domino reached into the mud up to his elbows and brought out a rib.

The familiars chattered as if urging Domino to taste the exhumed treasure. Horrified, Wicasah watched Domino smell the bone, flicked his tongue out to touch the browned thing. Domino pried his fingernail into the black-mold infested marrow, cracked the bone open, and flung splinters like spears into the grave. He yanked out a crawling insect and held the thorax tight. The bug's legs waved. Thunder rumbled Wicasah's insides. The bug tried to unfurl vestigial wings, but Domino put the bug in his mouth and bit down, chewing on the insect full of decay.

Mud washed out from under Wicasah's boots and he sunk closer to the hole. Disgust filled him at Domino's brand of witchery, something that hailed from how humans first emerged from the subterranean primordial ooze. The familiars gobbled up Domino's flung splinters and faded, some sinking into the earth. Domino threw his head back and sighed as if in great relief. Wicasah looked over Domino's shoulder and felt a thrill of terror course up his spine when he caught sight of the dark figure—that standing gatherer—in the distance. Watching. The crone, so far away, might not know what was going on, but she didn't move. Wicasah imagined a reaper—too close for comfort but far enough away to be a warning. Lighting flashed again, painting the hooded figure in gray.

Wicasah grabbed Domino's arm, scared to be caught grave-robbing. He didn't want that cloaked spirit coming for them, seeing what they'd done, to damn both of them. Domino didn't feel real. His arm was too soft and yet too hard. Domino smiled at the touch, transformed into this magic-drunk man Wicasah didn't know. Wicasah knew the sober Domino, the quiet Domino, not the bold witch who craved ossification like he needed air.

"Did you get what you needed?" Wicasah hated that his voice shook. Didn't matter. *He'd never leave.*

"Yes," Domino answered as the last of the familiars climbed up his face, kissed his cheek, and with a look of satisfied peace, absorbed back into his skin.

"This better be worth it," Wicasah said. "This transformation stuff. You look the same to me."

"Gotta let it sink in," Domino said. The pulsating power emanating from him slowly seeped away, casting Domino's usually darker skin into a wan pallor.

"I think it's time we leave," Wicasah said, hating how much of a caretaker he sounded like, demeaning, as if Domino couldn't think for himself. He helped Domino stand, slung his arm over his shoulder like he had when Domino was ill and manhandled him to his horse. Wicasah took Domino's reins, guiding them at a steady trot as he navigated through the flooded plains until he finally dismounted and pushed Domino into the rented stable house. Inside, the rudimentary camp home smelled of hay and clean manure.

He built a roaring fire and ventured out again to beg a carafe of coffee from the innkeeper. Returning, he found Domino seated in front of the sliding stable doors, wrapped in blankets, watching the last of the storm. Wicasah handed him a cup and poured the black gold, smelling acidic steam. He pushed his way next to Domino. When the thunder roared, he counted the seconds, wondering if the lightning weren't thunderbirds declaring supremacy, but birthing new warriors in the sky.

Domino rubbed his side, wearing a pained frown. Wicasah glared as his own insides rolled in response, woken from his sudden and indescribable fear, and knew his shadow-hounds desired to slaughter those dangerous familiars within Domino. That's how protective he'd gotten. *Christ.*

Domino let out a quiet breath. "I can feel your magic."

Wicasah's cheeks burned. "Sorry."

"Powerful stuff." Domino sipped his coffee with a grimace.

Wicasah shrugged. He didn't want to talk about his magic, the power he'd gotten through murder. He'd never been ashamed of it, but he felt terrible speaking of the domino effect his actions had, this guilt that he was the reason for Domino's path in life.

"You should talk."

"I'll wake up a different man tomorrow," Domino said. "I'll look like that poor crook from the grave. I'll check out the dig site, get hired on as a temporary field hand. Assess the state of things. Learn the lay of the land."

"Hopefully the skull will be dug out enough to extract easily," Wicasah said.

"After tonight, it won't be anybody's priority to dig. If they didn't cover the hole, it's probably flooded."

"They covered it," Wicasah said. "No way they wouldn't."

"After that, we get in and out. Ride away as fast as possible, collect the reward. You still feel uneasy about it?"

Wicasah shifted. He did, but the money seemed too good to be true. They had disguises and the place couldn't be that secure, not after this flash flood. Maybe he would haggle for more, get them cash to really go anywhere they wanted, take a sabbatical into the mountains where he wasn't bent over by the gusts.

"We can back out," Domino said. "No harm, no foul."

"No," Wicasah said, strong in his conviction. Two days of espionage and work? He knew he could handle that much. "What am I supposed to do while you're sightseeing? Twiddle my thumbs? What's my role in this?"

"There's power in patience," Domino said.

Wicasah snorted. "Patience is bullshit."

Domino responded with a grunt, rubbed his forehead, and shut his eyes tight.

Wicasah made a questioning sound.

"Hurts," Domino responded. "Migraine."

Wicasah tutted, surprised he could sound so motherly. It figured the magic would hurt—he'd always had the bellyaches after he worked anything immense that had him heaving up bile. A weight rested against his shoulder. Domino had leaned his head down, taken Wicasah as shelter. Wicasah sat without moving, reveling in the feel, even as the thunder crashed and the horses nickered. The fire crackled behind him, the wool blanket rough against his hands. He closed his eyes and felt home.

CHAPTER 5

WAITING ADDED WEIGHT to the day and increased the situation's power, especially when Wicasah could only cool his heels until Domino returned. He'd repacked his bag, cleaned his tools, checked the dry tinder for damp, worn a hole in the floor from pacing, and took a nap. He'd never been the one to wait before.

After the storm had worn out, he'd coaxed Domino to his bedroll. He'd tended the fire, then wrapped himself in his blankets, falling into a fitful slumber. When he woke, he had a new brother—some hunchback with broad features and crooked teeth that bespoke a beggar's life. Domino had departed soon after, saying the magic wouldn't last and that he'd get hired for the day as a shovel bum to suss out the dig's status. Since he hadn't returned, Wicasah assumed Domino had struck success.

He polished his boots and sewed up holes in his clothes. It was unnaturally humid. He waited.

The day waned into afternoon. When the sun cast the plains into shades of tan and the far-off town as black against the undulating heat waves, Wicasah caught sight of a dark shape barreling toward the stable. *Domino.*

Wicasah leaned against the doorway, a stupid grin curving his lips. This was *his* Domino, not the transformed man of before. As his brother approached, he looked exhausted. Lines deepened around his mouth. Behind him, the sun became momentarily blinding, overexposing the land and showing a flash of secondary movement far off. Close enough now, Domino grabbed Wicasah by the collar and pushed him through the door.

"We have to get out of here."

"What happened?"

Domino hastily threw things into his bag. He dropped the canteens and his saddle crashed to the floor. He put his hands around his head and let out an anguished moan. Wicasah laid his hand on Domino's back, felt the knobs of his spine, and was filled with instant relief that the bone was still there. Domino's panic seeped into him, filling him with the instinct to run. He'd seen this before, this tactic to hide and become small—some life lesson Domino had picked up living with Daniel. Fury tingled his fingers. His shadow-hounds ran laps around his lungs, desperate for release. Gripping Domino's shirt, Wicasah pulled his brother upright.

"Tell me what's going on." He was surprised at how calm he sounded.

Domino looked desperate. "Let's just go, get out of here, *leave*, I didn't know . . . "

"Domino!"

A woman's voice cut Domino's pleas off. The air sizzled and Wicasah suddenly couldn't breathe—it was like inhaling hot gas straight into his lungs. Just outside the door, backed by the white sheen of sunlight, stood a redhead, her face twisted in hatred. Behind her, it looked as if the earth was splitting. Black and red lava spewed from the cracks. Flames raced across the plains, setting the grasslands on fire in bursts, hotter with each syllable she uttered, "You skinless, bastard. You *coward*."

Wicasah waited for Domino's power—for the chittering familiars eager to defend their maker—but it was as if Domino's power had been stunted. Domino's eyes rounded in sick fear, the kind a beaten dog would have. That wasn't the Domino Wicasah wanted to see—that was the Domino waiting for Daniel to come home with words that never said anything but meant everything, words that echoed with the sentiment of worthless. Seeing it again made Wicasah shake in fury. He thought he had banished that look when he pulled the trigger of a borrowed gun and sent his father's brains sliding across the trailer floor like suds spilling from a bucket.

The woman blew through the door. The wood glowed with embers. "You think you can hide from me? You think I didn't sense you when you pulled your witchery, magic gotten from Christobel—you goddamn murderer—"

Domino turned, staying in front of Wicasah. "Benedicta, please, I . . . I . . . "

Benedicta grabbed Domino's hair, pulled him to her, and

smashed her mouth against his. Domino glowed from within and instantly transformed into an ash caricature. Heat emanated from the red-haired woman, who blazed as if on fire herself. Wicasah's own conduits stirred in response. He didn't have a plan, didn't know who this bitch was, but there was no way he'd stand for her putting that look back on Domino's face.

He yanked Domino and shoved his body between them. Benedicta's fire had caught on the rest of the stable, spinning it into a roaring blaze. The horses screamed for freedom. Wicasah focused on the harpy, his shadow-hounds uncurling from inside him, shaking up his throat, ready for him to release them.

Power had been in his blood forever, part of him like the love of adrenaline and the need for open space. He'd taught it to let him be its lover, he didn't need talismans to channel it. His magic came from the source and it exploded out of his body in an effort to scare this woman senseless and evict her from their life.

He snuffed out her fire by removing all the oxygen from the room. Domino and Benedicta turned to him, their mouths open and gasping, their lungs crinkling like prunes, nearly popping from the pressure. He felt the shades of his body change, grow amorphous. His shadow stretched out in front of him, far too black and inhuman, toward the edge of the charred door where a young girl—the girl from the inn, the girl with the soda-pop—watched him with astonished terror on her face.

Benedicta stumbled back. Wicasah allowed air back into the room—this little section of the world. He'd done this before, allowed the power to be fully unleashed, and he knew if he looked up he'd see the colorful threads holding this world together. While he couldn't destroy it, he knew how to reshape it, as if building pathways and changing the structure to create new threads by severing the old ones. He could make a web if he wished, a labyrinth that would ensnare and confuse this universe with others.

"Bless the aunts," Benedicta said. "You're Wicasah."

"Who are you?" His voice sounded deeper, slightly metallic.

She bared her teeth in a smile. "I'm your sister-in-law, or didn't Domino tell you about that?"

Married? Domino?

"Did he tell you that my sister and I taught him what it meant to be in the witchery? That he used that against us, killed her and her unborn baby, and then burned the building down? Did he tell you he pissed all over my dead sister? Did he tell you that?"

Domino dropped to his knees. Wicasah's second shadow, one that spiked from the first, sheltered him. Domino put his head in his hands, keeled over, his mouth open in a silent scream.

Benedicta stepped toward Wicasah. Terror shone in her eyes, backlit with a dangerous gleam, the kind that welcomed trouble. "I'm going to make him pay for it. What do you think I could do to you to make Domino's world a hell like mine?" She reached out as if to touch Wicasah's cheek.

"Absolutely nothing," Wicasah responded. This woman was in obvious agony from her loss—but Wicasah couldn't care. She could lose everyone she loved and he wouldn't give a damn. His magic flourished across his skin, skin that had become scaled and black. His fingers were wide and far longer than they should be. "You're going to wish you'd stayed next to your sister's urn. You're going to beg me to piss on your grave if you come near me and mine again. You think this is terrifying? How would it feel if I . . . "

He reached his hand out, open-palmed, and let the shadows snake out. Benedicta's mouth twisted as the shadows wound around her body. Her face went slack. Drool slipped down her mouth. Her eyes widened and turned red while she convulsed as if in a slight seizure. Any attempt to speak came out in a slurred question.

Wicasah curled his fingers into a fist, watched the shadows tied to her body respond in kind. They wrapped like a tourniquet around Benedicta's shadow, ready to sever it, capture it, bring it back to Wicasah as a gift to join their pack. Souls didn't live on the inside, no, souls were reflected in the changing sunlight and passing hours of the day. They weren't a bright shine housed within, but a physical follower bound at the feet. Nobody remembered the shadow. No one looked at the long line of darkness and thought it was something that should be protected.

Wicasah dragged Benedicta's shadow forward, prepared to sever it from her. Ready to absorb her power and meld it with his own. Erase Benedicta, leaving only Wicasah in her wake. Her hands twitched as if trying to grasp the floating darkness of her soul. He felt her power shift to become his own, making her magic the scissors that would sever the thread, when a screech broke his concentration.

"Mama!"

The young girl. Wicasah eased the pressure around Benedicta, glanced at the tearful eyes of Benedicta's daughter. So unlike her mother in many ways, but for the hands clenched in fists.

"Let her go, don't you dare hurt her!" she cried. Soot blackened her cheeks and her spectacles slipped down her nose. Her short dark hair stood up on end, but she looked ferocious, even if she hid behind the doorframe. "Didn't you hear me? Let her go!"

Another shadow—one of many—snaked out towards the girl and prowled around her feet. Her potential thrummed against Wicasah—a fledgling witch, her shadow quivering and vulnerable, and he sensed the future spanning between them, shimmering where he might cross it. Curiosity stalled him from claiming her mother, a bare shade of what he felt for Domino unexpectedly discovered in another person.

He released the mother. Benedicta stumbled and grabbed her daughter's hand, shoved the girl forcefully behind her. The girl stared at him in disbelief as if she wanted to sit him down and pick at what made his magic tick. Benedicta backed outside and summoned a line of fire to separate them. Through the flames, his reach faded. The women fled across the grasslands until they looked like nothing more than heat mirages.

The wildfire spread quickly. Soon, he heard the screams of the town's civilians and saw them begin to fight the burn with dirt and water buckets. The grass crackled, tinder for an explosion.

Wicasah retreated into the collapsing stable. Domino curled over his knees on the floor, sobbing as if he might break, surrounded by black smoke and rapid-burning hay piles. The shadows whimpered, cooed, and reached out to bind Domino in safety. Domino jerked as the tendrils draped over him and pushed the comforting touch away. He staggered to his feet and stumbled out the door, one hand clutching his stomach. Wicasah followed, his shadows galloping ahead of him to ensure the fire didn't singe him.

Domino bent to his knees again and tangled his hands through his hair, standing it on end. Sweat and tears shone on his cheeks. He looked absolutely *done*. "I didn't kill her," he said, nearly breathless as if he'd ruined his voice. "I didn't—she fucking killed herself. She killed our unborn baby because, because . . ."

"Because why?"

"She didn't want it to be like me. Like us. She bled out and let my child die with her." Domino punched the air. "Goddamn it, she did it on purpose, she chose that, and I hate her. Wicasah, I hate her so much."

On his feet now and pacing, tension and terror seeping from him in waves, Domino shoved the shadows away from him. "I loved her." He pointed in the direction Benedicta had fled. "And look what she did to our baby. She could do anything to me, killed me, but our baby? Our child? What kind of monster does that?"

"A witch," Wicasah answered softly, far away.

Domino screamed, rubbing his arms and clutching his gut. "Maybe, but she wasn't right. That wasn't right in any possible way."

Domino let the shadows touch him then, rubbing over him and cocooning him. Wicasah had an ache in his heart, an open wound that hurt like a clenched muscle.

"I can't stand it," Domino continued. "I can't handle it. I've thought about it. When I found her, I couldn't see the baby but I felt the stillness, that stillness that shouldn't happen after the quickening. I almost killed myself. I'll do it now. I'll do it tonight."

The shadows struck. Wicasah couldn't say no to them—saying so would be saying no to himself—and he lost control at that declaration. The shadows wound around Domino's throat, sunk into his mouth to follow the blood pathways until they cradled Domino's skull in a fragile, yet incredibly strong grip, threatening to crush. Wicasah wondered how strange it must feel, to have smoke in your skull. Domino choked, the light behind his eyes flickering, a black spot darker than his pupil coloring his iris and growing.

"Don't ever do anything like that," Wicasah growled. "You can say it, you can think it, but if you dare do it, I will keep you from doing so."

The shades twisted. Domino uttered a strangled gasp of pain. Wicasah didn't care because if Domino was hurting then at least he was still alive to feel.

"I don't mind being alone," Wicasah continued. "I don't need you to promise me you'll always be by my side. I do need to know you're out there, beside me or not, and you're alive—that you're existing in the same world as me. I want it. I might not need it, but I want it like I want food or drink or love. Do you understand me? Do you?"

Domino sighed and went limp, his head bobbing in some semblance of an agreement. Wicasah realized he'd grown into the heavens, taller than a giant and reaching the sky that was darker and lit with lightning. A beast for the beauty of this world. He released Domino and his brother crumpled to the ground, stared up at Wicasah with the same sublimity as the girl had earlier.

Domino reached out and touched the claws on Wicasah's feet. "I did good with you," he whispered. "I did good for you."

Wicasah's insides felt loose like he'd lost the tightness that made him grow. He began to shrink and brought himself back down to this realm where the colorful ties binding the world together didn't surround him, didn't flirt with him to play and transform them. He remained Wicasah—still monstrous, still shadowed—but Domino pulled him into an embrace, wings and scales and all.

Domino shook. Wicasah wondered if it had to do with what he had done, but he couldn't feel remorse. He had Domino again in the right way—alive in his hands, depressed and suicidal, but those things could be handled with therapy, love, and the healing kind of medication. He could handle that. He could deal with that.

Wicasah might be a powerful witch, but he couldn't summon gold from air. He needed money for the things Domino needed. With all this chaos, it would be easy for them to snatch the thunderbird skull and get the hell out of dodge. He grabbed Domino's shoulder and pulled back, ready to impart this new plan, but Domino's face twisted in a way that bespoke agony. He gripped his stomach tighter. His legs gave out. Wicasah yelled Domino's name as he caught his brother, but Domino felt loose and pliable in his arms. Domino malformed, as if his inner integrity had melted. He convulsed, mouth open in a wordless scream. His teeth disintegrated to dust, leaving gums striped pink and black.

Wicasah couldn't think, rendered immobile with shock. All of Domino's bones disappeared at once, leaving him jelly-like and limp, a long bloated body. A terrible pop filled Wicasah's ears and blood sputtered out of Domino's mouth. Wicasah screamed and screamed, but he didn't know where the bones went, didn't know how to heal, and he could only watch as Domino became mush. Domino convulsed, his face a deformed mass, lost in nothing but his own agony. Wicasah didn't know when it happened, only that Domino became still and that stillness lasted for minutes. No matter how long Wicasah cried out his brother's name, Domino didn't move. His eyes didn't flicker. Grease dribbled out of his ear.

A sharp poke in his chest and Wicasah drew back, blinking back tears, desperate to not look at where his hands had crushed Domino's arms into bruised pulp. A sharp jagged stick stuck out of Domino's flattened chest. A thin spear. It glowed and pulsed for a moment, illuminating an unknown language inscribed on it. Wicasah reached out to touch it but the hatred emanating from it made him hesitate. It was smeared with the scent of a witch. *Benedicta.* Somehow, she'd cast magic on Domino and killed him. He grabbed the spear—a fossil sharpened to a point—and yanked it out. Holding it white-knuckled, the pulse faded.

Wicasah gathered the remains of his brother to him and keened, clasping the spear until it cut his hand. The shadows released, chasing across the badlands to taste the direction she had fled. She had awoken the monster and taken it from him. There was no mercy within him.

CHAPTER 6

WICASAH TRIED TO bury what was left of Domino, but the ground had become char. In the end, he left Domino in the middle of nowhere under the blue sky, a lone tree on the endless plains, and shovelfuls of tanned earth that wouldn't grow a flower. The spear remained wrapped and hidden from sight in his satchel.

Shuffling back to the half-collapsed stable with a stone foundation streaked with black, he stroked the scorched hide of his fallen horses. His mustang appeared stiff, yet fragile, curved in from the heat. Exposed sooty bones. Lips pulled back to show yellowed teeth. Wicasah whispered condolences for not thinking of the horse's well-being as his world collapsed around him.

He tried to touch his grief, but it remained too deep and numb. Wandering back into town, he swiped items from those mourning the loss of their homes as the town burned to charcoal and headed out aimlessly into the prairie. The soft down of revenge began to warm the shocked numbness inside him, allowing him to nurse dreams of killing Benedicta in graphic ways. Soon, he succumbed to the magnetic pull of Domino's grave where he lingered until hours turned to days and days turned to weeks. Maybe he was cursing the place. Haunting it, pacing underneath the hot sun, until he wondered if he might become a shade himself.

Finally, he walked away, got a mile out, and fell to his knees. The high grass undulated around him like the ocean. His hand clenched in a fist against his heart. He didn't know where to go. What to do. He toyed with the idea of returning to Crazy Mary, but he wasn't sure he could bear her pity. Internally, he turned to face the villain of his loss, recognize it, accept it, try and move on.

He couldn't. The pain in his hand from where the fossil had sliced him throbbed. Benedicta had passed him her vengeance, killing one sibling to avenge another. Now, it was his turn. No other purpose existed beyond finding her and wiping the world clean of her.

His shadows released then, and he removed any filter so he would be able to see the real world unbound from mortal constraints. Flickering fireflies of creation floated around him. His shadows looped around the bobbing pinpricks, racing across the plains like streaks of night, searching for any scent of the woman that had almost become one of them. Perhaps they'd find her family. Perhaps he'd torture them all.

Looking down, he realized he'd transformed again, become a giant sitting with legs outspread in a field with fairy-lights dancing around him. He folded his wings and lowered his head, his claws clasped in his lap, and let his sorrow seep into the earth, wilting the grass as if from a frost.

The shadows returned at the edge of dusk with their offering. Benedicta had scrubbed her magical residue as clean as any hospital. Wicasah pet a shadow in his despair, seeking comfort, until it rolled over and explained it *had* found something else. A spotlight of power stronger than anything felt before, living at the edge of the Dark and Bloody. Wicasah queried, skeptical. After all, the last time he'd let the shadows full reign to search for Domino when he was young, they'd come back yammering about things that didn't exist, confused and forgetful of their initial mission. They had been so untrained, then.

The Dark and Bloody, they chirped now, circling him. *The Dark and Bloody.*

He looked over his shoulder, seeing the interconnected strings of color sway and bounce, trying to understand their legend and navigate to where that great dividing chasm might lay. The wind cooled his face, smelling like a goal. A direction.

Walking as a giant, he could cover ground much faster. No hitchhiking dirt roads. His strides ate up acres. He'd never gone so long with his shadows unbound, never let them scoot through the golden and rainbow threads of this world without a short leash. Yet they had been good, they'd earned it, and he needed to reach the Dark and Bloody in a hurry. The earth groaned under his weight. The land looked like a patchworked geological blanket below him. The shadows circled and bounced around him.

Show me the way, he told them. *Show me the way.*

———◆———

Somewhere in the middle of the great plains, the earth stopped supporting him. Each footstep left huge indentations in the ground. He slipped, felt as if he climbed mountains of sand. He called the shadows to him, and they reluctantly obeyed. Gathering them inside himself, he shrunk down to human size and swayed, unbalanced as if he'd plopped into a world that tilted the wrong way on its axis.

The dehydrated earth created cups out of the dirt, and they crunched as he picked his way across them. Old wagon and car tracks crisscrossed the surface, age-old markings that hadn't eroded. Stumps where trees and shrubs once grew stuck out as bleached landmarks. The ground rumbled under his feet as if wondering whether to collapse into a sinkhole. He squinted, wondering how fast a man could perish from heatstroke. Mirages undulated in front of him as if marking the long length of the abyss that waited beyond.

Without anything to think about beyond putting one foot in front of the other, his grief continued to thaw. Wicasah slumped, wondering how many invisible chains he dragged behind him. Tears clouded his vision. He couldn't stand the agony festering inside his heart, and he finally understood what his father went through when his mother was killed.

In the distance, a rounded shape began to take form—a yurt, the only dwelling he'd seen for miles. Beside it extended the chasm, a black rip in the country that only miners knew how far it descended. Wicasah's mouth dropped and he bypassed the yurt with its promises of rest to stand at the edge of the Dark and Bloody and marvel. Like a river, it scribbled into the horizon. He couldn't see to the other side. He imagined the quake that had parted the land, couldn't quite wrap his mind around how cities toppled into the deep, people scrambling for solid ground while cars and manicured lawns tumbled into the hole.

"Magnificent, isn't it?"

Wicasah jumped at the voice that came from behind him and he took a startled step closer to the edge. Pebbles crumbled over. For a brief moment, he imagined falling and watching the last shred of bright blue sky become a pinpoint. Would he scream? Or would he sigh, grateful for the darkness closing around him?

Shuddering, he backed away from the chasm and to the side of the woman who had spoken, standing beside him. He shaded his eyes. A magnitude of power towered over him, like facing a tornado and basking in its intensity before being swept away. The woman's arms crossed in front of her, but they looked bulky, her face on the side of too masculine, and Wicasah discovered with a slight shimmer of disbelief that the speaker was male, too. He straightened and gave a nervous bow of his head. He'd heard of two-spirits before, but couldn't say such a word out loud. It didn't belong to him, he didn't have the culture or history to use it, but what else could he identify this person as? Words had power and weight and all the ones Wicasah wanted to utilize weren't his.

"What do you think of it?" the woman asked, and Wicasah grappled for a pronoun, settling on *him*, but always knowing in the back of his mind that that wasn't quite correct.

"It's . . . like seeing your own death," Wicasah answered.

"Isn't that exhilarating?" The woman scooted closer to the edge and looked over. "What could be down there? A revitalized civilization? The land of the dead, perhaps?"

Wicasah's heart sang. "Do you think that's possible?"

"You've heard the trope."

He smiled.

"Anything is."

Wicasah licked his lips, unsure what to say, suddenly realizing he didn't know what he wanted beyond the basic who, what, where, and when.

"Were you the one who sent the spirits to come see me?" the woman asked. "Kind things. Like gentle coyotes."

"Yes," Wicasah managed, astounded that his shadows could be considered *kind*. "I'm trying to find someone who doesn't want to be found. They led me out here."

"Maybe you should stop looking, then."

Wicasah shook his head. "I have something of hers. I don't know what it is—a piece of . . . of magic, maybe. Can you help me?"

The woman paused, his hands tightening around each other. Wicasah balanced on a pinpoint, suddenly realizing he had a 50/50 shot of being denied. Hope twisted his stomach—the opportunity to not only find Benedicta at his fingertips but the chance to learn how this person knew about his shadows and didn't balk at the use of magic in normal conversation.

"Come inside." The woman gestured to his yurt. "I welcome the company."

Hope soared. He offered a small smile of thanks and felt his parched lips crack. The two-spirit held the hide-flap open and Wicasah hunched to fit inside. The sudden darkness blinded him and his eyes shut tight, inhaling the scent of leather and sage. He imagined sleeping in that darkness, curled up tight with blankets heavy over him.

A touch on the small of his back guided him into the dwelling. Embers glowed in an open fire pit in the middle of the room, the smoke snaking out the hole in the ceiling. A small child standing next to the stone circle tossed an ember back and forth between his hands. Her hands. *It*. Again, a surge of power washed over him. While the woman's power felt familiar—simply bigger and more powerful than his—this child's magic saturated the room, was something that could only have been pulled from the Dark and Bloody. It was that unknown, terrifying, and deep.

Face sloppily painted white. Eyelids and lips blackened. A shirt stitched haphazardly together out of scraps of cloth covered the child's potbelly. The shadows in Wicasah's stomach stilled like a predator might when in the presence of big prey.

The woman sat down cross-legged, pulling the child into a half-hug, and motioned for Wicasah to sit across from him. Wicasah did, feeling an ache take up behind his knees, finally understanding that his mind might be outracing his grief, but his body wouldn't be able to keep up for much longer without rest. He craved water. Inside, he felt a nauseous twist as a shade writhed up his throat, perching on his tongue behind his teeth as if waiting to strike. It tasted moist, like rain-filled mist on the horizon, light as cotton candy.

"I am All-Worlds," the woman said.

Wicasah licked his lips, grateful the woman had offered his name first. "Wicasah," he said.

"Wicasah," All-Worlds said slowly as if tasting the syllables. "Let me see this medicine of yours."

Wicasah pulled the spear from his pouch and unwrapped it. Still cradled in cloth, he handed it to All-Worlds. The woman brought the spear to his nose and sniffed it, his tongue darting out to taste it. Wicasah's heart ached. All-Worlds made a disgusted sound and handed the spear to the child, who twirled it around in her—*his, their*—hands without fear.

"Her name is Benedicta," Wicasah said. The child took the spear into their mouth and smiled widely around it. Wicasah tried not to grimace.

"It's a stinging fossil," All-Worlds said, watching the child. "A spell with evil intent."

"It killed my brother."

"An intent to kill a witch."

The unasked question lingered in the air, but he refused to elaborate. Wicasah didn't know this powerful woman, didn't know who or what he represented. Cautious inklings rose on the nape of his neck. He sat up straighter, alerting the rest of his shadow-hounds in case of attack. The shade in his mouth maintained a stillness that unnerved him.

"I can taste the soul on it," the child said. "I think I shepherded this one into Helia."

A cold rush of terror slithered down Wicasah's spine. The child must have misspoken because Wicasah had heard of hell, but to him, it was nothing more than a scaredy-cat story paired with the simple crosses of wooden chapels—something to make money at carnivals. Instantly, he remembered the bright lights, the dramatics he liked to do for the attention, the way Domino always had stage fright because he was so nervous one of them would fuck up. It'd never been more to him than that—no religious pandering of afterlife torture gave him a second thought, but now he wondered if it could be true and if everything he'd learned was a lie and somewhere deep in the pits, a demon was peeling off Domino's skin.

"The fossil killed him and sent his spirit to hell?"

"The spell only murdered him. Your brother was never destined to find his ancestors after the damage he'd done to his soul to become a witch," All-Worlds tutted.

"You don't know that," Wicasah said, his voice low. "Domino was a good person. He should be at peace."

"There's no peace in Helia for humans," the child said. "He's wandering the desert until he goes insane, or until he lets the dust erode him. He'll do anything down there. Maybe he's whoring—you can make a pretty penny with witch's blood."

The shadow in Wicasah's mouth struck. It dove into the child's chest, intent on strangling *their* shadow, bringing it out for Wicasah to devour. His shade bored deeper, seeking, until a sudden pain lanced, traveling from the shadow directly to him. He arched his back and wheezed. His shade cowered inside the child, suddenly surrounded by hundreds upon hundreds of shades all ripping into him, shredding him with nails sharp as knives. Wicasah screamed as his shadow turned to ribbons and was slurped up by those inside the child. The child's shadows reached to Wicasah, expressed as hands that encircled his body and rendered him motionless. They reached down his throat. He choked, gagged, as he was invaded. The hands gathered his shadows in their palms and squeezed until they begged. Wicasah thrashed, but it only strung his body further into stinging pain.

"You think these souls are yours? Come death, they'll all be mine," the child said. The hands squeezed tighter. Wicasah was sure his lungs would pop. Tension tight as piano strings convulsed in his throat and he wondered, fleetingly, if he'd ruined his vocal cords. "I shuffled your brother's soul into the dark and I'll splatter yours next to him."

The pain receded. Wicasah was strung in a momentary seizure before he collapsed. The shadows inside him—chaotic and bruised—tumbled as they tried to hide. He couldn't protect them or reassure them, not when the aftermath felt just as agonizing as the torture. It was a long time before he could sit back up again. Before he could speak.

"What are you?" he gasped.

The child rubbed his belly as if they'd just had a wonderful meal.

"What are *you?*" All-Worlds responded. "Where are you from? Where are your people?"

Wicasah thought he might vomit. How could he explain that he'd never known who or what his mother was? He didn't know what culture lived in his veins or where his shadows hailed from. Ever since he offered to the witchery, like his mother and her mother before her, he had no tribe. No culture. Nothing but evil in his veins, his past a land of smoke.

"Another mutt," All-Worlds said, looking to the child. "That makes this all the more difficult. This is a heyoka, a psychopomp taller than their shadow."

"A guide?" Wicasah asked, finally sitting up. The flames twirled in circles and the yurt seemed to spin. He focused on the child—*heyoka*—and tried to quell the terror turning his bowels to water.

All-Worlds nodded. "She's sorry for being rash, but you did attack first."

The heyoka only smiled.

"Did you mean what you said?" Wicasah asked, another sort of fear taking the place of his terror. "Where is my brother?"

"He's where all the other darkened souls go. Into the desert," the heyoka said. "I watched the funnel steal him."

All-Worlds made a disapproving hiss. The heyoka stroked his hair, whispering, "He's strong."

"Strong in revenge, strong in anger, strong in deceit," All-Worlds snapped.

"Spin his stinging spear," the heyoka said.

All-Worlds took the spear and tossed it into the fire. Wicasah cried out in alarm, but the spear floated above the flames. With a pointed finger, All-Worlds sent the spear spinning like a bottle. Wicasah held his breath, mesmerized. The heyoka put a hand on All-Worlds shoulder, her eyes soulless in the reflected light. The spear spun and spun. Firelight began to trace along its shaft, illuminating carved words of power like the hidden markings of beetles underneath bark. The symbols lit for a brief ember-bright moment before stuttering and fading. The spear hovered, as if deciding, but the brightness went completely out. The spinning halted and All-Worlds grabbed the fossil before it dropped into the fire.

"I'm sorry," he said. "The magic has been wiped from it. The witch who crafted it must have scoured her trace from the world. This remnant cannot pick up her location."

Wicasah wanted to howl. "Is there any way to find her?"

"Unless she uses her magic again, no."

"She has to use it again at some point. The spear can point to her when she does, can't it?"

All-Worlds fiddled with the spear. "The magic is a part of her, so it would be able to detect its master, but I won't spend my time spinning stingers for a mutt who only wants to make this world worse with his revenge."

Wicasah's gripped one of the rocks of the fire ring, scorching his hands. "What of Domino? What stole his soul? Why . . . why isn't he somewhere good?"

"Witches get what they deserve," All-Worlds said. "They make choices with consequences. They will never be reunited with their people."

"I have made an offering to the witchery," Wicasah said. "Will I go to the same place?"

"Yes," All-Worlds said.

"That's not fair," Wicasah said, his throat clogging up. He closed his eyes, but his tears still fell. "I was a child. I didn't know any better. I did it to save my brother—to save myself."

"You want to know what another strong witch like you did? A good man with good intentions and a bad past? Come outside."

All-Worlds left the yurt, the heyoka's hand clasped in his. Wicasah dragged himself to his feet, and followed the two out, stood beside them next to the Dark and Bloody.

"The last witch I knew did this," All-Worlds said. He cast his arms wide, chanting in a language Wicasah didn't understand. A multi-colored web appeared in front of him, the thin hairlike threads reaching out across the land as far as the eye could see and converging together to create a funnel. The crisscrossing mess extended into the Dark and Bloody like a covered slide, shimmering with the changing light and color.

"What is this?" Wicasah asked, feeling breathless and beaten.

"Do you know what a black hole is?" All-Worlds asked.

Wicasah only shook his head, his mouth open.

"It's a place with such a strong force that not even light can escape. It can bend time and destroy you before you had time to think. A witch—a good man, my man—stood out here in the middle of what once used to be a city and opened this black hole. He flung himself off the side because something terrible had happened to him and he wanted to make sure something equally awful happened to the living. He didn't want to hurt the earth, but he wanted to hurt the people. This black hole shuffles souls deep into the Dark and Bloody and spits them out somewhere souls shouldn't go."

All-Worlds took in a ragged breath. "Your brother might—*might*—have been destined for the starry road or heaven or whatever afterlife you believe, but that won't happen. Not while this funnel is here. It steals souls from the psychopomps. The Milky Way is probably a forgotten deer trail by now."

"They're going to hell?" Wicasah asked. "That's what you called it. That's what you said."

"I don't know for sure. I haven't died yet. From what I know, it's a terrible, desperate land."

"Helia," the heyoka corrected. "It's a beautiful place, really, once you take it in. Beautiful people."

Wicasah turned to the heyoka. "You've been there?" he asked. "I thought you said nothing could get out of the funnel."

The heyoka looked uncomfortable and fidgeted. "I'm a guide. I can move between realms."

"Then you can get people out."

The heyoka shook her head.

"Yes, you can," Wicasah pressed. His want saturated the air and if he said it, uttered the farfetched dream of bringing his brother back, it wouldn't be allowed.

"You're thinking so small. Some souls *should* go there—souls go wherever their next life takes them. A soul is dead—they know they are dead. Finding one among so many would be like finding a needle in a haystack. Nearly impossible. Bringing them back would mean making them remember life—what it means to be alive. Erasing the knowing of what comes after and taking them back to ignorance. It's magic I do not possess."

"Who has magic to do such things?"

All-Worlds put his hands on his forehead. "When I invited you into my home I did not expect it would create this much trouble."

"Who?" Wicasah asked again, pinpointing the heyoka. His shadows stirred and peeked out, still cautious, but seemingly interested in their witch's surge of hope.

"It wouldn't be just one entity," the heyoka sounded out slowly, looking sly. "The native folk of the land—demons to you, for lack of a better term in one so invested with your crossed-god's imagery—would be willing to help if you made the right offer. The other part, making a body for the soul to come back to, would depend on what kind of creature would answer the call for that kind of job."

"Help me contact them," Wicasah said. "I'll help you do anything. A witch made this? I'll help you close it."

All-Worlds clasped his hands and went incredibly still. "It's not our place to change the world."

"We would be putting it right again! We can't leave the souls there. They don't belong there. Domino doesn't belong there. Your man doesn't belong there. They shouldn't even *be* there."

The silence stretched.

"Set up a meeting. I'll find a way. I'll pray every night for something to help me. I'll learn everything from you. Please, help me."

"You'll have to master that ability to go into hell," the heyoka said. "The ability to pass through worlds."

"I already see how they're made up. These strands? I see them everywhere. I can reshape them. You want me to close the Dark and Bloody? I will."

All-Worlds looked stunned. "That's impossible."

"If you don't help me, I'll make my own hole into Helia."

The shadows inside him fluttered like wild butterflies. Wicasah realized he had grown, turned monstrous again. The earth creaked beneath him. The shadows spun out like ropes, licked along the webs, and pinged them, making the funnel hum as if plucking the strings of a guitar. All-Worlds' eyes widened in fear and awe.

"He looked like a demon," the heyoka said as she approached Wicasah. All-Worlds said something in a different language, but the heyoka raised her hand for silence. Madness danced in her eyes, a kind of reckless abandon that would have made him think twice if he didn't have images of Domino's suffering playing on an endless loop in his mind. The heyoka bid him to kneel. Wicasah did so. She put her hands around his roughened face, fitting her hands around the horns on his forehead.

All-Worlds shouted something, but his voice was far away. Wicasah wouldn't listen to him anyway—he wasn't about to lose his brother to an afterlife of agony. The heyoka wanted to help him if perhaps to only see what happened, but Wicasah didn't care about her motives. Magic he didn't understand surrounded him, but he could learn. He'd do anything to ease this pain.

"Think of the soul you want to find. Think on him. Tell me about him," the heyoka said.

A small hook pierced something inside him. A strange power that was not his own pressed against his brain. His shadows fought back uselessly, wrapping around the invisible hook as if to dislodge it. The heyoka grinned. Blood stained her teeth.

"Tell me about him," she urged. "Tell me the truth."

The hook tugged. Wicasah's mouth opened, his voice deeper from the magic inside him, and was surprised at what he said. "My brother is stupid. He thinks everything is his fault. He won't defend himself except against idiotic slander—a quip uttered accidentally, some pitiful come-at-me words. He's a good man. He did everything for me. He raised me."

The heyoka frowned. "Not good enough." She sounded older than she looked. Her childish face matured, nothing but a ruse. Whatever mask she wore, underneath she was powerful and ancient.

The hook tugged harder, pierced something meaty. The shadows spun, terrified. He felt raw and exposed, the hook ripping out things he'd never say or fully acknowledge.

"I should've acted faster," he said, hating that he sounded on the edge of tears. "I should've killed Daniel sooner. I should've protected Domino more than he protected me, but . . . but at the same time I *shouldn't* have."

Wicasah gasped for breath as if drowning. "I shouldn't have because it damned me. Even after Daniel died, we were separated and he left me—Domino left me—and didn't come find me. He had a wife instead, had a child instead, but he was supposed to protect me, even though it was my turn to protect him. See, I was supposed to make up for lost time, but he didn't come back and when I finally found him again, he left me. He left me."

Wicasah hated the ugliness, hated how he'd become a toddler again, the one he'd been one gruesome witch-burning night when the smell of gasoline made him ill and the rain brought on nightmares. He'd woken alone in a bed in a rented room, his father's snores filling his ears, and he'd realized he'd been abandoned. He'd sat in front of the door, waiting while the rain pounded, waiting to be remembered, angry that he had to be found again.

The heyoka breathed as if smelling something good and released her hold. Wicasah fell on hands and knees. He was full of all those contradictions and conflicting regrets. Back to human, his grief sharpened like a knife. The hook had flayed him open and he spilled out all the hurt and abandonment, everything he was too scared to know.

"I have a scent." The heyoka laughed. She turned and ran for the Dark and Bloody, reaching out to swing into the funnel, and disappeared in a flash of lighting.

Wicasah felt a hand on his shoulder and blindly grasped the offered hand. "I want him back," he sobbed. "It's all my fault and I want him back."

"Come inside," All-Worlds said, compassion softening his voice. "Come inside, little witch. Let's let you sleep. You've made a strange bargain with the heyoka, and she had taken something precious from you."

<hr>

Wicasah sat cross-legged on the edge of the Dark and Bloody and spun the spear again. It wound aimlessly until momentum failed and it fell once more to gravity's whims. Wicasah flicked his finger, sending the fossil circling like a compass needle. He sighed. The smell of roasting hare wafted from the yurt. Wicasah had caught the creature in a small trap and skinned it hours ago. All-Worlds had said he enjoyed the cooking work and chased Wicasah outside where he'd remained, spinning the spear and letting the sun bake his skin.

Months had passed since the heyoka had disappeared with Wicasah's memories in her pouches. In that time, Wicasah had become someone he wasn't sure he liked—bedridden with a depression he couldn't shake. All-Worlds had been kind, but each day revenge was the reason Wicasah roused from the pallet. He'd forced himself to take jobs: going to the closest trade post for goods, hunting, and mastering what magic All-Worlds would teach him. He spun the spear every day with hope. He plucked the shimmering web of the Dark and Bloody, wondering if the strands wrapped around the whole world were part of the makings of the universe. Wondered if the bottom of the Dark and Bloody was the soothing coolness of a dark cave padded with skeletons.

He prayed every night as if tacking a job posting on wood pillars in the imagined cities of gods that read: *Searching for a deity who can create a body. Specifically, Domino's body. Will pay in advance whatever's fair.* He amplified his prayer with magic, casting his shadows out into the world with one motivation—find mighty help.

The spear faltered again. Wicasah picked up the fossil and wrapped it in leather. He touched his heart, still raw where the heyoka hook had cleaved him. It hadn't healed. Maybe it never would. Maybe he'd always feel like his emotional guts were on the verge of spilling out.

He waited for his stomach to grumble; for anything to move in the desert heat. He didn't want to go back into the yurt where the blackness was a cradle that lulled him with the chance to grieve. Wicasah realized he wasn't a soul meant for revenge, but his dreams were harsh, especially the ones where he felt Domino's bones melting under his hands.

He'd been thinking about that for a while now—*loss*. About how if he could do everything right, cast aside the grief when he got Domino's soul back and found someone strong enough to craft Domino's body, he'd still be looking over his shoulder for Benedicta. Given the chance, she'd kill Domino all over again. The terror raking over him was a twin sister to his terror of Daniel. Of Daniel's rage anchored to Domino, how when Daniel looked at his oldest with that glare, Wicasah knew in the pit of his stomach something was going to happen, something that would rip away what Wicasah held dear.

He couldn't take that chance. If Wicasah had played his cards right, he could've had Domino beside him now. They could be looking into the rainbow web of the Dark and Bloody together and cheering to the insanity of the world. That was why he couldn't give up on revenge. More like an insurance policy, at this point. Domino couldn't exist in a world where Benedicta lived, because she would try to murder him a second time, reigniting the same cycle.

His hand ached from holding the stinging fossil so tight. He unwrapped it and tossed it to the ground again. It stopped, hovering for a moment before spinning like it would never stop. Wicasah tried to stopper his tears. He bent to pick it up again, but the spear ground to a halt like a bird dog that had caught a scent, quivering in the direction of south. Scarcely believing it, triumph engulfed him. *He had her.*

He grabbed the spear bare-handed and marched into the yurt. He was suddenly more alive than he'd ever been. The urge was back in his bones. The first step to finding Domino was to eliminate any other threat that would come for him.

All-Worlds looked up at him from the cook fire, eyebrows arched in question.

"I've got her." Wicasah sounded breathless.

All-Worlds eyebrows furrowed. "She used her magic?"

"The spear gave a direction. I can find her now."

All-Worlds shook his head and turned the hare on the spit. "You shouldn't."

"Why wouldn't I?"

"What do you have to gain? You're already doing what many cannot. What need do you have for revenge?"

"Who's to say she won't kill him again?"

"It's not right. Your obsession with resurrection."

"What's not right is having my brother die right in front of my eyes. *In my arms.* He did nothing wrong. He didn't deserve to be murdered."

All-Worlds let out an astounded chuckle. "It's always like that with you witches. You get so wrapped up in your own that you don't see anything beyond it. Domino clouds your judgment. Your thinking."

"Who's to say that? Because I think differently than you? I care for someone so much that I'm damned because of it. What do you think you could accomplish with that kind of love?"

All-Worlds backed away, and Wicasah knew he'd hit true. He couldn't let up. Not when this was on the line.

"I know exactly what you'd do with that kind of love. Your man made the Dark and Bloody. Were you helping him? Stopping him? Where were you when he hurt so bad he felt he had to do that? If that's your kind of love—sitting on the sidelines—I don't even want to fathom it."

All-Worlds rose, but his shoulders hunched. Wicasah felt the undertone of barely-controlled power, strong enough that it would destroy him. He didn't care—he remembered what the heyoka had said. If he died, he'd end up splattered in Helia. At least he'd have friends there.

"Your man was like me," Wicasah said, reckless with his words. "You'd do anything to get him back, wouldn't you? Or are you too concerned for the world's equilibrium to make that sacrifice?"

"Don't speak to me of things you don't understand, witch," All-Worlds snarled. "I've earned respect. I have walked this earth long before you. I know of love and hate. Tell me, when you're asked to sacrifice yourself, how much do you value Wicasah over Domino?"

Wicasah wondered if the floor was going to evaporate and seal him beneath the earth. He bit his lip. "I know my worth."

All-Worlds laid a gentle hand against Wicasah's cheek. Wicasah realized he was picking at scars All-Worlds already knew were there. They hadn't been easy with each other, but something quivered between them—respect, a shared sorrow, companionship in an empty land.

"You're old enough to have walked the future," All-Worlds said. "Didn't you see the warnings there? The messages?"

Wicasah closed his eyes and remembered the older Wicasah, broken to collapse. The look of hope and awe on his face. "Yes."

"And is this still the path your future-self would have wanted you to take? To kill this woman? Will revenge make things better?"

"It will make me feel safer," Wicasah said. Acknowledging it filled him with relief. He pulled away from All-Worlds and saw the tears shining in his eyes.

"You know your path," All-Worlds said. "It's pointless to sing new songs to witches when you're enamored with the sound of your own voice."

"I'll fulfill the promises I've made," Wicasah said. "I'll make this world safe for Domino to come back to."

All-Worlds' hand fell away. "The world doesn't have to end in flames."

"Then why does it seem like everything's doused in gasoline?" Wicasah said.

He walked out of the yurt and transformed with each step into the monster he was under the flesh. His footsteps sounded like thunder as he traversed the starving land to find the woman he planned to kill.

CHAPTER 7

THE BURNING LIGHT emitting from the fossil spear shone like an electric spotlight. It quivered near Wicasah's outstretched hand, pointing to the front door of a darkened townhouse. Behind him, cookie-cutter homes lined the pavement street. Wicasah plucked the fossil and covered it, dousing the light. He picked his way around to the back and climbed the cheap chain-link fence.

He knew next to nothing about Benedicta, but he knew she couldn't resist using her magic. He'd lost her scent somewhere while crossing the plains and spent a month twiddling his thumbs in some railroad town. Once the stinging fossil spun and pointed, though, the off-and-on trend continued. The fossil led him in a zigzag down the country, the frequency increasing with the passing year. She must have felt safer, figured him for a passion-of-the-moment kind of man who would let time heal his wounds. He couldn't wait to laugh in her face.

In passing, his mind wandered old paths to relive nighttime fears: that the heyoka had lied, that his chance to find Domino disappeared with All-Worlds. Sometimes, he wondered if he'd gone mad with the waiting. Then, the fossil would catch a direction again, and it would be back, the hope, the remembrance of relief, the knowledge that the threat would be eliminated.

He snuck through the townhouse's back entrance, bypassing a small square foot of a yard that had been overrun with clay pots and a sagging laundry line. He picked the lock and eased into the kitchen. Silently, he padded his way over the tiled floor into a hallway that opened up into a parlor looking out into the front street. A nice home, but by no means a rich one. A green slim-cut coat draped over a coat rack. Shoes—high heels and boots with bows—were heaped together. The stairs creaked as he ascended them.

Upstairs split into another hallway with a study and half-closed bedroom on one side and the master bedroom on the other end. Adrenaline pumped through him as he slunk towards the larger door. A purse sat on a small bench beside the stairway. Perfume wafted around him. He was used to dust, fresh air, and sunlight, not the distilled bottled remnants of flower petals. His shadows lingered against his tongue, eager for violence.

His hand rested on the doorknob, prepared to open it, when the door yanked opened and Benedicta, clothed in a nightgown, stood in front of him. His heart stilled in the spare moment before she uttered a high-pitched screech and raised her hand. Fire shot from her palms.

Wicasah dodged to the side as the wallpaper scorched into ember curls behind him. He unleashed his shadows. A second ring of fire exploded from Benedicta and Wicasah barely managed to roll away from each burning bolt. The wooden floor beneath him glowed red-hot, searing his feet and clothes. His shadows reared back as the flame shot through them, dissipating momentarily in lifeless smoke. He gritted his teeth—this witch had obviously learned new tricks.

Billowing smoke obscured his vision, stung his eyes, but his shadows finally landed a strike, causing a gurgled cry from Benedicta. His lungs ached with each breath. The floorboards groaned. He rose and let his rage flood him, let the transformation begin. He cast his shadows out again, felt them strike and grab an ankle. Benedicta screamed as he yanked her back through the wall of flames to him. She rolled onto her back and put ember-pulsating hands into his eyes.

He bellowed, reared away from her, and heard a crack just before the floor gave way. Wicasah clipped his leg on the stairway as they crashed to the ground floor, landing in a heap of smoldering ruins. Benedicta scrambled out from under him, kicking him in the face as she sprinted for the front door, and Wicasah growled, pouncing after her.

"What the hell is going on here—*Benedicta!*"

"Holy shit, Mom!"

Wicasah's head snapped up to look for the distracting voices. A bespeckled man stood over the hole in the floor and a girl—that short-haired pixie—crouched over the jagged ruins. Wicasah snarled and launched for them, knowing that if Benedicta felt anything, it would be for her family.

Sudden pain raced through his shoulder. He rolled to see Benedicta pull out a sharpened shaft from his body. Her arm arched to stab him again, but his shadows whipped out, caught her across the stomach, and sent her flying. She hit the wall with a thick thump. The father and daughter above cried out in distress. Black blood smoked from his wound. Wicasah grimaced, crawled to his feet even as Benedicta shot another blaze of fire at him.

He smelled burned flesh, realized huge patches of his scales had crisped back to expose angry pink skin. He leapt for her as her mouth opened, shouting words that engulfed the whole house in flames. Fire licked at Wicasah, charred a second layer of skin until he resembled a walking meat monster. Blood smoked from him. Heat threatened to boil his eyes. Agony in each step. Screams echoed behind him and he knew she had damned her own husband and child, leaving them in a collapsing townhouse pyre. His shadows writhed, but obeyed like hunting dogs to his call, baying at the moon and wrestling Benedicta to the ground. They wrapped around her, held her in a seizure-like form. She choked. It wouldn't be like before—no, Wicasah wanted it to be quick and violent. His shadows dove inside her, ripped the shadow rooted in her soul like pulling a weed, and shook the earth to ensure nothing of it remained.

Her blood-red shadow arched within Wicasah's shades' grasp, but they brought their new sister back to him. He devoured her, shredding the shadow with his teeth as her remaining magic burned his lips into bubbles and made them curl back into a rictus grin.

The rush was incredible. His head sank back and he shivered, barely realizing he might die in this house going up like tinder. Benedicta's body dropped, limp. The fire licked her skin and caused her to curl up like a piece of flash paper. He spotted his bones peeking through his charred muscle. He was hurt. Stumbling to his feet, he lurched through the broken doorway and staggered into the fresh air. His foot caught and he tripped, landing on his shoulder. The impact jarred him.

Shrieks and jumbled chatter cut through his shock. Citizens, those with water buckets and those standing far enough away from the blaze to remain safe, stared at him, horrified.

"What the fuck is that?"

"Kill it! For the love of god, kill it!"

I HAVE ASKED TO BE WHERE NO STORMS COME

A thrown shoe hit him in the shoulder. A rock followed it. Wicasah rose to his full height as a new screech pierced the air—one that wasn't a scream of the unknown or fear of the monster, but one of fury. He glanced back and down through the hole in the roof to see the red-haired witch's progeny standing on a sliver of the floor, the last piece of flotsam floating in a sea of fire. She pointed straight at him, her lips moving in a way he couldn't read.

Benedicta's shadow pushed against his heart. The taste of ash filled him. He knew what Benedicta wanted and something settled next to her shade's pressure—he'd never felt it before, but it felt strangely akin to what he felt for Domino. Love. The shadow forced her way into his mouth and pushed against his teeth. Without thinking, he reached down and engulfed the girl in his hands, gently so as not to hurt her, and lifted her up and away from danger.

Cradling her gently, he thundered away, his strides the length of streets yet growing smaller until he could barely see the glow of the fire above the rooftops. The girl rolled out of his hands as he shifted to his human form and collapsed. Smoke curled from the outline of buildings to the stars as if the whole world had been lit on fire. His skin scraped against the cobblestones, making him grimace. Trying to stand became useless and he slumped against a brick wall. Through watering eyes, he watched the girl crawl over to him. A deep lung-wrenching cough from smoke inhalation shook her. She sank beside him and peered at him with eyes slit and red. He realized in a detached way that he was telling her *to breathe*, gasping in time with her until the shortness eased. The rasping cough remained. She wore a pair of wire glasses, the lenses scratched and blackened.

"You need a doctor," he whispered.

She glared at him, her arms tight around her torso as if to hold still from another cough.

He didn't know what to say. Here was a girl-woman somewhere between ten and sixteen, who had just lost her mother, who he had saved. He remembered her father—the man with the spectacles standing at the top of the stairs—and an awful dread settled in his stomach. He hadn't yet processed that Benedicta was gone. That this world was safe for Domino once more.

"She killed my brother," he said, as if that could do anything to rectify it. "I had to do it, but I'm sorry."

"Did you plan to kill me, too? Leave me here in the streets? Think it's a fitting end for my last memory of my father to be of seeing him as a scorched skeleton?" Her ragged voice had an alto huskiness to it.

"What a wonderful cycle," Wicasah said with a sigh of defeat. "I kill your family, now you're going to kill me."

"I know what you are, motherfucker. Don't play games with me. Don't pretend like you care. You only wanted to kill her for power."

"You think this power was just earned? Your mother killed Domino. She asked for her death when she crossed me." Wicasah swallowed hard. His rage felt quenched, but the shade of Benedicta, or whatever remained of her until it forgot, filled him with a yearning to make things right with the short-haired pixie girl.

"You got other family?" he asked. "Anywhere I can take you? Least I can do if you don't plan on killing me."

She smirked at him. "In a way, you *are* my other family."

The realization hit him hard, like a sledgehammer. He let out a laugh. "Oh, sweetie, no."

She smiled back, crying at the same time. The red shade nudged him and before he knew what he was doing, he let the shadow spill out of him. It wrapped around the girl, who ran her fingers through the fading red tone.

"Mom?" Disbelief coated her words.

Wicasah hissed, keeping a close eye that the shadow didn't try to reach inside and pull the girl's shade out.

"You stupid bitch," the girl said, her voice thickened with sobs. "You drag me across the whole country, drive Dad crazy, abandon us, and then when it comes to a fight, you set the whole house on fire? You killed Dad, you selfish *whore*. What the hell were you thinking?"

Wicasah put a comforting hand on her shoulder. If he apologized again, it would only be empty words. He might die at the hands of this girl, but that was the risk when you murdered people who still *had* people in this world.

"I know what you are," the girl said to him through the shade that covered her face like a veil. "I'm like you, too. Now, you've got her remains and you've got all the answers. She never told me much about what I am and now I have no way to take my power.

That's why she was like she was, wasn't it? She was scared I was going to kill her."

The red haze tightened around her. Wicasah felt it again. Loss. Regret. Wondered if that had ever passed through Domino's mind. That Christobel had killed herself to avoid matricide. He petted the red shade until, like a skittish dog, it backed away, but he'd been a good master. He'd let the shade out to see her daughter one more time. The shade nuzzled back and he finally coaxed it inside himself.

The girl stared at him with an unreadable face. "Think if I kill you it counts?"

Wicasah shrugged. "Better chance now than you'll ever have."

The girl's lower lip trembled. She looked away, blinked hard, but the tears cut paths down her cheeks through the soot.

He could say it better now. "I am sorry."

She shut her eyes and her chest rose and fell rapidly. "Take me to the aunts."

Wicasah wanted to say no. At the same time, he wanted to leave this girl on the doorstep of strangers, but he could only see a young, sooty, tear-stained Domino standing at the witch burning of a woman Wicasah sometimes saw in his dreams. The kind woman with the cookies.

Witch burnings left and right. More orphaned children. More revenge. More witches.

"Okay," he sighed, feeling defeated.

"Naomi," she said. "My name is Naomi."

Wicasah bit his lip but he couldn't do it. He couldn't give his name back to her.

———◆———

Fog padded him as Naomi figured out how to access what savings her parents had to buy train tickets. He took his seat without so much as a peep. Steam and coal flakes filled the air. The sound of people laden with luggage jogging outside the dulled scratched window irritated the pounding headache threatening to crack his skull. He stared at Naomi across from him and wondered how he'd gotten here to this moment with her. She pushed a spare pair of black-rimmed spectacles up her nose. Nothing remained after the fire—no clothes, no papers—and yet she'd somehow found a blouse, trousers, and boots. Her short hair was plastered with sweat to her temples, but he could pick out long-haired Benedicta in her profile. He looked away and the silence stretched, too familiar. They hadn't spoken beyond courtesy declarations of where they were going. Wicasah didn't understand his compliance to stick with her, but it felt obligatory. Expected. Or at least, until they found the aunts. Whoever the fuck they were.

Not like he could take care of himself at the moment, anyways.

The train whistled and chugged to a start. Wicasah's eyes drooped, but sleep lent more to exhaustion, especially when his dreams pursued him. Where Domino burned at Daniel's hand and Wicasah spent precious moments casting veils off corpses searching for a fire extinguisher. Where the screams followed him until he opened his eyes and sensed that he was running out of time.

The fog felt good, though, like he'd accomplished the first movement of a very complicated opera. Still, he couldn't shake the exhaustion, or the aches wracking him. It would pass. Just like the mountains slowly sloping into the plains, it would pass.

"I remember Domino," Naomi said, out of the blue. "He was there when I was born. I remember holidays, birthday cakes, and visits just because his apartment was on the way to wherever we were going next."

He didn't expect her story to hurt so much. The twist tightened. He peeked a look, taking in her bright tear-stained eyes, the way the burned skin peeking out of her arm bandages still carried the heat of the fire.

"My mother hated Domino," Naomi continued, a desperate edge to her voice, as if she'd been holding it inside. "I remember him being kind to me. Quiet, but kind. She practically lived with him when Christobel was pregnant. She would drop me off with my father and I wouldn't see her for months, but I knew where she was. With them."

Her breath hitched. "She lied to me a lot. She was good at it. I didn't pick up on it for a long time. Didn't understand that she was keeping me away because she didn't want me to come into my power. That, or I was a substitute for Christobel when she died, dragging me out of school, making me cross-country in the search for Uncle Domino."

She paused. "I guess what I'm trying to say is you didn't do me a disservice. She and me were already heading for a disaster. There were a lot of times where I was scared out of my mind because of her." She pointed a finger at him. "You didn't do right, either. She was still my mother. I still loved her. I'm just saying you took an evil situation off my hands. Get it?"

Wicasah nodded. He knew she wanted him to say something—after all, it was the most she'd spoken since the fire—but all he could do was turn his head back to the window and watch the brush pass by.

Within weeks, they were walking up to the Victorian that looked so out of place on the prairie. Ragged, with faded paint—yellowed and beaten from the wind. Behind the roof, the sun cast a haloed glow. Perhaps Crazy Mary had been right about ancestors and haunting. This home looked so out of place, it had never truly settled from its uprooting.

Naomi took the front steps with a familiarity that astounded him. He approached carefully and stepped into the front hallway, cluttered with stacks of old books.

Children's books. Slender and hardbacked with a fine cover of dust over the hand-drawn characters. Mail piled up haphazardly in a corner. He stifled the strange urge to bolt.

Naomi navigated around the piles away from him. "Hey, Kit."

A second woman's voice rose in excitement, and he picked his way from the front entrance to the kitchen. A large woman, her hair short and hanging like straw in front of her face, puttered around a counter and pulled a pan out of the oven, which looked new considering the ambiance of the house.

The woman—Kit—smiled at Naomi, full and broad with teeth stained with either tobacco or chocolate. Her pink-flowered dress caught around her ankles. She slid a pan onto the stove to cool and then embraced Naomi with so much love it made Wicasah's heart hurt.

"How are you?" Naomi asked, but even Wicasah saw the question was more tradition than anything.

Kit still kept her arm wrapped around Naomi and gestured to the pan. "Pot pie. Had a craving. Tastes good every time."

"Where's Fia?"

Kit touched a flighty hand to her temple. "Bad day. Forgetting again."

Naomi's face scrunched in unhappiness. She turned to look at him and he wished she wouldn't tell him. She could keep her secrets. She should've cut and run from him at the train station, but he supposed she was grieving just as he was prepping for his next plan. The plan he couldn't quite put together with the exhaustion that hounded him.

"She's got Alzheimer's," Naomi said, almost angry at him like he'd asked for an explanation. "Can't remember much. And Kit is . . . well."

Wicasah understood. Kit wasn't all there either. He could see it in her face, the way she spoke high-pitched like a child that didn't fit the fifty-some body she inhabited. He swayed, feeling sick, and bee-lined for the white-painted table, sitting down heavily.

"You're Domino's Wicasah, right?" Kit asked. "Domino used to come here. Fia thinks he's buried out back with Christobel, but the books have told me he's actually with you."

Wicasah blinked. Bit his lip. "Not anymore. He died."

"Benedicta finally got to him?"

Her openness staggered him. "Yeah." His voice sounded so small.

"Didn't see that coming, but she never did get over Christobel."

Naomi slid into a seat beside Wicasah and scooted her chair closer to him. He stared at her, wondered when he'd earned the right to be in her space. He hadn't been much good in their trip out here—sat and slept and hurt while the girl handled everything.

It wouldn't last. All her attention had been on him because she'd planned revenge, but now, in a place where she obviously felt safe, he couldn't understand her trust.

Kit cut the pie and portioned it out into two bowls. She placed the food in front of him. Steam rose from the crust. Wicasah's stomach groaned. Naomi laughed. A blush built up on his cheeks. The pie hadn't settled and looked like a gooey mass of peas and gravy, but Wicasah burned his tongue anyway shoveling the first bite into his mouth.

Kit sat down with her own bowl and blew on her food. They ate in silence until a crash echoed from another room. Kit paused, her fork half-suspended to her mouth.

"She's getting worse," Naomi said out of the corner of her mouth.

Wicasah paused, realizing she spoke to him only. "How long?"

Naomi hunched further over her food. "Year or so. She tried to get Mom to move back to help out, but . . . well, she wouldn't have, even if you didn't kill her."

"Now that they have you they won't have to worry."

Naomi stared at him, her eyebrows slanting into a glare he'd become familiar with.

Kit continued to eat. "You're planning on staying the night? Bed upstairs is fixed up. Don't know where we can put *you.*"

"I'll be on my way soon," Wicasah said and meant to stand, but he couldn't force himself out of the chair.

"Better rest. You've been burned to all hell. Need a doctor."

"I *look* fine," Wicasah said. His skin had darkened back to its old hue and while he hadn't stared at a mirror in a long time, by no means did he appear bad enough for a doctor.

Kit shot him a look—*well, aren't you the idiot?*—and placed a stack of books in front of her. She opened a Dr. Seuss and poured over it like a valuable manuscript.

"She, uh, means your other form," Naomi said. Her legs swung off the chair and she scooped up their empty bowls.

"Two sides to everything," Kit said. "Here, I'm the mentally ill one. There, I'm a genius. Here, the books speak the language of children. There, they're prophecies."

"You'll always be my favorite aunt, Kit."

Kit beamed at Naomi. "You're my favorite, too."

"What do the books say today?"

Kit studied the thick cardboard paper. "Webs are still being spun. Although, they won't *get* spun if that one doesn't take care of himself."

Naomi began to wash out the bowls.

"You should change," Kit said, staring at him.

Wicasah didn't have to ask her meaning. "I'd break the house."

"You're killing yourself."

He glanced nervously at Naomi, as if wanting her permission, but the young girl kept her back turned with the sound of soap and scrub cleaning the dishes. Maybe her suggestion would help him battle the exhaustion that never seemed to get better.

It hurt to transform. He didn't complete it, kept his size as small as he could until he merely towered over the table. Kit was right—he was an absolute mess. His usually hardened skin had become scabbed, gristle with oozing pus on his arms and thighs. His head drooped and, with a chill of shock, he realized he wasn't exhausted—he was on the verge of collapse.

"Go lie down," Kit instructed.

"Where?"

"On the floor. Outside. Anywhere. Just *sleep*."

Wicasah lurched to his feet, suddenly at the mercy of this non-witchery witch and her commands, much like he would be when Domino asked without asking for him to take a nap. *You'll feel better in an hour, just trust me, okay? You won't be missing anything.*

He thumped back the way he had come and curled up like a dog against the foyer. It was the only place he would fit. His eyes drifted shut. His hole-ridden wings wrapped around him. Somewhere within the fog, his shadows remained deathly quiet. The lull of Kit and Naomi's voices drifted to him coupled with the clang of dishes, the opening and closing of a cold box, the sound of pages being turned.

He didn't know if the nightmares came, but when he woke, he had a blanket laid on top of him. Naomi loomed over him and he wondered, vaguely, if this was the time for his death. He couldn't defend himself and hoped the Dark and Bloody would accept him. She cast a secondary shadow over him. Hands on her hips. Deciding.

She pattered up the staircase and sleep tore talons into him again, casting him into the other side of *awake*.

———•———

Coolness breezed over his face. Shivering, no, *freezing*. A woman, her face lined in every way possible, knelt in front of him and smeared lotion over his open wounds. He jerked away, but she hushed him.

"Don't do anything rash. Who knows how long I'll be here until my brain fucks me over again." With a shaking hand, she brought a dead cigarette to her lips and tried to pull a drag. "Made this salve for you. Well, I made it for someone years ago. Never figured out for who, but it's yours now. Don't know why you have to be so ugly when your brother was so handsome, but I guess that's Thessaly for you."

A cold tingle spread over his body. His shadows bounded around him like bunnies, rejuvenated. He'd never seen the woman before, but he knew without a doubt that this was Fiametta.

She stood up and pointed a finger at him. "I'm tired of getting you out of scrapes, Domino. Either fix it with Christobel or get out." She pattered away, pulled her shawl closer around her shoulders, and yelled for coffee into the empty kitchen.

I HAVE ASKED TO BE WHERE NO STORMS COME

Wicasah stumbled to his feet and got a good look out the window through the lace curtains. Time—how much had passed? Adrenaline poured through his blood. The exhaustion had evaporated and as his claws tapped on the floorboards, he realized he hadn't been well, that the side of him he'd always considered unstoppable could in fact be put down.

Already he could feel the salve doing its work. The chill eased into a soothing elasticity like he could move without tearing his scales open. He pattered into the kitchen, keeping his shape small, but unnerved at how this place felt so . . . familiar. Looking through the doors flung wide open was an old experience, even though he'd never seen the waving grass against the horizon from this place before, and he'd never seen it through these witchery eyes. Strings of existence crisscrossed like a cat-gnarled bundle of yarn across the sky, shading it with twilight purple.

Kit puttered in a garden overgrown with wild prairie grass, a straw basket slung over her arm. She bent to pluck the stalks, and Wicasah's stomach curled into a knot. Malformed heads broke through the soil like melons. Shoulders emerged like tubers. A tug played in his chest, and without thinking, he unraveled his shadows. They bounded across the fields like wild hounds.

Wicasah wondered about the past, these places Domino had been, what walls he'd leaned against, what words had vibrated the walls, and he hated that he had to see things through Benedicta's memories instead of having his brother beside him to walk him through his past.

"Best sit before you fall over," he heard beside him. Fia glared up at him, the sun shining across her face as if it might light up her decaying mind. He lowered himself beside her, growing larger all the time, and held out one of his wings, casting shade over her while the scent of her lit cigarette mingled with the fresh scent of far, traveled winds and grasslands.

"What is she doing?" Wicasah asked. Kit shooed one of his shadows away. "Fia, can you see them, too?"

"See what?"

One of the shadows sniffed at an upturned face and snuck through the head's nostrils. The face reanimated like the opening bud of a daisy, empty eye sockets popping open, the mouth curling into a too-broad smile. Another tug in his chest twisted into throbbing discomfort and another shadow crawled out from him like woodsmoke, clutching the ground.

Benedicta barely clung to her form. Her hair waved behind her in a mass of red-tinged gray. Shackles twisted around her throat and arms, binding them back to him, but she crept toward the nearest growing body. Pity filled Wicasah, and he waited until she almost reached the vessel before he stopped her, disintegrating her shape until she was nothing but a cloud and yanking her back to him.

He gently cupped her face in his claws. "Even if I could, I won't release you." Saying it felt like the aftermath of adrenaline, the way he felt when he saw the blood pooling on the floor after the ringing gunshot, the way Domino's face had paled to a ghost when Daniel had died. Terrible, exhausting, the weight of consequence his own shackles. "What powers do you hold?" he whispered. "Would you return somehow? You'd slaughter me, take everything from me. It's better to keep you here until you forget. You've destroyed what I love. Revenge is fierce and no mercy would save me if I let you free."

"Who are you talking to?" Fia asked, her voice wary.

"I'm sorry," he whispered but knew it wasn't enough. Whatever semblance of a good man he could've been had been dragged through the mud. Magic and guns had been placed in his hands, tools he'd used willingly. No one forced his hand. He'd accepted the hurt and evil. He knew what he did was wrong, but being right, being good—it left him with nothing.

A hand crashed through Benedicta, scattering her to the winds. Looking up, Kit's furious face loomed above him. "Wrangle your damn shadows! They're ruining my garden!"

"I can't remember jack shit, but I know you two aren't speaking my language," Fia said, ignored.

Wicasah blinked as if emerging from a trance and saw bodies rising like zombies, staggering like stiff dolls toward each other, faces wide open with delight.

"Pests!" Kit yelled, pointing at them. "Call them back!"

"How did you do that?" Wicasah whispered, the solution to a question staring him in the face. "How did you grow flesh?"

"You're ruining my garden!"

Wicasah whistled, sharp and piercing. The bodies dropped like their strings had been cut. Dark masses surged out of them, barreling into Wicasah, happy to be home.

Kit's face turned red with anger. "Look what you've done."

Wicasah peered around her and saw the mess of half-reconstructed bodies scattered around the field. Chaotic and broken.

"I'm so sorry," he said, and this time meant it. "I should've been paying attention."

"You can't keep track of your magic." Kit wiped her mouth with her hand. "I decided to let you stay here because of what my books say and what happened to you and Domino has always been a regret of this family. We let you down once when you were young, but Naomi told us what you did to Benedicta. Why would you help Naomi if all you know how to do is kill?"

Wicasah's wings trembled and he fought the urge to explode upwards, larger and stronger than any of her magic could be. He couldn't tell them about Benedicta's shadow—they might make him release her—but he had to know how Kit had created vessels for shadows to fill.

"I killed my father," he said. "Shot him straight through the head. No one ever stopped to help us, even when they knew things were bad. Now, it sounds like Benedicta wasn't the kindest mother to her daughter and while I killed her, I also know what it's like to be an orphan. I knew we were family through Domino in some way. I helped her because I knew it was the right thing to do."

"We tried to help you," Fia said, sounding shaken. "Domino called us one night, begging us to leave you all alone."

"Domino never knows what's good for him," Wicasah said, sharper than intended.

Kit looked to Fia. The cigarette in Fia's hand had eaten its way up to her fingers, turning her skin black. "What do you want from us?" Fia whispered as Kit yanked the cigarette out of Fia's hands and snuffed it in the dirt.

"You know my path," Wicasah said, turning to Kit. "You've read it in your books. You see the same things I do—the shadows, the piano strings holding this world together."

"The beating heart in the mountains."

Wicasah paused, uncertain, but played along. "Exactly. Listen to me, I'll leave you alone. I'll go far enough away you'll never see me again, but I'm here for a reason. To learn how to make flesh out of nothing from you."

The wind picked up, throwing Kit's straight, rough hair in front of her face. Wicasah followed her gaze, saw the pulsating strings converge in a spot far away in the distance.

"What can I give you?" he asked.

"That you take care of Naomi," she said softly. "I can't, not with my sister the way she is. How can Naomi learn anything about what she is through me? I only have Brightside magic."

"Why would you entrust that with me?"

Kit smiled. "Maybe so that she can come into her power by destroying you."

"I'll accept that risk."

Kit sighed and looked into her basket, pulling out a long black thread of shadow. It flopped over her arm like a fish, shredded at the ends. "The graveyard existed here before we did. Sacrificial, I think, for the serpent skeleton that emerged after some archeological dig of Christobel's. I couldn't go outside for the longest time because I was so scared of the bodies in the yard. Then I found a bit of shadow, nothing but a sliver that had been split from its owner somehow, and I put the shadow piece in the graveyard. It slunk into the remains of a small bunny, eaten by hawks. I managed to repair the body, built it until the shadow burned out and the bunny was gone again. It's my power. A small gift, when faced with something like yours."

"It's monumental." Wicasah wanted to leap into the air, bring the Brightside witch under his protection. The puzzle pieces, which once seemed so unattainable felt within his grasp. Hope tasted sweet. His shadows leaked from his mouth, bounding around Kit. She uttered a slight eek and held her hands up around them.

"What use is the spirit without the house to live in? Don't you understand what you're capable of?" Wicasah asked.

Kit turned away, a sheen of tears coating her eyes. "It's garden magic."

"If I asked you to grow a body for me, what would you need?"

"A piece of the original body—a bone."

"Flesh? Soil where the body was buried? What?"

Kit looked uncertain. "It's not that accurate, just something of the body's essence."

"But I'd need a shadow to fill the body. I need the soul for complete reanimation."

Kit's face scrunched up in fear. "I'm not sure what you mean, but I assume so, yes."

"That's more than enough," he breathed, knowing he sounded insane. "That's more than enough."

"What are you trying to do?" she asked.

Wicasah didn't hear. His eyes focused on the far spot of pulsation in the distance, over the plains where the mountains began. The lines lead there, and he could see his plan as clear as the strings of destiny, unexpectedly converging for him.

CHAPTER 8

THE DIRT WRITHED with maggots and earthworms. Their pale pink bodies slipped between Wicasah's fingers as he sifted the garden-earth into a glass mason jar, careful as any gold panner. Fingers peeked and waved through his hastily dug hole like curious roots. Dirty nails touched the creases in his tough pants and scraped gently at his wrists as he cupped handfuls of soil. If what Kit said was true, resurrection magic infused throughout this earth, the ability to grow new flesh empty of soul. If Wicasah could harvest enough, he could re-bury Domino inside it, nurture that boneless casing in this womb of soil, glass, and tin top. Wicasah could grow back what he'd lost, coax Domino alive like a mint plant sprouting after a long winter. While he tended to this new body, he'd search for the spirit to fill it.

Hope, so longed for, now lassoed his heart.

The half-crescent moon shone down on him. The porch light from the aunts' house drowned out the stars, keeping the galaxy-path above dimmed. At some point, he heard the screen door squeak open but paid it no mind until he felt the cold slide of a shotgun barrel tap the back of his head. He exhaled evenly and carefully poured the garden dirt into the mason jar before holding his hands up and out wide. The barrel slid around the circumference of his head until Naomi came into view. A long black robe patterned with roses and violets wrapped around her wiry frame. Her short hair had been braided around her head like a crown. Muddy boots were laced up her feet. Wicasah smirked. She'd obviously taken her time watching him muddle around in the dirt, that she showed him with her dress she'd been awake long enough to plan, that her boots were made for walking.

"What are you doing?" she asked softly.

"You know very well what I'm doing," he hissed. He hated

playing dumb, hated wasting time explaining his actions to those who would never understand. To those who would think they knew better, being on the outside and numb to the ache inside him.

"Kit thought you might do something like this," she said. "That you'd cut and run with her soil, after everything we'd done for you and yours. She won't stop you, said there'd be no stopping you."

"As should you." Wicasah glared up at her. His shadows curled against his hard palette, eager to strike even as Benedicta infected some with a flavor of reluctance. Affection permeated the shadows, some wishing to protect Naomi, others excited to consume her so that she joined their ranks. "If you're going to kill me, don't hesitate."

"I'd come into my power then, wouldn't I?" she said, pressing the barrel deeper into his skin. "Kill a family member and I'd be a powerful witch, too."

Wicasah didn't say anything, kept his face impassive.

"But I don't want to do that, not yet."

The metallic push suddenly left and she grabbed the back of his head, yanked him closer before he could think, her thumb digging into his forehead. Heat traveled from his forehead down his cheeks like lava. That burn centralized in front of his bottom teeth—a searing pain branding his lower lip. Blood filled his mouth. He bit down on a scream as the cold touch of the gun was back against his forehead. Naomi's fingers dug into his scalp, holding him still, as endless types of pain rocked through him.

"What did you do?" he asked, a thin wet spread of blood and saliva slipping down his chin. The magic smelled of her—young and untempered—but had the aged notes of a mature witch. Give her an evil deed and she'd be strong.

"Branded you like cattle," she said, fingers tightening until a bright searing pain throttled the back of his head. "You can try to run and disappear, but I'll always know where you are. You try to do anything? I'll know about it. I may want to kill you, but you've got to teach me first. The aunts are too far gone to help me. You're the only one with the ability to help me hone my witchcraft. You can't run before you can walk, but that's what all you plains-magic folk do—run and stumble and roll without the basics. I won't be like that."

"You can't *keep* me," Wicasah said, rage glowing like a forge inside him. She could rope him in, set the barriers of his roam, and the thought of being so captured made him want to scream. His words had bite, sharp as a rattlesnake. "Kill me now, girl, or I'll fight you with everything I am."

"You won't kill me." She sounded shaky. "I don't believe you would. You have a good heart. Don't prove me wrong."

Wicasah wanted to tackle her, push her mouth and nose into the dirt until she went still under him, but her accusation had grounds. He'd murdered her mother, burned her house down, and then chaperoned her to her next of kin out of guilt.

"You can leave, but you'll take me with. We're in this together, and while we travel, you'll teach me."

"I have nothing to give," he hissed. "I barely understand my strength as it is."

"Then we learn together," she said. "Anything is better than nothing."

"Until you decide to kill me and come into your own."

"Yes," she said, moving the gun barrel away. The shadows grumbled back to their sleep. She was right. He wouldn't kill her, not when she was in her youthful prime, the woman she would become slipping out in the lines of her body, the plump freshness of a teenager already being eaten by age.

"I'm not staying here. I have to go back." He licked his lips, his tongue tentatively brushing over the brand on the inside of his lip.

"For your brother," she said. "For Domino."

Words suddenly felt mundane to explain the ache inside him. "You don't understand. He did everything for me and got nothing in return. Now, he's in Hell for sins that aren't his own, for situational wrongs that left him no choice. I can't leave him there. He doesn't deserve to be there."

"All right," she said, as if overwhelmed. She knelt in front of him, and plunged her hands into the earth, sprinkled the clumpy dirt into the mason jar. "But we do it right. Supplies, money, boots, clothes. At dawn, not in the middle of the night, and after proper goodbyes. We can take the train back, buy some horses at the waystation. Where do we have to go?"

Wicasah coughed his gratitude away as he topped off the jar. He sealed it, held it close to his chest. "We go to where I buried him. Plant him in this soil. I'll be making a deal soon with the demons of the underworld to get his spirit back. At least, I think I will be."

I HAVE ASKED TO BE WHERE NO STORMS COME

"Okay," she said softly and smoothed the earth back over the hole, burying the waggling fingers. He didn't understand her tender interest, the way she agreed without stipulations or lectures that his love was more like obsession, but his tongue probed the scabbing brand and knew he had to trust somewhere along the way.

—————◦—————

Soil became the guideposts leading him closer to that bright sun of hope.

Rich magicked earth sat deep under his fingernails and lined his knuckles as Kit patted his hand and whispered, "I'm sorry about the brand. She's Benedicta's, and family, so I had to help her. I hope you understand."

The wind blew the tall pale grasses sideways as the aunts gave Naomi a tearful goodbye. Dust devils and tumbleweeds swirled up along the road, showing Wicasah the way. He swept his tongue over the looped sigil—posh magic, no doubt with roots on the other side of the Dark and Bloody. Naomi prattled the tale as they walked away from the old Victorian toward town, saying how the aunts had followed love driving them west, that Brightside society had let them sink their money into putting that old home on the prairie. Wicasah studied the way Naomi's backpack of canvas and leather was strapped tight to her, the water bottle of metal dangling from twine and clips. He carried a change of clothes, hardy food wrapped in checkered cloth, and in the middle of it all the precious mason jar.

As a trade for stories of Domino and Christobel, of this family he only had ties to through marriage, he taught Naomi the way of the lonely—how the constellations could be strung together into tales, how to sniff out the stick of a good fossil, how to see the rainbow spiderweave embroidered around the world with the grounding knot tied to the Dark and Bloody. Lessons passed from All-Worlds to him to her. Maybe she'd make more use of them.

The dark velvet soil of the garden disappeared when they hopped on the train heading farther into the heartland, giving way to dry topsoil aching for a drink. Naomi's sleep, once rough and pitted with anxiety, soothed into the deep slumber of the growing. Wicasah took to laying his jacket over her shoulders to keep her warm. Strangely, she accepted him and he wasn't sure what it meant. The flat roll expanded before them, the sky plumeing with earth coal burned into energy.

The earth around the tree he'd buried Domino under was dried out to white and had a sandy texture. The black branches reached into the sky and rattled when the prairie gusts wound around it. Wicasah spit his hair out of his mouth. Something hardened within him.

"This the place?" Naomi sounded doubtful. "How can you tell?"

"I buried my brother here," Wicasah snapped. "You don't think that moment is skewered into my brain?"

She looked thoughtful. The late morning sun cascaded over the bridge of her nose, leaving her profile in stark relief. "I don't remember where we buried my mother. Did we bury her, even?"

"Nothing left to bury, really." Wicasah looked away from her. The flavors of their grief both amused and fascinated him, and he found himself analyzing the way their nature and nurtured life had brought them to stand shoulder to shoulder on the same path. He knelt at the base of the tree and put his hand flat on where the roots dug into the soil.

"Does that make me a bad person?" Naomi whispered. "I didn't even think about my father."

He looked up at her with a severe frown. "I'd say it makes you a better person. It's good to be able to see what wrong has been done to you, call it out, shoot it down. You know your mother was bad to you. I wish . . . " he paused, pursed his lips. "I wish Domino could do that."

"Did you hate your father?"

"That man was the worst thing that ever happened to me," Wicasah said, speaking nothing but truth. "I'm glad he's dead. Glad I was the one to do it. That sin is on me, not Domino."

"You two share wrongs, then? He takes one, you take the other?" She huffed a laugh.

Wicasah shrugged. She wasn't wrong. He dug his spade into the ground and shoveled until the dry dust turned to layers of clay and darker dirt. It wasn't long until he uncovered the scraps of Domino's body. The rough leather of his skin had been eaten to scraps, the clothing dusty and cold, familiar blonde-brown hair wisping across the twisted mask of a face.

"Sorry," Wicasah said softly to the corpse. "Sorry about leaving you here."

A touch on his arm. He wiped his elbow over his eyes. Pulling the mason jar out of the backpack, he unscrewed the lid as Naomi took the spade and cleared more dirt off his brother. The heavy scent of moist earth reached his nose, the kind that lets fucking tulips survive in a wasteland. "I don't know what parts to take," he admitted.

Naomi reached down and snipped off a piece of Domino's hair. "Little bit of everything, I imagine," she said.

A scrap of skin, then. Fistful of hair. Bit of the grave dirt for good measure. He formed a deep hole in the mason jar dirt, laid what he could in it like a spring bulb, and covered it. This, he cradled to his chest and padded it in his pack.

"Now what?" Naomi asked.

"We go back to town, get you a room. Next step, I get his soul back."

"And how you going to do that, exactly?"

He wasn't sure he appreciated her tone, the way she started throwing his own brand of sass back into his face. "I gave . . . a memory scent to a psychopomp. I hope the heyoka is finding Domino's scent in hell."

Helia, the heyoka corrected in his mind.

"Sounds like malarkey from where I'm standing." Naomi gave him a sloppy smile, something that spoke of recklessness.

It brought Wicasah up short. "What do you think we're doing here, you and me?" he asked, feeling shocked, uncalled for rage go through him. This wasn't a game.

"Something more than ourselves," Naomi answered.

"Definitely not that. I'm selfish as can be. This is all for me, one hundred percent." If Wicasah didn't do this, he'd end up drinking himself to death with his ribs clanking like wind chimes for the rolling winds of loneliness that threatened to push him over. This wasn't about anything but his own personal survival, same as seeking out water, same as hunting for food. Emotional, mental survival. Because everything else out there? All these landscapes and people? They weren't safe. They couldn't fill the ache of bereavement inside him. And he couldn't just let himself starve now, could he?

"Sure is. This is one of those grand epics about love, but if you don't want to see it, none of my business. We'll set up camp here," Naomi said as she began to rebury Domino. "Take some time here. I like sleeping outside, less chance of you trying to leave me. Tell me what the strands look like, Wicasah."

"Try'na distract me." The idea of filling the hole back in made him feel nothing. This grave wouldn't be a grave for long. Soon, it would be a landmark of remember when. Remember when you died, Domino? Remember when? "The strands are thin here," he said softly, plucking a pink shimmering white thread. It rang like a harp. "They're thin."

CHAPTER 9

"WHO ARE YOU?"

Naomi's sharp tone cut through the dreamless black of Wicasah's sleep. Blinking, he saw a blinding blaze of orange and blue fire devouring the dead branches they'd cut from the tree in their makeshift fire ring. Moisture sizzled on the blackened rocks. Above, the stars swirled in smears of twinkling light, but Wicasah couldn't reach for their shapes and stories. His arms instinctively tightened around the mason jar cradled between his arms. *Safe.*

Naomi held an ashen stick draped over her lap, her blanket thrown over her shoulders, and her dark gaze peered just past the campfire with suspicion. Wicasah followed her line of sight and scrambled to a sitting position as a jagged creature shambled towards them.

The heyoka entered their campsite lightning struck—off-centered lips, one eye askew, but grinning madly. Dawn surrounded them like a halo as if she'd brought a new sun into the midnight darkness. Wicasah rose and stood in front of Naomi, but the heyoka gripped his wrist fast.

"Don't touch him," Naomi growled, scrambling to her own feet, grabbing Wicasah's shoulder. "He belongs with me."

Wicasah shook her off as the heyoka's dawn washed over his face with desert heat. He tongued the brand against his lower lip as the heyoka's jittery laugh filled the night.

"Will your owner let you prove your worth?" the heyoka mocked. "Sounds like you've made too many promises, witch."

Wicasah flinched, but even so, struggled to keep the eagerness out of his voice. "You've found Domino's soul?" In his hope, he looked down at his feet, but it was as though the world too had become lightning struck and mismatched: one foot stood in Kit's garden with the bones of a dinosaur under his feet; the other foot on a thin fine dust of Domino's grave. Naomi's pinched mouth uttered words that had become unintelligible. Above him, the lines of fate throbbed.

The heyoka's smile broadened. "Never promised that. Never said that might happen."

Wicasah's hope withered on its fragile vine. "That was our deal," he said.

"We made no deal." The heyoka waved a finger. "You have yet to make the deal. I've only found you dealers. Do you know the price for entering Helia?"

"No," Wicasah said, full of confusion and crushed hope, "but I know you took something from me to find Domino. Now you're saying you have nothing?"

"Summer-child, I have everything."

The heyoka plunged her hand against Wicasah's chest, right above his heart. Pressure increased on his breastbone until he felt the plate fracture. Weakness spread across his ribs, down his spine, embedded in the thick sturdiness of his thighs. His bones were melting—just like Domino's had.

In the heyoka's hand, his wrist flopped like a limp noodle. Wicasah's body collapsed in on itself without any internal structure. The heyoka reached up and plucked one of the shimmering rainbow-colored strings above. Naomi's cry of denial was swallowed as the Dark and Bloody suddenly loomed in front of them like a flat ocean on a black night, the darkness alive like staring down the throat of a whale. The rainbow strands cut through the black, colliding into a twister leading inside that crawling depth.

Wicasah tried to scream, tried to fight, but the small bones of his throat were gone, the cage of his lungs disintegrated. The heyoka held him fast. Wicasah's legs slithered behind until he couldn't help but be morbidly fascinated by his own distorted body. The glimmering funnel brightened, hungry for a new soul. Before Wicasah could say anything, the heyoka lifted him and tossed him inside of Helia.

He landed on fine sand. Heat burned through the pads of his claws. Scaled plates ran over his chest like armor. His wings pinched tight and protective against his back and exposed neck. A canyon loomed in the distance, a landscape of gray and brown plateaus, and before it, three creatures stood silent with their arms clasped in front of them.

"Is this the human?" one of them asked softly. "He smells more like a demon."

"He must be human up there," a female creature said. "I still smell life on him."

"How is that possible?" the third one snarled. "We were promised a witch."

"I think that *is* the witch, Manit," the female said.

"We wanted a witch who could get rid of the human souls, not a demon possessing flesh!" Manit snapped.

"Who are you?" Wicasah rasped. The sharp barbed bones inside him felt like pillars, something he leaned on for gratitude. Here, his internal structure had been returned.

Manit snorted. "We were promised to meet a witch in great need, a witch with something to offer us. You look like something chewed and spit back out."

Wicasah stumbled to his feet. His mind whirled in confusion and he knew he'd been thrown into a deep pool with no choice but to sink or swim. The heyoka was nowhere to be found. "The funnel will do that to you," he said.

The demons fell silent. Wicasah had no idea what promises had been made and unmade, but Wicasah was used to guesses and lucky shots, liked the rush of impromptu deals crafted from words, shaken hands, and spit-seal. "I hear you have a soul for me," he said, using his wings to steady him, hoping the anxiety of his insides didn't match the lazy swagger on his outside.

"Presumptuous," the first demon whispered, his body like a smoky whip. "Don't you agree, Aiyana?"

"I do indeed, Ickto." The female demon glared at him through round, watery eyes. Her slenderized nose flared. "But, human, we're the eyes and ears of Helia and employ the best trackers around. We have the scent of, what I assume, is the soul you're looking for, but why should we help you, witch? You'd be more use to us sold or drained for your blood."

"Terrible hospitality," Wicasah tutted. "Out of the goodness of my heart, I'm here—up to my neck in souls, by-the-by—and I'm looking for one itty-bitty one." He loosened the choke-chain around his shadows. They spun from him like unraveled yarn, then circled the demons as wolves. A smile spread across Icko's face, something too wide with teeth. Aiyana let out a sound of delight, her sharp cat claws petting the patterned scales around her cheeks.

"From what I hear, human souls aren't supposed to be here," Wicasah continued, thinking fast. "Up there? In my world? I can see the funnel connecting our two realms. I've bound these souls to me. Maybe, if I wanted, I could do that for you."

Aiyana looked uneasily to Ickto. The shadow-demon studied Wicasah like he'd enjoy nothing more than possessing Wicasah's body. "They're a plague," Ickto said softly. "The first one landed here like a comet. Our people cared for him, but his terror infected all he saw. Called Helia a hellscape, called us demons of the damned. Then, the souls became like meteor showers, infecting everything with their fear, turning Helia into a place of horror, using our rituals for their own purposes."

"The sand and dust are the bones of our people for Helia to speak through," Manit said, "but the humans grind our bones and make drugs from it, instead. They're addicted to us."

"You want them gone?" Wicasah asked as his shadows sniffed and explored the new realm. "I can bind them to me. Tie them all to me and then go back to my land. Destroy the funnel and ensure nothing is left here but . . . demons. If I wanted to."

Aiyana smiled, her teeth like broken glass. "You're making quite the deal for one measly soul. These promises are grand. Too grand for the price you're asking."

"I can prove it," Wicasah said and then winced. *Brazen,* he heard Domino say in his mind. *Too impulsive.*

"The humans are your people," Ickto said, syrup-sweet. "Wouldn't your heart bleed for them? Wouldn't you rather save them than imprison them?" He stepped aside to reveal a man hog-tied behind him.

Wicasah tensed. His wings stilled.

"We caught him selling demon bones as dust-drugs," Ickto said lazily. "He was the first scent associated with your lost soul. Tried to sell . . . *Domino* for his witch blood, didn't you?"

The man whimpered behind the cloth gagging his mouth.

"How would you punish this human, witch?" Aiyana said to Wicasah. "Where do your loyalties lie? My guess says it won't do me any favors."

"But perhaps you'll prove us wrong. The heyoka has great faith in you, and they're the only good thing to come out of your world," Ickto finished. "The only good thing that followed the souls here."

Wicasah fell silent and the demons followed, as if giving him space to consider. The desecration of the demons' rituals seemed to be a crime worthy of a terrible punishment. Perhaps, they were testing him to determine how far he'd go. This man was a gift to prove Wicasah's abilities, but Aiyana was right—his promises were too grand. He still didn't know how much effort it would take to make every soul a shadow and bind them to him. But if he could prove that demons were just as important—even more so—than human souls . . . he might buy enough time to figure things out.

After all, Wicasah was a witch. Hadn't he been told that over and over? Witches weren't good for anything but evil and selfishness. Why wouldn't he get what was his, even if it was more precious and temperamental than any gold, woman, or booze? He was bound for . . . well, the equivalent of Hell in his Christian-cultured world because he couldn't think of anything else. If he ended up here or there in the end, so be it.

How far would he go for Domino? To the ends of the earth.

The armored plates along his chest rippled like shedding snakeskin. It felt unnatural, letting his monstrous suit slip away into his soft body with Thessaly's eyes and Daniel's mouth. The demons parted as he approached the bound man. He untied the gag around the criminal's mouth. That was how he needed to think of this soul—not as someone with a family, or someone desperate to survive, but someone who sold flesh and murdered.

"Please," the man said, his mouth dry and cracked. He looked up at Wicasah with tearful eyes. "Please, don't hurt me."

"What's your name?" Wicasah asked.

"Evan," the man said, eyes darting between Wicasah and the trio of demons surrounding them.

"Tell me about Domino," Wicasah said softly, stroking the man's sweat-damp hair. "If you do, I might be able to help."

Aiyana made a guttural sound of denial but Manit grabbed her shoulder before she could act.

"We didn't mean to do it," Evan said so quickly Wicasah knew it was a lie. "We'd simply hoped to make some money. There's a strong market for witch blood. It's good for spells and Domino should've shared it with us. We were his friends, after all. We could've been safer out there if he'd helped us, but he kept it all to himself."

Wicasah's mouth pursed into a moue. "How selfish."

"Right? You understand. You know what it's like. Every man

for himself out here. So we bound him like a pig and took him to a witch-slaver. Fetched a high price. Gallons of water. But then, word was, his power blew the trade post to bits." Evan's eyes widened as if the confession had been forced out of him.

Wicasah hummed in sympathy. "I see. So, you betrayed my brother and sold him down the river for water."

"No." Evan looked from Wicasah to the demons. "No, that's not what it was."

Wicasah's shadows swirled around him like tentacles, reading the violence as it was heated and folded in on itself to create a sharp blade. He grabbed the back of the man's shirt and hauled him to his feet. A terrible inkling played in the back of Wicasah's head, something cruel. Just beyond, the sand shivered as if responding to his inner desires. Suddenly the shape of a horse appeared—glossy with vitality, its broad chest rounded with muscle. A hellion corpse straddled the horse, her throat slit, an anatomist's cut slicing her down the middle.

Wicasah turned Evan to look at the horse with a woman on its back. Evan's mouth dropped open and Wicasah felt a slice of glee fill him. Aiyana let out a sound of surprise.

"How much did her bones fetch you? Beautiful thing, she was. Did she deserve what you gave her?" Wicasah asked, glancing to see the expressions of the demons—outrage, grief, and interest.

"Let's go see her, shall we?" Wicasah nudged Evans closer to the horse.

"What? No, no, please," Evans stuttered and twisted to free himself. Shadows gripped him even as Wicasah guided him to the corpse and horse. "Leg up," Wicasah said, helping Evan to mount the horse and then lash him face-to-face with the dead hellion. Evan sobbed. Wicasah tightened the bonds.

Facing the three demons as if daring them to object, Wicasah slapped the horse's rump and watched the creature gallop through the desert toward the canyon. "How far should I let him go?" he asked.

Aiyana licked her lips and glanced at her fellow demons, but a hot, eager light filled her eyes. "Until insane," she whispered.

Wicasah nodded and unfurled his wings, half-flying and half-striding to catch up with the riding duo. The horse had lightning in its hooves, and the dust clouds exploded behind it like nebulas as it galloped into the canyon. Evan's screams filled the air. Wicasah smirked.

Wicasah knew he was an evil thing. He'd killed his father. He'd let Domino take the blame for it. Evan deserved to be in this hellscape, not Domino. This bastard on the horse was one more man who betrayed his brother, one more man who made Domino doubt the good in humanity, doubt the softness of living. One more man who brought the hunted, dog-whipped look to Domino.

The canyon opened up with sun-blasted rocks and boulders interspersed with huge bones—most likely Helia's earliest inhabitants, those who rose and fell and who now littered the plains. The sand had a glittery quality to it, like black and silver vermiculite. The sound of a gun blast followed by the whine of a bullet exploded from the canyon sides and Wicasah ducked as a patter of gunfire destroyed the path near the horse and rider. On its heels rose the mechanical screech of a plane alongside the high-pitched whine of a bomb being released. Horror filled him as the earth in front of him exploded. Particle and bone fragments rained down on them. Helia shuddered, the tiny earthquake the land's warning, and Wicasah glanced down just before his foot stepped on the half-buried remnant of a landmine. Old and matte black, half-covered in sparkling sand.

Rapid-fire gunshots. The sharp tang of sulfur. The deafening whine of another bomb. Wicasah sought cover behind a boulder and realized he'd led them straight onto a battlefield.

The horse continued on, unfazed, dodging flung dirt. Soldiers emerged from the crannies of the canyon, gaunt and hunted. Rifles and bayonets clutched in their hands. Helia rolled, dislodging them and they tumbled to the ground, hitting landmines and sending body parts scattering across the sand. The earth slurped the blood.

Helia was alive—not in the way Wicasah was alive, but the rocks and caverns all had animation, and Helia did not like these soldiers any more than he did. Ahead, Evan tried to pitch himself off the horse, but the dead demon slumped into him instead until they held each other in a strange neck-to-neck embrace. Wicasah dodged forward, listening to the micro-rumbles of the sand to bypass landmines and whizzing bullets. He barely kept his head attached to his shoulders when a new kind of crack fill the air.

Lightning. The sizzle of petrichor. The twisted tentacle glimmer of fulgurite zipping across the sand. The heyoka stood amid the battle shucked of her mismatched form. Long black hair flowed down her back, her eyes the overturned richness of dark earth, a bold power dancing between her fingertips. One long-clawed hand clutched the arm of a soldier in buckskin pants and a white tunic, his dark brown skin matte from dust. A rifle tapped against his shoulder. A bow strung across his back. Beaded necklaces roped around his neck. The heyoka lunged for Wicasah, her clawed nails piercing the veined leathery span of his wing, dragging him closer until she filled his vision.

"How well can you hold shadows?" she hissed, gripping the hook inside of him and wrenching it forward. Pain made him a panicked doe, trying to outrun a rifle scope. He collapsed to his knees. Ants, determined to save their hill, swarmed over him. The heyoka widened the hook except it wasn't a hook at all, but an anchor, something deep in the still waters of his insides. The brand against his lower lip throbbed and opened up in a gush of blood. The heyoka gripped the anchor and wound the soul of the man beside her to it like a braided chain. The soul shimmered, becoming amorphous like a bundle of stars pockmarked with familiar shadow-darkness.

"Take this one back to earth with you," she whispered.

The world tilted. Just beyond, Wicasah glimpsed Evan, tied tight to the horse, disappear further into the canyon with the hellion corpse resting slack-mouthed against his shoulder. The horse would keep running for miles, Wicasah thought, feeling woozy. The horse wouldn't stop. Evan would be bound to his victim that decayed in his arms until . . . until . . .

"This used to be a sacred place," the heyoka said. Rage layered her voice like the strata of a rock. "Until war, greed, and bombs rendered it into nothing. Just because it's been desecrated, doesn't take away its value."

Wicasah swayed with the heft of anchor inside him. The shadow-soul was smoke in his lungs, cataracts in his eyes, arthritis in his joints. A cotton-candy dawn surrounded the heyoka, making the world shiver in a mismatched way. He had one foot in Helia, and the other in prairie grass under a blackened tree. Each piece of him began to mismatch—his intestines crooked, his spine bending, his legs bowing. The heyoka reached up, plucked the rainbow strands of the funnel that glimmered in Helia's hellfire sky like clouds, and then broke every cell of Wicasah with electricity.

Wicasah screamed until his voice had no meaning, until a scream meant nothing but a sound like the lapping of waves and the rustle of leaves—a call that simply *was* without cause. He was a mule carrying a shadow, a river clam protecting the shadow-meat he was forced to clap around, his smooth inside abalone-purple and pearl-white. Helia dismantled around him. The rainbow strands caught him, a hundred fly-fishing lines launched from the sky, penetrating his skin, and reeling him up and into a realm of familiarity.

Briefly, he remembered this place as a gravesite—unmarked, unconsecrated, un-sacred. Just a slab of dirt without any shimmer or shine, nothing but the bones of his kin resting inside it. Only now the campsite has become a smooth-sided smoking pit and the blanket mattress had transformed to a yurt-hide dwelling.

The heyoka loomed before him and yanked on the anchor. Shattering the clam into two sides. Splitting timber into logs. Breaking the mule.

The shadow spilled out from him like steam, loose with curls. Wicasah grasped that raw ache inside of him, his hand over his chest, as the heyoka untangled the spirit he'd carted away from Helia. Cupping it between her hands, it shone like a star. With an upward glance, she reached up and with forefinger and thumb, pinched the Milky Way, dragging that starry road down and nestling the star on it. The sky wobbled like tight elastic. Wicasah swayed as the rainbow threads stretched and twanged like too-tight guitar strings.

"Imagine binding all souls to you," the heyoka whispered, her eyes still trained on the stars even as she let go of the night sky. It wobbled and settled. "That was only one."

"I lied to them, then," Wicasah gasped, spilling this ghastly truth, thinking of the demon trio. Bruises lined his soul, the shadows belonging to him limping, the anchor inside him dragging him down. "I can't bind thousands of shadows. Not like that. Not again."

"Yes," the heyoka mused, "but we can find different ways to take the souls out of Helia. Set up territories and reservations, map out the land like the European-half of your blood has done for a century." The heyoka's smile spread into a cruel grimace.

"But Domino," Wicasah whispered and everything lay within those words: his hopes, his grief, his love. His loss.

"You'll get your brother," the heyoka said. "The dealers were impressed. You put on quite the show." She leaned down, her clawed hand stroking his chin. "But you will not tell anyone about the souls I give you. You will have your brother and they will have their fresh land and I will have the souls I want. Do we have an agreement?"

"Do I have a choice?" Wicasah asked. He could barely feel her touch.

"Do you want your brother?"

"Then, yes," Wicasah said, hoarse.

The heyoka shrunk, the wide glory of her compacting into a different shade as if pushing her essence into an ill-fitting body. "Grow the soul a body," she said. "Then, you'll need to find the lady-slippers queen. A psychopomp to lure your Domino out if he is found."

"The lady-slippers queen?" Wicasah asked. He was nothing but a blue and white magpie, collecting words like baubles, lining his nest with tidbits and advice.

The heyoka softened and tapped his lower lip, plumping it out until the opened brand burned. "Ask your owner. She's had time and training, now."

The rainbow lines trembled into a pastel slide of color. The heyoka gathered a fistful and tested their elasticity before disappearing down their lines, leaving Wicasah smoking on his knees in the middle of a prairie. The black tree stood before him, the gnarled branches trimmed with crinkling buds. Cottonwood? Below it, three rock cairns lay under its shade. The brand on his lip stung and, as if in response, he pivoted, looked behind him to a yurt. The door was open and the inner firelight illuminated a woman in the doorway. He knew that dark hair, those black spectacles, only this Naomi had grown by years. The teenager was gone, leaving the lean lines of a young woman.

"Wicasah?" she said softly. The brand glowed in recognition and he felt her tug on it in experimentation.

"How . . . how long?" he asked, horror like a waterfall crashing in his belly.

"Three years," she whispered, coming closer. Wicasah shut his eyes tight. He didn't want to look at her. He didn't want to know by the erasure of her youth that he'd lost so much time.

How much lightning had filled his world in the time between then and now? Count the miles by the seconds between the strikes. That thunder had been traveling for years when it finally arrived:

the too-slow sound desperate to follow the map of bright purple and yellow. When it landed, it rumbled Wicasah's bones loose. When the peal sounded, it vibrated the glass of Wicasah's spirit. The thunderclap shattered his mind.

CHAPTER 10

TIME DISMANTLED AROUND HIM, coalescing into the pixels and motes of three years. Had it really taken that long for the heyoka to pressurize his body to hold shadows? For Helia to collapse around him? For the funnel's rainbow strands to trawl the depths until its net entangled him?

The monstrous form hovered around him like a lens flare. Desperately, he wanted to step inside that larger, terrifying shape. The armored plates and leathery wings felt safer and more familiar than this soft, fleshy mold. Yet he couldn't quite shift. He'd been lightning struck and had curled into a ball while the last remnants of thunder left him fragile.

Naomi curved over him. Warm hands slid around him. He looked up into her face, dazed. "You don't look like her," he blurted out.

A soft smile crossed her lips. She knew his line of thought. "I always took after my father."

"How . . . how old are you now?"

"Nineteen," she said.

A hysteric laugh eeked out of him. The night held the brisk chill of fall shaking off the heat of summer and slipping into a bone-chilling winter. A neat cairn of rounded stones piled underneath the blackened tree and tears peppered Wicasah's cheeks. "You build a marker?" he asked, his fingers reaching out and wanting to touch.

Naomi let out a soft huff. "You left me without much to do," she said. "Come inside." Taking his elbow, she helped him stand. He teetered into her. She was firm and wiry as knapweed.

"Why did you stay?" he whispered.

"You're the link to my power. Plus, I have a lead on you." She tapped his jaw and he tongued the tender, raised shape of his brand.

I HAVE ASKED TO BE WHERE NO STORMS COME

You could've desecrated Domino's site and earned your power. Why didn't you? After all us Bluepoint men have done, why are you showing me kindness?

She pushed open the tacked-down door flap, and they entered the cozy dwelling. A fire licked happily in a half-buried pit, the smoke rising out the hole in the roof. A rickshaw table stood off to the side, full of herb bundles, prairie grass, lupine, and yucca. A woman braided pieces of hay together and when she looked up, Wicasah's knees gave out.

"All-Worlds," he breathed. The fragile barriers of his mind shuddered as if being battered by a gust of wind.

All-Worlds rose and cupped Wicasah's face in his hands. Wicasah blinked back tears, overwhelmed.

"The Dark and Bloody trembled with your departure and split wider with your return. My small home was in danger so I followed the strands that pointed here to Naomi."

The rawness in his chest, where the heyoka had tied and anchored a shadow to him, throbbed. When he covered the pain, he felt the oversensitive hook shrink back. His shadows wrapped around it like gauze, and for a moment, Wicasah felt as if their protection might stop his metaphysical guts from spilling out on the ground.

"All-Worlds has been teaching me many things," Naomi said, her fingers gently touching All-World's shoulder.

"You could've had your power by now," Wicasah said and flattened his palms against the dirt ground. "You should've . . . I don't know. Finished school. Got drunk at the local bar."

"Who's to say I didn't?" Naomi shared a look with All-Worlds.

Wicasah opened his mouth, knowing he sounded petulant and ridiculous, when the reflective shine of a glass container caught his attention. Bigger than a mason jar, round like an ether container, and arranged like a planter, it sat propped near the table. Lichen-coated rocks and dark soil propped up the lax face of his brother. Youth and age warred on Domino's shiny-slick yet wrinkled skin. Long eyelashes curled like lace against his closed eyelids. The softly parted moue of his lips balanced in the deepest sleep. Wicasah crawled to the container, pressed his face and palm against the glass. "It worked?" he asked. "He grew?"

"Several times," Naomi said, crouching beside him. "The first growth was odd and began to rot six months in. The second one came through crooked. This third one has taken, though. I haven't seen any anomalies."

"Thank you." Tears pressed against Wicasah's eyes and he closed them briefly, imagining the frustration and despair he would have experienced if he'd had to bury Domino over and over, half-grown or not. He'd do anything for Naomi for this. The brand seemed like a small price to pay. "You can have my life," he whispered to her. "Strike me dead anytime you want. Take your power."

"I'll consider it." Her expression was calm, but sorrowful as if he were an abandoned barn kitten. Mewling and sad, waiting for milk. Wicasah swayed, listing into Naomi's arms.

"I have to find the lady-slipper queen," he whispered to her, fearful All-Worlds would hear.

Naomi's brow furrowed in confusion.

"You'll have to wait until spring, then," All-Worlds huffed, much closer than Wicasah had imagined.

A storm built in the corners of Wicasah's vision. The dark clouds rolled through to ground any higher thinking he might possess.

"I'll wait then," he managed just before the rain began to fall, drumming his consciousness into wet splotches of sleep. He turned into Naomi's shoulder and whispered, "He's protecting you, Naomi, but wait until you're selfish. Then, he'll turn his back on you."

—————◆—————

The gray skies of a prairie winter sent whipping wind that cut straight to the bone and gave voice to an otherwise flat land—a howl that outstripped even a lone wolf call. Wicasah shivered in the midst of the snow squall, standing like a stubborn and foolish juniper brush. The wind pushed his shoulders further into a hunch. The chill circulated in his caverned marrow. Flurries danced on thermals in lieu of the birds. Ospreys perched on fence posts with their wings closed tight, studying as Wicasah defied the elements.

Spring felt like a dream in this never-ending winter. A tug on the hook inside him had led him here. He'd responded to the heyoka's demands, but lightning had no claim here.

Loneliness crept over him the past few months with a detached frustration. All-Worlds was no guide for him. Despite Wicasah's questions, the woman had erected a barrier between them. To All-

Worlds, Wicasah hadn't earned the answers to his questions. For Wicasah, there wasn't time.

"The stories you demand of me are earned through years of dedication and mastery," All-Worlds had finally snapped at him. "They are rewards. Do you wish to become a shaman? A medicine man? A healer or doctor? Put in the training. Only then will I give you the tales of the lady-slipper queen."

"I don't have years," Wicasah had hissed. "What does it matter if I'm a healer or a warrior? Isn't it part of my right to know the stories of the land I'm from?"

What a glare All-Worlds had thrown at him. "There's nothing pure in your blood," he shot back. "Nothing but mutt-blood and mutt-magic."

And so on and so forth. Now, when Wicasah studied the bunchgrass rattling like maracas in the winter breeze, he felt no ties to them. He gathered no pleasure from cooing to the downy silver leaves of white moss and shrubs curled close to the ground. He had no idea where he came from, who his people were, except that evil muddied the ocean of his blood like spilled oil. This homeland that he'd walked on was just as foreign to him now as the Brightside. He had no claim to the land he'd been raised on. He never would. That realization felt like a twisting knife.

Now more than ever, his one tie lay with his brother. Domino shared the oil-ooze of evil, the same suffocating thorn-studded vines rooted them together. Wicasah might not belong to the land, couldn't claim or tell any of the stories that enriched the earth he stood on, but Domino belonged to him. He belonged to Domino. As always, the only semblance and stability of home was a person, not a place.

The hook stung as if ripped off a fresh scab. Against the horizon, a shape struggled with the squall—a woman wearing a tanned hide as a cloak, her long straight hair blowing against the whiteout sky like spilled ink.

She'd called to him. Wicasah had responded, slipping out of the yurt after another well-trod argument with All-Worlds, where Naomi had wrung her hands and sought to keep the peace, but no peace could be found in the battle between good and evil.

"I thought I might have to convince you to come, especially after last time," the heyoka said, her mouth a dark rose slash across her face. The childish mask she'd worn before seemed ragged, a well-used sheath showing its age.

"I can't go back to Helia," Wicasah said, cutting her off. "I barely survived it."

She cocked her head to the side, considering. "The damage is always extensive when you are shuffled through a death-funnel. Does this mean you are not interested to hear that I've spoken with the demons on your behalf?" She grinned at the word demon as if it were a simplistic term for a much larger concept.

Wicasah's hope sung a note as crystal-clear as a bell. "Three years you kept me," he growled. Ice embroidered along his braid, stiff over his shoulder.

"They're getting closer." The heyoka held out a closed fist to him. "It means going back to Helia, though."

Wicasah tongued the brand on his lip. It had healed again and now that he'd gotten used to it, the link between him and Naomi suspended like a swinging bridge over a river. He could feel her, just as he was certain she could sense him.

"Tell me," he said.

"They've acquiesced that binding all Helia's souls to you is impossible. They've accepted my solution of setting up allotted spaces for the human souls, instead. All contingent that you're able to do the magic, of course."

Wicasah slowly held his hand out to accept the gift in her hand. She dropped a cotton ball into his palm. A pinprick of reddish-brown stained the center. The shadows inside Wicasah tensed in excitement. One pressed against his hard palate, eager for a taste. *Domino.*

"Is he hurt?" Wicasah asked, desperation clogging his throat. He shielded the cotton from the squall, slipped it into the bag he wore.

The heyoka shrugged. "How am I to know? Aiyana and Manit demand you prove that you can wrangle the human souls if you cannot extract them from Helia."

"What does Ickto want?" Wicasah said, remembering the smoky whip of the third demon.

"If he can possess your brother when they find him."

"Absolutely not." Wicasah suppressed a shiver as the wind blew past and the two of them leaned closer, like a buffalo herd weathering the storm. "Spring is close. I can't leave to negotiate with them only to discover I have to wait for the seasons to change again. I need to find the lady-slipper queen. All-Worlds won't help me. Naomi won't help me."

"It's difficult, to be alone," the heyoka said, her bitterness sudden. "Know this, though. I will not take you into Helia again without the promise that you will bring back another shadow I've chosen. That is my price."

Wicasah swallowed hard. "Like I said. I barely survived."

"But you survived. The price is high for everything you want. Once, I would never have asked for a price. I would have asked for trade, but times change, and there are so many different blood origins inside you. I don't know what rules you honor."

Shame boiled inside Wicasah. The frigid air dissolved any flush he might've produced. "My mother was a witch. My father a mixed bag. That's all you need to know. I honor *my* rules. I honor what it takes to get my brother back."

"Then to Helia we go." The heyoka held out her hand, the tips of her fingers white-blue from frostbite.

Wicasah took a breath and accepted. The pastel rainbow strands swirled around him, cocooning him and splitting his world. Again, he stood with one foot on the wintered plains and the other on the fragile precipice of the Dark and Bloody. Again, the funnel sucked him in like a summer twister as his bones melted to convince his mind he'd died so he could enter Helia.

The hot rush of a chinook wind felt like a balm to his frozen soul, chasing away the nauseating chill. Grass and shrubland had been replaced by endless sand. A desert surrounded him. The trio of demons loomed over him—scaly hellion, ram-horned fury, and sly smoke.

"The heyoka gave you your gift," Ickto smiled.

"We're glad you still want to trade," Manit snarled.

"What do you propose?" Aiyana asked. "We have brought you more humans."

Wicasah groaned as he stood on clawed feet. Ants crawled over his scales. The memory of the feather-light cotton ball lingered on his fingertips and he thought of Domino's blood staining the sand, thought of protection symbols he used to craft with marker and love. Aiyana extended her arm to encompass the shantytown in front of them. A tarp covered a hole in the ground, a post with wind-whipped papers tacked to it, a makeshift, white-boarded church with unknown symbols painted on the door.

"I need rocks," he gasped out. "Wood. Anything that can be painted on."

Ickto and Manit exchanged looks, but Aiyana knelt and tapped her long claws against the sand. The ants swarmed away from Wicasah and Helia offered up the requested items as if they'd bled through from another world. Long flat sandstone. Black felt-tip markers.

"What are you going to do?" Ickto asked, sitting on the ground beside Wicasah.

"If I can't take them out, I can seal them in," Wicasah said, uncapping the marker and putting felt tip to smooth surface. Protection. Barriers. Magic half-concocted from memory and spellbook. Magic crafted out of love and intent.

By the time Wicasah put the final touches on the spell, his sandstone fence encircled the shantytown. The demons watched his work with interest but remained silent until he sat back on his haunches, exhausted. A migraine threatened to encompass his mind in clusters and he breathed the acrid air deeply, hoping to settle the tightening around his scalp and horns. He heard the rumbles of thunder far away and fear clenched his heart.

"Bring them out," he managed to say.

His shadows bounded around him, wobbly with fatigue. Aiyana smiled and reached to run her hands through their amorphous shapes. Manit whistled and, as if acquiescing, Helia shook the earth, making sand fall on top of the tarp and collapsing it inside the hole.

Wicasah heard shouts, watched as humans climbed out of the hole. Seeing the demons, they shrieked, levering shotguns and blunt shivs at them. Gunshots exploded, the sulfuric fire of old gunpowder shooting through the air and hitting the protection barrier. Round bullets ricocheted off the wall, pinging back towards the humans. Some screamed and clutched bleeding legs. Others tried to climb over the sandstone barriers and were pushed back by an invisible wall.

Manit finally wore a pleased smile.

"Incredible," Aiyana breathed.

"You'll need to care for them," Wicasah told Helia, patting the sand. "They won't be able to fend for themselves on their reserve. They won't have anything."

"Fine by me," Aiyana said. She brought her claws to her nose and breathed in deep. "You'll have your soul soon."

Wicasah couldn't watch the panicked humans scrambling for

freedom. He couldn't focus on the demons, delighted that he'd upheld his end of the bargain. They promised to find Domino. He promised to continue lassoing human souls throughout the inhospitable Helia with drawn barriers.

The heyoka stood along the horizon line. A shadow of a woman graced her side. She motioned to him. Ready to let him shuffle spirits again. Ready to let thunder rattle his soul into madness.

CHAPTER 11

BY THE TIME Wicasah crawled back to Naomi, the hook in his chest had become a scarred nub deformed from many crossings, and Naomi neared her thirtieth year.

He found her in a saloon on Main. Black canvas clothed her legs and a white-shell button-down shirt accentuated her rail-thin body. Small polished stones gleamed in her ears. She laughed with a group of men, laid down her corner-bent cards, and took the pot while they saluted her by finishing their whiskies.

The town had expanded from when Wicasah had last been there. Ore and pyrite became staples. Dirt caked into the wrinkles of the bar-drinkers, indications of how they spent their waking hours. No one cared for dinosaur bones anymore, not unless it could be pumped out of the core as sludge and rendered into brown gold.

Wicasah nudged Naomi's shoulder and she turned to him with a surprised, delighted grin. Her kindness still unsettled him. He couldn't understand where it came from, only that it continued to soften over the years. The brand on his lip was as fresh as the day she'd placed it there.

"All-Worlds told me about Fia," he whispered to her.

The corners of Naomi's lips crumpled as if holding in a grief that had been masked over with cards and laughter. She pushed up her small lens spectacles. The dark frames caught the candlelight. "I just got back from the funeral," she managed as a barmaid filled her glass with a shy, coquettish smile.

"And Kit?" he asked.

She shrugged. "Still there. I thought about bringing her back with me, but the house is her world and she likes it that way."

"Maybe you should move back," he suggested.

She turned to glare at him, her bangs braided out of her face.

By All-World's deft hand, he had no doubt. "You can't get rid of me that easily," she snorted. "Who else is going to drag your drooling body out of the snowstorm?"

"That was one time," Wicasah said, holding up his finger.

"Or when you appeared in the creek, shivering with pneumonia."

Wicasah winced. That one had been bad. The heyoka had tied twins to him that time, souls that wouldn't risk separation. That crossing had come on the heels of crafting a huge reserve in the wasteland spiral of Helia and he'd already felt the strain. The world had come back to him in snippets. Dying of thirst and never being able to drink a drop. Seeking out the river packed with ice floes. Becoming disoriented in the frigid waters until he heard Naomi sharply demand he follow her. The burning of the brand when he didn't follow her orders.

He'd been sick for two months. The crackle in his lungs sounded like brown packaging paper being crushed. All-Worlds had forced willow-bark down his throat at Naomi's behest, cursing witches all the while. Naomi had bathed his skillet-hot body and piled blankets on him, fretting about fetching a town physician. All-Worlds had given her a look that would've broken pottery. Wicasah didn't miss the way Naomi had been chastised, and gave a small kiss to All-Worlds' in apology.

Wicasah had eyes. All-Worlds doted on Naomi. She was the prodigy-witch he'd sought, the one Wicasah could never be. But Naomi was still a witch, with the amoral glazing her bones.

"Point taken," Wicasah said and opened his palm, "but not for much longer."

Naomi squinted at the blood-soaked bullet in his hand.

"They found him," Wicasah said, unable to hide his trembling happiness. "He's almost ready. This time, his body will be ready, too."

Domino's regrown body had upgraded from the ether glass to a long planter box inside the yurt. White moss and tan and red mushrooms dotted around him. Once, Wicasah's shadows had possessed his brother's body in a moment of Wicasah's diverted attention. Wicasah had been terrified when the body had stumbled out of the yurt with a simpleton grin on his face and nearly pitched into the fire. It had taken years for that body to bloom. He couldn't imagine what would happen if this one failed.

"For once you're around in the spring," she said, even as her eyes glistened with jest.

"I just need to find the lady-slipper queen. All-Worlds has to tell me about her," Wicasah said, fervently, and played his own cards, hoping she didn't call his bluff. "Will you help me?"

Naomi glanced sharply away. "Haven't I done enough for you?"

Wicasah stilled. He'd feared this. That at the time when everything aligned it would all fall apart. "Please," he whispered. "I promised you my life. You can come into your power once Domino is back."

"I don't want power," she snarled. "Not anymore. What am I going to do, Wicasah? Witch blood runs in my veins. If I kill you for it, All-Worlds will never forgive me. But if I don't, then I wonder if the latent power will kill me, instead. It's like burning coal within me that won't die."

Wicasah saw the familiar press and pull of a conduit seeking release against her throat. He reached out and placed his finger on it, like locating a tumor.

The lacquer on the bar top split as if an ax had sliced it through. Naomi let out a sigh and rubbed her finger in the mark her anger had manifested. "I've done the time for you, Wicasah. I trained to be a shaman. I've earned the tale of the lady-slipper queen. For you." She closed her eyes. "Why do you think I'm here right now? All-Worlds is furious with me. He wished to keep the story secret, but I'd earned it. The witchery is strong inside of me, and he knows I'll give the tale straight to you. But if he kept it to himself, it would invalidate his beliefs." Naomi reached out and took his hand, holding it tight. "I'm using everything he believes in and turning it against him. Just like a witch."

Wicasah tried not to squirm. Intimacy was strange and uncomfortable to him. Nights spent with women were unenthusiastic events that left him numb and melancholy on the inside. He wasn't a good lover, his friendships minimal at best, and he felt unsafe being so physically exposed with strangers. Touch was difficult because he knew it meant he'd be required to give something. He had nothing he wanted to part with.

Naomi wanted reassurance, but by the way her eyes glittered, he knew she wanted more. He forced himself to keep her hand in his.

"If I tell it to you, you have to promise to take me with you," she said. "I want to be one hundred percent in this now. Like partners."

Wicasah stared at her. "Why?" he asked softly. "What would you find? My whole life I've been told I'm selfish and wrong. This . . . quest is nothing but me trying to save the last good thing I know."

"I know," Naomi said and her dark eyes hardened, "but it's the most love I've seen anyone have in my whole life. My mother didn't love my father. All-Worlds loves me, but there are limits to it, complicated ties I can't help but unbind. You and Domino . . . " She inhaled deep. "I want to see this to the end. You trust me, don't you?"

Wicasah turned his hand until he could interlace his fingers with hers. There. He'd done it. "More than I care to admit."

"So, let's get the fuck out of here. Let's grab the rose-colored strands and find the lady-slipper queen," Naomi said.

Wicasah signaled for another drink.

———◆———

"The lady-slippers queen," Naomi slurred as she gathered only the pinkened rainbow strands cascading throughout the sky, "is the psychopomp born from the Dark and Bloody."

Wicasah handed her a bouquet of the pink gossamer threads. They tugged in the direction of the mountains looming far in the distance. "I thought the funnel sucked all souls away from whatever afterlife they were intended for. Now, you're telling me that this queen shuffles the souls there?"

Naomi tested the strands by tugging at them and made a pleased sound when they twanged with tension. "She blocks other death-guides from tearing the funnel apart and fetching the souls they should have taken."

Wicasah frowned, thinking of the heyoka stitching souls to him. Thinking of how she'd placed those souls along the Milky Way. He hadn't told Naomi about that, yet. "Why would she do that?"

Naomi shrugged and held her hand out. Wicasah tentatively gave the bullet to her. The sooty plumes baked along the side of the brass casings looked like ink in water. "All-Worlds said his lover opened the crevasse and the queen emerged from it to drag him inside." Naomi nestled the bullet in the nest of pinkened rainbow strands which shimmered like a dew-dipped spider's web.

"She's a woman whose spine is the crest of the mountains and her womb the darkest cave. With her slippers, you can tread there and find a soul that's forgotten it has died. All-Worlds says the Dark and Bloody twisted her, though. That she'll take everything from you."

"You spent how many years getting that story?" Wicasah threw his head back and laughed. "What bullshit. If I'd gone the right way and apprenticed and that was all he told me, I'd have killed him."

Naomi's tight-lipped smile told him she disagreed with his methods, but that she too felt the payout unworthy. "I asked to know more, but the story is a personal one, Wicasah. It's not just about becoming a shaman or a magician. It's learning about how to connect with All-Worlds so that he feels safe enough to tell the tale. Somehow, he was involved with the complete transformation of the world and lost the man he loved. He has reason to be cautious."

Wicasah's laughter died. He'd come to terms with the fact that All-Worlds and he had very different methodologies when it came to the concept of love.

Naomi gestured him closer. Tension sung within the rainbow strands, as if they were quivering for release. His shadows unraveled from him. Benedicta's red-tinted shade wrapped around Naomi, even though Wicasah knew she couldn't quite remember her daughter anymore. Naomi uttered a soft sound of surprise, then tentatively reached out to slip an arm around his waist. Her breath brushed across his chin. His shadows enveloped them tighter until only the pink glowed like a sunset between them. The sharp tang of booze combined with lavender and sage filled his nose from her hair. Naomi's dark eyes reflected the light, casting them as warm pools that he could sink into. His mouth went dry. He was stunned by her—not just the way she'd grown from youth to young woman, but that she was still here, at his side, helping him do the impossible year after year.

"Hold on tight," she whispered, sounding breathless.

The threads snapped out of her hands. The world crumbled into pieces of a puzzle, a familiar sensation he felt whenever the heyoka yanked him in and out of Helia. This last time, Ickto had placed that bloodstained bullet into his hands and said, "He was difficult to break. It was hard to make him forget he was dead."

The prairie fell away. Wicasah's stomach dropped as if he were flying with the barnstormer and fairy lights dotted the night. When he felt the world reassemble back around him, his shadows loosened, and he saw they stood in a valley. The jagged line of a mountain range surrounded them, jutting like teeth. A pool glimmered at the mouth of the cavern, reflecting a rainbow spectrum of blue to teal, yellow to purple. Small bubbles boiled to the surface.

Wicasah stumbled out of Naomi's embrace, astounded at her power. He knelt and held his hand out, feeling the heat emanate from the water. "How do we get across?" he whispered.

"There." Naomi pointed across the pool as the shape of a woman emerged from the cave and stood on the opposite bank. Hair thick and curly as a buffalo, her rose-gold eyes seemed to glow. A petal-thin and veined cloak graced her shoulders. The lines of the world converged around her and looped around her skin like yarn. Somehow, though, these seemed different than the ones spun through the world. Thicker, somehow. She sucked in a deep breath and whatever scent she picked up seemed to displease her.

"Back again, All-Worlds?"

Wicasah shook his head. "I am not with him. I come to take an alive soul that's caught in your funnel."

"I only capture the dead," she said. Tilting her head to the side, she began to walk across the water surface. "I have no resurrected life here. All-Worlds wears many faces. How do I know you're not here for Anxius?"

Wicasah exchanged a confused look with Naomi. The bullet rolled in his hand and the rainbow strands clung to it, like gum tendrils. He held it out towards her. "Look here," he said. "Take this and know I speak the truth."

The psychopomp reached them, yet still lingered in the shallow depths of the hot spring. She accepted the bullet and placed it under the waters of the pool. Blood coated her fingers and spilled across the spring, transforming into images. Wicasah's breath caught as he saw Domino's face again. Animated. Road-rashed. Resurrected.

"You are a witch of great evil and love," the lady-slipper queen said to Wicasah as her fingers trailed through the images. "You are like Anxius in that way. He too envisioned grand plans to boil the core of the earth and cleanse the land of those who saw what they could take instead of what they could give. He had great love for

All-Worlds, but his evil poisoned his love until he no longer saw the good in anyone. There would be no Heaven or Hell or starry road or reanimation after the Dark and Bloody. People would no longer kill and torture and traumatize in the name of gods or angels or spirits or familiars. Instead, there would be eyes in the birch, teeth in the peaks, fear of the earth. That was his choice. He will hold the funnel up forever. It was his creation, after all."

"I promise you," Wicasah said, his hand covering his heart. "I want only the soul that you see before you."

"You already have many souls tied to you," she whispered. "What is one more?"

"This one is my home," Wicasah said, hating the thick catch of devotion in his voice. Naomi had gone still beside him. "There is forgiveness for me in him. There is a future with him. I can heal with him. There is peace."

There is a quiet life for us, he thought in addendum. *One where no blood needs to be spilled. One not marked by magic.*

The lady-slipper queen studied him, then stepped onto the bank. Her gnarled hand covered his over his heart. The golden flecks glittered in the rose quartz of her iris. "I know the heyoka's mark," she said, sounding wistful. "Although, she is not truly a heyoka, is she? She's chipped away at you. If you continue on as such, you'll go insane, but I cannot let you into the caves. I don't think you'd give up your power."

"Once I have that soul back, I won't have to work with the heyoka anymore." He curled his hands around the lady-slipper queen's. "I can give you my power. Have it. Take me. Just let me inside."

"Who says I want you?"

Wicasah's mouth went dry. It still hurt, to know he would give up everything and it still wasn't enough.

"You're chased by thunder," she mused and seemed to pluck at stray lint along his shoulders.

"Do you want the heyoka?" Wicasah asked. He was reckless with his wants.

The lady-slipper queen's pink mouth was caught between her teeth. "Would she come?"

"For me, she will," Wicasah said.

"Give me your name then," the lady-slipper queen said. "Anxius will want it. Another witch for his chains."

I HAVE ASKED TO BE WHERE NO STORMS COME

"Wicasah, no," Naomi hissed and reached out, putting a hand on the lady-slipper queen's arm to hold her back. "If you give her ownership of your name, then she can use your powers. This Anxius will hold you hostage."

Wicasah studied the psychopomp and saw no deception within her. "I'm doomed either way," he said. "Take it."

"*Take it.* Another one of Anxius' favorite sayings," the lady-slipper queen said. She stepped out of her shoes. "Who's going to shoe your pretty foot?" she asked.

Wicasah yanked off his own boots, ignoring Naomi's protestations. He stepped into the shoes—white delicate flowers shaped like clogs. The petals enclosed around his ankle and molded to the conforms of his feet.

"Don't take them off," the lady-slipper queen whispered, "or the darkness will take you and the colors will boil you. Anxius will siphon away your power with time, but if you lose your shoes, he will eat you in one fell swoop."

Her words were a smear to Wicasah. He only saw the final gauntlet which to pass. Wicasah stepped out onto the boiling water, his heart clogged with fear that he would be burnt alive. Instead, he seemed to float. The last thing he saw was the psychopomp urging Naomi closer to her, their heads bent together in sudden conversation before the cavern of the lady-slipper queen closed around him.

———◆———

The darkness enveloped him completely. The shoes glowed with golden-white starlight as he padded blindly into the cave. Inside, it smelled of cold, damp earth. The pinkened rainbow strands stained his hands with bioluminescence, giving him meager light to see by. Pale tan stalagmites shot up from the floor. The ground pulsated around him, expanding and compacting from tiny breathless pockets to huge catacombs. He felt as though he walked through the long-dead skeleton of a massive deity. The earth was his sky and sea.

Perhaps, he crawled through the body of a god.

At some point, he began to wonder if his body *was* the cave. Stalactites curved down over the flat plane of his breastbone to merge with the diamond-hard ladder of his spine. Oil and coal filled his muscles, heavy with a fracking's harvest. His lungs were hollow packets of talc that panted and wheezed. His stomach

257

gurgled like an onyx pit. His brain was a green malachite mass. His skin sloughed off flakes of mica. Yet only his heart squeezed and stuttered, wet with life.

Sometimes, the silence rang with music. The chime and clank of chains rattled within the rushing pulse of his blood as he walked into the chamber of kings. Ossified pillars surrounded him. Holding his hands up, the fading light blooming on his hands illuminated the matured shape of Domino's bone familiars. Wicasah's jaw dropped in awe, like a boulder finally being split in two. The rounded eyes and surprised childish mouths of the familiars were now grim. These bone kings loomed with rock-swords immobile in their hands as warriors, holding vigil over a small pink flower in their protective circle.

A bitterroot. A resurrection flower.

Wicasah inched closer to the fuchsia sharp-bladed bloom. In a way, it reminded him of an urchin clinging to a rockpool. Closer to the center, the pink hue faded into a throbbing golden center. Wicasah's breath caught in his throat. The life that had marked his from birth lived in that fragile bitterroot, so close to the dark ebb of death, barely hanging on to life. Bending down, Wicasah plucked the starburst bloom and cradled it between his palms, holding it close to his chest.

The music of chains rattled the chamber. Wicasah curved over the flower to protect it. A long mournful cry vibrated throughout the cavern, making it shudder as if with earthquake. Wicasah looked up and felt his heart stutter in his chest. The bone kings had shifted. Where once they stood straight and motionless, now they were arched, their swords drawn, their mouths carved into snarls. Another cry rumbled the cavern, the tonality like that of a monster. Stalagmites tipped and crashed to the floor. Wicasah shut his eyes and when he opened them again the bone kings loomed over him, the tips of their swords angled at him.

One pointed a bony claw into the darkness, though.

Fear cascaded throughout Wicasah and he blinked again, only to see a second king point in the same direction even as the sword points had gotten closer. His breathing came out in desperate pants. Holding the bitterroot as if it were glass, he forced his earth-body to plunge in the direction the bone kings pointed.

The roar sounded again. Stalactites shivered on their perch. Wicasah dodged as one crashed down, tripping over the sharp edge. He felt a delicate tear, and with a muffled cry, glanced down to the ripped side of his lady-slipper.

When he looked back up, the bone kings had split up. Four loomed over him while another set remained behind as if in defensive sacrifice. The cry shook the cavern, originating from somewhere deep inside the earth.

For a moment, Wicasah envisioned being buried alive, slowly watching the crumbling dirt snuff out the fragile resurrection flower. The agonized scream came again. A sprinkle of soil rained on his face and he pelted into the darkness. He couldn't look back. Shattered rocks sliced through his slippers. A burning sensation crept up his toes and into his heels, nearly paralyzing his tendons. The bitterroot shuddered. Petals lifted and broke off, floating behind him to be crushed.

When he glanced behind him, only three bone kings remained. Their swords raised as if to defend against some unknown terror. Tears blurred Wicasah's vision, yet he kept running even as the burn upgraded to an agonized throb. He didn't know where he was going or what waited for him on the other side of the darkness.

The sparse light from his hands disappeared. Open rings of white floated in and out of his sight, making him wonder if his eyes were open or shut. A sob crowded his lungs. Even if he made it back to the pool, he wouldn't be able to cross. The shredded petal-shoes clung to his skin like a second layer, slick with his blood.

Another beastly roar shook the darkness. Behind him, only one bone king remained. The bitterroot curled in on itself, the innermost petals wilting.

Then, ahead of him, like the first hint of dawn cascading over the mountains, emerged a green light. The green flash as the sun descended, the green burst of a new day. The bitterroot's inner gold flickered like the last dregs of firelight caught in a heavy wind, but Wicasah knew that embers could smolder for days.

He flung himself toward that last flash of green light and into the vast incomprehensible void of the beyond.

PART IV:
PLAIT OF POWER

CHAPTER 1
DOMINO

HE WOKE TO LIGHT—bright light, God's light, blinding light—searing his pupils and frying his brain.

This must be a new torture. Domino thrashed, wrenching his arms up to shield his eyes. What if he lost his eyesight to this pure, white fire?

He kicked out. His foot slammed into something solid. He was scrunched up, curled like a baby in the womb. His arms flailed, hitting a wall with a hard thump. A loud, unbearable alarm suddenly went off, splintering his skull, piercing his ears until he shouted to make it stop. What new level of Helia was this?

His tongue felt bloated. Was that dirt in his mouth? He bit down and tasted blood. Wires sprouted out of him. Gauze obscured his vision. He thrashed again, filled with insensible rage to escape and destroy. Being trapped in claustrophobic light was just as bad as being in the dark.

Rapping, like knuckles on glass. A whoosh, like rolling down the windows while driving too fast. A hard grip on his ankles. He jerked and felt himself pulled until he slid, wet and petrified, confused and lost, into the next torment.

His breathing came in hitching gasps. Someone clogged his nose. More fucking wires. He could make out a blurry shape . . . Wicasah frantically talking to him with those dark eyes narrowed in terror. Domino started to cry with relief, which transformed into terror because he had been sent to a bad afterlife and somehow his brother had joined him.

"Domino, calm down, I have you. You have to calm down."

The shrieking alarm transformed into a continuous beep. Domino grabbed a fistful of wires protruding out of the back of his hand and yanked. Wicasah let out a plaintive no and put his hand over Domino's.

"I'll take them out, let me do it. Jesus, you got blood everywhere."

Blood. Familiar. It spurted out of the widened holes in his skin, dripping onto a dirty carpet. If there was blood, he must be somewhere he'd been before. Hell would soak it up. He began to shake from head to foot and looked down at his chest.

More wires, only these looked like roots budding with petals of blue, green, and red. A howl of rage rattled loose from him. The more he yanked on them the more the beeping became one long drone. He smacked his own face. The wires led up to his nose and it felt like a new piece of defilement. He let out a sob and watched Wicasah go from panicked to distressed.

"Let me do it, Jesus, just let me take it out."

Domino calmed long enough to feel his brother's fingertips prod his nose. Wicasah unhooked something and then the unpleasant experience of shooting out a slimy nasal wad made Domino sneeze.

Were those . . . pink petals coming out of his mouth?

He sucked in a deep breath as though he'd defeated an avalanche. Wicasah kept talking while gently removing the futuristic wire-roots hooked up to him. He choked out another cry when he realized he was stark naked and saw the catheter and the broken tubing swaying off the end of it.

The smell of piss permeated the air. A swinging bag connected to the incubator he'd been housed in, leaking all over the floor. He snarled at the intrusion, took the catheter with two hands, and Wicasah slapped him away. Domino screamed at him, for god's sake, he'd seen what the horrors hellhounds would do to bodies to make them unrecognizable, what were they planning to do to him?

Wicasah eased it out in one smooth motion, leaving Domino empty. Shame crashed through him. Full of useless situational fury, he whipped around, grabbed a chair, and smashed it into the incubator. He needed to destroy the unknown, the place he'd been bound.

Why did it look like a planter box?

Wicasah grabbed his shoulder, trying to ease the chair away. "Don't touch my dick," Domino stammered. The chair transformed into chunks in his hands. A crack splintered down the glass planter.

"Stop being one, then," Wicasah roared back at him and then abruptly sat crossed-legged on the floor. Domino continued to smash things, even though he recognized Wicasah's tactic. Domino had done it when young Wicasah threw a tantrum: sat down, hands on his knees, head cocked to watch the anger play itself out. Wicasah wore the same look, too. The one that said *you're behaving like a brat and I'm judging you every second it continues.*

Domino's sides heaved. He dropped the chair remnants and sat in front of Wicasah, their knees touching. He twitched and tried to control his hyperventilating.

Wicasah cleared his throat and reached for a bottle that had rolled off the side table Domino had knocked over. He unscrewed the top and pressed it into Domino's hands.

"You need to drink this. Can you drink it?"

Domino didn't know, but he would try. As soon as he smelled the foul mixture, he blanched and tried to give it back.

"You're dehydrated, you have to drink it," Wicasah insisted, pushing the bottle back into Domino's hands.

It smelled like urine, but that could be his own, really, but it also had a scent of lemongrass and sage, rose hips and despair. He took a shaky sip. The lukewarm liquid hit the back of his throat and rushed down with a minty aftertaste. Wicasah urged him to drink the rest all in one go, his hands steadying the bottle at Domino's mouth, helping him tip it back.

Finished, Domino let the bottle fall on the sopping carpet. He blinked. The world came into focus. Was it possible for a soul to feel heavy? Like the concoction has turned his spirit to concrete, which now sank into the ocean of his blood and bone. The thought made his stomach roll. A heave coursed through him.

"Don't throw up," Wicasah said, grabbing the back of Domino's neck and forcing him to bend his head down between his crossed legs. "That brew was expensive. I don't have enough to make another batch. You have to keep it down."

"Don't talk about it," Domino choked.

"What? Throwing up?"

"Don't say it, don't even say it." His tongue felt heavy, his words leaden.

Wicasah let out a chuckle.

"Not funny," Domino gasped, trying to ignore the warm rush

of saliva pooling in the cup of his lower lip, heralds of the final act of gastrointestinal defiance.

Wicasah petted Domino's head and didn't say anything else, but Domino knew Wicasah smiled, and some things really never changed. He gagged but kept it down, even as the acidic burn climbed his throat and slid back down. Finally, he put a hand out and leaned into Wicasah's shoulder, bringing himself back into an upright position.

"Feel better?" Wicasah asked. Deep crevices of worry marred his forehead. Domino didn't remember them being there before.

"Don't know," Domino whispered as Wicasah threw a blanket over his shoulders. Domino looked at the big oblong glass rectangle with a beige tarp. The incubator for a premature baby or fragile imported bulbs.

He didn't have the slightest idea where he was. This could be another of Ickto's dreams. The thought almost had the vomit coming up again.

Wicasah stroked his cheeks. Domino jerked back. "Please, stop crying," Wicasah murmured.

Domino wasn't crying. Crying was useless in hell. Yet, when he reached up to touch his own cheek, his finger came away shiny and wet. "How?" he croaked in disbelief.

"You've been crying since you woke up," Wicasah muttered, tucking his hand into his sleeve and wiping it against Domino's jaw. The blue material came back stained.

"I need to go outside," Domino said suddenly. He struggled to stand and leaned against his tall brother, heard Wicasah say, "No, why would we go outside, you just got out of hell, you're practically comatose, why would you want to go outside?"

"Gotta go outside," Domino reiterated. His knees gave out. How had he become so fragile?

"Why?" Wicasah asked, tucking Domino under his arm, and every desperate thought was in that question, every desire to understand, but Domino wouldn't know where he truly was until he was outside.

"Just take me," Domino growled. It sounded like a mewl.

"You're a pain in the ass," Wicasah snapped. "Don't even got you back for five minutes and it's all demands and *take me outside or I'll go on my own.*"

Domino didn't know exactly what Wicasah was getting at, but

he thought it was as close to an agreement as he was going to get, so he said, "Yeah."

Wicasah picked him up. The world tilted. He heard a creaking door and smelled fresh air that filled him like an answered wish. He looked into the dark night sky.

Everything had been wet: the piss, his blood, the tears, the drink. He soaked it up like a sponge. But as Wicasah steadied him, he strained his neck upwards to see the dark sprawl pinpricked with twinkling lights and a full harvest moon. His whole being felt as though it were coming apart at the seams. Those tiny reflections of light, millions of years away, were the truest thing he could cling to. The thing that defined this sky from Hell, because Hell didn't have stars. Not one. Not one blinking galaxy in the whole realm of fire.

——·——

A yearning woke him.

He sat on a creaky chesterfield saddled up as close to the front room's barred window just so he could see the same three stars of the Big Dipper's panhandle.

Wicasah sat scrunched on the other end of the sofa, burned out from magic and the stress of Domino's recovery. Seeing the night sky of the living overwhelmed Domino. His body was disorientated from being alive after it had been committed back to the earth. Wicasah had eased white pills onto his tongue.

"What did you do?" Domino asked, and leaned into a drug-slack slump against his brother.

"Grew you a new body," Wicasah answered, drunk-slack from bitter whisky. "Dug you up. 'Scuse me. Exhumed your corpse. Whoo, did you smell."

"Disgusting." Domino hiccupped.

"You. You were all shriveled. No bones. Could've fit you right in my arms." Wicasah crossed his arms to make a cradle.

"That's adorable," Domino said. He suddenly wanted to punch his brother in the arm, roughhouse with him, get on his nerves.

"Had to do it. Made the stupidest deals. Burned my feet off." Wicasah looked at him with wide eyes.

"S'why you gotta keep me around. Gotta stop you from doing dumb shit like that."

"First body didn't work. Naomi told me. Second one grew wrong. This one did the trick, though. You's gassy near the end." Wicasah patted Domino on the knee.

Domino went quiet, imagining how he must've grown like a tumor. "I wasn't gassy," he finally declared. "I was dead." Domino's head lolled to the side. Another thought crossed his mind. "Had to clean my shit up, didn't you."

"You changed my diapers. Thought it was an even trade."

"You were a baby," Domino said, raising the stakes. "You giggled while I did it."

"I think it would've been creepy if you giggled while I wiped your ass," Wicasah guffawed. "Fucking doesn't matter, though. Fucking worth it."

"Gonna hafta tell me how you did it," Domino said, putting on his big brother tone. This had been big, soul-altering magic. It was dangerous to fiddle with the forces of nature.

"Will," Wicasah huffed, rolling into Domino's shoulder. "Tomorrow, though. Gotta take it easy. Just got you out of fucking Helia and you're gonna start on the riot act? Can't a man have a break?"

Domino pressed his new lips to the crown of his brother's head and remembered this easy trust from when Wicasah was young and space wasn't necessary between them. Domino drifted, seeking sleep.

He drifted, dreaming of want until the yearning became an ache. He desired the calm of demon dust, the way the powder burned his nostrils. Gnawed on his lip, he nearly laughed aloud when he wondered why his body didn't crave the stuff like an addict's should. Soul-addicted, he realized. Hell was no place for bodies, and in that realm of souls, Domino's pleaded and twisted for the dust like a worm on the hook.

He slipped away from Wicasah's radiating heat and snuck into the bathroom, convinced he was going to be sick. Hunched in front of the sink, his brain churched with need even as his body showed no indication he needed a fix. Looking up, he studied this resurrected stranger and wanted to smash the mirror to pieces. He looked too fresh and smooth. He wanted the familiar landmarks of his scars and wounds.

There wasn't any hint of the man who had been tortured to insanity by three demons. Nothing of the thousand lifetimes he'd endured in Hell, to the point where he'd become fond of its starkness. And the ache continued.

Kitten-weak, he pulled on Wicasah's coat and zipped it up to his chin. It engulfed him. The door creaked open and closed, the night air smelling vaguely like garlic. Wicasah had rented a room in a men's boarding house in what appeared to be a town's mining slum. He wandered, knowing it wouldn't be long before human calamity found him. Always the same, up, down, and all around.

A woman with long legs leaning against a log-sided building whistled at him. He paused, knowing the signals of *you help me, I help you*, before staggering to her. She smelled like cheap tulips.

"You look like trouble, old man," she said and lit a cigarette. "You look like you've got a bad need."

"Dust?" Domino croaked, his throat parched. "You have some?"

"Angel dust? The aesthetic?"

Domino laughed in her face. "Angels don't exist," Domino cackled. "You can't make angel dust without angels."

The woman's confidence collapsed. "Don't get snarky with me, asshole. Look, I don't got none of that, but maybe something close. You got money?"

Money. So archaic. "I can give you a spell," he hedged, and almost broke down at her blatant confusion.

"You're crazy," she snapped, her mouth half-cocked like her hip. "You've lost your goddamn mind."

"Do you have dust or not?" Domino demanded. It was an awful letdown when she shook her head and backed up farther into the wall.

"Just get out of here, man, just leave, okay?"

"Okay." Domino leaned in close enough to feel her tremble. He knew the small woven pouch was smooshed inside her suffocatingly high corset. He pressed closer. She swiped at him with her long nails, leaving marks down his chin and jaw. He reached for her and palmed the bag, as she uttered an outraged squawk. He gave her one short but violent push into the wall. She gasped but didn't follow him as he shuffled off.

He wanted to curl in the dark doorway and sleep. He completely forgot which street was his and wandered the block for a staggered length of time.

Slumping into a building's stonewall, he fumbled with the woven bag. The beeswax lining crinkled and he winced at the sound. He put his finger in the white powder and rubbed it against his gums. He felt nothing.

"Domino!"

Harsh hands shook him until his shoulders banged off the wall. Suddenly, he felt ashamed for what he'd done to the alleyway woman. Wicasah, eyes round enough to see the whites, hissed wordless threats at him. Domino leaned into him with unspeakable relief.

"What the fuck?" Wicasah yelled, hauling Domino under his arm and tugging him in the opposite direction Domino had thought about walking. "Wake up and you've disappeared, goddamn gone. What were you thinking, you idiot? This isn't a game."

"I'm sorry," Domino whispered and wished he could feel something.

"What is this?" Wicasah said, snatching the bag out of Domino's fingers, and smashing it underfoot. "Is this fucking drugs?"

"No," Domino pouted.

"You're on drugs right now, aren't you."

"I needed dust."

"Dust?"

"Yes, demon dust!" Domino nearly exploded. "It calms me. I need it!"

Wicasah stopped in the middle of the street and wrenched Domino around. "You take drugs again, and I will whoop you raw, do you understand me? Dad wouldn't have been able to beat you as bloody as I will."

"You can't do that. I'm older, idiot."

"You're the idiot," Wicasah roared and steered Domino up the front stairs to the boarding house. Domino tripped, but Wicasah clearly didn't give a damn and hauled him by the scruff of his neck into the room.

"Your eyes are dilated," Wicasah snarled. "You think running away is a good idea?"

"I'm sorry," Domino whispered again as Wicasah threw him down on the couch and lorded over him, arms crossed. He wished Thessaly were here. She would understand.

"You better be. Do you understand what you put me through?"

Domino paused. "This is real, isn't it?" He rubbed his hands up and down his forearms.

"What?" Wicasah demanded, thrown off balance. "Of course, it's real."

"It isn't, though?" Domino said shrilly. "This is another trick. This is a hallucination. Another dream."

Wicasah's face softened. "Domino, no. This is real."

"I've done this. I've been through this before. And I've seen you before."

"I swear to you." Wicasah dropped next to Domino and took his hands. "I promise. Hey, would I lie to you? Have I ever lied to you?"

"No," Domino stammered, on the verge of tears.

Wicasah licked his lips. "You know who I am, right?"

Domino missed his mother so badly he thought he might actually cry out for her. He nodded anyway.

Relief crossed Wicasah's face. "Then you know I wouldn't lie to you. I wouldn't take you somewhere you shouldn't be. I promise you this is real, okay? I promise."

"Okay," Domino said and this time an escaped tear trickled down his cheek. "Okay."

CHAPTER 2
WICASAH

WICASAH SHUT THE door to their rented room and carefully locked it with a muted click. He waited on the other side, motionless, listening for any sound of distress. Nothing but silence.

Wisdom had been hard to come by, especially after the series of horrendous mistakes he'd made when it came to his brother. He'd forgotten that Domino wasn't his old self, or a quiet complacent child, but instead a Helia-trained and tortured soul settling into an earthen-grown body. The first time, Wicasah hadn't noticed Domino sneaking out until an hour had come and gone. When he'd finally tracked him down, he couldn't shake the lost look Domino had given him, as if he waited for Wicasah to shatter the realness of this reality. The way his eyes had flickered and gone wide when Wicasah had hauled him back to their room, shouting the entire way. Domino had fallen into a deep, deathless sleep afterward, upon which Wicasah had obsessively studied him from across the room, waiting for a sign.

A sign. What kind of sign, he didn't know. Something that would tell him everything would be okay. That *being okay* would take time, but it would be worth the investment. That, one day, he would wake up and thump downstairs and find Domino fixing eggs, offer him that cock-sure smile and they'd shoot the shit about everything and nothing.

Though Domino hadn't woken for four days, Wicasah still locked the door. Perhaps Domino's soul was settling into the body. Taking root. Discovering the soil.

He stuck his hands in his pockets. The long dark braid laid over his shoulder was shot through with dirt and ragged at the ends. Inside, he felt eroded, like a stone finally worn smooth so you could see the beauty of it. The afternoon sun cast a bright yellow glaze on the small town. Old gray timber had been used to construct horse troughs and Brightside car garages. Not much wood out here on the plains. With the way the wind blew, it made for nothing but twisted trunks and spindly branches, anyway.

But long grasses swayed with the gusts. They tickled Wicasah's fingers as he took a dirt road out of town and then diverged to follow the compass throbbing against his lower teeth. Rocks and dry slabs of earth crunched under his boots. Golden stalks full of rough pods melded into a landscape of tight pale green shrubs and sun-bleached tumbleweeds. The big sky rolled out like a carpet above, a blinding blue. Naomi stood framed by it all and at her feet the dirt caked and split, drying into a semblance of a desert. Conduits in her throat bobbed and Wicasah's pulsated in response. He was irritated at being bound so.

"Didn't think I'd see you so soon," he said, his bitterness a frozen lake that they both stood on.

Naomi turned. Exhaustion left lines around her small mouth. She pushed her spectacles up. Her bangs had been braided back from her forehead. "Being mean doesn't suit you," she said.

Wicasah felt the ice creak. "All-Worlds nearly destroyed Domino's body," he hissed. Fear swam in the depths of Wicasah's bitterness, a beast of unfathomable magnitude. It thrashed as Wicasah's hands cupped in remembrance of that fragile resurrection flower. How, when he'd emerged from the caves, the two of them had ridden the rainbow funnel-strands back to the body, and each moment another petal lifted and floated away, turning to a gray husk on the wind. How they'd run into the yurt to find the glass planter box overturned, Domino's body spilling out of the dark rich soil, and All-Worlds holding a rock over his head to smash it like a squash.

Wicasah's shadows had wound around Domino's still body, dragging it sharply away and into Wicasah's arms. All-Worlds had cried that Wicasah had given up too much, but All-Worlds didn't understand there were two end paths of love. In grief, one could accept, or in grief, one could fight. Wicasah would never understand how All-Worlds could be content with his sorrow, not when Wicasah's was of the parasitic nature and had eaten him from the inside out.

The bitterroot had laid perfectly on Domino's slack-jawed

tongue. The light in its center flickered weakly, and then barbed roots wrapped around the tongue, seeming to burn into the soft palate of the earth-grown body's mouth. But by then, everything had been destroyed. The planter, the soil, and Naomi had decided to stay behind as All-Worlds cried into his hands and Wicasah had fled.

"He was trying to save you from yourself," Naomi said, as if this was a worn-out conversation.

"I gave my name and power freely," Wicasah said. "What right does he have over me to tell me no? To warn me and assume it means anything?"

He's not my father. He's not my mother.

"Don't you understand, yet?" Naomi asked, her expression crumbling. "It means everything. You've fought so hard to have a second chance, but how long will that chance last? Another entity owns your name and power, Wicasah! It can use it for its own purposes. You're tallow, ready to be burned. All Anxius has to do is light the wick."

"Doesn't matter." Wicasah's lips thinned. He replayed All-Worlds destroying the home by a makeshift grave under a lone prairie tree, could hear All-Worlds saying between sobs, as if no one was listening, *He can't keep taking names, can't keep taking power. What will be left?*

"It does matter," Naomi said and took a step closer. When he looked at her, it seemed as though she'd created cracks in the sky itself. "What is Domino going to do when you're dead and gone? Do you think he's going to be able to live through that?"

"Yes," Wicasah said. "He won't have a choice. Why would it matter to you? Did you think I was ever going to do something good with this life? I killed my father when I was a teenager. I murdered your mother out of revenge and bound her soul as my slave. You don't think I know that the end of my rope isn't anything but a dark and bloody end itself?"

A soft huff flowed out of Naomi, as though she couldn't believe what she'd heard. "All-Worlds was right," she said and stepped away into the cracks in the sky. "Witches are no good."

———◆———

The fuchsia shade of a late summer sunset colored the bitterroot petals, yet every time Wicasah looked down, the sharp-pointed tips had begun to curl inwards. His breathing came out in gasps.

I HAVE ASKED TO BE WHERE NO STORMS COME

He couldn't bear to see his feet, bloated and sloughing off reddened skin with the final remnants of the lady slippers melted to his flesh. Naomi sheltered him as they landed in front of the yurt. When they pushed inside, the smell of fresh earth filled his nostrils, eager to take life and nurture it from bulb to root to stem.

All-Worlds stood over Domino's slack body. Tears ran down his cheeks. He held a rock between his hands, poised above the calm youthful slackness of Domino's empty body. "You did it," All-Worlds sobbed. "You actually gave your name away. You're just one more name to him, one more source of power. You're just like the rest of them."

Wicasah's shadows whipped out and wrapped around Domino, yanking the body to safety just as the rock landed with a puff of earth on the ground. Somewhere, Naomi spoke fast in a soothing tone, but Wicasah had lived through this before. He'd lived through men trying to destroy what Wicasah held dear and he wouldn't live through another one. His shadows struck and shoved All-Worlds to the ground. Power swelled within All-Worlds as if he wanted to lash out, but a thin layer of burlap suffocated it.

"You just give and give," All-Worlds said, "and not recognize that it's thievery. You've given him everything and you'll get nothing in return. I tried to stay out of it and it still did nothing!"

Wicasah couldn't breathe. Everything inside him screamed to find somewhere safe. Domino's body slammed into him and he stumbled back. Naomi wrapped a comforting hand around All-Worlds bicep, her words like a smear to Wicasah's ears.

All-Worlds lunged for him, clawing at his protective cradle around the flower. A choked-off sound wrenched out of Wicasah's throat and his shadows dropped Domino, weaving a wall between him and the enraged shaman. All the color had leaked out of the flower. Wicasah gripped Domino's slack jaw and forced it open, shoving the flower onto his tongue . . .

A shudder racked Wicasah and he blinked, staring at the mold stain in the sky, like a damp infestation in wallpaper, that Naomi's strangled magic had left behind. She'd chosen to stay with All-Worlds. She'd ripped through Wicasah's shadows and had stared at him, aghast. He should've never expected her to come with him. After everything she'd done for him, he had ignorantly assumed that would persist, even if she'd planned to keep him around to take her own power.

The crack in the sky darkened. Fingers seemed to fight through, digging past the plaster of blue to widen it. The heyoka's black hair spilled in front of her face as she forced her way through the leftover mark Naomi had made, her face a grimace of irritation. She fell to her knees and staggered to her feet. Her hand extended to him and, for once, Wicasah could look at her without expectation, without want.

"I need you," she said and gravel ground together in her voice, the sound of an oncoming storm. "Come with me. Helia calls."

Wicasah took a step back. "I don't need to go into Helia anymore."

"You don't just stop owing someone," the heyoka hissed. "You'll always owe me for what I gave you. And now I need you. The demons need you."

Wicasah shook his head and clenched his teeth against the fear. "I've done enough."

The heyoka stumbled as if she couldn't keep the pieces of herself aligned together. Lightning-struck. Thunder shook. Her hand struck to wrap around his wrist and tugged him forward.

He dug his heels in. "No."

The nub in his chest throbbed, scraped raw by her presence. The heyoka hooked her claws into that nub and gave it a tug. Wicasah tasted blood.

"No," he said again.

"I'm not done," she said. "I haven't found the right people yet. The souls that we've released, not all of them were right."

"I can't," Wicasah said, thinking of how time passed. He couldn't leave and come back five years later only to hunt for Domino again. He couldn't let his brother believe he had abandoned him, not when everything had abandoned him already. If he went to Helia, he didn't know when he would come back.

The heyoka wrenched on the hook in his chest. Wicasah released his shadows, taking off the leash and collar, removing the muzzle, and letting them run.

The heyoka screamed. A pressurized bubble of power surrounded him and he saw—

They stood in a field, newly planted, newly destroyed. The drills had created craters, unearthing the ancient bones of beasts that roamed the earth before without a thought. With a creak, the machines began to pump and spray chemicals into the heart of the earth, poisoning it to get at the liver, the gizzard, the delicate guts.

"They can't do this," a man said, and Wicasah turned to see someone he'd never seen before, his face dropped in agony.

"They can do whatever they want," the heyoka said, only it wasn't the heyoka—it was a woman with a strong jaw and dark black eyes, a line of fury between her brows.

"This place is dead now," the man said again, and Wicasah watched a much younger All-Worlds wrap his arms around this unknown man and hold him close. "We'll make it better," All-Worlds whispered. "We'll save the next one."

CHAPTER 3
DOMINO

HE WOKE HALF out of his mind in terror, convinced he was still in his coffin cell, his blood and magic being siphoned. A fine sheen of sweat slicked his skin. His eyelids fluttered in exhaustion, but he couldn't sleep, not with the dream so fresh. Soon, Ickto would arrive with the next dream and call him little soul, but never his name.

This world was a clever conceived trick. Wicasah was a lie. Domino was damned, stuck thinking he could live again. But maybe now he had a chance to fight back.

Trembling, he rolled from the bed and gathered a duffel bag full of guns and goods, and crept quietly through to the bathroom, glancing at the long sprawl of Wicasah snoozing on the chesterfield. This Wicasah had returned in a daze, quaking as if with tremors, and had collapsed in a heap on the couch. Domino closed the bathroom door, eye fixated on the construct that pretended to be his brother. Wicasah was alive, not rotting down in the pit. Soon, that fake construct would wake. Domino didn't have much time.

He clicked the door shut and slid the lock in place. Pulling out a purple piece of chalk, he drew warning symbols on the floor and wards of protection along the wallpaper to keep all kinds of monsters out. Magic zinged through his blood, sparkling like champagne. Ickto had gotten sloppy letting him access this kind of power. He dug out herb bundles and dried flowers from the duffel and arranged them on the sink and along the doorframe. Whatever planned to come through to get him would be met with a whole lot of intent and witchery. He covered the floor with more symbols and crushed rosemary and lavender. Then, once everything had been laid, he climbed into a white clawfoot tub to wait.

I HAVE ASKED TO BE WHERE NO STORMS COME

Scum had dried in a ring a hand-width from the lip. He leveled a shotgun against his shoulder and tried to calm his breathing. His heart jackrabbited in his chest, making his stomach roll with queasiness. He realized if he didn't control his hyperventilating, he would pass out soon.

A shadow moved past the door. A struck match, then lantern-light flickered in yellow pulses from underneath the sliver between floor and door. They were probably getting ready to slide him out of his coffin-cage. Ready to inject something vile in him. Turn him into a drooling fool who didn't know reality from the living.

The knob jiggled.

"Sweet god, fuck," Domino whispered. The knob rattled and turned violently to the side, but whatever hunted Domino stayed on the other side. He fought the urge to level his gun at the door. His hands shook too much. The shot would go wild, and then it would be a wasted bullet. He could wait until the monster broke through and then he would decapitate it point-blank. A whimper crawled out of his throat at the thought. Calm. He reached for the calm he'd cultivated when he was young and indestructible.

The doorknob stopped jiggling. Domino waited, knowing his eyes were just a touch too wide and burning. A scrape and scratch. A new sort of wiggling. The lock being picked. He put the butt of the gun into his shoulder, ready to absorb the recoil, and braced the barrel over the tub. His finger curled away from the trigger.

The door gave way and opened a sliver. Someone called his name in an exhausted voice, but it was just an illusion.

"Domino, it's me."

That voice was real. That voice was true. How had Wicasah gotten into hell?

"Get the fuck in here," he half-yelled. "Get in here, or they will get you."

His little brother disturbed the herb line as he slipped into the bathroom. Domino motioned with his hands to get into the bath, *for god's sake, do you want to be turned into meat? Close the fucking door.*

He pointed the nose of the gun up into the air and scooted to the other end of the bathtub, flinging his legs over the rim as Wicasah folded himself in the empty space beside him, mimicking his position.

"Were you asking to get shot?" Domino demanded. The

monsters were too close to him, thus too close to Wicasah. Too close to the boy Domino had sacrificed his life to protect, the boy he'd lost for far too long.

"Calm down," Wicasah said. Dark circles had deepened under his eyes. "Where do you think we are?"

"Where do I think we are?" Domino mocked. "Any moment they're going to burst through those doors, you idiot. Shut up or they'll hear you."

Wicasah fell silent. They were smooshed together, shoulder-to-shoulder. Never battle-ready, his brother. Domino refused to take his boots off—too terrified he'd have to escape without them. He jumped at every noise, creak, and shiver in the old room. His muscles ached and his neck felt weak as though he couldn't hold his head up. Slowly, he felt it drifting to rest on Wicasah's shoulder until he jerked back awake.

Wicasah shifted and dragged his feet into the tub, moving sideways until his back rested against the rounded curve of the porcelain. His legs bent to his chest. Time continued to pass and Domino watched it slip away between snatches of a nap and panicked consciousness. Every time he looked at his brother, Wicasah met his eyes, solemn.

At some point, Wicasah stretched his legs onto Domino's lap. "What are you doing?" Domino snapped and tapped on his shins. "Stop getting comfortable. We need to be ready."

"Tub's too small," Wicasah complained. "Need to stretch. Need to sleep."

Domino swallowed his sound of frustration and scooted around so they faced each other. Wicasah shifted in response until his legs propped up on either side of Domino, his smelly feet tucked against Domino's armpits. Domino made a face.

"You're going to get us killed," he snapped.

"Maybe we should go get a bigger tub tomorrow," his brother said instead, leaning his neck back. "One of those hot tub numbers where they have lounge spaces for you to actually lie back."

"What would we do with that, huh? Cart it around all day? You wanna go shopping for tubs?"

"If you're going to PTSD all over the place every night, I'm gonna need a bigger place to put my legs."

"Tub's the fucking safest place in this whole goddamn apartment," Domino snarled, ticked off and a little hurt at his brother's insinuation. This wasn't a joke, this was real, there were things outside waiting to hit and tear, take and maul, and Wicasah was making jokes. "Where do they tell you do go during a tornado? Fucking tub. Where do you go if there's an explosion? Fucking tub. You're telling me I shouldn't get into the fucking tub when demons are out to get me when it works just fine as a defense against the elements?"

"Just saying we should get a bigger one is all."

Domino glared at him.

"Gonna be sore in the morning," Wicasah continued. "Gonna be grumpy too, and guess who has to deal with it? Me. Who has to make you coffee? Me."

"What's your goddamn point?"

"That we need a bigger tub."

———•———

It was Domino's first morning out, and Wicasah took him to a mom-and-pop diner on the street corner, where the linoleum on the tables had so many scratches in it Domino could read the names and initials of a hundred folks who sat down and prayed for a five-dollar meal. He scraped his finger along the dirty gum holding the table together and marveled at how everything felt starker here, more real, but almost like a dream at the same time. An edge of uneasiness sat in his gut that made him look side to side out of the corner of his eyes.

Wicasah kicked him hard in the shin underneath the table. He smiled at Wicasah, to be encouraging, a simple little lie to put his brother at ease. It felt like the first time he was in hell, when everything was fresh and startling.

The waitress put a tall glass of water in front of him. He chugged the whole thing. Ice cubes, wide, smooth, and thin clinked against his teeth. He took three and shoved them into his cheek, delighting in the way the melting ice made his whole jaw ache. He swirled the newly made water around his mouth, erasing the parched leftovers of Hell like a desert's rainy season.

Wicasah ordered for him, a mess of syllables he didn't really hear because the window looking out over the narrow street and into the solid graffitied brick building across the way had a message for him.

Hell is empty, he read, as a bubbly chuckle formed like champagne inside him, *and all the devils are here.*

Wasn't sure if it was one of those break-down terror laughs or a disbelieving one. He glanced at the yellow yolk of the egg, cooked sunny side up. Bacon on the crispy side. Browned hashbrowns. Wicasah had two cups of coffee in front of him and dumped small sugar packets and doll-sized buckets of cream into one. He handed Domino the cream-colored one and cradled the black coffee between his own hands.

"I drink it black," Domino said.

"No, I drink it black," Wicasah said. "You pretended to like it but I'm not an idiot. 'Sides, sugar's good for you. You look like you're gonna keel over."

"Am not." Domino sipped, the sugared cream sliding over his tongue. He let out a rumble of pleasure, easing back into his booth seat, and swore he could taste the metals in the well water the coffee was made from.

Wicasah dug into his omelet, cheese bleeding out the corners. Domino noted his straight white teeth glinting past his lips, good dental hygiene still maintained after all these years. He wondered if Wicasah still felt him sliding the old toothbrush between his clenched lips, running the splayed bent bristles up and down his baby teeth.

"What's so funny?" Wicasah asked, attention still on his food.

"Nothing," Domino said, sipping his coffee, savoring every drop.

"You were laughing at something earlier," Wicasah said, taking a drink out of his own mug. "Crazy laughing, too, to top it off. Could've flirted with the waitress, but no, you decided to act insane."

"Just wondered if it's true."

"If what's true?"

"The sign." Domino nodded toward the black spray paint message.

Wicasah brought his cup to his mouth and stared at the two lines. His eyes flickered back and forth as if he saw something different.

Domino broke the silence. "Maybe they're after me again."

"No one is coming after you," Wicasah said quietly, yet he still stared, still stared.

"Haunted," Domino told him, bacon halfway to his mouth. "I'm haunted."

"It's just a fucking line from some story, okay?" Wicasah snarled. "Fucking need to wash that shit off. No one needs to hear that kind of bullshit."

"Language," Domino reminded him softly, the bacon greasy, mingling with the leftover coffee.

"No one's coming after you. It doesn't mean anything. It's just some kids thinking they can be deep by plastering Shakespeare on a ghetto wall."

"Okay, kiddo," Domino agreed, egg whites buttery and slippery. "I believe you." He looked at Wicasah fondly, a tight twist in his heart as Wicasah's mouth screwed up and his eyes wrinkled. Signs of a temper tantrum coming.

"I'm serious, Domino."

Domino kicked Wicasah's shin under the booth. Wicasah grimaced. He tasted the bland hashbrowns and added a blurb of ketchup and pepper to the mix. He didn't want Wicasah mother-henning him more than he already did, but Domino was a good liar and would keep his eyes peeled.

It wasn't a coincidence that a warning appeared in front of him after he'd been pulled out of hell. Hell itself had taught him that, full of her prophets and psychics. He hadn't avoided the demon hunters and hellhounds for so long on luck alone. Domino was a fate man now, and those words weren't just child's play, they were a goddamn oracle. If he could come out of the pit, then it would be easy for the monsters to follow him out, too. *Empty. Hell is empty.*

"Stop it," Wicasah growled. "Thinking too hard."

"Contingency plans," Domino noted as the waitress refilled his cup. He took a long slurp before setting it down. Wicasah made a face and stole the cup as soon as it touched the damaged tabletop, scooting it to him and adding sugars and cream.

"I'm not a child," Domino said, raising his eyebrow.

"Stop acting like one then," Wicasah retaliated. "You want sugar and cream? Have it. You've died once already, not like it's going to kill you now."

"Cleaning up my shit really gave you a big head," Domino said, using his toast to soak up the yolk.

"I've done a lot worse than that," Wicasah said with a smile.

"Then the devils are *here*," Domino said, raising his cup in a salute.

CHAPTER 4
DOMINO

THE HEADLIGHTS OF the ancient car cast a foggy gleam on the bug swarms coalescing around the flat dirt road. Nature must've known the beams were unnatural as the darkness seemed to douse it. Domino knew he was unnatural, but with time, his grasp on reality strengthened. Along with that came a brewing storm that built within him like a beckoning.

Wicasah had a different storm inside of him. One with a cyclone of rabid energy that had frothed at his mouth for weeks. So, it wasn't surprising to Domino when his brother slammed open the door to their rented room, dangled keys in front of Domino's face, and said, "I'm driving."

"Where did you get that?" Domino asked, already hearing the roar of an engine.

"Borrowed it," Wicasah said. "Never mind where. Never driven much before. Have you?"

Domino had smiled in response. Wicasah cinched the keys into his palm and left the room, expecting Domino to follow him and, for a moment, Domino wondered if anything had changed between them. They could still be young and reckless without the chains of their past hanging from their wrists.

Wicasah slid into the driver's seat and turned the engine over. Domino pressed his face against the rain-streaked passenger window as his brother pulled out and onto the road. His fingers touched the cool glass, watching the oil and heat leave a marking that at times both evaporated and remained. The engine rumbled under his feet, nothing like the Shelby's kitten purr. When Wicasah shifted, Domino delighted in the smooth jerk of a mini-coast before the car chugged up to higher speeds. Wicasah maneuvered the car from the rocky dirt road to a paved road that wound like a snake up a mountain. When he looked out and beyond, it seemed as though the whole of heaven were laid out before him. They descended into a wide meadow.

"Stop," he said breathlessly. "Stop here."

The steering wheel creaked as Wicasah tightened his hands around it. Domino glanced at him. A small hollow appeared in his lower lip where it seemed he was sucking it in. They drove another ten miles before the wheels grumbled under the rocky terrain of the roadside, unhappy to leave the pavement. The engine jittered as old cars do, telling Domino just how it felt about this midnight ramble. Domino opened the door carefully and stood in the humid air with the electricity of the night washing over him.

The black asphalt road lay straight as an arrow into the dark gray-blue of an outbound storm, a black dimensional border to the green field dotted with bright yellow flower heads. Mosquitoes buzzed close to his ear. He could feel the prick of long spindly legs on his forehead and over his forearms. He rubbed his arms and shifted his feet in the rusted dirt pushed out of the way for the new road. Lightning hit the sky like a rocket. Purple-white light flashed in a bolt and lit up the long profile of the mountain range. Black and hunched they were, silent and obscured by the cloudy storm. Handfuls of purple light tossed inside the rain illuminated the low clouds like firecrackers. Braver bolts chased across the horizon.

He could see the darker shadows of Wicasah's face through the bug-spattered windshield, hands dropped from the steering wheel with one eye on nature's show and the other detailing Domino's changing mood. It should have made Domino itch, the coddling, but it swept through him warm with affection, instead. It felt good to have someone worry about the simplistic yet crucial things, like his mental health, now that demons no longer chased him. Domino had carefully rebuilt his sanity, but his foundational base was Wicasah. Wicasah who assured him this world was real—that he could trust it—and Domino believed.

Behind the car rose a golden teal sky from the horizon. Domino felt quaky seconds before a thunderclap shook the clouds. Gooseflesh broke out along his arms and he heard the car door squeak open and close as Wicasah stepped out. He loomed close to Domino, then stood in front of him so Domino had to view the lightning over Wicasah's shoulder.

Wicasah.

Domino swore the lightning cracked his brother's name. When the lightning lit the inside of his lids with crooked branches, he heard another call, like Thessaly shouting for them, but this was something age-old, something he heard in the shuffle of his nightmares.

Wicasah.

"Let's go," Wicasah said.

"Why?" Domino craned his head to hear the message in the thunder better.

Wicasah didn't turn around, but his shoulders hunched higher as if trying to block Domino out completely. "Let's just go, okay?"

Domino walked closer to his brother and brushed Wicasah's elbow. He tasted petrichor along with the electric sizzle of ion-ridden air. Another flash of lightning cascaded against the teal sky and blinded him. The lightning tendrils exploded like a volley of arrows into him, hitting the small bones of his spine and zinging numbness along his nerves. A nebula swirled in the back of his mind, threatening to revert the gravity of his being. Domino gasped, his mouth open in wordless pain.

Magic. Terrible, world-shattering magic. Yet it didn't come from him. It didn't come from Wicasah.

Through the light, Domino barely made out the gray outline of Wicasah's profile. The once, almost regal, sloping nose and broad cheekbones had become disjointed. When the thunder hit, it rattled Domino's bones loose. Could the sky roar?

A new figure stepped from out of that teal-yellowed expanse—a creature as mismatched and jagged as Wicasah. Her eyes glared black fire and a swath of broomstick straight hair flowed behind her. Domino bit back a cry as he picked up the hot dry sensation of Helia following her. He'd believed this world was real, and now, this reality was shattering, showing the truth behind the curtain. This . . . demon, he supposed, reached out with a snarl, and dove her hand into Wicasah's chest. A sound seemed trapped behind Wicasah's bared teeth. The creature twisted.

Lightning still penetrated Domino's feet, bolting him into place, but it couldn't imprison the age-old lesson baked into his soul that his purpose on this earth was to protect his brother. Shadows erupted from Wicasah like smoke, whipping around the creature like a cat o' nine tails.

The old panic of uncertainty joined Domino's wondering fear, but if this was still Helia . . . if this was still damnation . . . well. Domino knew what it was to die.

It had been a long time since he'd called on his powers. He had no components or ingredients, only the catacomb of marrow deep within his body. The thunder had already shaken pieces of him loose. It was time to release it all the way.

The familiars rattled through his bones like maracas. Pouring from the ossuary of his body, the thumb-sized creatures pushed past his skin to swarm the demon-hellion wrenching Wicasah to his knees. Domino's ribs expanded, as though his lungs were over-inflated balloons pushing their cage to the limit. A crunching, lancing pain skewered him, but kings lived in his witchery. Domino's skin peeled and curled away, leaving the glowing white phosphorescence of his structure to emerge. His arm extended to become a broadsword pockmarked with breaks, yet he knew it would hold if tested with steel or silver. It felt as though the bone king—his familiar matured—stepped out of Domino's flesh and descended on the hellion-creature with a fury to match the storm.

Baked in his bones: protect his brother. That bedrock would not be shaken. Especially now.

The king's sword arced and caught the edge of golden lightning-glow before crashing on the arm connecting Wicasah to the thunder-creature. The smaller familiars opened their mouths wide with glee and swarmed over the thunder-woman, their bony fingers digging through her flesh to reach the source of her blood.

The sky roared again, providing a voice for her agony. She stumbled back and the sky seemed to eat her, sucking her in and finally up and away. The shadows wrapped Wicasah in a shroud, but when Domino bent toward them, they twitched in recognition.

Marrow blood dripped from the king's sword. Domino brought it to his mouth to taste it and felt the black hole pull of consequence engulf him.

CHAPTER 5
WICASAH

THEY SAT AROUND *a fire barely hanging on from the relentless wind and couldn't look each other in the eyes. Cups and hollowed-out horns had been filled with bathtub gin and gut-rot whisky, but after what they had seen . . .*

Ancient trees uprooted, the soil ripe with lichen and moss like ripped silverskin, spilling out the guts of the earth. Mountains blasted with cheap dynamite, the portraits of erosion and sun-bleached cliffsides fallen into rubble. A cemetery of petrified wood had been used for target practice. Battle blood and gunpowder stained Wicasah's fingers and face. He didn't know these people, but somehow, he knew that the man on the left was one of his closest friends and the woman on his right had once been his lover.

He knew that before him was All-Worlds, young and thin, tightly holding the hand of another man.

"I don't understand how they could do that," All-Worlds whispered and turned to his beloved. "Anxius, how could they do such a thing?"

Together for years, they were. They'd sworn fidelity and immortality to each other, promised happiness and sorrow. Wicasah knew this, but he did not know the names of anyone else around him.

Anxius rubbed All-Worlds' hand, even as his mouth hardened into a stubborn line. "They only know how to kill power, not nurture it," he said, his voice hoarse. "We tried. We failed. We know what we need to do next, don't you agree—"

The name Anxius spoke was like nails on a chalkboard. It was a slew of incomprehensible, piercing sound. When Wicasah realized Anxius had addressed him, had looked at him, he felt his mouth moving without his permission and heard his voice say, "If we bind our powers to yours . . ."

"We have enough power to barricade those corporations from harming anything else," Anxius interrupted. "We're five incredibly strong witches and shamans. By making us one entity we are as infused as the roots of the earth, the core of magma heating this world from the inside. I know you're scared—"

Wicasah winced as Anxius said the unknown name again. It was a thunderclap piercing his eardrums. He swallowed hard.

"—but this is the best chance we have to break the bindings on the earth and let it express itself. Let it be the horror it's evolved not to be. Let the ocean have a voice, the trees have eyes, the ground fangs. Don't you want that?"

Wicasah's voice was not his own. The familiar tremble of it broke past his lips. "We would give you our names, Anxius, but then you would own us. We'd be stripped of ourselves and our powers."

"Gradually," Anxius said. "When you lose your name, the madness of chaos doesn't set in until later."

"But it still sets in. Any idea of time is relative."

"She is right," All-Worlds whispered.

Anxius' bit his lip. "You trust me, though, don't you? You know I'd never do anything to hurt you. We wouldn't be one ruler. We've been one entity with no ruler. No head. No king. I'm the caverns of the earth, the roots in the soil. All-Worlds, my paintbrush, you are trees that reach for the sky and —"

The other names became screeches to Wicasah's ears.

"—are the lightning and thunder," Anxius finished.

Wicasah hesitated. "It's not that I don't trust you, it's that giving you so much power over me is a lot to ask."

"But if you could save the petrified woods?" Anxius persisted. "To save the bluffs that you roamed as a child, where your mother once lived, where the ancient bones of the animals of the past once were. Would you do it for them?"

Wicasah looked away. His heart ached in an unimaginable way and he knew it wasn't just a homeland that had been destroyed but the memories, too. The people who enriched those pieces. The bluffs weren't only rocks. They were belonging. The plains weren't just fields of tall grasses full of lupine, but the *privileged myths of his lineage. He'd wanted his children to roam there. He'd wanted his bones to feed the lichen.*

But it was all just ash now.

"We will bind our names to you," he said.

"Yes," Anxius said, his excited tone one of victory. "We bind our names and thus our power to one person. I will be the conduit, you the tent poles. We will infuse our essence with the earth and break the boundaries keeping our sentience separate. They won't dare unearth another tree without permission."

Wicasah took an unsteady breath. He reached out and clasped the hand of the woman next to him. When he turned to look at her, her face had been erased, as if all her features had been molded back into a flat terrain of ruined clay. "As long as we're together," he heard himself say, only the voice wasn't his. It hadn't been this whole time.

He heard the voice of thunder and lightning. The voice of the heyoka.

CHAPTER 6
DOMINO

WICASAH COLLAPSED AND the shadows unraveled to reveal that his brother's human shape had been shucked. Black leathery wings spread out around him and Domino crashed to his knees, unsure what to do about the pulsating throb of magic bruising Wicasah's chest.

"What do I do?" he asked the shadows. "Help me, please. I don't know what to do."

Missing Wicasah was its own kind of injury, and Domino was only just recovering from his time in the underworld. Right now, that wound stretched to splitting.

One of the shadows with a belly stripe of crimson slithered into his mouth, latching to the nerves and synapses that controlled his arms. In jerking motions, he watched his fleshless hands cover what looked to be an exposed rounded hook. The sparks of a beginning fire warmed his hands. Whether it was his magic or the red-shadow, he didn't know.

His bones began to glow from white to gold to red. Domino gritted his teeth against the searing agony. The fingerbones blackened and crisped, the embers burrowing deep inside his puzzle-piece palms to smolder. The charcoal sticks of his fingers scraped against Wicasah's scale-plated chest. Beneath, the plates turned rubbery and melted, cauterizing the thunder-creature's magic that festered within Wicasah. Forming a seal.

Domino's hand trembled against Wicasah's chest. In a detached way, he watched his hand flake away even as an ocean of despair froze him. The other shadows writhed around them as if caught up in some kind of madness, driven by instincts Domino couldn't understand. The teal sky brightened for a moment, lightening to a summer-warm morning, when it cracked like a splintering earthquake. Fear filled Domino, convinced the thunder-creature had returned. He had no clue how to defeat such a monster.

A young woman wearing thin glasses stepped out of the sky-rip. Suspenders looped over her shoulders, blouse a dusty black, and the concern on her face made Domino's breath halt in his chest.

Another witch.

One that hadn't made the sacrifice yet. He could tell by the eager, bulbous push of the conduits against her throat. Domino's head spun at the heady potential of her power. She knelt beside him.

"Domino," she said softly and offered him a strained smile.

Domino reeled. A black hole lobotomy scrambled his thoughts with a pike through the pupil. How did she know him? The crimson-streaked shadow nestled against his soft palate, like a mouse hiding in a newfound den.

"I'm a friend," she said quietly and touched Wicasah's motionless chest. Wicasah didn't even flinch. "I only know how to cut and tear, though. I can't fix anything." Her lips pursed in dissatisfaction before saying, "She came again, didn't she? Tried to take him to Helia."

Domino's hand gripped hers. He fought for words. The shadow tongue-tied him, her tendrils slinking down his throat to his bones, and threatened to move him like a puppet. "Who . . . who are you?"

A pained look crossed the woman's face. "I'm Benedicta's daughter."

The black hole inside Domino's head widened, making him reel. He could see it now—her father's sharp face, his near-sighted eyes passed to her, the way Benedicta would look patiently irritated whenever his name came up reflected in the moue of her thin lips, the tilt of her chin.

"Naomi," he breathed out, trying to compare the tiny bundle he'd held in a backwater hospital to this grown witch before him.

"I'm disappointed Wicasah didn't tell you about me," she said but the black hole expanded to take over everything until he saw nothing but a glowing blue nebula of light and unconsciousness.

"Not surprised, though."

I HAVE ASKED TO BE WHERE NO STORMS COME

For a moment, just before he opened his eyes, Domino pretended it was Sunday. Not much happened on Sundays. Worship was for Brightsiders and holier-than-thou types, all before Daniel's conversion. Daniel slept off his bender and Wicasah was tucked into his side on the double bed they shared. When he woke, Domino would sweet-talk him into sneaking pennies for low-brow coffee, eggs, and stale bread. They would race into town. Wicasah would have him in belly-aching chuckles. The morning would slip into robin-egg's blue afternoon as they wiled their hours fishing in a trickle of a stream and meandering through the fields looking for grouse. They wouldn't see Daniel all day.

It had been so long since Domino had had a Sunday.

The bellow rattled Domino's newly sheathed bones and shredded the memory. He jolted away from the yawning black hole sucking him in and thrashed against the arms that held him up.

"Goddamnit, would you hold still? You fucking idiot—"

The grip released him. He fell, his one hand splayed out for him to glimpse the vast, unfathomable tear in the sky between the web of his fingers. His stomach dropped. He should be tumbling through that open expanse, but he remained suspended on the fragile bridge of Naomi's power.

"Stupid fucking witch, damn you—"

Domino wrenched his gaze away at her voice. The long black shadows extended from Naomi's hands like rope and cocooned Wicasah. She hauled him toward the sky-rip like pulling a sled. Inside the sheath, the beast writhed.

"A little help?" Naomi cried out.

But Domino's world was still dismantling around him. One side, he saw their borrowed car and an abandoned moment. On the other, he saw a room whose walls were littered with shadows from a blazing fire.

Wicasah thrashed, his howling inhuman. Domino crawled toward his brother.

"Leave him be!" Naomi commanded and hauled him closer to the rip.

But Domino had no reason to obey her pleas. His brother was trapped, hurt, crying out. A gelatin-like substance oozed over Domino's bones, a translucent sheath of his own. He didn't know if his organs had disappeared when the bone king familiar removed his flesh, but he felt something flutter against his ribcage. He brushed back the shadows to see Wicasah's face—if his brother could just know that he was there, maybe it would stop the inhuman agony erupting from his throat.

Wicasah glared at him with eyes transformed from man to monster. The whites had sunk into the familiar brown like cataracts. His fangs gnashed and tore into the shadows that crossed his mouth. Blood pooled on his tongue. Scales plated down his neck and chest. Whatever shrieked was no longer Domino's brother.

"Wicasah," he whispered and reached out to touch him, but Wicasah arched and screamed like a caged thing once more. Domino glanced up to Naomi. Her arms strained as she pulled Wicasah through the rip, her face transformed into a paroxysm of determination.

One wing pushed free from the shadows. The shadow still clinging to the inside of Domino's mouth vibrated like a cat about to pounce. Domino could either help Naomi or leave Wicasah's future up to fate. He had never been one to put his faith in destiny. He lunged for Naomi and put his weight around the shades, lent his strength to her endeavor.

They tumbled through the crack and into the strange room. The black hole's gravity swirled and sucked him back in, leaving him momentarily lost in time, waking only when he felt a soft breath waft over his face.

Wicasah was curled against him, encased in a cocoon of shadows. One tendril floated free. Domino put his hand along Wicasah's too-sharp jawline. Uneasiness clawed at him, as if he saw the shell, not the ghost who occupied the corporation. He smoothed the shadow back over his brother's face, terrified of what had happened, of the extreme swing from animal to coma that had sling-shotted his brother.

His own gelatin flesh had hardened but still felt too pliable. Naomi's sky opening had spit them out into a yurt. Beyond Wicasah's shoulder, he saw Naomi stagger to her feet and collapse in a heap next to an unknown person hunched over the fire. Sitting up, Domino pulled his coat from his shoulders and draped it over Wicasah, hoping if Wicasah woke, he'd know he wasn't alone.

"Come to the fire, Domino," the unknown person snarled in a

deep bitter voice. "After everything that's been done to rip you from Helia, I'd at least like to see if you're worth it."

"All-Worlds," Naomi admonished. Her face was pinched with exhaustion. When All-Worlds wrapped her hand around a steaming cup, it shook in time with her hands.

Domino swallowed hard but joined the duo. *Watch your back,* Thessaly crooned in his mind. He sat cross-legged between them. Naomi's lips tightened into an unhappy line as All-Worlds reached out and took Domino's chin in his hands, twisting him back and forth until Domino smacked his hand away.

"I can't see the resemblance," he said in a low tone that Domino wasn't sure how to interpret.

"Maybe you can tell me why my brother is tied up, instead," Domino said. "Why he doesn't know who I am."

All-Worlds scowled and poked at the fire with a charcoaled stick. "Your brother is going insane," he said. "It doesn't help that a thunder-goddess is after him to shuffle more souls out of Helia using his witchery."

"Was that what it was?" Domino asked, remembering the black-haired thunderclap that had shaken him to his core. "What do you mean shuffling souls?"

The fire flickered in the depths of Naomi's dark eyes. She took a deep breath. "You didn't get out of Helia because of good behavior, Domino," she said. "Wicasah made a lot of deals to make you remember you were alive. Bounty hunters to find you. Demons to make you believe you could live again. In exchange, he had to give up his name and power."

"I warned him." All-Worlds waved at the shadow-wrapped creature behind them.

"You didn't," Naomi argued. "You thought ignorance wouldn't iron-clad his will. Wicasah would not be stopped."

I'm not worth this. "If we get his name and power back, will he be himself again? How do we do that?" Domino asked. The shallow shoals of his ocean of fear melted. Terror lapped at his feet while he stood at its shore, staring into an endless horizon.

Whatever it cost, I'm not worth it.

"Good question." Naomi looked irritated at All-Wolds. "I haven't advanced in my training far enough to know the exact connotation of that request yet."

All-Worlds glared into the fire. White streaked his plaited hair.

He licked his lips. "This story isn't for free," he said and turned a steel-gaze on Domino. "Now or later, you'll have to pay for it because I hate to tell it. I hate that you witches are forcing me to remember the worst part of my life."

"It's Wicasah," Naomi said and thick devotion stuck in Domino's throat. She felt the same as he did. "We can't just leave him like that."

"You very well may have to. Wicasah made his decision. You must accept his sacrifice for what it's worth," All-Worlds said.

Domino frowned and glanced at Naomi, hoping her passion still shone bright. Naomi sipped her drink and pointedly refused his gaze. Dread scalded Domino's devotion as he realized that Naomi had pinpointed their location without a map nor compass. "How did you know where we were?" he asked, the same flat expectation of Hell seeping back into him, making him wonder if this was all a dream.

"Put a marker on him." Naomi tapped her lower lip. "I'm a hero, remember. Came to the rescue." She smiled as if the whole thing was grim.

"How will that marker serve when he's lost in Anxius' chains?" All-Worlds demanded, taking Naomi's drink and sipping it himself.

"Tell us, then," Naomi said in a voice unbearably soft as she took back her cup. "The story is poisoning you. You've wanted to speak it for some time now. What do you have to lose by doing so? You hate witches for their selfish ways, but they are drawn to you like a moth to the flame. Help us this time."

Domino put his hands on his knees. A Helia-taught lesson of adaptability rang through his mind. He settled in to learn and observe. The past was a haunted place, and Helia wasn't the only world that used it to her advantage. This was just like plotting to get another hit of dust, sitting through endless bargains until he had what he wanted. All it took was patience and time.

"You're not a witch." All-Worlds reached out as if he wanted to shelter Naomi.

"Not yet," she whispered.

All-Worlds studied her as if memorizing her face. Time became a slippery thing. Domino made a frustrated sound, but Naomi swiftly motioned for him to be silent. Finally, when All-Worlds did speak, Domino heard a deep well of power lace his words, as if something had been untied and released.

CHAPTER 7
WICASAH

WICASAH GAVE HIS name to Anxius.

It oozed from him, leaving him slightly empty. A pinprick abyss. His power built between them like a charge and then shot away from him in an explosion of dusky twilight and gold to electrify Anxius. Next to him, and in turn, the others who he could not name gave Anxius their identity. Anxius' witchery braided their powers like sage, sweetgrass, lavender, and yucca into a thick plait of personality. It only needed the ends to be bound and tied off, something only a shaman's power could do.

Anxius glowed with their combined strength as he turned to All-Worlds. All-Worlds, the last horsehair that would cinch their braid tight. Anxius held a hand out to him, fingers curled slightly with fondness. Behind him, the sun drifted behind that unwavering horizon of the plains, and Wicasah wondered if he would see a green flash. All-Worlds' fingers were worried together above his heart. His eyes flickered from his hands to Anxius and filled with tears.

"All-Worlds," Anxius cried, those softly curled fingers extending out in a demand. "Give me your name. Your power."

All-Worlds hesitated. Wicasah had seen it before. Despite all the years together, the outcasts from tribes, churches, societies, who had sought safety in the cradle of the woods or the mountain tops or the open fields, All-Worlds would doubt. Betrayal crept over him like a slug and he wished he had a pillar of salt to dissolve the mess of it away. All-Worlds had spoken his fears around their fires when they were in deep conversation, but they'd soothed his worries with promises and vows. Wicasah thought it would be enough. That his love of Anxius would be enough.

"This is what we've worked for," Anxius said because that was what Anxius did for All-Worlds. Permitted him to trust, the space to doubt, the support he needed to decide. "The world will have our magic and our sentience. It will defend itself against those who seek to tear it apart."

Still, All-Worlds hesitated. Wicasah knew Anxius would prevail. If All-Worlds doubted, Anxius was the sun that they orbited around, none more so than All-Worlds.

"Remember the lake?" Anxius said. "The wetlands where the ducks floated and minnows peppered the surface with tiny ripples? Remember the blue herons that stalked the shores with their long legs. The pelicans that flew by, their beaks heavy with fish and water. Remember how they dumped raw sludge into it and how that clogged the surface? We found that trumpeter swan drenched in oil. Remember how we laid with it and outstretched our wings and begged for forgiveness."

All-Worlds' fingers twitched. They tightened as if holding onto something precious. "I can't," he choked out. His voice sounded as dry as a riverbed parched with drought.

"You doubt me?" Anxius asked, the same betrayal ricocheting between all of them. The braid of their combined power began to fray.

"Yes," All-Worlds said and the word was one of agony, an admission that had been nurtured in the dark. "I always have. This is too much. You ask for too much. We will not be ourselves when you are done. We will be the wetlands that you ruin. I told you this. How many times did I tell you this."

Thunder rumbled inside Wicasah, a hurricane threatening to collapse in on itself. The braid loosened, the integrity falling.

"If you don't complete this, we will all be lost," Anxius cried.

"You're not strong enough to hold us all. If I don't join, there is some chance for us to recover ourselves."

But Anxius' face transformed into a rictus smile as though he'd grown weary of this well-trod argument. Wicasah felt his power be wrenched, used with and yet without his permission. "All humans are like this," Anxius hissed. "If I cannot give my sentience to the earth, then I cast all souls from it. Why should they be allowed to walk the Milky Way, the Heavens, any paradise, yet still believe they can harvest its stars too?"

Power siphoned out of Wicasah. The earth rumbled as Anxius

forced all their names and powers into a barbed spear through the mantle and core to shred open the endless realms and underworlds. The barriers became a mangled rip of linen, glistening like a cobweb weave. Rainbow frays filled his sight, like an endless refraction. A barbed spear would shred more coming out.

Somewhere, far away, Wicasah felt All-Worlds release his power. It clawed against the braid, trying to untangle it, but All-Worlds had always been a desperate fool who never saw the big picture, only those who lived inside it.

A crack shot across the ground, broadening into a huge chasm. A new horizon line of them all to see. Anxius gathered the strands and they whooshed like magnets furious to be this close together. Wicasah could feel the negative force with his body, even as his spirit felt battered from All-Worlds' power. The magnet brought other things to it—souls of the dying and dead, ripped to its hungry wants like a vacuum. Wicasah did not know where they would go. He couldn't stop watching the beautiful weave of the braid fall apart.

The core of the world shook as if expunging something new. Within the dark chasm they'd created, the dirt looked rich and red as if stained with a rose bloom. The earth gagged again and out of the rainbow funnel rolled a capsule. A white petal slick with afterbirth unfurled until Wicasah recognized the lady-slipper queen. Her rose-quartz eyes gleamed feral. The cyclone intensified as she screeched in hunger. She lunged for Anxius, even as the braid unraveled and became links in a chain that bound them all to him. Anxius fought, threw every ounce of power into her famine of a vortex. The lady-slipper queen clawed at him and with her hand full of his chains, she dragged him into the darkness.

Wicasah realized, suddenly, why the heyoka had no name. Why she had taken on the mantle of an honored creature of lore to resonate with the thunder in her bones. He could not speak her name, or the name of any of the others, because they had all been forgotten. They had all been consumed.

The lady-slipper queen took her first souls into the Dark and Bloody. She took her first souls into Helia.

CHAPTER 8
DOMINO

THE END OF All-Worlds' story reverberated inside Domino as a reverent come for its piece of flesh. A story of friends and promises, of betrayed love and world-destroying power. Anxius might have tried to protect the natural beauty of the world by animating it with humanity's vices, but he did so by damning his made family, instead. And that undead wraith now had its rotted fangs in Domino's kin, even if Wicasah had been the one to spit and shake.

"If Wicasah got his name and power back, would he be better?" Domino demanded. He'd launched his boat into the ocean of his fear, a tiny fishing boat trawling for hope. "Would he become sane again?"

All-Worlds studied the fire. "Who says what is sane and insane?"

"Insanity is that shadow-wrapped nightmare." Domino's voice cracked. "Insanity is the brother who doesn't know who I am."

"You know her," Naomi said, flabbergasted, her rounded eyes staring at All-Worlds as if she'd never seen him before. "The heyoka was your friend. You never *said*."

"I can't even speak her name anymore." All-Worlds' lower lip trembled. "When I think of her—when I think of any of them—I can't recall what they look like. I remember the sensation of her in my heart when in her presence. I think that's why, when she came to me along the Dark and Bloody dressed as a heyoka, I let her stay with me."

"Did she know you, then?" Naomi asked.

"I think she knew *of* me," All-Worlds said. "It happened on the heels of the final earthquake, when the extravagant homes and machinery drilling into the earth collapsed into the Dark and

Bloody. She emerged not long after. Disheveled and lost, mimicking a tale that might have come from her people or one she'd stolen. I don't know. I never asked. We were all outcasts for one reason or another. Kidnapped, stolen, runaways, witches . . . whatever it was that had separated us from where we'd come from. Magic was what we had in common. Asking about the past was an understood taboo."

"You should have said something," Naomi whispered. "You should have warned us. We're not like *them*. We're the hatchlings under your wing, and you let us fly without telling us how."

"There are no good witches." All-Worlds' voice had gone flat as if repeating a long-held mantra.

Domino didn't care about the canvas pulled taut between Naomi and All-Worlds, about how All-Worlds' story threw more paint in thick, dripping lines on the picture, transforming it from tragedy into a mash of brown. He wouldn't trade anything for such a tale to take up his time again—time he now knew was dangerously short. Wicasah's sanity was the net cast in his ocean of fear: weather-worn, storm-tossed, and on the brink of shredding. Domino had thought their lingering days with each other had been the slow start to a drawn-out meal of life. Now, he realized they were but a meager supper and he was starved for more.

He would forage for more. He would beg and steal for more. This *more* rested with Anxius. As Naomi and All-Worlds stared at each other in stunned silence wondering if everything between them had been ruined, he knew what he had to do. Domino was good at deals, his poker face was legendary, and he liked to go all in. This was just another game to play.

Dry thunder rumbled, tickling the bottom of his feet. He almost ignored it, until the vibration soon interfered with the steady, if frantic, beat of his heart. A background noise that could drown out anything. The fire flickered irregularly.

Naomi studied her cup. "What is that?" she asked in a soft hush.

Domino yanked the cup closer to him to see ripples spreading across the surface. The air seemed charged with electricity. A moment of dread filled him as he caught Naomi's eyes. The realization shot between them—negative to positive—in a firing of thought.

Domino leapt to his feet, spun, and lunged for his brother as the tacked door flap blew open. The sizzle of hide and smell of charred flesh filled the yurt as the heyoka stepped through. Her long dark hair was frazzled and frayed, her russet skin glowing with the leftover sparks of heat lightning. The sparks shot from her and collided with Domino, sending him catapulting into the hide wall. His palms skidded on the ground, tearing open his hands. A sharp pain exploded in his head, triggering the nebulous roil of magical aftertaste to become a clustered migraine. He'd forgotten the consequences of his witchery and he hadn't paid for the bone king yet.

Power thickened the air like added flour, making it doughy. The lights blurred as he squinted up at them. They arrowed into his skull. Pain radiated down into his gut and, for a moment, he feared his body would shut down without his consent. Near blind, he peered around until he saw Wicasah as a mesh of blackness before him.

He could reach his brother. That was all that mattered. After that, it was a simple matter of escape. Escape and find Anxius. Cut the chain that bound Wicasah to Anxius, or make a deal and swap one brother out for the other.

A new flavor of magic illuminated the yurt and a series of black witchery-rips filled the air. "Leave us alone!" Naomi screamed as the rips cut across the heyoka's cheeks. Lighting zipped in and out of the rips as though they were open doors. Thunder followed on their heels, making Domino's ears ring.

"With my prize, I will," the heyoka said, her voice rich and bitter. She stepped closer to Wicasah and All-Worlds flung out his hand, freezing her in place.

The heyoka laughed in disbelief. "You'll fight me now?" She took one step forward as though fighting to make her body work in ice-floe water. "After all this time, this is what you needed to act? You coward."

"I never meant to betray you," All-Worlds said and even Domino could hear the endless nights the shaman had spent doubting and regretting, heartsick and lonely. All-Worlds pulled a pouch that hung from his belt and emptied the powder within into the fire. The fire transformed colors and the heyoka's face grimaced at the same time with discomfort. "Yet my fears were realized. I wouldn't have been able to make a difference. We would all have ended up chained to Anxius at the bottom of the Dark and Bloody."

I HAVE ASKED TO BE WHERE NO STORMS COME

Domino crawled toward Wicasah, feeling blindly for his brother. The shadow in his mouth pulsed like his heartbeat, a tick guiding him in the right direction.

"But you did!" The lighting-woman bared her teeth at him. "We were the only thing each of us had in the world and you turned your back on us to live the life you chose. You left us!"

"Then take me," All-Worlds said. "What use do you have for two tumbleweed witches?"

"I want my family back," she said, and as if with the sheer force of will, broke All-Worlds' spell to shuffle forward another step. "We were all sucked into Helia when the Dark and Bloody opened. Left there to forget and wander, to become shades of our former selves. Did you know that? That we all went mad? I want to save us, but I need a vessel of transport." She looked to Wicasah. "This tumbleweed witch has helped me bring their souls over to the other side."

"They're already gone," All-Worlds shouted, the strain tucking in the corners of his mouth. "They're already deranged shades."

"Then they can be free to go to their paradise!" the heyoka screamed.

The next thunderclap rendered Domino momentarily senseless and seemed to encompass the stars, the skies, any celestial orbs rotating above. He reached for his familiars, but they were slumbering beings tucked against his skeleton. They needed bone to *be* bone. *Eat from me,* he thought uselessly. He barely had anything left to give. Even to his own witchery, his offer was still left wanting.

The heyoka took another step and fell to her knees beside Wicasah.

"You can't have him," Domino whispered, his hands reaching out for the shadow-shroud.

She flashed a dagger-sharp grin at him. "I'll have him. He'll shuffle as many souls out of Helia as I want him to before he fades like an overworn shirt. Are you worried about him being taken by Anxius, Domino?"

Domino swallowed hard when he heard his name in her mouth. The image of her was burned on his retinas. He saw her outline like a specter every time he blinked.

"Yes, I know you," she said. "The scent of your nightmares still fills Helia. Never fear. I won't let Anxius get what he wants, the bastard. With me, Wicasah will never be in the Dark and Bloody."

Domino's hand landed on the shadow-shroud and pulled the

form closer to his chest. Wicasah screamed at the touch. More cuts of the ripped sky appeared around the heyoka, but she smirked and the lighting coalesced into one bolt, shooting through the doors and striking the unpromised witch in the chest. Naomi grunted in pain, her shirt bright with lit embers, as she collapsed with a hand against her heart. All-Worlds cried out and dropped to his knees before her. His power unraveled around the heyoka, leaving her to once more walk freely.

She bent and ripped into the shadows covering Wicasah's chest. Domino pushed her back, but touching her was like gripping an electric fence. The reddened scab of Wicasah's cauterized wound lay exposed, the hook raw and oozing pus.

Domino surged forward to grip her shoulder, the black lay of her hair bunching under his hand. He held on as though she were his one lifeline in this tempest of untamed magic.

"I promise you, I'll keep your brother separated from Anxius," she whispered to him. Her hands flickered in the air. The shimmer of rainbow strands appeared around them. She tugged on the spiderwebbing strands as if testing the weight to ring a bell. "I promise," she finished.

The thunderclap vibrated Domino's bones to pieces, jumbling them like runes and casting them, but he had no prophecies to give, no fate to follow. Wicasah was ripped away from him. The heyoka's magic dismembered him into eroded pieces of marrow just before she took his brother and disappeared in a bolt of light.

———•———

Domino woke to see the eroded curves of his bones underneath the translucent sheets of his skin. His ribs looked gnawed on. Divots pitted his femurs. A small familiar tilted its head at him.

"Nice of you to show up," he told the thing and held out his newly formed finger bones for the creature's inspection. The tiny thing mouthed it, learning the texture, before scraping minuscule teeth along it. The rasp made Domino uneasy, but his witchery had failed him when he needed it most. He'd failed it by not giving it what it needed. He'd failed Wicasah by losing him.

With a groan, he managed to sit up and saw Naomi hunched next to a newly stoked fire. Her hand clutched her chest. Domino crawled over to her and paused when he glimpsed the bandage wrapped around her torso, stained red from blood and green from salve. She smelled of peppermint.

"Nice to see you again," she said with a wry smile and then gasped in pain.

"What happened?" he asked, hand outstretched and hovering. Fervently, he wished he'd been able to help her, take away her pain, after everything she'd done for him and his.

"Lightning to the heart," she said. "All-Worlds bandaged it up, but I have a suspicion he's holding me together with nothing more than his own brand of magic. Should've . . . taken Wicasah up on his offer. Should've killed him. Then I would've been strong enough."

Domino's hand retreated.

"Indeed, you should have," All-Worlds said as he stepped through the charred opening of the yurt. He dumped a tumbled mess of antler sheds, jawbones, and owl pellets in front of Domino. The little familiar gnawing on Domino's exposed finger glanced at the offering with a note of disdain.

"Thank you," Domino said, picking up one of the pellets and tearing it apart, glad to have two hands once more. He extracted a needle-thin rat's leg bone and handed it to the creature. The familiar sat back and munched on the offering. Domino sat back with a sigh. The more it ate, the more Domino felt the migraine receding. Inside him, the bone familiars were pulling his thunder-rumbled form back into some semblance of a human again.

All-Worlds knelt before Naomi and lifted one edge of the bandage. He took a whiff, smelling for rot. She withstood his ministrations until swatting his hands away. "I'll be fine," she said.

"You're barely standing," All-Worlds pointed out.

"Rips are my specialty," she said. "This one? It's just a graze."

All-Worlds brought her hands up to his mouth and laid one kiss on her fingers. "Just a graze."

The gelatinous layer of Domino's skin began to harden, but he still felt a give where some of his skeletal structure hadn't quite aligned yet. Wicasah's shadow still lingered in his throat like a gossamer cobweb layer. It rolled as if shaking off the heyoka's power as well. "A good thing it's just a graze. I'll need you to guide me to Anxius."

"Your brother is lost," All-Worlds said. "There's nothing left for you in him. How can you ask this of us after everything we've given you?"

"If I cut his chains to Anxius, I can save him," Domino said.

"He will still be insane. He will still die."

"Then I bargain with the man. Make a trade."

"You can't give up your life," Naomi hissed. "It would desecrate everything Wicasah has done for you."

"Already died once, didn't I?" Domino said.

All-Worlds shook his head in disbelief and spoke to Naomi. "See what I've been saying? Witches are nothing but trouble. There is nothing in them but selfish wants and gains." He turned to Domino. "Destroy yourself if you must. But in the end, no matter what you do, your brother will die or lose himself. The cost of a bargain does not simply disappear."

Domino squared his shoulders and refused to respond. He couldn't let his brother become one of these restless, nameless, powerless shades. He wasn't worth that sacrifice.

Naomi bit her lips, considering. "Where would we have to go?"

A sharp sound of denial eeked past All-Worlds' clenched teeth. "After everything Wicasah has done to you, you'll still try to help him? It is a lost cause. He killed your parents. Why would you want to help him?"

Naomi laid a hand on All-Worlds' shoulder. "You forget that I come from a line laden with witches. If I can be the one good witch you know, it will be enough for me. I still have some claim over Wicasah. He bears my mark. There is still something to bargain with."

All-Worlds shoved her hand from him. "Go to the Dark and Bloody, then."

"You have to see that all this love has shaped your world, don't you?" Naomi said. "Come with us. We need your strength. I need your strength. You love this man. He will listen to you."

All-Worlds studied her as though he'd never seen her before. His dark eyes flickered to Domino and Domino glanced away to the familiars that had multiplied in his hands. Five of them gnawed on the sharp edge of an elk shed with unmitigated ferocity. "She's right," he said. "You know Anxius best."

You're our guide in this unknown land, he thought. *You've walked these paths and sung these sorcery songs, but you're a reluctant mentor.* "You're scared the past will repeat itself," Domino said his thoughts out loud and couldn't help but snort. "You're scared you'll lose it all again."

All-Worlds shut his eyes and Domino ignored the tears that fell down his cheeks. Calmly, he fed his familiars the wild bones and started to think about Helia again. Thought of being washed up on demon's spit and the rush that comes with harmful spell casting. If Anxius was the source of the Dark and Bloody, he was also the thing that kept the funnel steady and alive. Maybe, if Anxius died, the funnel would collapse.

But what would happen if Wicasah died before the funnel collapsed? Would he be stuck in Helia without Domino? Would Domino be cut off from that land of terror, forced either tomorrow or in his old age into a new type of paradise or eternal torment with no chance at reconciliation?

No. He'd make sure he followed Wicasah to whatever afterlife existed for them. Even if that meant facing Helia's tortures once more. This time, if he went back, it would be worth it. He wouldn't leave Wicasah to wander the landscape like a tumbleweed scattered to the wind. Not with a shattered mind. Nameless. Powerless.

"I'll go," All-Worlds said softly.

"Good." Domino stood, losing just a touch of height from the pitted shield of his patella, and felt the bone king inside him roll in slumber. Dreaming of war. Dreaming of battle.

CHAPTER 9
WICASAH

LOST IN HELIA, *Wicasah sought out the lady-slipper queen. He learned the shape of the rainbow strands she left behind whenever she visited and when he finally saw her thick head of hair and the gleam of pink-quartz eyes, he'd begged for his name and power back.*

"Why would you want it?" she asked. "You can't remember who you were anyway."

"I know that I could make lightning with my hands," he sobbed. "I remember my heart rumbled with thunder instead of a beat. I remember I had family who I'd found like sea glass on the shore."

The lady-slipper queen looked sad as she released a new soul into the dust-devil ridden desert. Demons set upon it and tore the man limb from limb. "The chains of Anxius cannot be broken or else I would be destroyed. The funnel to Helia would collapse. I would have no purpose, no realm to oversee. I don't want to cease to exist. You're integral to his prison, just like his friends. I will only add to his bonds, not take them away."

"Why would you tell me this?" Wicasah asked, breathless. "Can't you replace me with another?"

"Find me a witch as strong as you," the lady-slipper queen said. "It won't matter, though. You'll forget this conversation in a century. The lightning in your brain is strong, but it too will lose its charge."

I will find my family, Wicasah vowed. I will find them all and release them from this place and when I do you'll be sorry you ever crossed me and mine . . .

I HAVE ASKED TO BE WHERE NO STORMS COME

"Can you focus?"

The question came from far away. The words bit him like a mosquito, sucking at his essence, leaving behind an unbearable itch. The brickwork of himself fragmented, the mortar binding him together chipping and stale. His name was Wicasah. He had never been to Helia. He was not a lightning-struck goddess.

A piercing pain spread throughout his chest. Looking down, he saw a leash clipped to the hook in his chest. The heyoka tugged the braided rainbow lead in her hands to get his attention. He blinked and saw that they sat beside a flat wetland pond, the surface glassy. The sky was the gray-navy of an oncoming storm, reflected in the water, giving everything a dark glow. The heyoka stood with one foot in the sirocco winds of Helia and the other in the flat blue stretch of land in the here and now.

"Focus," she whispered and reached into the portal to Helia to stretch a soul across and toward the hook. She tried to wind the gossamer thread, but the puckered hook was too scarred to take anyone but himself. Wicasah swayed and grinned at her, knowing it to be crazed. "Too slippery," he said, feeling the soul slide away.

The heyoka made a frustrated grunt and flung the soul back into Helia. "Focus," she urged him. "Control your power."

Wicasah opened his mouth to tell her no, but instead a story spilled out. "You didn't realize when you'd gotten out of Helia and stepped into the land of the living. Your old home. You didn't recognize it. Didn't understand it. It wasn't until you met me that you saw a chance to recover what you'd lost. In his rage, Anxius created another earthquake to kill all the Brightsiders who lived along the edges of the Dark and Bloody, who fracked the inside of it, and watched as they all tumbled into the darkness. He laughed all the way. That's when you got out. In that earthquake."

For a moment, any oncoming storm had stopped. The smell of petrichor evaporated. The heyoka watched him with widened eyes. Wicasah felt a strike of victory that he had surprised her once and for all. The rainbow braid slackened further and she stepped completely out of Helia. Wicasah eyed the open rift with trepidation. Other spirits waited at the edge of it. In the back of his mind, Domino's voice warned him not to enter. That if he did, it would shred what little of his identity he still clung to.

His chest bled. Not just a cascade of red, but his own shadow. The witchery-soul of him oozed out like black oil. Enamored,

Wicasah put his fingers in it, rubbed the sticky coat between his thumb and forefinger. The drops fell to the ground.

"Don't do that. Anxius will start to know your scent," the heyoka stated, stroking the rainbow braid binding them together. He shuddered in response and sucked hard on the inside of his lower lip, obsessively tonguing the brand and pouring whatever power he still possessed into it. He didn't know why it was important, only that it was a mark of survival connecting him to his past.

"You're reading my memories," she said.

Wicasah's wings drooped behind him as he nodded. The bound shadows galloped around him like feral dogs who'd forgotten domestication. Biting, clawing, chewing off their own legs for freedom.

"You're slipping quicker than expected." Her dark eyes narrowed at him. "It's why I can't drag you into Helia. There's not much left to drag."

Her story nudged his tongue and he let it spill out. "You keep binding the wrong people to me. You can't remember what they look like. The sound of their voices. Their names. You have a memory of a memory. When you try to match it up with all of Helia's souls, something just isn't quite right. You might have even gotten the right people out and you wouldn't know because you can't remember."

"Stop it." Her mouth pursed into an angry line. A sudden wash of tears made her dark eyes starry.

Wicasah couldn't stop. He was she. Only the truth of her life existed between them. "You're scared that if you bind another soul to me, it will be the wrong one, and I'm not going to live much longer. You're scared if you give me to Anxius, he won't give you anything back, but if you take me into Helia, you know I won't survive it and I'll be his anyway. You don't have much to gain, but your window of opportunity to gain something is shrinking."

She let out a soft sigh. Any sign of the mystical being she'd been faded away until he saw the ghost of her, the powerful witch she was once upon a time. "If you can see so much, do you know my name?"

Her hope tasted like rosemary on his tongue. Maybe that was part of it. Perhaps it was what her name used to mean. He shook his head. "No. Even your face is a blur."

"Do you remember their names?" she asked. "The others?"

"It's nothing but a screech," he said. "Soon, you won't remember my name, either."

She turned to look at the sky, her mouth half-open in desperation. "I wanted to save the plateaus," she said quietly. "The flat tops and the ragged walls that held them up. To me . . ."

"They always looked like citadels of the gods," Wicasah finished for her, seeing the red striated rocks, the burnished orange glow and stripes and how the greenery seemed that much more vibrant in comparison. Through her memories, he could see arches of stone, the tapered cylinders cleaving the sky, cliffs she could climb and let the wind whip through her hair.

"You were abandoned," he said. "Your mother thought you were cursed. The rocks became your home—"

"*Enough.*" Her hands folded together, an ancient action of safety, as if to hold her anxiety close to comfort it. Wicasah knew all this. He knew it all because she was part of him now, bound with the rainbow braid until he lost the final shreds of himself. Like plucking the petals off a flower. Does she love me? She loves me not.

The heyoka studied the horizon where thunder-bumper clouds grew once more. Virga streaked from the white bullheads. The smell of petrichor returned, stronger than ever.

"I'm so tired of rain," they said at the same time.

She closed her eyes. He thought about asking what she was going to do, but he already knew.

He already knew.

CHAPTER 10
DOMINO

THE DARK AND BLOODY squiggled through the dried-out dirt like an ink spill, and Domino thought that even though All-Worlds and Anxius believed they'd failed to save the world from human influence, they'd succeeded in other ways. No one wanted to cross that canyon-sea. No one wanted to build anywhere close to the droughted land around it. The whole place remained relatively untouched.

Standing at the edge of it, he peered into the deep well of darkness and knew someone looked back. A powerful witch, chained with the powers of his friends, interested to see what he would do next. It had taken them days to arrive here, at the edge of the world, using a series of wagons, trains, magic, and finally old-fashioned walking. Domino turned to see Naomi clutch her chest with a wheeze and lean against All-Worlds. All-Worlds whispered soothing words to her and she smiled thinly at him. The swell of power washed over Domino as All-Worlds placed his hand over Naomi's wound and he wondered how much of her he was keeping together. Perhaps it was All-Worlds' power to freeze and solidify that saved her life right now.

The stolen shadow from Wicasah that clung to Domino's mouth burned like too hot water, singeing his soft palate. He swallowed hard and tried to ignore the raw sting.

"Let me help," he said and reached out to take Naomi from All-Worlds. Her slim form slumped against him.

"Thanks," she whispered. "How are we going to do this?"

"I'm figuring it out as I go." Domino gave her a reassuring squeeze. He had a sheathed knife in his pocket and his magic broadsword ready. He'd had worse odds.

I HAVE ASKED TO BE WHERE NO STORMS COME

All-Worlds stepped closer to the Dark and Bloody. "I lived next to you for years," he said and sunk to his knees. He took a handful of reddened dust into his palms and let the soft breeze lift and brush the fine dirt away. Naomi breathed hard, her face screwed up into a grimace. A henna-brown fractal line stained her neck like a reaching root system. Domino frowned, knowing he hadn't seen the full extent of her injuries. He shifted her button-down shift aside just enough to see the blood-soaked bandages crisscrossing her chest. He pressed his hand over it as if he could keep her alive for All-Worlds, just as All-Worlds was trying to keep Wicasah alive for him.

"You came to me twice, asking for me to complete the braid," All-Worlds continued as more dirt slid through his fingers. "The lady-slipper queen dragged you back each time. The final time, the earthquake shook all the homes on stilts into the darkness. The frackers came back deranged from what they had seen. A reverent you were, a spirit I could not shake. Saying your name made you haunt me until I got rid of everything that was linked to you. Everything, except this."

All-Worlds pulled out a small plait of fuzzy white sage, the softness of little bluestem, and peppered with the crinkle of black-eyed Susan's yellow petals. "You gave this to me when we first . . . when we first loved each other. I'm ready to talk now, Anxius. I'm ready to complete the braid."

For a moment, Domino thought the rumble was the arrival of another thunderstorm. He cast his eyes to the blue horizon, looking for any sign of coiled clouds, a red sky of warning. But it was the Dark and Bloody that shook. Pebbles danced across the surface. Rocks cleaved off the canyon and tumbled into the darkness. The edges widened, making the ground underneath All-Worlds fracture and float like its own island.

"He's going to fall," Naomi said, frantic, and shoved Domino's arm off her. "He's going to fall."

"That's the least of our worries," Domino breathed out, even as Naomi screamed and reached uselessly for All-Worlds. Domino grabbed her shoulder and wrenched her back as All-Worlds sank into the darkness. The Dark and Bloody was expanding, with Domino and Naomi petering on the edge of a shifting leviathan. Other toothpicks of land broke off and floated out until crumbling into the darkness. The land rolled, sending both him and Naomi to their knees.

"Here, take my hand," he yelled and felt the reassuring grip of her thin hand slide into his. He wrenched them both up as the crevasse continued to widen. Land broke apart like a puzzle being dismantled. A sharp spike of anguish filled Domino as the black cracks spidered out along his feet and into the distance. What use would they be to Wicasah if they died in this earthquake?

Please, please, don't let it end this way, he pleaded, even as they limped and struggled across ground that split and flaked under their feet. He was on a ship without sea legs and couldn't find his gravity. Another roll had him pitching to the side. Naomi cried out his name as their hands were ripped apart. She fell on all fours as the earth separated them. Her wide, horrified eyes burned into his before the darkness devoured her.

Domino didn't know how to scream. There was no one left to call out to. He sprinted as fast as he could, but the rumble that followed him was more terrifying than the heralding thundercracks of the heyoka. The ground pitched once more and he lost his footing, just before the Dark and Bloody tilted up like a bird with a fish and swallowed him whole.

He tumbled into the darkness with a wordless shriek. His head collided with the side of the crevasse. He fell for what felt like an eternity until he landed in a crash of broken bones.

Dust puffed around him like gentle fog and he groaned, wondering if it was Anxius' kindness that had let him survive or pure luck. Blinking, he looked up to see he was in a huge cave with the rip of the Dark and Bloody as a crack of white light above him. Stalagmites rose as mounts from the floor, larger than Domino. He braced against one as he stumbled to his feet. Quickly feeling his pockets, he realized his knife was lost. A weak bioluminescence shone on the ground, leading him further into the cave. Crystals glimmered with pastel colors of twilight embedded in the walls— hints of lavender-purple and dusky blue. He kept to the darkness as he followed the sound of the voices, all the while listening to the ones in the back of his mind.

"Domino, nobody asked you to keep protecting me," Wicasah said.

"Nobody has to protect you," he shot back. *"You think it's all about you? What about my life without some semblance of meaning? Face it, kid. You're that meaning whether you like it or not."*

I HAVE ASKED TO BE WHERE NO STORMS COME

Soon, the weak glitter led him into another massive cavern. Domino's mouth opened in a perfect circle as he studied it. An altar stood in the middle, a rounded pedestal with colored chain links stringing from all directions and binding the stone golem creature perched on top. The chains seemed to move and breathe on their own, and swells of power ebbed and flowed throughout the room, making Domino feel the uneasy shift of lightning about to strike, the uncanny scent detritus of undergrowth, the howl of wind kept stagnant.

All-Worlds knelt in front of the pedestal, his fingers twisted together. Their exchange was mush to Domino's ears, a language he did not understand, one that had died long ago. Anxius—the stone man—twisted as All-Worlds' spoke, as though fighting the uncomfortable string of his bonds. The earth gave a gentle roll and Domino was shoved forward by earth and mineral, forced to kneel next to All-Worlds with a whoosh of power.

"So, this is your new witch," Anxius boomed with a voice as dark as onyx.

Domino fought against whatever force held him inert. He met All-Worlds' hopeless gaze and knew what the shaman wanted to ask. *I don't know where she is,* he thought back.

"Not mine," All-Worlds said in a hush.

"You have my brother," Domino said in a rush. "I'm a straightforward man. I want him back."

Anxius shifted his hands, straining them together, and opened his fingers to show Domino a blue lace agate polished and gleaming in the center. "Ah, yes. The witch who never knew his mother and murdered his father, a powerful beast who can hope and hop between realms. The lady-slipper queen holds his name and soon she will gift it to me." Bitterness coated the air. "Another chain to strengthen the funnel. At least that was the good piece of my legacy. Souls banished from the land they desecrated." He bared his teeth, quartz pillars in lieu of canines.

"What if we could free you?" Domino asked. "Break the chains?"

Anxius snorted in derision. "Do you wish to take my place, instead? I will give you your brother if you will do that willingly. Even though he will still be dead and his soul in Helia. The last soul for Helia and the funnel."

Domino swallowed hard. No matter what he did, it seemed Wicasah would perish.

"He is not strong enough to hold such power," All-Worlds said softly. "He would collapse the Dark and Bloody."

"Yes," Anxius mused. "Always the logical one, All-Worlds. Always seeing the flaws in my plans. How many lives between the coasts would be snuffed out? Would you rather save this one witch or damn all the other souls? I know you, All-Worlds. No matter what this witch means to you—to him—he will never be worth the cost. You were . . . still are the love of my life and you would not do that even for me."

All-Worlds closed his eyes tightly. "I did not think you would become this."

"Give him back to me, then." The rock dust clogged Domino's throat when he interrupted. "He's not yours. He's replaceable."

"The lady-slipper queen has his name," Anxius reiterated. The marble orbs of his eyes rolled, the blue swirl acting as an unnatural pupil and iris. "I cannot give him to you until she gives his name to me fully with his death and dismantled sanity. Even now, he's barely hanging on."

"Take mine, instead." Domino knew he sounded desperate. He held out one of his hands, letting the blade of the bone king emerge, knowing the king's broad ribs bracketed around him like wings. Still ossified and hunched around him, requiring ossification to devour.

"I will not," Anxius said and he lifted his shoulders, as though the whole underworld rested upon them.

"What could I give you for him?" Domino said, making deals he had no right to make. The blue lace agate's polished surface caught the light and within the shades of white, ivory, and angel-blue, Domino caught a glimpse of the universe spiral contained in its middle. The universe of Wicasah. Domino's universe.

The good of the world over the fate of one. One was a universe. One was a matter of life or death. The bone sword of the bone king rippled into being and Domino swung, shooting every fiber of his witchery into his transformation. He would cut the chains. He would take that blue lace agate promise and Wicasah's life back into his own hands. There was no other choice for him. His world ended a single way: with the fate of one.

CHAPTER 11
WICASAH

WICASAH NOW KNEW the lady-slipper queen of old and new. She was a dusted-off discovered relic and he marveled at how she had impacted his life and the life that wasn't his.

He knew the heyoka had decided. He knew this because he was riding shotgun in her mind and memory, bound by the leash connecting them. Her thunder had been the first peal that shook his sanity loose and now, as the shape of his name became a faint recollection of ownership, he realized the lady-slipper queen's final claim was imminent. He knew he was Wicasah, but who was Wicasah, exactly? What defined it?

How could he know he was dying? Time spanned out in moments of waiting without purpose. Blank slats of moments full of the heyoka telling him where to go and what to do. She tried once more to take him into Helia and bind souls to him, which had ended in a black swath of unconsciousness, and the oozing witchery-soul of him became more viscous. He was of no more use to her. He was nothing but a cursed penny, a bad bet, and now she was going to claim whatever prize she could before he disappeared completely.

Shades haunted him now. He glimpsed souls without faces dipping in and out of his peripherals. The souls of minerals and gems waved from below. The sky was full of moonlight and sunlight and all the refracting particles in between. His name flickered in and out of thought like a lost and longed-for fact. The shadows that bounded around him were now his friends, except they nipped at his ankles and wrists, leaving them bloody.

Now, he stood at the edge of the hot spring pool, the surface a shifting blue from mountain valley to Caribbean paradise, clear as glass. Wicasah's mouth dropped open in childish awe and dipped his fingers into the sizzling depths. Water was so precious. You could have wars over one tiny aquifer, and now he was at the source with all of humanity's leftover tears spilling into this pool of sorrow. His heart clenched like it might collapse in on itself, as he edged closer to the shore, his feet crunching on sulfur pieces and mineral deposits.

"I have him," the heyoka called across the hot springs. "If you want him, I'll need something in return."

A tall shape shifted across the way and the lady-slipper queen stepped on the surface of water. "What could you possibly want?" she sneered.

Wicasah could finally see the steps she had taken to stay alive. A new entity birthed to serve the Dark and Bloody's funnel, conceived from the wild, combined powers of those wanting to keep the earth sacred, it made sense that she'd made that goal part of her reason of existing. Yet, she was lost and scared, alone and confused. No one took her hand and led her to the stream to drink. The bonds of her own existence lived within the funnel, her purpose to keep it ever-churning.

The rainbow strands of the funnel floated by him, and he ran the bloodied stumps of his fingers along their glimmering edges. He cast away the belief of significance, seeing only her want to have a hearth to warm next to, the body of another who would laugh at her antics and murmur well-kept secrets for her to keep.

The heyoka tugged on his braid, but there was nowhere else for him to go. He could walk into the hot spring and melt apart, instead he knelt as the lady-slipper queen came ever closer.

"I want my name," the heyoka demanded. "I want my power back. My true power."

A cold gray fog billowed around them, a great storm rolling in with thunderheads. Wicasah waited for it, ready to take it on. Steam rose from the pool, muting the spectrum of colors around them into a wash of monochrome. Somewhere in the midst of it all,lightning flashed.

The lady-slipper queen laughed at the heyoka. "Will your wants ever cease?" she asked. "You asked me that once before and the answer is the same. Some things cannot be taken back or reverted. Anxius is my beating heart. Your name and power are the veins pumping power to make me live but also to hold up the funnel of my existence! Why would I take away from the integrity of it? Why would I ever sacrifice myself for you when it was you who made me?"

Wicasah shuddered as electricity zinged up from his shared consciousness with the heyoka. He tongued the brand across his inner lip, taste-testing the cold metal of the runes imprinted on his soft flesh. He couldn't remember where they'd come from, but they gave him a sense of peace. His shadows tugged, desperate to run into the funnel. One had already escaped. Or had it escaped a long time ago?

"Then give me the names of those who have been lost so I can find them!" the heyoka screeched. "They don't belong there. All you've done is transport us into another land to fill with our mistakes."

"You've taken enough from Helia already," the lady-slipper queen snarled. Lightning illuminated the surface of the spring, but also the outline of the skeleton inside her humanoid form. The bones within her were larger and more monstrous than whatever she showed on the outside. Her pink-quartz eyes glared at the heyoka, stoked with a new light before Wicasah felt tension string throughout the rainbow strands and the sudden whip of their release.

A dull faraway shock of pain filled him as the rainbow strands severed the links to his shadows, leaving them decapitated or limping. Others galloped into the arms of the psychopomp and the cave behind her. The more they fled from him, the more disjointed he became. A roaring agony followed the heels of that realization and he looked down to see he's been nearly cut in half. Strands dug into his arms. One hung barely off his elbow. His neck gushed blood.

The braid tugged on his chest and he peered up to see the heyoka balanced before him, protecting their link from being severed. Yet, it had been wounded, hanging on by a fraying thread. She was even more mismatched than ever before—only now, the funnel strands had taken chunks out of her flesh and gouged out one eye to leave a gaping maw of red meat behind. Lightning exploded, making the steam sizzle.

"Don't fade," she commanded. Wicasah picked up the limp ends and felt himself fray as well, becoming a shadow of links. He saw her try to reach through the fog and steam to wrench open a portal into Helia. He smelled the hot dryness of the desert, suddenly wiped out by the mineral-thick sensation of the springs.

"Don't fade to him," she repeated, the layer of determination in her voice making him smile. If he could feel her, perhaps she could feel him.

"Your brother is Domino," the heyoka stuttered out as if against her will, telling his memories to him as surely as he had to her. "He raised you when no one else could and he died because of his foolish heart and you brought him back because this world hasn't lived up to your expectations and the only one who ever did was him."

The rainbow strands tightened again until they quivered with tension. The lady-slipper queen wrenched her elbow back. Soon, they would be the final saw cutting into the wood of his life, wiping him away, chaining him to Anxius. The witchery ooze of him puddled out and into the water, leaving an acid burning layer that contaminated the spring.

"You still think it was worth it," the heyoka sobbed as the rainbow strands twanged and released. Before he felt the pain, she said again, "You stupid idiot, somehow you still think he was worth it."

"The only soul I ever saved," Wicasah whispered.

There was nothing left for him but to succumb to the storms of his life and become the new chain to Anxius.

CHAPTER 12
DOMINO

DOMINO'S BONE BLADE sunk into the chain closest to him and the sound was like steel on steel radiating throughout the Dark and Bloody's catacomb structure. His familiars rushed out of him and climbed the braids, gnawing at them with their power, burrowing to seek the source of bone. His flesh receded from him. A black hole erupted in his brain, a cathedral of consequence. His blade sunk into the plait as though being sucked into quicksand. He pulled and wrenched back, only to feel the uncanny yank in response. The braid twisted and the blade broke. Domino screamed as the loss radiated up his arm. Anxius' laugh rumbled around him as the braids struck and wove around him like a rattlesnake. They squeezed until he felt the crunch and slide of his bones against each other.

Anxius suspended Domino in front of his face. The granite face twisted in some semblance of a smile, showing the opal glimmer in his lips. "Take my place," he whispered. "You want this place damned. So do I. This soul you came to save will become part of your chains. Isn't that the point? To save what you love? What safer way than to have him with you."

"He would still be dead and alone in Helia," Domino gasped before the braids tightened again. Dark spots dotted his eyesight. His spine rasped together before an unsettling collapsing feeling overwhelmed him. Could his bones be used for power? His remains a magical ingredient for some future spell?

Maybe it was better this way. Domino would die in Anxius' grip. Wicasah would follow. They could be in Helia together until Wicasah faded into a shell of who he used to be, no longer responding to the gentle guide of Domino's hands.

Not like this. Domino gasped and twisted his head to see All-Worlds watching him in sorrow as if accepting Domino's fate.

The muck and withered grip of Anxius' power pressurized his breastplate, crumbling like plaster. The braids sought out his twister-ridden witchery-soul, the one that had been wiped clean of ancestry and lineage, another witch that made a mistake long ago and would be paying for it ever since. He thought of Wicasah and how they'd clawed to have some kind of future that wasn't marred by gunshots and curses, and found it to be just part of their fate. They were bad men and the endings for men like them were nothing good. He tried to gasp for air and scramble for power, but everything was gone but that consequence cathedral.

Suddenly, a black rip parted in front of him. The braid holding him captive shredded. Anxius immediate grinding scream made Domino realize the rip was actually inside the braid and that it kept expanding. The Dark and Bloody shuddered. The stalactites quivered like a dozen swords about to fall. The rip continued to widen and a fragile hope bloomed in Domino's chest. *Naomi.*

Anxius' scream dug into Domino's core, but at least he could move his arms now, and he slashed at the braided chain with the mutilated ends of his own sword. The strands frayed and gave like a steel cable collapsing, sending Domino hurtling towards the ground. He landed with a thump and a moan of agony, but there was no time for pain. Another rip opened in the next chain, exploding it in power. The released end sling-shotted across the cavern and took out the sidewall. The Dark and Bloody shivered again, only this time in fear instead of anger.

Domino frantically looked for Naomi, but all he could see were her small black rips embedded in the chains and dismantling them along fault points. The stone monster of Anxius tilted like an unmoored ship, uncertain what to do with his weight.

The third braid snapped into a slew of dangling pieces. Wherever she was, her untrained witchery electrified the air and danced along Domino's skin. He couldn't help the devil-may-care grin spreading across his face as he watched her tear Anxius apart.

Anxius gripped his chains as though trying to regain his balance. New magic floated around them, making the cavern shake with a brand-new kind of earthquake. With a furious roar, he began to topple over. Rocks fell and cascaded like a deluge, obscuring everything in a cloud of dust. Domino coughed, the ossified sacs of his lungs full of dust that sunk to the base of whatever organs remained.

A sharp hand on Domino's shoulder guided him to his feet. All-Worlds held him tightly. "Can you see her?" the shaman demanded. "Where is she?"

Domino looked at him helplessly as another black rip opened up and split the next chain apart. It was no sword or blade that destroyed Anxius, but a rippling power of time that spoke of deterioration, that made organs sag and give, bones bend and collapse, the tearing rips of mortality spreading out around them. He peered into the dust and barely made out the slump of a human in the distance. He pointed and All-Worlds disappeared from his side, returning with Naomi in his arms.

Domino took her face in his hands, saw her face streaked with dirt, a huge gash marring her cheek. Her dazed eyes barely focused on him, even as the conduits bulged and pressed against her skin. He pressed his hands over her chest, finding it sticky with blood. "Hold on," he whispered. The next braid slammed into the wall, making stalactites fall like released spears.

The black hole inside him had become a yawning vortex and Domino threw whatever scraps of power he had left to strengthen Naomi's onslaught. His familiars crawled over the remaining braids and onto Anxius like a swarm of ants. Stones could be bones and he sent them to dismantle the ancient witch.

The familiars dug into the granite flesh, seeking the organic infrastructure keeping him alive, ready to eat the glowing layers. Domino gritted his teeth as he felt them burrow and finally explode, sending shards of rock hurtling around them like a bomb.

All-Worlds grunted and suddenly toppled. A triangular rock shard stuck out of his side. He pressed his hands around the gushing wound even as one hand reached out to protect Naomi as he had always done.

Naomi reached the extent of her power. The final braid tore and fragmented, releasing like a whip and creating a boom that rendered Domino momentarily deaf. He gripped her and felt the soft give of her body, that quiet collapse when magic had been spent. Fear raced through him. Without her, there would be no rips to run into, nothing that would let them escape.

There was only one thing left to do. Desperately, he took it all in—the fallen witch, the collapsing cavern that had defined his life, the braids of power being destroyed. The funnel to Helia would face the same fate. They needed to get out of here and somehow find Wicasah before it was all too late.

One of his familiars bounded to him and handed him a stone. The polished surface felt slick as he studied the now cloudy roundness of the blue lace agate. The small universe throbbing inside it had been cracked and a keening wail built inside of Domino. Wicasah was near gone to him.

Another explosion of rock sent more shards speeding throughout the air. Pain peppered Domino's cheeks. Soon, they would either be shredded apart or buried alive. Even if he could die, he couldn't let Naomi and All-Worlds meet the same fate.

He had to be the one good witch All-Worlds knew.

He let the bone king overtake him, the final dregs of his power letting him shuck his skin and grow into the giant witch that he'd always hidden and never fully let out. He bounded into the next cavern and eased Naomi and All-Worlds into the cage of his ribs, next to his exposed heart, and hoped they would hang on. His hands dug into the walls, his feet scrambling for purchase as he began to climb.

The schism of light above him grew bigger and broader. Boulders fell into the depths of the shifting canyon and he dodged them as best as he could. One smashed into his shoulder, but he shrugged off the fragmenting pieces of that shattered clavicle to climb out of the Dark and Bloody. Another rammed into his knuckles and he slipped, suspended in the air by one hand. Screams came from inside his chest, but he managed to swing his skeleton hands to find new purchase.

He had one singular focus. To reach the top.

The funnel to Helia was collapsing. Rainbow strands whipped around him and scored into his bones, leaving lesions. They couldn't die here. He couldn't fall. They were so close.

The white light became a sliver of blue and he lifted them over the edge of the Dark and Bloody only to discover they had emerged at the edge of a hot spring. Rain coated his face, along with the scent of freshness. Somewhere, he could taste the lingering leftover of lightning.

Exhaustion pulled him into a sprawl and he gently removed Naomi and All-Worlds from the safety of his chest. He placed them on the ground as if they were bird eggs. Once they were free, his magic collapsed like a star, pulling him closer to that black abyss waiting to claim him. He shrunk, letting his human form emerge into the bloodied destroyed thing it was.

Naomi crawled to him and took a fistful of the torn remains of his shirt. She pointed to the slumped form against the bank. "Is that . . . ?" she asked, her voice nothing more than a croak.

Domino gripped the blue lace agate tight in his one good hand. *Too late,* he thought.

Always too late.

CHAPTER 13
DOMINO

"WICASAH," HE GASPED as he ran for the motionless figure alone along the bank of the hot spring. A black coating, like the skin of milk, floated on top of the waters. Sinking to his knees, he pushed the slack form over and tried to fight back a swell of tears. "Oh, no," he whispered, putting his hand over the raw acreage of carnage that marred his brother's chest. He felt for breath. "Oh, no."

A charred length of something twisted and dark was attached to the hook protruding from Wicasah, as though whatever had been on the other end of it had been obliterated. With a trembling hand, Domino slotted his fingers up and under Wicasah's jaw, searching for any kind of heartbeat. Around him, the rainbow strands fell like cottonwood seeds, their unique colors fading like blooms facing winter.

A stuttering faint thump. Something barely there. A triphammer that had finally gone still.

His sob was inhuman. Faced with this kind of destiny, he wanted to howl against their very existence. Wicasah didn't deserve to be in Helia. Not alone. Not without a guide. Someone who knew how to navigate the madness that would dodge him even as the ever-changing Helia would test him. He brought his brother further into his arms, holding him close. *Think around the black hole,* he pleaded. *Please. What can you do?*

The stolen shadow in his mouth tickled the back of his throat and sent the scent of charcoal into his nose like an offering. He gasped, wondering at this gift, and thought back at the crimson-streaked creature. *Yes.*

A burn began to encompass him. A window existed for them

to be together on one plane. They could fade at the same time. Even as the funnel was collecting its last soul, maybe it could collect two. *Maybe.*

He laid down beside Wicasah, face-to-face. Just beyond, he saw Naomi turn away from them, even as All-Worlds watched, possibly as a witness, but Domino would put down a bet that it was to make sure these witches stayed good and dead.

Domino took in Wicasah's face—the closed eyes, the ragged black hair, his mouth moued pink—and laid a final kiss on Wicasah's forehead. Cold to the touch, the remaining clamminess drying and evaporating. All the effort of Domino's life had gone into making and growing this person in front of him. A strong surge of pride struck him even as the shadow inside him combusted and burned him from the inside out. He had done this. He didn't have the slightest clue how, but no matter what anyone else said, he knew he'd raised a good man.

He didn't understand it, but the smoldering wildfire popping the pinecones of his bones felt cleansing in a way. Something new could grow here. Helia would no longer scoop up souls. Maybe, the souls could finally go where they were meant to be.

His eyes drooped, the embers of the shadow making the moisture inside him sizzle and spit. His breath came in short gasps like he'd forgotten how to breathe, but it must be because his lungs had popped from the heat. Everywhere, he felt fragile with trust.

He knew where Wicasah was going. Wicasah was going to Helia no matter what. The funnel was gone, but in the final moments, it would take Wicasah with it. Domino wouldn't let him go into that land alone. He would ride on the heels of that destroyed power and squeeze through the closing door.

The shadow inside him burst into a roaring flame. His bones blazed golden-red, scorching his skin from the inside out. A familiar whoosh like gasoline taking spark engulfed him. Crackles. Roaring. He saw his brother's face one last time before they were both consumed by fire.

Bodies of kindle. A bonfire full of their baneful bones.

Domino didn't say a word or utter any kind of hope, but he thought it. *Just wait. Just wait until the next life.*

CHAPTER 14

WICASAH

HELIA SPREAD OUT before Wicasah in a color palate of reddened sand and hellfire sky. His own touch had transformed the world. His magic had marked reservations for human souls. He'd upheld his bargain with the demons who'd walked these plains long before a whisper of humanity had come here. It seemed fitting that he had been ejected from the land he'd been born on to end up here, another lost soul for Helia's maw.

No shadows rested inside of him, nothing bound that coiled and leapt to him. There was no division between human and beast anymore, either. His hands ended in curved black claws. Diamond-shaped scales patterned down his chest to encircle the scar of where a thunder-goddess had left her mark.

But he knew his name. He could say to anyone that he was born of Thessaly and Daniel, that he had an older brother named Domino, that he murdered to keep what he loved, and that he was a witch who'd finally made it to Hell.

Yet, he didn't know what to do. Where to go. After all this time, he'd never asked his brother what it was like to live in this ever-changing landscape. No map or compass could lead his way. As he studied the flat horizon in front of him, as though it too waited in anticipation for his next move, he tongued the throbbing brand on his lower lip and uttered a sharp bark of laugher.

Even here, in an underworld that could no longer be accessed by humans, he still bore Naomi's living mark.

If she wanted, perhaps she could find him. Maybe, she made the sacrifice and had untold power at her disposal. Maybe she desecrated someplace sacred. Maybe she'd killed him.

He couldn't quite remember how he'd died. The wind pressed

against him, urging him to move, but he swayed in its path instead and let the slow slink of time erode him.

At some point, the presence of Helia slunk away, leaving only a brickwork road of destiny in front of him, if he so chose. Not a worthy soul for torture, he thought with a smirk of derision. What did it hope to give him that he hadn't already suffered through?

He realized, at some point in the eclipse of hellfire and the tundra of the night, he was grieving. Grief for himself, for his family, for those he'd twisted out of shape on his way to this final damnation.

A strong touch encircled his shoulder. In his chest, his heart gave a mournful stutter. Just Helia, he told himself. Messing with his mind. The touch remained, though, a steady weight that told him to take his time. His heart spread its wings, taking flight with newfound hope.

His own hand covered that touch, his black claws digging in just enough for him to believe in the reality of it all. The hand squeezed back, a familiar pillar which Wicasah had leaned against his whole life. He turned slowly to look into the face he'd fought lightning and mountains and death itself for.

And now they could ride into a land where no storm would fall.

ACKNOWLEDGEMENTS

I once sat in a band rehearsal guest conducted by David Maslanka. We'd fumbled through a difficult passage of music and he had his hands perched near his mouth, trying to find the words to express the needed improvements. He finally looked up and said softly, "Think of it like this. This passage is like you're in the bottom rung of hell and for the first time in a hundred, no thousand, years, you've finally glimpsed a ray of light." He then went on to say, "I've written many variations on this same theme. After a while, I decided that I was done with it, but sometimes you find yourself writing variations on the same idea, anyway. Sometimes, the theme simply isn't done with you."

Both of these sentiments resonated for me during the composition of this novel. I've written numerous times on the theme of magic, the underworld, and resurrection, and at times, I'm convinced that particular muse will never be done with me. Yet, this story had a much more personal touch in it. It's a story first built from the skeleton of gathered shiny stones of myth and lore that seem thrown around easily and without explanation on my side of the United States and in my homeland. I have these bare glimpses of memory as a child visiting a dinosaur museum and hearing mention of the great thunderous birds and water serpents that also defined the scientific names alongside the fossils. Two Medicine in Glacier National Park remains a place of great importance to me, and yet the significance of it eluded me until I took a good hard look at the etymology and lore signified. The long flat prairie of the High Line, the castle-esque plateaus rising against the big sky, the mist rising from Flathead Lake, the formation of the Badlands National Park and the Prairie Badlands, all had me thinking: where exactly is the magic here?

Where are the witches, seen in the Germanic forests? Where

are the weather witches of the Highlands? Is there any magic in these seemingly flat, dry places and the stark beauty of the mountains? What are the stories beyond the breathtaking experience many seem to speak about? How do I find them?

This took me on a long personal quest, analyzing those small magpie-gathered stories bouncing around in my imagination, digging for said land and lore, finding that yes, there is such bountiful magic but it is something guarded, and not meant for my eyes. And thus, this became a story of living on a land where its stories don't belong to you, but where they still surround you and influence you, and what it might be like to experience that world in both an altered country, but also an altered underworld.

And, of course, not book can grow to fruition without a village to support it. To my husband Shay, for endless support. To my parents, for encouraging me to write in the first place and taking me to places I'm sure they never thought would influence me in such a way in a million years. To my found family of friends who tease me mercilessly about why I write what I do, but always preorder and read my strange tales (to my mortification, out loud and around a campfire), and send me ideas for the next novel. To Joe and the Crystal Lake Publishing team who said, *this dark fantasy alternative history weird west isn't something we usually publish . . . but we absolutely love it.* To Monique, my editor, who slashed my crutch words and shaped this into a better story. To Felipe Kroll, for gorgeous artwork. And, of course, to those people and places who let me ask my questions and gave me my answers. Thank you.

THE END?

Not if you want to dive into more of Crystal Lake Publishing's Tales from the Darkest Depths!

Check out our amazing website and online store.
https://www.crystallakepub.com

We always have great new projects and content on the website to dive into, as well as a newsletter, behind the scenes options, social media platforms, our own dark fiction shared-world series and our very own webstore. If you use the IGotMyCLPBook! coupon code in the store (at the checkout), you'll get a one-time-only 50% discount on your first eBook purchase!

Our webstore even has categories specifically for KU books, non-fiction, anthologies, and of course more novels and novellas.

ABOUT THE AUTHOR

Gwendolyn N. Nix has had a variety of weird jobs from casting producer, to shark researcher, to evolutionary biologist, and is currently an Entertainment Editor with Aconyte Books. Her novels include the Celestial Scripts series (*The Falling Dawn* and *Seams of Shadow*), *Sharks of the Wasteland*, and *I Have Asked to Be Where No Storms Come*. Her short fiction has appeared in a variety of anthologies, such as *Pileaus Symphony No. 1*, *Where the Veil Is Thin*, and *Apex: Worlds of Dinosaurs*. She lives in Missoula, MT. Find her online at gwendolynnix.com, on Twitter at @gwendolynnix or Instagram at @gwendolyn.nix.

Stories of famous monsters in an equally famous anthology.

"A star-studded lineup that succeeds in giving its audience a chance to fully immerse themselves in B-movie horror."
- Publishers Weekly

Readers . . .

Thank you for reading! We hope you enjoyed this novel.

If you have a moment, please review *I Have Asked to Be Where No Storms Come* at the store where you bought it.

Help other readers by telling them why you enjoyed this book. No need to write an in-depth discussion. Even a single sentence will be greatly appreciated. Reviews go a long way to helping a book sell, and is great for an author's career. It'll also help us to continue publishing quality books. You can also share a photo of yourself holding this book with the hashtag #IGotMyCLPBook!

Thank you again for taking the time to journey with Crystal Lake Publishing.

Visit our Linktree page for a list of our social media platforms.
https://linktr.ee/CrystalLakePublishing

Our Mission Statement:

Since its founding in August 2012, Crystal Lake Publishing has quickly become one of the world's leading publishers of Dark Fiction and Horror books in print, eBook, and audio formats.

While we strive to present only the highest quality fiction and entertainment, we also endeavour to support authors along their writing journey. We offer our time and experience in non-fiction projects, as well as author mentoring and services, at competitive prices.

With several Bram Stoker Award wins and many other wins and nominations (including the HWA's Specialty Press Award), Crystal Lake Publishing puts integrity, honor, and respect at the forefront of our publishing operations.

We strive for each book and outreach program we spearhead to not only entertain and touch or comment on issues that affect our readers, but also to strengthen and support the Dark Fiction field and its authors.

Not only do we find and publish authors we believe are destined for greatness, but we strive to work with men and woman who endeavour to be decent human beings who care more for others than themselves, while still being hard working, driven, and passionate artists and storytellers.

Crystal Lake Publishing is and will always be a beacon of what passion and dedication, combined with overwhelming teamwork and respect, can accomplish. We endeavour to know each and every one of our readers, while building personal relationships with our authors, reviewers, bloggers, podcasters, bookstores, and libraries.

We will be as trustworthy, forthright, and transparent as any business can be, while also keeping most of the headaches away from our authors, since it's our job to solve the problems so they can stay in a creative mind. Which of course also means paying our authors.

We do not just publish books, we present to you worlds within your world, doors within your mind, from talented authors who sacrifice so much for a moment of your time.

There are some amazing small presses out there, and through collaboration and open forums we will continue to support other presses in the goal of helping authors and showing the world what quality small presses are capable of accomplishing. No one wins when a small press goes down, so we will always be there to support hardworking, legitimate presses and their authors. We don't see Crystal Lake as the best press out there, but we will always strive to be the best, strive to be the most interactive and grateful, and even blessed press around. No matter what happens over time, we will also take our mission very seriously while appreciating where we are and enjoying the journey.

What do we offer our authors that they can't do for themselves through self-publishing?

We are big supporters of self-publishing (especially hybrid publishing), if done with care, patience, and planning. However, not every author has the time or inclination to do market research, advertise, and set up book launch strategies. Although a lot of authors are successful in doing it all, strong small presses will always be there for the authors who just want to do what they do best: write.

What we offer is experience, industry knowledge, contacts and trust built up over years. And due to our strong brand and trusting fanbase, every Crystal Lake Publishing book comes with weight of respect. In time our fans begin to trust our judgment and will try a new author purely based on our support of said author.

With each launch we strive to fine-tune our approach, learn from our mistakes, and increase our reach. We continue to assure our authors that we're here for them and that we'll carry the weight of the launch and dealing with third parties while they focus on their strengths—be it writing, interviews, blogs, signings, etc.

We also offer several mentoring packages to authors that include knowledge and skills they can use in both traditional and self-publishing endeavours.

We look forward to launching many new careers.

This is what we believe in. What we stand for. This will be our legacy.

Welcome to Crystal Lake Publishing—
Tales from the Darkest Depths.

www.ingramcontent.com/pod-product-compliance
Lightning Source LLC
Chambersburg PA
CBHW060856210726
48293CB00006B/1826